THE BRAMBLES

THE
BRAMBLES

ELIZA
MINOT

ALFRED A. KNOPF
NEW YORK
2006

Fic
Minot

THIS IS A BORZOI BOOK
PUBLISHED BY ALFRED A. KNOPF

Copyright © 2006 by Eliza Minot

All rights reserved. Published in the United States by Alfred A. Knopf,
a division of Random House, Inc., New York, and in Canada
by Random House of Canada Limited, Toronto.

www.aaknopf.com

Knopf, Borzoi Books, and the colophon are registered trademarks of
Random House, Inc.

Library of Congress Cataloging-in-Publication Data
Minot, Eliza.
The brambles / by Eliza Minot.—1st ed.
p.   cm.
ISBN 1-4000-4269-0
1. Mother and child—Fiction.   2. Married women—Fiction.
3. Motherhood—Fiction.   I. Title.

PS3563.I474B73   2006
813′.54—dc22   2005044421

Manufactured in the United States of America

FIRST EDITION

7/24/04
BT 95
23

For Eric

To infinity, and beyond!

—BUZZ LIGHTYEAR

THE BRAMBLES

I

L et's keep him," said Florence. They were about to sign the lease.
"He looks like he likes it here."

In the flowerbed, a small cement statue, two feet tall, robed,
bearded, in mid-step looks down at the rounded rim of the swimming
pool. In one hand he holds a spade, in the other a plume of kale or
chard. The house's previous occupants had left him. Or maybe the
occupants before them. A frost of green moss along an eyebrow. Part of
a finger fallen off. Coin-sized circles, charcoal gray, of lichen.

"Saint Fiacre," said Arthur. He'd recently seen an article on him in one
of the gardening magazines. "Also known as Fiacrius, I believe. Fiachra."

"Mmm," said Florence. She was already tearing up some weeds in the
raised bed next to her hip.

"The patron saint of gardeners," said Arthur.

"And women who can't conceive," said Florence, bent over, uprooting
tall grasses. "And taxi drivers."

Arthur laughed. "Nonsense."

"And potters, tile makers . . . hemorrhoids."

"Hemorrhoids get to have a saint?"

"That's what one of your magazines told me," she said. "I read it on
the john." She stood up straight. "Do you think we could bring out a
part of that rambler rose? Plant it right here?" She shimmied her arm
up, a move from one of her dance numbers a long time ago, to demonstrate where. "A trellis?"

Arthur stood at the pool's edge, watching the water's surface get
spackled with light. "I don't see why not," he said.

Florence surveyed the place, massaged her chin with her thumb and forefinger, playing the part of someone surveying, considering, left behind a soul patch of dirt underneath her bottom lip. "Can't we put bulbs in the freezer to *pretend* winter's happening?"

"Certainly," said Arthur.

"Those other roses," continued Florence, "the sweet midget ones, could be over there."

"Dwarf. Of course," he said.

Florence looked up to see him standing at the edge of the pool as if he might upend it. "Look at you," she said. "You'll never step foot in that pool."

"It's remarkably clean."

"It better be clean."

"I'm not looking forward to keeping it clean."

"Roy told me a young man does it for practically nothing," said Florence, ambling toward the garage. "The kids will love it."

"Sure they will," said Arthur, without irony, with true warmth, thinking of his daughters, Edie diving in, her body coated in a shaft of glass. Margaret with her new baby when it finally comes, bobbing it up and down in the water the way mothers do. He could place his son, Max, lazing in the chaise with a baseball hat on top of his face. Arthur had a hard time believing any of them would ever make the trip across the country to visit.

Florence answered him, reading his mind. "They'll be thrilled to come visit us. Who doesn't like sunlight? Who doesn't like California?"

Arthur raised his hand. "Me," he said, pointing down to himself from above. "Me."

"Too bad about you." Florence smiled.

Arthur watched his wife busying herself, familiarizing herself with this new place, how to make it hers, placing her scent everywhere. He watched her circle trees and look under plants, gently gathering tall stalks like a ponytail to inspect their roots. He watched her poke around in the garage, kicking at boxes, and peer over fences on tiptoe, imagining things to be done, things she would do. She looked the same as she always had, spry and young to him, trim and hearty as she moved gracefully about her new garden. Her white hair, her sea-glass eyes with the elfin squint lines around them.

An infomercial personality from Baltimore had bought the house they'd lived in for the last thirty years in Merrick, New York. They learned, after closing, that he was planning to subdivide it, build a Tudor thing on top of the rock garden, put a tennis court and sauna arrangement where the old lilac bushes had been. "It's just as well," Florence had said in the living room, sitting back in the old chair covered in Indian fabric with elephants all over it. She tossed a handful of peanuts into her mouth. "The house as we know it is *finito*."

California. A one-story house they could practically leap over. Dry green hills in the distance, spines of ridges lumpy like the backs of stegosauruses, sets for Westerns, sets for M*A*S*H, scratchy-grassed meadows that made you wonder where Reagan's ranch was, where was Neverland. A plush gray cat looking at Arthur from underneath their white rental car. The smell of menthol from the eucalyptus trees. Florence with the hills behind her, a small mountain her belled-out cape. The dusty colors flattering her tawny skin, leaping from the page of a catalog with names like ecru, stone, sand, olive, pumice, leaf, bone. The sunlight crackling on the pool's puckering surface with every breeze. Arthur watching a fuzzy seedling, a starry orb, sail from one shore to the other. Florence looking aimlessly for a garbage can, her hands full of weeds.

Arthur smiled. "Taxi drivers, eh?"

"Do you see a trash can?"

"Does that include limousine drivers? Shuttle vans?"

"You'll have to ask the pope," she said.

"By the door, my dear. Over there."

Florence spotted it, veered with renewed purpose in its direction, a replica of their garbage cans back home, dark green plastic with flip-top lids from Sears.

"Margaret will be in San Francisco next week," said Florence. "Did I tell you?"

"No, you did not."

"If we lived here, she'd come visit. See?"

"I'm concerned that she's too pregnant to be traveling."

"Not yet."

Arthur squinted, perplexed at why Margaret's job would bring her out of New York. "I don't understand her job."

"You don't need to, sweetheart."

"Has Edie gotten a job?"

"Arthur."

"Yes?"

"Let her finish school."

"Yes."

"She has a fine job waiting tables."

"Yes."

"And she's tutoring those children."

"Yes."

"Max might start working on a movie in Los Angeles."

"You told me. Yes."

"It would be nice if he's there and we're here."

"Now there's a job I thoroughly don't understand."

"That's because you've never wondered about how a movie gets made," said Florence.

"They get made, is all. A person films other people who act."

"I'm sure plenty of producers and directors never wondered about your job either."

For most of his life, until his recent retirement, Arthur had been the lead lawyer for a watchdog company that managed the recalling of consumer goods.

"I'm hungry," said Florence. "Let's go to that Mexican place by the beach again."

"Wonderful," said Arthur. He looked at the statue of the saint, its small hooded head looking delicately away.

·

Now a green garden hose winds like a snake on the lawn, uncoiled, dead, the last thing Arthur was doing when he went to sit down on the wrought-iron chair at the glass-topped table. He sat there for some time, wondering if he was having a heart attack, on top of everything else, as he stared at the rear neighbor's avocado tree on the other side of the tall stockade fence, trying to ignore the pain in his chest and abdomen.

Arthur sat still, puzzled and uncomfortable, while he mustered his strength to get up and turn off the running water that was piling into puddles on the drought-ridden grass. Then he made his way, sidestepping soft-shoe, keeping his balance, through the open back door on his way to the bedroom, not bothering or, rather, *unable* to wipe his feet on the doormat on the way in, thereby tracking mulch and wet dirt onto the cream-colored carpet. Florence would've shrieked at him laughing—*Ack! Take off those shoes!* But now, alone without her, he is concentrating pointedly on simply making it to the bed, feeling like he'll vomit or soil his pants or pass out or all three, where he lies crush down on the firm mattress, belly-flopped, head askance, the cotton against his cheek a sure and familiar comfort.

Then, dusk. All about him, circling the house, things carry on. Cars bleat along the small streets surrounding him, heading to the Shop and Save, heading home from the beach. Silver beads of airplanes Etch A Sketch across the sky. Kids on bikes shout to one another, disappear down the hill. Miniature treeless mountains stand like upthrust chests, slope-slicing into the ocean along Route 1 where traffic has stopped to watch a pair of whales in the channel spout like steamships.

The sun slips, coloring the ocean with an oily orange film. It is dusk, not day anymore, not night yet, the way life has become for Arthur Bramble these last couple of weeks, right in between, perched at the wait, one way or the other, which way to turn, until, finally, there comes the simple settling—*this is the way it will be now*—toward an elegant purgatory. Each day is more animal than the next, more pared down, more unmistakably stripped of future. Each day—but are they days? They blur like nights of heavy drinking or the mind's eye of a child—has taken on the mysteriousness of Africa, a velvet darkness at every periphery, what comes after we stop living, the honor of the inevitable—*here he is*, grown old and dying—what lies ahead? Out of the air it is coming to him. It blazes in the afterglow that glimmers wildly through the trees. It whispers through the swipes of clouds that are plastered still and scarlet against the massive sky up above. It calls to him, *yoo-hoooo*, in a voice he hasn't heard in a long, long time.

In the morning from his bed he hears his nurse's car come sputtering up the skinny driveway alongside the flattened house. He hears her— Alice—on the other side of the window. The *thwack* suction slam of a door. Through the closed muslin curtains, the shadow of her shape is elongated, distorted, Gumby-like, an alien coming to take him to space. He hears the back hatch squeak open, the girlish rustle of plastic grocery bags being collected together.

Arthur thinks of the stroll Alice must have just taken through Von's Market, entering and leaving effortlessly, pain-free and regular, passing through the automatic doors that hum open as though for royalty, framed by cheerleader pyramids of flowers, each pot wrapped in purple foil. He thinks fleetingly of how probably he will never go alone through a market again.

He hears Alice struggle with the back-door key, first locking it since it was never locked, then unlocking it, then opening the door, letting in the airy hum of the world outside.

Arthur calls to her when the door opens. "Alice?" He clears his throat. "I've been in bed since yesterday," he announces.

After a moment, a stripe of sunlight falling across her chest like a Miss America banner, Alice appears in his doorway, the weight of the groceries pulling on her arms like a prairie girl's buckets of milk. She looks at Arthur frankly, eyes him slowly with a half turn of her head. Alice hardly ever smiles, let alone laughs, which gives her an air of constant comedy since she has a fine sense of humor. Alice sighs. "Oh, Mr. Bramble," she says.

"You'll be pleased to note that I've put my pajamas on appropriately," Arthur points out, though he barely remembers when he managed to do that.

Alice looks Arthur over. He's not lying down all the way and he's not sitting up all the way. He's slouched in between, one pillow pinched under his head and another one rolled into the twirled shape of a strudel pinned between his elbow and chest like a football. "How do you feel now?" Alice asks him. She scans the room. Everything seems to be intact. A glass of water, still full, sits on the bedside table.

"Fine."

"You should've called me," she tells him, moving about the room. She puts the groceries down on the cedar chest at the foot of the bed and flings a fallen bedspread back into place. She opens the curtains and cracks the window to let in some fresh air.

"Well, but here you are," says Arthur, straightening himself up.

"You call me, Mr. Bramble," she says loudly. "That's what I'm here for."

"Certainly," he says.

"Have you eaten anything?" she asks. She picks up his glass of water, dumps its remainder into the potted amaryllis on the dresser, and then holds the glass daintily in front of her belly button like a ballerina.

"Yes," says Arthur. "Your marvelous pot pie."

Alice frowns at him. "I didn't leave you any pot pie," she says.

"Your marvelous pot pie," he says again with a nod.

"I left quiche. A frittata, really."

"Precisely. Your marvelous frittata."

Alice cracks one of her tiny smiles. "I'll fix you some soup. Or bacon and eggs?"

"Bacon and eggs, please."

Alice props him up better on some pillows and brings him some fresh water. She moves about him efficiently, smacking at some pillows so the dust flies up, swarming in the sunlight like sea monkeys. She wipes at the bedside table, shines it up with her bare hand, and then shakes out a blanket with a military crack.

"The most competent woman in the world," Arthur told his daughter Margaret on the phone, referring to Alice, pronouncing the word *wurld*, swirled up into a wet whirlpool, his ancient Boston accent sprouted like a crocus from England centuries ago, now at the end of its line like his family's money, an accent practically extinct. ("I didn't know your father was British," his children's friends would say. *He's not!* Arthur was always the oldest father. "Is that guy your grandfather?" his children's friends would ask. *He's my dad!*) "A wonderful *gurl*," Arthur said to Margaret about Alice. Can't get much better than that, thought Margaret, unable to recall such a compliment out of her father's mouth about anyone, including herself.

Alice brings him the newspaper. "Thank you," says Arthur, but he barely gives it a try. Reading's become a sort of carnival game. The typed words pinwheel and make him seasick.

Alice heads into the bathroom to see what needs tending to in there. She refolds a clean towel that's slipped to the floor. Some of the framed pictures on the wall are askew, tilted at cockeyed angles—what went on in here? she wonders, imagining Arthur tipping about in the dark, pawing at the walls, mussing the pictures. Alice looks them over: His daughter Margaret in a pink bikini with her husband, smiling in a pool somewhere, two toddlers clasped onto their backs like barnacles. Max and Edie as teenagers, both of them smiling on a porch, puffs of breath beside their pale faces, evergreen garlands twined around a column near their heads. In a big silver frame, Arthur's wife, Florence, young but not too young, glamorous in black and white, laughing up into the air, perfect teeth, her mouth open as though waiting for a tossed grape, in a photograph taken for a magazine.

Through the open bathroom door behind her, Alice can hear Arthur speaking as though he's having a conversation with someone. She listens as she straightens a frame. "If only," she hears him say animatedly, as if he's happily explaining something, "if only I'd *held* her every night." A burble of laughter. "Why didn't I just hold her every single night?"

Alice returns through the door. "Are you talking to me?"

Arthur looks at her, startled, though it's unclear to Alice whether he's startled at her appearance or startled that she wasn't there to begin with. He looks quietly out the window and then turns to Alice abruptly. "There are things," he says to her, "that keep coming to my mind."

"Like what, Mr. Bramble?" she asks. She's standing at the foot of his bed.

"They pace around," he says quickly, Cagney-like.

"So let them out." Alice shrugs. She mostly enjoys this speaking in code that she falls into periodically with Arthur. It reminds her of word games that her family used to play on long car rides. It makes her think of a modern dance performance that she saw on PBS once, everyone wrapped tightly in white sheets, tipping left, tipping right, catching one another and then spreading like dominoes.

"I open the door and they look at me," says Arthur. He turns his head to look at Alice with a blunt expression to demonstrate.

Alice shrugs. "So maybe they don't want to be let out." Alice is imagining dogs. "Maybe they want to be fed," she says. "Or patted or something."

Arthur turns a smile upside down and dips his head sideways in an expression that says, Now there's an idea.

Alice sits down on the side of the bed. The mattress dips. She waits for Arthur to continue. She watches him bring his hands together, the pads of all of his fingertips touching their counterparts, forming a cage in the shape of a ball. It's pompous mannerisms like this that bug her, that make her think of her own husband when he's had too much to drink. But Arthur here—well, give him a break, she tells herself. Sometimes the things he says stick with her like lines from a movie or lines from a song: The time they were sitting in the back, Arthur deadheading the bleeding hearts hanging near his head, the pool at their feet still and undisturbed, jelly-like, looking like a giant tub of aqua shampoo. "What a waste to be afraid," Arthur had said, almost wistfully, out of the blue, letting his arms fall loosely on his lap. "Really. The most ridiculous thing."

Arthur jiggles the ball cage he's formed with his fingers as though he's trying to shake free a grain of rice that's stuck to its inside. "A promise—" he says, distinct and forceful, the start of a sonnet, the start of a poem, but the word zips aimlessly free into the air with nothing following it.

"—is a *promise*," Alice finishes for him.

He looks at his nurse. "That's right," he says. His dark brown eyes hold traces of the boy, way in back. "But," he says. "No," he says. "What?"

"Promises," says Alice. She's thinking of the rehab in Malibu. Isn't that what it was called?

Arthur continues. "If I promised my wife something . . ."

"Probably a promise to keep." Alice winks, wondering whether it was Ben Affleck who went to the Promises place or Ozzy Osbourne's kid. Or neither. Maybe both.

They sit quietly for a moment, Alice wondering if she's ever passed the entrance to Promises—it must be off the Pacific Coast Highway— while Arthur tries to subdue something that passes in and out of his head like a roaming housefly, something his children don't know, something he's not sure they need to know. It all seems so vague and unfamiliar, so difficult to approach.

"I miss—" Mr. Bramble sighs. It just comes out. So he keeps going. "I *miss*—" he says, putting a lot of emphasis on the word. He starts chewing on his lip. The wrinkled ravine between his eyebrows hooks into a question mark. He stares at his legs under the white sheets, two pole logs under snow.

"Your children?" prompts Alice. "The Eastern Seaboard?" as she's heard him refer to it.

"I *miss* my wife," he says, with a bow of his head as though saying, *That's* what it is I feel, like he's solved some great riddle, like finally things are coming around, finally things are getting somewhere, falling into place.

"Your daughter will be here this afternoon."

"Yes."

Alice gently pats Arthur's leg through the covers. "Let me get you some food, Mr. Bramble," she says, and leaves him there listening to various birds that he can't see come and go: the occasional pneumatic-tool sound of a woodpecker driving its beak into the palm tree, rat-a-tatting the silence; the dulled clack of it pecking at the car door.

2

Birds tick along the telephone lines that swoop from pole to pole like blank lines of music. Mother after mother and nanny after nanny plop babies into their cribs, wipe at food and snot on small faces, struggle with snow-plowed wheels of strollers that are stymied by fault line lumps in the sidewalks where roots erupt through the pavement. Women wearing Tevas and women wearing clogs call after kids in soccer-coach voices that they never even knew they possessed until they became mothers, their maternal barks now drifting swiftly with authority like lassos over front lawns and front porches, to large-headed toddlers who bumble toward the road, who teeter on edges, who veer near small goldfish ponds hirsute with brown algae.

Arthur's firstborn, his daughter Margaret, her straight hair shining in the morning sun, piles her three kids into the silver Odyssey, headed for the doctor to check on the two oldest to see if they have strep. Her littlest, Florence (three), just got over it, and now Stephen and Sarah (six and five) both have slight fevers, though their throats don't seem to be an issue.

"Little Rosemarie's got Coxsackie," says Brett, the know-it-all neighbor, watering his lawn out front in a manner that drives Margaret crazy. He holds the spray nozzle low at his hip, fans it back and forth in quick jerks, the fast shoot of water pelting his flowers and shrubs mercilessly like riot control.

"Who's Rosemarie?" asks Margaret, scooting Flo into her seat, wondering if the name's not actually *Rosemary* and Brett's given it his customary stamp of incorrectness.

"The little girl in the pink house up the hill," Brett tells her. "The new people? She's about two or three."

"Yuck," says Margaret, thinking it yucky on varying levels simultaneously. First, the house he's referring to is yucky with its vinyl siding, the pasty pink color of Flo's leftover amoxicillin that's still in the fridge. Second, the fact that Brett already knows the little girl's name. And third, she remembers when Sarah had Coxsackie—the dreaded hand, foot, and mouth disease—blisters like a horror show all over the inside of her toddler mouth, her limp body draped over Margaret's hump of a belly, which was, at the time, Flo in utero. There was that worry too, she recalls, about the pregnancy and would it somehow be affected if she was exposed. It was summertime, and Sarah's chubby feet, the size of mini éclairs, were unbelievably hot.

Margaret recalls something else, seems like way back, working at a job in New York during her freelance days. (Was it that decor magazine with that British blonde? Was it the swimsuit calendar?) Her new office mate, Nanette, who had her own sort of trademark in wearing a lavender item every day—a barrette, a shirt, a belt, like a blind date: I'll be wearing a lavender scarf—didn't show up on her third or fourth day of work. In her place on the swivel chair at her desk next to Margaret's was what Nanette had been reduced to: a pink message slip upon which the receptionist had written, with a fat-tipped black Sharpie: *Nanette won't be in today* (Tues.)—*she has Hand Foot & Mouth disease, VERY contagious.* Someone took it from the chair and eventually taped it to the doorframe of Margaret's shared office in the style of the Black Death's red **X**s, since the note was such a riot. The entire office was giggling about it, all atwitter—What *is* it, hoof-and-mouth? Is it *mad cow?*—laughing at the gross name and then getting somewhat serious, hoping, of course, that Nanette was okay. Hoping too that they wouldn't catch it.

The entire office, probably, Margaret thinks now, was childless, other than maybe the people you barely saw: the producers in charge behind sealed doors or the producers in charge of the producers, who rarely made appearances but when they did they almost always looked concerned and hurried, their long cashmere overcoats flapping behind them as they went.

A different era, those days living in the city, thinks Margaret as she heads back into the house to collect the rented DVDs, already a couple of days overdue (*The Incredibles* for the tenth time—she should just buy it—and *About a Boy*, which had actually made her cry quite a lot, had actually sort of inspired her). She wore better clothes then, clipped down the sidewalk smoking cigarettes in high-heeled boots and excellent cream-colored leather pants that would look ridiculous if she wore them now. Back then she looked in mirrors at herself, Rollerbladed the days away, saw movies, lots of movies, sometimes alone, sometimes back to back. She dawdled in secretary stores, trying on shoes, trying on sweaters, taking her time. Yoga class at 9 *p.m.*, dinner *afterward.* The days when she met Brian. She and Brian staying in bed all day some weekends, surfacing on a spring afternoon that had turned evening already to get some Vietnamese food or gorge on sushi maybe, the excellent *shumai* at their favorite place topped with weird wispy noodles that quivered like anemones. Then afterward show up—presto!—at the nearest movie theater to check out the best option. To show up anywhere spontaneously? She couldn't remember the last time.

She used to sit gladly through any movie as long as there was a fair level of production value and she had some Twizzlers on her lap. Now she can't tolerate it if the film's only a little bad, if the dinner out is only average, if the salesclerk at Target is taking too much time changing the tiny paper roll in the register, looking for serial numbers, whatever. Any time solo, without the children, needs to be spent with top-notch efficiency; otherwise it's infuriating; priceless time down the tubes (time is premium) and money wasted—on the movie, the meal, the babysitter—all, in the end, like crumpling up bills, ripping them up, and tossing them down the toilet.

A far cry from those carefree hours of yesteryear! The city! Summer at night! A Cuban sandwich, mango salad, grilled corn on the cob encased in butter and black pepper and Parmesan from the stand-up stand, beers with lime wedges at a round table on the sidewalk, cars slowly chugging by at parade speed through the small downtown streets, their dark reflections in the restaurant window ballooning slowly, shrinking slowly, passing like giant fish trawling an aquarium's floor. A black SUV, its darkened windows vibrating bass. On the sidewalk, a middle-aged woman with a buzz cut, somewhat harried, asking for directions to the Brooklyn Bridge. A little girl jumping rope, ponytail whirling, watched by an old woman sitting in a foldout chair, her elbows resting on its metal arms, her shoulders forward in a permanent shrug of disbelief and boredom. A chic young woman in an orange halter top and a brown skirt below her outie belly button, speaking in Italian into a miniature phone. Water dribbling, cool and inviting, from the fire hydrant that's been clamped off. A man in flip-flops lazily walking his dog. A cell phone rings somewhere among the tables to the electronic tune of *"Nessun Dorma."* Later, another to the *Star Wars* theme. She and Brian watch a man and a woman run into each other on the sidewalk in front of them. They are old friends, maybe old lovers. Maybe, possibly, they are divorced. The small drama of it, badly acted. When they part, they don't kiss good-bye. The man is clearly angry. How the woman feels, not so clear. Someone on a bike goes riding by, the blur of a straw basket, the ticking wheels, gone. Brian takes a drag of his cigarette—they both smoked then, pre-family—puts his hand on Margaret's thigh under the table, then tucks his hand under it.

The way life threads itself through change. Margaret can't remember the last time she and Brian sat idly anywhere enjoying a beer alone, except, of course, on the patio in the backyard, which was pretty lovely sometimes, she had to admit. The crickets and cicadas buzzing and rattling, whirring like alarms, sizzling like a table saw or meat dropped onto a frying pan, the winking ember of fireflies, the hulking trees sunken into the warm dark like giant blots. Suburban jungle noises: water running, muffled shouts, a necklace of laughter unclasped out a window, the sputter of a sprinkler. A plate clanks in a neighboring kitchen. Down the road, a car guns it. An airplane grumbles, nearing Newark. Through the trees, some faint hip-hop.

The lunatic sounds of other people's children pleading, wailing, the wild bedtime hours. An entire house yelps out the yelp of the child inside. The smug feeling that tonight the noise is not theirs. Upstairs, their kids are asleep in their underwear, Flo in some pull-ups with a mermaid all over them, no covers, fans whirring at them with the determination of army generals while the curtains drawn over their windows glow white-blue, pearly, with the fading daylight from outside. Down the hill, some moron starts up his lawn mower in the twilight, sure to wake someone's sleeping baby.

Aside from the bore of sunblock and prickly heat, it certainly beat wintertime, particularly after the past winter, The Winter That Would

Never End, as her sister, Edie, called it after the April blizzard. Summer certainly beat winter, which was primarily a house-arrest situation, a jumble of marrying mittens and filling up vaporizers, administering medicine the color of maraschino cherries and searching for hats and good warm socks. Crowds of dirty underwear, layered winter clothes, gathered like exhausted bodies in the laundry room. The thin glue-like glazes on the kids' cheeks from smeared runny noses. Outside, bare trees rising up all over the place, looking like gigantic raw nerves. Ice regularly fusing the Odyssey doors shut, making Margaret feel, ice chipper in hand, blinking against frosty winds, as though she is on an expedition in space, desperately trying to get back to the mother ship.

The days with small children, she has come to accept, *blend*. "Face it," Brian said to her when she complained years ago that she wasn't getting any work done, "you've been thrown into neutral." Neutral it is, non-aligned and patterned. It's the movie *Groundhog Day*, Bill Murray stuck in a sort of purgatory, the same midwestern day over and over, waking up at the same deadpan time every morning to the same ensuing motions. Flo wakes first, sometimes tamely, sometimes wildly, but always unable to speak quietly, sliding into bed next to Margaret, poking her feet between Margaret's knees, bossing Margaret around about which way to lie, which way to face, where to put her arms, which way to breathe so her morning breath doesn't go puffing into Flo's mouth and nose, and then finally Flo getting up and pulling on Brian's pillow—I want to go downstairs. I want to go downstairs, Dad. I want to go downstairs. I want to go downstairs, Dad. I want to go downstairs— Flo's ordinarily sweetly high voice sounding shrill and awful enough to make Margaret, exhausted as if drugged, want to hurl a pillow at her small daughter or shout very loudly.

Brian gets up, the snap and crackle of the tiny bones in his feet as he shuffles downstairs before his shower to get Flo some yogurt and blueberries, the yogurt in one bowl, the blueberries *in another, Dad* (which cost a *fortune*, roughly five cents a berry, Margaret figured one insomniac night) to eat as she watches *Dragon Tales*. And so the day begins: Stephen sliding down the banister, leaping down the stairs, Sarah pouring her own Froot Loops all over the floor, various feet crushing them into a fine powder like colored chalk; and then the kiddy arguing again as Brian slips out the front door silently, dressed like an adult, on his way to work, an enviable job (despite mediocre pay) of helping rich people and companies decide where to give away their bountiful amounts of money.

Everyone else getting dressed, the fighting for the last *this*, the struggle for the last *that*, Stephen demanding to wear the one Billabong shirt that smells like sour milk, twisted wet like a cruller in the dryer that never got turned on, Sarah refusing to wear long sleeves in the winter and short sleeves in the summer—the transitions of seasons apparently really tough for her—the demands, the laughter, the tears, the car, the gas, the dropoffs, the pickups, the groceries, the struggles, whining, lost tempers, Margaret raising her voice, bargaining, distracting. Every day an encapsuled love affair with three different people: the misunderstandings and supplications, the forgivenesses, the push and pull, the lunatic jealousies, the heightened sensitivities, the beginner neuroses, the starter complexes all being born and fostered.

The mania! The intense elation, the unbelievable excitement—at least her kids all liked one another. How they laugh spasmodically over something about a Mister Porpoise Pants says *Ahhh* (Margaret has no idea), as true a love as ever exists, looking out for one another: "Mom, Sarah's a little mad that Flo has one" (Thanks, Stephen); "Let's get that for Stephen, Mom!" (Not today, Sarah); "Where's Sarah?" (Flo, abandoned, crestfallen because the house is empty when she wakes from her nap); "Where's Steve?" (it was inevitable, after all, that he'd be called *Steve*); Margaret in the kitchen overhearing Stephen in the TV room, "You okay there, Flo?" or Sarah, being diplomatic, "Okay. If you really want to."

But whatever rosiness existed was soon followed by utter despair; oh, the misery and human despondency unleashed, unchecked: "I hate my house!" Nothing manufactured in their brains yet, practically, to hold things in—"I don't *like* you, *Momma!*"—to keep it together, the life in them bursting out at the seams, in shambles. "My stupid *stupid* life!" It was both heartbreaking and hysterically funny to watch. And infuriating. And humiliating. Finding herself prone on the floor looking under dust-clogged furniture for ridiculous finger-sized action figures that bore more character and weight than any human beings outside the house, arguing like the captain of the debate team for a solid ten minutes with Stephen in the kitchen and then, finally, looking at his little body standing there, realizing that this kid is *six* and she is thirty-four. Searching through the wet garbage pails outside for the coveted sticker of an octopus that she offhandedly pitched. None of them listening to her as she pleads with them longingly, aware of the fact that she's been reduced to too-tight grips as she grits her teeth ("Oh, did I pinch you?") and idle threats (Hey *kid.* Look, *buddy.* Listen, *mister.* Wait a second there, *princess*).

Finally, after the most likely peak hours of nonsensical meltdowns, there's the end of the day, *the finish line*, the lights dimmed down in the swept kitchen, the dishwasher chugging along heartily, Margaret and Brian sitting in front of the TV or lying flung onto the bed. Wherever they are, the rest of the house disappears like a set on a stage where the lights are turned off.

But slowly, day in, day out, through the blended doughy (Play-Dohy!) days, emerge these children, growing, something happening after all, something so wildly different from before when Margaret didn't have them, and how did it happen without her seeing? Small legs getting longer, traces of adult faces emerging from their babyish containers, the characters that were there from the beginning, encased in those luscious chubby baby bodies, those distinct personalities looking out from behind those clean baby eyes now efflorescing, becoming more so, more themselves, the selves that were always there to begin with, like a color that deepens, the sky as the sun goes down, still the same but still changing.

But what, meanwhile, was happening to *her?* To Margaret? Not much. Simply, she is here. *In the moment,* as they say, behaving like a waitress, a handmaiden, a love slave, alternately ill-treated and then adored, worshiped by the little people. Humiliated and adored. Part goddess, part foot soldier, every day varying, yet every day the same. The general departures from the regular are similar to the weather forecast (unpredictable, kind of important, but basically beside the point), which Margaret listens to and reads about with great zeal since it demands so little effort, is sometimes achingly beautiful in its descriptions, feeding a certain famine of charmed language in her life, and is so informative, so crucial in the plans of how best to pass the time with the children, how to dress them, what to wear, where to go, who to call.

Margaret listens to the weather so astutely, so regularly, that some-times—she can't help it—forecasts for the household abound in her head.

Friday: Fussiness and cranky crying will give way to good humor late in the day with the appearance of the ice cream truck and again with Dad. Evening will bring fair temperate conditions in the TV room. Possible nightmares toward midnight.

Saturday: A jubilant Sarah will busy herself in the lower portions of the house throughout the morning, causing exasperation as well as a few laughs for a tired older brother.

Tuesday: Very boring. Frustrating. The next several days will be the most tedious of the current monotony.

Some obvious differences do come along sometimes, livening things up like a splat of color on a piece of wet cardboard, for better or for worse. Usually they're problems. The big differences lately for Mar-garet? She, as they say, *compartmentalizes* them. The differences start small, the minute and specific which seem the least important but actually tend to be the most important and, at bottom, very much affecting everything, disrupting her day (it's all about day to day, alas, hard to look up from the water when you're swimming with three small people who can't swim very well), and then they progress outward, rippling out toward issues beyond, rings from a stone tossed into the water. Moving from small ripples to large:

1. The Popsicle situation. The massive supermarket is either con-stantly out of or no longer carries (she can't get a consistent answer) the fruit juice brand that's vital to her household and line of man-agement (i.e., disciplining, bargaining, placating, etc.).
2. Stoned Wheat Thins. The massive supermarket doesn't carry these coveted crackers anymore.
3. Flo's Dora the Explorer backpack. Left at the playground at the top of the slide. Gone upon return (after crushing Sarah's Lil' Bratz car while backing out of the driveway, and then, as a result of ensuing backpack search, missing Brian at the train station, who proceeded to walk home and along the way was bit on the ankle by a leashless dog that he had to beat on the head until it ran away).

4. The stamp machine at the post office. Still busted.
5. Funny smell in the Odyssey. Burning rubber, rotten eggs.
6. New neighbors a few doors down. Margaret still hasn't greeted them. Hunches with a sheepish wave as she drives by when she sees them outside.
7. Her friend Sally's new baby. Still hasn't gone into the city to see her. How old now? Two months? Five?
8. Dishwasher making a grating noise at start of dry cycle.
9. Ants in the kitchen. Tiny microscopic ones, hundreds, trickle single file from the wall onto the counter to ensnare a solitary crumb. A reluctance to kill, kids regularly watching *A Bug's Life* and *Antz*.
10. Vaguely leaking washing machine.
11. Voice-mail messages. Choppy and deranged, they are often indecipherable, particularly when they sound pressing.
12. Roadwork being done downtown. An already desperate parking situation rendered hopeless.
13. Sarah and Stephen's fevers. Possible Coxsackie?
14. Debt.
15. An impending rise, again, in their property tax.
16. Code orange? Amber alert? War.
17. Her father is coming to live with her.
18. Her father has cancer.
19. Her father is dying.
20. Her mother is dead.
21. She has an irrational urge for another baby.

See, so there are changes! There are things happening! The last one, both on her mind and not, at the forefront of her mind and then again at the back of her mind, makes an all-encompassing corral. The one before that, her mother, is not so recent but recent enough: almost three years ago. There on the kitchen counter, its Formica faux granite surface speckled like a duck egg, is the bad reminder recalling it, the newspaper article amid the pads of paper taken from Stephen's cleared-out first-grade desk. He'd used it for a newscast report that he was assigned for school. Margaret wasn't sure if it was ghoulish or reckless of her to allow Stephen to use it, given the people involved, but thought too that maybe it was a good way for him to approach it. At least it was an approach. Margaret wasn't sure. It was a tough call.

Stephen had first rehearsed it for her and Brian at the kitchen table. Seated across from them, he looked up, smiled brightly—"Ready?"— and then started with gusto, putting on his imitation talk-show/anchor voice, the semifurrowed brow, the smart-alecky tilt of the head. After relaying the first few words with real oomph, Stephen's head lolled forward, his body slumped, to read the rest of the first paragraph of the article in the dull staccato reserved for beginner boy readers reading out loud.

At least he's not pretending it didn't happen, thought Margaret, Stephen's words droning on as she tuned him out. Brian's helpful (constant) prompts were muffled as though through water. Margaret was purposely trying not to listen, thinking the entire thing utterly strange: her only son reporting on her only mother's death, his little body, his little male mind, reaching to get his head around mortality. Or was he simply being dramatic for his friends? It was too odd, too bizarre, too *sad*.

She'd recently become more adept at deflecting things, turning thoughts away, transforming them into something else (or perhaps she'd always been this way; it was just that now, with a house of small people so intricately involved around her, such traits of psychology became more apparent). So many times, all day long, her extreme passions, like the children's, were brought to the fore. She needed mechanisms to maintain her sanity. All in a single day, she'd never been so frustrated, so besotted, so bored, so pleased, so proud, or so annoyed.

What struck her as most odd, as she watched her son's snapdragon mouth move up and down, as his words blurred across her ears like a lovely rain, what struck her as unbelievably magnificent as well as absolutely strange, was the feat that this boy, this incredibly good-looking little kid who was managing to pepper out sentences all on his very own, was her *son*; that she'd somehow managed to carry him— *him!*—in her belly for forty-one weeks; that she'd somehow managed to rear him until right now, this second—and now here he was, with his own . . . *everything*. His own tongue that lolled comfortably between his lips as he tried to think of something. His own eye rolls and prickling hangnails. His own haircuts and reflexes, tendons and impulses. His own future. His own past. His own pleasure at having his scalp scratched. His own boyish preferences already so clear: the caricatured style of comic book characters, the look of snowboard riders with the thin modern lines and retro graphics, hats pulled tightly down low on his head, particular shades of orange and blue, strawberries, his science books jam-packed with illustrious pictures, skateboards, hockey skates, brown-eyed girls with ponytails, his favorite teacher, Mrs. Bradley.

Margaret loved Mrs. Bradley too, wished that the woman could somehow morph into becoming Stephen's new grandmother. What would Mrs. Bradley think of this report? Distasteful? Progressive? Margaret wasn't sure. She tried again not to think about it. Brian thought it was fine. "Whatever the little guy needs to do." He shrugged vaguely, as if he was stoned.

•

In Margaret's hands at the sink, the zinnias with their fuzzy leaves were splotched with milky white mildew. Out the window the dark greens of September; the sun coming sideways, autumnal, long across the house; Brian lying on the lawn after mowing it while all three kids came running onto it, like a floor that's finally dry or clean ice at the rink when the Zamboni's at last pulled off.

The floor was sticky with some spilled lemonade. Margaret's feet were bare. She stood on one foot, her other big toe tucked up into a rope anklet Sarah made for her at day camp. The zinnias were the color of bubble gum, the color of Tang, their petals tight like the scales on a fish or pinecone.

When she picked up the phone she didn't even say hello, absorbed in deleafing each of the stems, stripping them of their sickly leaves, wondering where the best vase had gone.

It was her brother, Max. "Maggie?" he said. She had to turn the music down.

"Well, finally," she said, poking fun at him. "Where have you been, Timbuktu?" Then immediately regretted it since she sensed something, fear, a little late, maybe in the tone of his voice, maybe in the way he was breathing or pausing.

"There's been an accident," he said.

For a giddy second Margaret thought he was joking. But then it was as if she could smell him through the phone, see his face trying not to uncork. She was swiftly displaced, relocated to someplace dark and claustrophobic, an abandoned mine, a sinking ship, speaking to her brother through something flimsy like a Dixie cup.

Out the window in front of her face, the shadows long, Margaret could see all three of her kids sprawled on the grass like a Balthus painting, though she still had the feeling—a stone tossed into her guts, sinking there, a rock through hammocks of spiderwebs—that her brother was calling about one of them. Brian was out there too, laughing, his hands clasped behind his head, but she had a flash vision of him collapsed in the middle of a midtown crosswalk, his light blue shirt still clean, his hair whisked to the side across his forehead as though he'd just come up from underwater.

Max continued. "The plane from Hunter, Maggie."

Sarah was making whooping sounds, doing slow somersaults on the grass. Brian now held Flo by the ankles, swinging her upside down like a pendulum, her downy hair fanning out behind her.

"You're kidding," said Margaret softly. She listened to her brother's breathing. A sensation was rising, swelling up from the base of Margaret's head that seemed to be telling her, *Of course. Here we go*—the misleading voice that clarified things incorrectly for her during nightmares, pulling her up slowly like a balloon, *Of course. This* is what's been happening all along, the background awareness; this is how things *really* are: the sensation that something awful had already happened and now was happening again, compounded, tumbling on top of itself.

She felt herself starting to panic, seized but alert. "But *where?*" she asked, her tendency to redirect, as if maybe her brother was simply flat-out wrong, as if maybe he didn't have all the facts in order. "When?" she demanded. As if it made a difference.

•

The clipping is still rumpled up among Stephen's things (spiral note-book, clear Super Ball with an eyeball inside it, a pint-size shin guard swiped with grass stain) near the DVDs she's come indoors to collect.

Outside, her children sit waiting in the idling car, bait for a carjacking, sitting ducks for an abduction, one small face looking left, another looking right, child daydreamers imagining worlds.

Margaret brushes it aside to get at the movies. She'll never need to read it again to know exactly what it says:

FIVE DIE IN SMALL PLANE CRASH
INFANT AND MOTHER AMONG THEM

A Boston-bound Stafford Express flight out of Hunter, Maine, plunged into the Atlantic ten miles off Barriscotta on Sunday morning around 8:15. All five people on board are assumed dead.

The FAA is investigating what exactly caused the plane to plummet into the ocean. Hazy weather made for poor visibility.

The missing have been confirmed as Cassie Simpson, of Hershey, Pennsylvania, and her ten-month-old daughter, Lauren; Florence Bramble, of Santa Barbara, California; and the two pilots, both residents of Portland, Maine, Troy Jenkins, a thirty-year veteran of flying, and Bob Mackie.

Cassie Simpson, who until last year taught first grade at Hershey Elementary School, and her daughter are survived by Cassie's husband, David P. Simpson, and the couple's three-year-old son.

Florence Bramble, 62, a retired dancer and model who appeared in numerous fashion magazines in the fifties, is survived by her husband, Arthur, 73, of Santa Barbara, California; a son, Max Bramble, 29, of New York City; two daughters, Margaret Bright, 31, of Magnolia Heights, New Jersey, and Edie Bramble, 27, of New York City, and three grandchildren.

Troy Jenkins, 51, had been flying since he was 20 years old. He was the owner and founder of Puddle Jumpers Inc., a charter outfit out of his hometown Raymond, Maine, that flew passengers and goods about the islands of Penobscot Bay. He is survived by his daughter, Lana, and three grandchildren.

Bob Mackie, 43, of Portland, Maine, is survived by his wife, Janelle, and a son, Robert Jr.

Plunged into the Atlantic. It made it sound like fun. At least it hadn't been her, as in *she herself*, Margaret thought (regularly) and then felt terrible about thinking it, cramming the thought backward like an embarrassing piece of trash. And at least it hadn't been her husband. Again, she felt terrible. What sort of warrior would she ever be in dire times? Would she be the one who flees, fends for herself, hoards and manipulates in order to save her family at the expense of everyone else? Probably.

But Brian wouldn't allow her to be so cowardly. "I'm here to serve you," Brian had said to her, shortly after they met, like a fairy god-angel falling from heaven, looking straight into her eyes. "I'm here to make your life better." They were standing on a street corner, and Margaret heard a satisfying *thud* somewhere near her feet—she didn't bother to look away from Brian's face to see what it was—something landed on the ground, the package she'd been waiting for suddenly delivered, suddenly found. Boy, she loved him! He was strong and gorgeous and funny too. He knew everything and was capable of anything, sometimes exhaustingly so. Her only complaints were his tendency to leave bottles and jars loosely capped in the fridge and his habit of putting the button edge of the duvet cover by the pillows instead of at the foot of the bed. Not in her wildest dreams did she ever think she'd find him. It was that simple. She dreamed regularly, however (particularly around the births of her children, during that watery time where time is gone), that he wanted a divorce or was sick of her, that he was having an affair or blatantly in love with someone else. Was she petrified for her security? Was she more petrified now that her mother had been killed? She wasn't sure.

Coming back out onto the front porch, bouncing down the front steps in a hurry, Margaret looks up to see Brett still watering and is reminded of the horrid Coxsackie prospect for her feverish kids. In pre-children New York, hand, foot, and mouth disease might have sounded dangerous and exotic, even funny, but out here in the world of child rearing there was not a thing funny about it. It was, very simply, an agonizing bore that lasted a week, possibly two or three if it got swapped around, kid to kid, and then sometimes playfully passed back again.

At least none of them were infants anymore, that scary time, so tiny, with an older sibling sick: *Stay away*, she'd say firmly, sticking a protective arm out over the pink baby, warding off the poor sick older child, a baby still but looking like a third-grader in comparison to this minuscule person. In a bartender's voice, *Back off*, she'd tell the sick one, usually Stephen, as he'd daintily approach the sleeping infant. Stephen, feelings hurt, would crumple to the floor, hopeless, rejected, wailing for her with arms upstretched, wanting her. They always wanted her. Awful mother, she'd tell herself, and hurry to collect him, let him cry all over her, let him smear snail trails of snot on her sweater, on her neck, let him try to touch her skin anywhere with his hot hands and cheeks. Once the upheaval was over, she'd head to the bathroom to disinfect herself—hands, neck, breasts—as thoroughly as a surgeon before putting on a fresh sweater or shirt, back to the new baby with her sleeping eyes like a pup's.

Let's pray, Margaret says to herself, mounting her driver's seat, that this isn't what the fevers are heading toward. *Please, God, please: no Coxsackie. Please, no SARS. Thanks.* They're a compulsion, these kinds of prayers, quick and brief. Although she means them, she's hardly aware of them. In fact, if anyone ever asked her if she prayed to God regularly, she would answer, Oh, God, no, hardly ever, when really she prays probably four or five times a day. Her technique—fast and simple—hasn't evolved since grammar school when she was primarily asking for the attentions of a particular boy named Andy Means in the grade above her. It's almost always requests, the requests of a ten-year-old rather than her adult self, beginning regularly with *Please, God* or *God, please* said silently in her head. *Please God don't let him be mad anymore.* Or, *God, please let it be fun!* Occasionally there's the add-in of her own sort of religious patois: *God please bring unto us some money. Please let thy child's nap last until three.* And, when she thinks of it: *Thanks.*

"Mom?" It's Sarah in the way back, her new preferred seat.

"Yes, honey?"

"I don't have a sore throat, Mom."

"You've made that clear, sweetheart. You do, however, have a fever," says Margaret, groping around on the floor at her feet, feeling for her wallet. Its hidden home is under the driver's seat, along with an extra set of car and house keys, slid under a metal ridge that Margaret has never actually seen so can only picture in her mind, like the top level of the Brooklyn Bridge.

Over the years her wallet has evolved, unlike her prayers, from the immense leather backpack bag she'd schlep around the city on her right shoulder (which, she believes, caused irreparable damage to her back).

That was when she was waitressing (her uniform folded neatly inside), working at Shakespeare & Co., babysitting for eight-year-old twins, or serving as an intern in wardrobe for *Another World*.

Then, when she was working in midtown for a photographer named Butch, there was the red calfskin snap accordion purse that her mother gave her, which had lots of credit-card slits and endless compartments for change and phone numbers that she kept in a cute black Prada-esque vinyl clutch that she bought on the street for ten bucks but was problematic because she had to *clutch it all the time*, which made life diffi-cult if her hands were cold or if she wanted to read something on the subway, the bag loose on her lap, up for grabs, which led her to the awful black-leather fanny pack that she wore front-facing, which was a bad look but, let's face it, did a good job of accentuating the waist as well as being incredibly convenient when she was trekking around the city getting props and supplies for one boss, Glenda, who did extensive window dressings all around town.

A summer job with an ad agency brought with it the embroidered canvas wallet in the miniature orange silk dupioni pocketbook that she bought on the street, big enough for her wallet, her pack of smokes, a lipstick, her keys, and her miniature red cell phone. This was the arrangement that she stuck with, relying on a white bag made of sail-cloth for the larger items she had to lug to and from shoots and jobs as a full-fledged freelance stylist. Then came the diaper-bag ordeal, some-thing else entirely. . . .

Next, with the move to the suburbs—where the car became her pocketbook, basically—was a turquoise satiny-silk change purse from Chinatown, a remnant of city living that she repeatedly left on the roof of the car while she buckled some small person in; it would fall off somewhere on Fielding Road and be brought to her door by a distant neighbor down the street until, one day, it was gone for good, which led to this final evolution, nestled on the Odyssey's floor: simply, her cash card, her New Jersey driver's license, and her Visa card, held tightly together by one of Flo's fluorescent hair elastics, a receipt from the dry cleaners tucked into its loop, as well as a twenty and a spare check.

She picks it up off the floor, notices some raisins down there like shriveled sheep turds on the soft camel-carpet contours of the car's floor, and slips it into the side of her bra. She never seems to have pockets anymore. But in her head she has plenty memorized. The stuff of cards and wallets. Their health insurance number: YLJ 142-8735; the group number: 23BX; the Visa card: 5873-1420-3566 exp. 04/04; the reference number for the bulk granola (1468) at the natural market; all the kids' social security numbers, Stephen's: 53—

"Mom?"

Margaret looks up into the rearview mirror as she efficiently buckles her seat belt like a stuntwoman, without looking at her hands. "Yes?"

Stephen sits behind her. "I *do* have a sore throat," he says. "Sort of."

"Roger, Stephen," she says, going into reverse.

"Who's Roger, Mom?" asks Flo.

"It means I hear you," Margaret answers. She backs out without turning her head around. She closes an eye, sharpshooter, lining up the line of the car with the line of the driveway's Belgian-block curb.

"Roger," repeats Stephen.

"Mayday, mayday," says Sarah.

"That's niner niner niner, Mom," says Stephen, into an imaginary lavaliere microphone.

"Over and out," says Margaret, suddenly exhausted. She spins the van backward in a crescent onto Fielding Road, then revs forward past Brett, who waves at them with his hose. Sunlight gets caught in the spray of his water, a sphere of moisture, mist like ice crystals. Margaret sees a rainbow in the vapor, there and then gone. She nods her head at Brett's tiresome face, is tempted to say *creep* under her breath for no real reason other than his being a general snoop—a stalwart busybody—but it's the kind of thing she can't say around the kids anymore. They hear too much, their ears wide open all the time, crazy curled funnels for their rapid learning, their brains desperate for information, starving for it. The questions turn endless, puddles of questions, lakes of questions, serious, intense, desperate to understand.

What do you mean *creep*, Mom? The splish-splash of questions. We don't like Brett? That's not very nice, Mom, is it? What *is* a creep exactly? Does *Dad* like Brett, Mom? Mom? Is a creep like a creepy-crawly? Is a creepy-crawly a bug? Why do some bugs have so many legs, Mom? Plus it's a bad example to say something rude in front of them, particularly about someone they know.

The last thing she wants is for one of her children to turn out as a judgmental rude person. Well, the *last* thing she wants is a nuclear holocaust. And after that, the next-to-last thing she wants is for another person in her family to die. And after that, a major terrorist biological attack, or dirty bomb, poisoned water, or whatever, in nearby New York City, but close to the top of the last-thing-she-wants list is for one of her kids to turn out to be a jerk. She drives on by, glances at Brett. "Nice shorts," she mutters instead, unable to contain herself.

She pokes a CD into the player, a mix burned by her brother, Max, of downloaded songs, starting with a kid-friendly song from the original *Shrek* sound track so it goes over fine with everyone, avoiding a loud struggle, though she'd rather listen to something edgier or NPR or sing along loudly with two corny tracks on Max's mix that she puts on repeatedly (replay, skip, skip, play, replay) like an insane person when the kids aren't in the car. NPR, meanwhile, serves as her umbilical cord to culture and the world beyond her home and its walls, her town and its goings-on. She relies on it desperately, is ashamed during every fund drive that she never bucks up and gives them the money they deserve from her but takes pride partly in the fact that she does continue to *listen* through the appeals.

Now that school's out, however, it's as though news of the world is suspended as well. It's summer, and the kids are home all day like they're babies again; 10:05 a.m. and there they are, watching something terrible on TV until Margaret tries to herd them into the backyard. The kids getting bored, the kids needing rides, the kids getting sick, she and the kids, me and them, they're coming with me, we'll be there soon, we're running late, we weren't home yet, we'll be in the back, we'll be upstairs, we'll be downtown, we'll be next door, we're heading down, we're coming up, we're heading out, wee, wee, wee, all the way home. . . .

Routines are all askew. It's a Friday for Christ's sake and here they are all together in the Odyssey on Oak Street at a red light. Ordinarily she'd probably be at a client's house, measuring windows or swabbing a sample of paint on their wall out of a can the size of a jam jar, Cumulous Cotton or White Satin, Full Moon or Beacon Gray— some of the names were the best part—or over at Giovanni's borrowing books of fabric, or simply drinking iced tea with some jittery or bored new homeowner, suggesting whatever it was she thought they should do.

It was when her friend Linda, loaded Linda who's come and gone, jet-setted into town for less than a year from New York upon the impending arrival of her second baby before moving to London and then Kuala Lumpur. Linda moved into a pretty house, a turn-of-the-century center-hall colonial that needed new paint in every room, curtains, the works. Linda insisted on paying Margaret (Margaret being a *stylist* and all) to help her pick colors for the walls and suggest basic ideas like layout, decor, vibe, etc. For five hundred bucks, Margaret chose colors for each room and picked a few fabrics, suggested a type of rug, maybe new cabinets here and there, even scanned the garden possibilities.

Loaded Linda went on to sing her friend's praises at the many cocktail parties and play dates she hosted at her big house. Soon word spread through the larger homes of Magnolia Heights and its environs, and Margaret Bright had her own fledgling industry, making *suggestions* for people who could afford them. Her business card was tasteful, her name all in lower case—that e. e. cummings thing had always bugged her, pretentiously playful, but seemed to work here. It just looked better, clean but warm: the letters in chartreuse, the cards a nice weight. Underneath it, *ideas for your home*. It made Margaret want to barf—*ideas for your home*—it sounded so bed-and-breakfasty, so Hallmarky. But that's really all she did, and the alternatives were even worse: *consulting* (too vague), *decorating consultant* (too professional), *suggestions* (too vague), *suggestions for your home* (implying that the home sucked), *decorating* (she wasn't decorating), *house beautifying* (too complicated, too silly), *better home* (ditto, plus like the magazine).

Margaret's eBay problem began as a result of a woman she met at the fabric store who told her she'd bought her dining room set on eBay, along with a Balinese bed, both for a song. "It's the shipping costs that get you," the woman told Margaret, "but the rugs can be great." Margaret noticed that the woman was looking through the book of the most expensive French fabric. Margaret watched her unfold the eyeglasses that dangled on a gold chain around her neck. The woman put the glasses on and looked at Margaret conspiratorially over their top rim. She mouthed the words exaggeratedly while whispering, "A Feraghan Sarouk for next to nothing."

At the time, Margaret had no idea what a Sarouk was. But now she knew, boy did she know, after cyber-browsing through masses of Persian rugs: orientals, gabbehs, Caucasian Kazaks, kilims, Hamadans, Ghoochans, Kashans, Shirazes, chobis, Gharajehs, Tajiks, Qashqais, Sarouks, Shirvans. She knew quite a lot about knots-per-square-inch counts, vegetable dyes, Persian vs. Indian gabbehs, you name it. She wasn't an expert by any means, but she was well informed and ready, all right, when it came to eBay and its listings.

The first one she bid on, a big bright-red, semiantique runner from Pakistan, she bought for ten dollars.

"This'll be interesting," said Brian, when she told him.

"It said the market price was like two thousand dollars," she told him brightly.

"Sure it did, sweetheart."

"I can always return it. Minus shipping and handling."

"How much is that?"

"Seventy dollars. Or something."

"Well, there's a bargain. One-forty to return a ten-dollar rug."

"At least I don't have a problem with Ameritrade or something. Shelly said she was going nuts trading online."

"At least that way maybe you'd make us some money," said Brian.

Margaret continued, wringing out a shirt of Sarah's in the sink. "This rug stuff. I have a good feeling about this. I have a feeling this rug's going to be fantastic."

The rug came, and it was fine. Quite nice. Not the most beautiful in the world, but for ten dollars . . . ?

When she spread the news to her friend Regina, Regina was ecstatic. "This could be a major breakthrough for me, Margaret," she said. Margaret wasn't sure what she meant, but it sounded encouraging.

Margaret then mentioned it to a client, Diane, a friend of her friend's friend, Jackie. Then she thought better of it. Why give away this secret? Why be bidding against someone rich like Diane?

Diane didn't seem to be a threat. She was flummoxed, aghast even, wrinkling her nose. "Where do they come from?"

"Different rug dealers." Margaret shrugged. "All over the country. Some directly from overseas."

Diane's eyes bugged out. "Are they *clean*?"

"Um, sure," said Margaret. "The first one I got came from North Carolina. Chapel Hill or somewhere. Some dealer called Persia Bazaar."

"Persia *Bazaar?*"

"I've noticed there are a lot in Florida."

"Florida?" A sour face. "How do you know there's not, like, anthrax or something sprinkled in the fibers? Smallpox! Anything!"

Margaret shrugged. Diane clearly wouldn't be competition on the bidding page. Margaret thought fleetingly of the book she'd read last summer about the plague being brought to a village on a piece of fabric brought by a tailor. The village quarantined themselves so they wouldn't infect anyone further, all nobly agreeing to stay within the walls of their town so they wouldn't bring the plague upon anyone else. The richest family, though, who basically employed most of the villagers, took off, breaking their word.

Next on her list, after rugs, which was an ongoing quest, was outdoor furniture. "Two teak chaise lounges!" she told Brian in the kitchen when he came home from work, the two of them wading through the children who were rosying around them. "For forty dollars!"

"Something's wrong," said Brian, downing a glass of water. "Who's that?" he asked, pointing his chin toward a small redheaded girl sprinkled with freckles.

"Cynthia. Flo's friend from gymnastics," answered Margaret, getting shoved from the side by one of the kids.

"Hello, Cynthia," said Brian. He made a hat-tipping gesture to the oblivious little girl as he placed his glass in the sink.

"I'm just an excellent bidder, honey," said Margaret.

Brian flipped through the mail. A small hand reached up and grasped one of the envelopes. Brian plucked it back. "How much was the shipping?" he asked, dubious.

"Free!"

Four days later, a tiny package arrived. From the living room, she could hear Brian laughing, a childish laugh that turned suddenly uncontrollable as though he'd suddenly lost all his senses. "Margaret!" he called finally. He rarely said her name. She came rushing in, already smiling, feeling frolicsome, ready for something funny. "Your lounges have arrived." He smiled.

"Are those for me, Dad?" asked Stephen. "Are those for Flo?"

Brian placed the two miniature steamer lounge chairs, teak, on the big table in the kitchen as a centerpiece.

Flo squealed, "Batman can sit in there!"

"Yeah," said Sarah. "And Barbie."

Just last month, the strangest of all eBay incidents. She'd called to Brian: "Honey?"

He was attacking Stephen downstairs. Stephen was all whoops and haws. Margaret peeked around the corner down the stairs. The girls were oblivious to the racket. Sarah was making a macramé bracelet and Flo watched her, attentive as can be, her tongue plugged out of her mouth in concentration, eager to master her sister's skill.

"Sweetheart?" called Margaret furtively, aiming it toward him, trying to insert it between Stephen's cries. She felt a frivolous thrill, an effervescing excitement. "Honey!" she called.

She looked back into the bedroom at the little packet, small like a roll of goat cheese from the Fresh Foods market. It sat plainly, like an egg, on top of the new kilim that she was unpacking, unrolling.

The roughhousing ended. "Brian!" she yelled more loudly, impatiently, in order to finally get his attention.

A few moments later, he came up the stairs, his hair mussed like a child's, pink-faced from the activity. "Please don't yell at me like that," he said. "No wonder our kids yell all the time."

Margaret paid no attention, started whispering, ushering him into the bedroom. "Look at this," she said.

Brian stood in the doorway, shook his head. "No," he says, frowning. "This one isn't as nice. That other one was better."

"Not the rug. Look." Margaret pointed.

"I have no idea what you're pointing at. Why are you whispering?"

"Right *there*," she said.

"Your clogs?"

"Not the *clogs*! *That*!"

"That . . . bag thing?"

"It was inside the rug."

Brian shrugged.

Margaret looked at him.

"And?" he said.

"So," said Margaret, whispering, her nose twitching, "what *is* it?"

"Maybe it's a freshness thing. Like for salt."

"What? Oh, those. No."

Brian reached for it blithely.

"No!" said Margaret. She touched his hand, and then whispered, almost maniacally, "What if it's anthrax or something?"

"Are you serious?" Brian started laughing. "Anthrax?" Downstairs, the Nelly Furtado song about turning out the lights was just beginning, thumping up the stairs, coming to get them.

"I don't know," said Margaret. "Some weird chemical?"

Brian shook his head back and forth. "Oh, honey," he said, with amused exasperation. He picked it up. He held it. "It's squishy," he reported. He raised an eyebrow at her. "Like it's full of powder."

"See? It is?"

"Calm down," Brian told her. He started to peel back a layer of white tissue paper, the crinkling, a gift.

"Wait," said Margaret, touching his arm. "Seriously. What if it's something?"

"Like anthrax? Ebola? Sarin gas powder pellets?"

"Yeah," said Margaret nervously.

"Or smallpox? Monkey pox? Botox? Clorox? Goldielocks?" He was opening it up.

"Yeah," said Margaret. "Orange Alert, remember? Or Red. Yellow? Something."

"Relax," Brian told her. Something powderlike poufed into the air slightly. "Ahhh!" said Brian, joking into a cower.

Margaret, not joking at all, picked up a T-shirt strewn on the edge of the bed, and waved it in the air nonsensically.

"Sweetheart," said Brian. "I'm joking."

"What *was* that, Brian?"

"I promise you it wasn't anthrax."

"I'm going to tell the kids to go outside—"

"Honey." He put his hand on her shoulder. "Shhh."

"Okay," she said quickly. "Then what is it, Mr. Smarty Pants?"

"Shhh."

"I mean, Brian, these rug guys are mostly all Arabs," said Margaret, nodding.

"Oh, honey." Brian sighed. "Easy."

"I know. I'm just *saying*."

Brian ignored her. He sniffed at the stuff. "I think it's baby powder," he said.

"Is it cocaine?" asked Margaret.

"I think it's cocaine," he said. He took a tiny sample on his pinkie the way detectives do on television, dabbed it onto his tongue. His face registered: *Boing!* "This is cocaine," he said, nodding.

"It is? It's kind of a *lot*."

Brian weighed the little log in his hand. He sat down on the bed. "Who sent the rug?"

"I have the invoice upstairs." Margaret moved quickly, went up into the attic to the computer. Brian could hear her traverse the floor above him.

She came back and closed the door behind her awkwardly, edging someone out. "Mom? Ouch!"

"Flo! Sweetie, I'm so sorry. I didn't see you there."

"You stepped on me."

"I almost stepped on your foot," corrected Margaret.

"Mommy? Will you come make a bracelet with me?"

"In a second, honey. Let Sarah show you how to make one."

"Sarah already did."

"You know what, Flo? I don't know how. Why don't you learn from Sarah and then you can teach *me*."

"I want to learn *with* you."

"You go down and get all the stuff ready, okay? I'll be right down."

"What's that?" asked Flo. The tiny roll in her father's hand looked like a miniature roll of cookie dough.

"Nothing," said Margaret. "It's some glue stuff of Daddy's."

"Glue stuff?"

"You make glue with it," said Margaret, giving Brian the hairy eyeball.

"That's right, Flo," said Brian, eyeing Margaret back. "You make glue with it."

"Dad, will you come make a bracelet with me?"

"You go down and get everything ready, honey," Margaret told her.

"Okay." The small voice, soft and dejected, headed away.

"Get everything ready?" asked Brian, putting a hand up under Margaret's shirt. The other reached up to her bum through the legs of her shorts. Her husband could ravage her the way no one ever did before.

"I don't know. Find string and stuff," said Margaret, falling back on the bed, looking for Brian's mouth with her own, pushing her forehead against his. They both looked sidelong at the doorway, saw the top of Flo's head disappear down the stairs, and turned back to each other. All clear for the moment.

•

Margaret, her cargo of children strapped into their spots, guides the van along the gradual leafy hills, past the homes nestled closely together with their porches and sunrooms, peony bushes puffed up, their flowers dead and messy, top-heavy, diving toward the ground. Prehistoric-looking hostas the size of wheelbarrows around walkways and stoops, the pretty Victorians the color of desserts with their airy porches, their scalloped slate roofs, their Rapunzel-tower spires like ice cream cones turned upside down.

She turns onto car-clogged Greenfield Avenue, looks into the rearview mirror back at the kids, all of them buckled in, ready for blastoff. Flo is already nodding off—but it's way too early!—her eyes fluttering, neck buckling like she's been given a tranquilizer. The other two gaze out the window, thinking about something, she'll never know what—skateboards, squirt guns, braids, bikinis—singing softly along with the music, hitting the high notes:—"*All that glitters is gold*"— tipping their heads slightly side to side.

Margaret veers onto the circle in front of the mediocre branch of the town library that she hardly frequents, momentarily recalls a *Blue's Clues* video that must be long overdue there. She bears right around the bend toward busy Grapevine Road and stops at a yield sign.

The sandpapery sounds of thick traffic when she cracks her window, the fresh air wafting in lovely and free, the faint sting of exhaust. She listens to the music, looks for a break in the many different cars, big

ones, little ones, cars with names that imply journey and hope and faraway adventure—Explorer, Discovery, Voyager, Outback—wondering
whether the band wrote the song before the *Shrek* movie or whether they
were commissioned *specifically* for *Shrek* or possibly—*ka-whack!* The van's
jolted forward. A big iron crunch. A royal shove. Move!

Margaret's first reaction: *How rude!*

She turns quickly to look at the kids. A dark hood, a windshield, she
can't tell what exactly, looms large in the rear window. More important, she registers the children's faces. All are surprised. All are okay.
Stephen's expression borders on the thrilled; Sarah appears to be holding her breath. Flo looks as though she's about to cry since she's been
woken up.

"Oh, boy," says Margaret, thinking of the damage, thinking of the
hassle. Her armpits prickle with released adrenaline. "Everyone?" she
calls, the leader of the troop. "Is everyone okay?"

"What happened, Mom?" Stephen smiles.

"We got hit, honey."

"I'm okay, Mom," says Sarah.

"Flo, sweetie?" asks Margaret. Flo's practically still asleep, though her
brow is tense, her mouth wide open, a cobweb of saliva. "Flo?" For a
micro-second Margaret thinks Flo is hurt, the electricity of adrenaline
there again, tingling through her, then Margaret sees Flo moving.

"Mommy," Flo whines, stirring. She rubs at her nose. For the first
time all morning, Margaret notices that Flo has silver glitter dusted
throughout her hair.

Margaret pulls over onto a wide shoulder probably there for the sole
purpose of similar accidents. Indeed, she spies a cracked piece of a
brake light that she crunches over. The big car behind her—she can't see
what it is yet—lurches next to her. She sees it's a Range Rover, which
makes Margaret mad to begin with, shiny and black. Oodles of money
from neighboring Greenville.

The big Range Rover pulls up in front of her, chugs to a stop. A
thickset wide-hipped woman with a frizz of blond hair gets out. She
looks frazzled to Margaret, like she probably has too many kids, or one
that is a major handful. She walks toward Margaret on the idiotic side
of her car, the side where traffic is whizzing past her, dangerously close.

A decision like this, Margaret observes, Well, maybe she doesn't have any kids. Margaret watches her approach. The woman's shaking her head back and forth, smiling, *Silly me*, pinching the bridge of her nose with two fingers, looking down at the ground, seemingly unaware of the many close cars, the death weapons, that are firing past her within an arm's reach. When she looks up, squinting, Margaret can see her face. She has the skittish mien of an albino rabbit: the pink nose, the chapped-looking area around watery eyes, the permanent look of having just yawned.

"Oh, boy," whispers Margaret, recognizing what she's about to contend with.

Margaret sits back and sighs, rubs her neck as she watches the woman come bumbling toward her. "Oh, for crying out loud," says Margaret, full-voiced, a phrase straight out of the archives of her mother's phrases and said with the same arching lilt of annoyance, the same resigned exasperation.

The last time Margaret said it, same phrase, same tone, wasn't very long ago, at the antics of her little sister, Edie, in the kitchen during her last visit from the city. Their conversation about moles (of the skin) had snaked its way toward the topic, by way of cancer, of how their father would make his way east to Magnolia Heights.

"Little kids fly alone on airplanes all the time," said Edie. She was at the sink washing dishes after dinner, letting hot water come bulleting out of the faucet in a torrent, wasting gallons. Margaret had already turned it down to a slower flow twice and Edie, oblivious, had turned it right back up again. Margaret couldn't help but focus on the water, watch it, listen to it, torturing herself to keep from turning it down again. See, thought Margaret, if Edie had kids she wouldn't be wasting water this way.

"What is that on your arm?" Margaret asked her, trying to take her mind off the water.

"A stamp. As long as he makes it here; that's what's important."

"That's not what's important," said Margaret. "It's important that we take care of him." Which is hard for me to do because I have *three kids*, she wanted to say, and Max has one and a marriage in possible crisis. And it's expensive, Margaret wanted to scream, taking the red-eye, flying all the way out there. She couldn't afford it, but she still went. Edie has no idea, thought Margaret, looking at her sister. Edie has no idea, for instance, what a feat, what a victory it was that all three of Margaret's children were sound asleep and it was barely eight o'clock *and* everyone had already eaten dinner. Edie probably thought kids just went to bed and that was that, no effort involved, no *training*.

"Well, it's been hard to take care of him," said Edie. Then, like she'd read Margaret's mind, "I want to give you some money for some of your flights."

"A stamp for what?"

"This thing I went to last night. This fund-raiser thing."

"A fund-raiser? You're such a glamour-puss."

"For orphans in Nicaragua. Like eighty percent of the place must have been doing ecstasy."

"Lovely. Nice."

Edie rubbed lazily at the fading blotch with her wet finger, back and forth like some form of acupressure, trying to get it off. "I don't know what it is. A wheel? It looks like the Pentagon." The black ink was turning purple.

"A cog," said Margaret. "Have you seen Max?"

"I never speak to my brother anymore," Edie answered. Margaret always liked it when Edie referred to their brother as "my brother." Edie did the same thing with their parents. *My* dad. *My* mother. Margaret liked it, protective and sweet-sounding, especially when she imagined Edie saying *my* sister when she was talking about Margaret to Max or their mother—or—well, their father. *My* brother. As if Margaret had no idea who he was. Edie continued. "I called him last week, and that assistant—"

"Miriam."

"Yeah. She kept asking me if I was Chloe, even though I told her it was me."

"I haven't been able to reach him," said Margaret. "I wanted to ask him about Dad's stuff. He told me he packed some more things the last time he was there." Margaret wanted to get to the subject, but she also wanted to avoid it. She threw in, "You look great, E," and pinched her sister's waist, as a way to say something, to circle the topic like a lioness.

"You mean I look fat?"

"No. No, I mean you look great."

"You think I should have been out to see Dad more," said Edie, now really letting the water run plentifully, no longer even washing. "That's what you mean, isn't it, when you say *we* haven't been taking care of him. You mean *me*."

"No." said Margaret. "But how many times were you out there, twice?"

Edie looked at her, stunned. Somehow she thought maybe no one had noticed.

Margaret reached over and turned the water off.

"Why do you keep doing that?"

"There's a drought," snipped Margaret, knowing it was a record-breaking month of rain.

Edie looked at her sister through a slant of hair. "You'd like me to go get Dad," she said.

Margaret pushed a cabinet door closed with her knee, picked up a wet pot to polish with her dish towel. "Didn't you want to sell your car to someone in LA or something?"

"Jesus," said Edie, her voice trilling high. She was smiling the reddened smile she made, eyes gone beady, when she was angry. "Why didn't you just *ask*? Why don't you just *say*?"

"Oh, for crying out loud," said Margaret, putting the back of her wet hand to her forehead. But Edie was right. It was exactly what Margaret wanted her to do. After all, Margaret had been out there a lot: four times, in just the last three months. Not that she minded going, for the most part. It had been one of the coldest winters she could remember, the skin cracking on her hands like an old person's, her feet constantly cold and brittle except when she was in a hot shower. The sun, albeit California winter sun, made her shoulders feel as though they dropped an inch or two, her limbs and joints more pliant. Plus, the flight was like a frigging spa: peanuts, snoozing, magazines, smiling people serving her things for five or six hours, no one interrupting, no one squawking, no one *talking*.

Sure, it was disturbing to see her father ill, and it caused major uproar to be away from the kids for a night or two, but partly she enjoyed it. Alone again. The quiet after a loud party when your ears keep screaming. She'd wake up throughout the night in the guest room with the fleur-de-lis wallpaper to—nothing. The pool's generator kicking in. A volley of dog barks. The honk of a horn muted by space and air. A distant rumble, possibly an earthquake, possibly an airplane, possibly the waves down the hill rolling endlessly onto the shore in the dark.

In the morning, her father. Sometimes genial, sometimes difficult. She knew him intimately but hardly at all. All her life, practically, she'd only been alone with him for a few hours at a time. He worked in New York, and when he was home he was usually immersed in some project, a major one, like building a new bathroom. He'd hurry off to the dump, head out to the golf course or the hardware store, settle into his garden, the knees of his pants skidded with dirt, enmesh himself in some fix-it project down in the basement, shovel snow, clean out the gutters, glaze the windows, leave to get firewood as soon as the Thanksgiving meal wound down. Now sick, he was her captive, practically, when she was out at his house, an arrangement made familiar to her from her kids, and she had him all to herself. She wasn't so sure she wanted him all to herself, but the novelty, the desire to be alone with your father, the apple of his eye—well, does that escape anyone?

There was, no question, this ineffable feeling that she got when she was around him sometimes that she hadn't remembered, that she maybe partly remembered having as a little girl at certain times, when he arrived home from somewhere, when he held her hand, when he read to her in bed, when he listened to her with what looked like a smile even though he wasn't smiling. "My dear," he'd say to her, a brief nod in greeting as she entered a room. That was all, and there she'd be, conjured. Lifted and pleased.

Her father would still busy himself—he wasn't *that* sick yet—but with lesser tasks. He'd replace door hinges or rewire a lamp or a light fixture, dismantle the ceiling fan in the guest room halfheartedly, causing all sorts of commotion.

One morning she woke to the sounds of him taking apart the mahogany frame of his bed, a larger endeavor that he'd clearly been waiting to do during one of her visits. The scrapes on the headboard had been driving him crazy, he said. "Look at them," he said, disgusted, once the headboard was at his mercy, flattened like a patient on his workshop table in the garage. Margaret could hardly make them out. "They're like fingernail marks," he said lightly.

Margaret shivered, a sudden image of him in his bed unable to get up, scratching at the wood. What concerned her, however, putting other thoughts of his declining health aside, was that the value of the bed would be diminished. She'd learned about the danger of refinishing on *Antiques Road Show*. She mentioned it. "It might mess up the value, Dad. Refinishing it."

He looked up from the yellow can of Minwax and gave her a look that said *Not you too*, as if she'd slipped briefly into the realm of imbeciles who concern themselves with such things as money and value.

He'd still venture out on his own a bit too. Amble off in the car to the drugstore for shaving cream, the liquor store for ginger ale, the art store for some paint for the carved birds. "I'll be back in due course," he said to her one day, as he got into the car. She was sitting in the lawn chair reading a profile on Sean Penn. Her father poked his head out the car window as he backed out. "Remind me to name a boat *In Due Course*," he told her. "Or maybe *Due Course* would be better."

"Okay, Dad."

"I suppose I could name this car," he said. He lingered there, the engine puttering, looking his daughter over. "You have a nice arrangement," he said to her. Beside her was the pitcher of iced tea she'd made for the both of them. At her feet, the telephone.

"I'm enjoying myself," she said.

He stayed there, looking out his car window as though it were a porthole, surveying the small backyard, the garden, his daughter, thinking for a split second about dying, how everything remains despite it. "Hummingbirds! Hummingbirds!" he said softly, eagerly, pointing them out with a nod.

Margaret looked. They hung there, two of them, striking and sweet, bobbing like puppets on strings at the red feeder that dangled from the tree. She could hear the silent sound of their movement. Margaret always had a strange urge, the athlete in her, to whack them with a badminton racket, see how far they'd go.

One of them disappeared. The other buoyed up and down, extracted red sugar water with its needle beak, then dove away, floating fast through the air, bobbing, uncorked.

Margaret looked at her father.

He nodded to her. "So there," he said, and backed out.

3

Edie, a woman more like a girl, has been acting like a man the way she jumps into the car every morning and takes off as if she's got no kids. Which she hasn't. "That's right!" she yells to herself, stupid music blaring inside the sealed compartment of her car, pulling away from motels with hurricane fences around dingy half-filled pools, pretending momentarily that she's leaving people behind. "*Ciao for now!*" she's been booming out loud to herself, zooming away from anywhere like a solo fugitive—a Louise without Thelma, a Thelma without Louise—along roads like ramps, roads like rivers, and then racing track roads with easy curves through fields of grass the color of light brown hair.

She motors on west, through deserts with the windows open, whizzing past blue-jeaned guys in front of dusty shops, then up into mountains with melting snowdrifts molded like donuts around the biggest red-trunked trees she's ever seen. She passes people in hats and sunglasses, sporty cars with thick tires and fluorescent snowboards, surfboards, kayaks, canoes, then twirls her old Volvo down from the mountains, ringing around fresh green hills to arrive at the flat-bellied stretch alongside the coast.

There's plenty of time. Someday. For what, exactly, she's not sure. The great mass of air hovering above the water beside her seems prescient somehow, containing possibilities, her future, more than what she has now. The tinfoil flicker of the water. The mercury gleam of the horizon. But for now she's been driving and driving, through towns she doesn't know the name of, over small mountain ranges of which she's unaware. She's been gone for a few days, thinking absentmindedly of nothing much at all, occasionally panicked that she's without a plan in the grand scheme of things, but for the most part she's simply glad to be going, glad to be on the move, and with her mission, at least as an immediate objective, to collect her father.

At least she has a job. She's a clip coordinator at *Chew the Fat,* an obnoxious talk show hosted by a blond comedienne named Beverly Dodd who has a strong penchant for bronze (lipstick, nail polish, car, leather, shoes, silk) and takes pride in hosting a show with a quasi-political bent. The events that occurred on the last day before hiatus last week, a typical day for Edie: her intern getting blamed for losing the petty cash envelope that was brought on a remote, two passes for Edie to a media screening for Nicolas Cage's new movie, a cold call message for Edie left with the receptionist from the actor Jack Rawlings's production company, which was clearly a mistake, or a joke being played by one of the show's writers or one of Edie's own siblings.

Things heard around the office on that last day before hiatus, a typical day, snippets filtering out of offices as Edie walked through the hallways, stood at the Xerox machine, or got some coffee out of the snack room: a female producer talking as earnestly as if she were battling for the rights of all women, "I told him that if the Dove/Hawk sketch can't have the *hawks* diving at the *doves* in the studio, forget it. It's pointless without them, pointless! So what if they hit the lights?

Edie's friend Colleen, in charge of casting, possibly the only regular, sane person in the entire office, was on the phone. "I'm sorry," Colleen said, squinting into the mid-distance, a pained look on her face. "I'm sorry about this. . . . That's right," she said. "The four fattest people you can find. It's called"—she winced—"the Blimpie sketch." Here, Colleen's head collapsed onto her hand, a visor at her forehead. "Right. The guy who ate all those sandwiches."

Downstairs in the studio, a flamboyant film director from Spain, the first guest, was in the greenroom when Edie slipped in to grab a few Mrs. Field's cookies from the buffet tray. The Spanish director was being told that the show was taped live so please avoid swearing during the interview. I understand, the director said, his accent playful. *No problema.* As Edie closed the door, leaving, she heard him finish, asking, "But can I say . . . *pussy?*"

A lobbed yell down the long hallway—"Hey, Ted!"—followed by a hurrying writer eating a folded slice of pizza. "Does she like the leukemia-guy idea? Will she wear the burka?"

Edie, returning to her office via the conference room entrance after having a cigarette downstairs, finds it full of Marilyn Monroe look-alikes and a couple of Hillary Clintons. Rick, one of the writers, a long ponytail down his back, was asking the curviest Marilyn, "And will you be willing to wear this French maid outfit"—holding it up—"with garters?"

A segment producer, Fred, calling Edie's name from behind as Edie's getting money from the ATM machine next to the commissary. "Edie! How's that footage coming?"

"What footage?"

"What footage?" repeats Fred, appalled. He was hurrying toward her down the long windowless hallway.

"You haven't asked me for anything, Fred." Edie leaned over the ATM screen protectively as he approached to hide her measly balance. She once went into Fred's office to search for a tape on his chaotic desk and came across three large dog-eared paychecks, uncashed, dispersed throughout his heaps of papers.

"The baby? The baby in utero?" said Fred.

"I have not received this request," said Edie. With Fred, when he's keyed up, he has a tendency not to listen, to twirl his ideas around, to blame things on whoever he's speaking with, to make them crazy. Edie has found it easiest to communicate with him in monotone, almost robotic, sentences.

"Yesterday," says Fred. "The morning meeting."

"I was in the studio," responds Edie.

"The day before, then."

"The only request I got was B-roll. Wild horses. Protozoa. Recent film trailers."

"Oh," said Fred. "Well. I need a baby. That *Nova* stuff."

"Okay."

"For the Anti-Baby campaign."

"The what?"

"You'll see. We need it by tomorrow."

"Tomorrow we're all on hiatus," said Edie.

Fred began to play the excuse back to her. "Tomorrow we're all—"
He looked sideways without moving his head, glinted his eyes at her
apprehensively. "We are?"

"Yes, Fred. We are."

•

It was best when she had a lot to do. The day raced. Like when she was
a waitress in college or working for that catering company. The shifts
and parties that were incredibly busy were the most rewarding—they'd
speed by at a hustle and she'd have a mound of cash at the end of the
night. At work at the show, when she had a lot to do, she'd have various
lists on nice colored Post-its on the wall by her desk: a list for needed
footage, a list for footage that needed to be bumped up, a list for
footage that needed to go to the edit bay, a list for still store, photos she
needed to get, photos she needed to take to the control room, things
they needed to buy, things that needed permission, things that needed
to be waived. . . .

It was best when there was a lot to do because otherwise, sometimes,
she'd get so bored, so tired, too many cookies at lunch, her butt heavy
and uncomfortable in her seat, too many magazines borrowed from
Research making her feel carsick, the lack of natural light causing her
immune system to feel feeble: headachy, chills, awful. Regularly putting
her head down on her desk, feeling pathetic, wanting *air*. The drone of
televisions all around her.

•

She'd woken at dawn at the desert motel earlier in the morning, extra
early, craving sugar, wanting to get moving. She felt guilty that she
hadn't called Margaret yet, was aware of the possible pay phones that
she was passing when she passed them. Behind the wheel, she drove
without thought in the dawn's early light, dangerously hypnotized,
miles passing with nothing to recollect about them. An emphysemal
wheeze under the dash from time to time. Dunkin' Donuts coffee, light
cream, the warm cardboard cup like sunlight against her inner thighs.
The ashtray full of mutilated cigarette butts. On the radio, the classic
rock of any-year anywhere America: this time, "Leather and Lace."

As the sun came up, there was some commotion ahead. A female cop on the side of the road, the wind blowing a jagged part in her hair. A box truck was holding things up. Edie thought of radiation, a TV series in the California hills. The thought of being *right here* for the big bust of a terrorist cell. She immediately placed herself in a movie: the flashy trailer, the deep-voiced narrator. *She* was on her way to get her sick father, but a simple drive turned out to be *not so simple*. (A rapid series of images, shocked faces, terrified screams: *Oh, my God! I can't hold on! Is he in there?* Angles of trucks and cars, a close-up of a likely terrorist's sneer, a match being lit.)

A patrolman waved her on perfunctorily with an orange flag. Edie glanced sideways like everyone else to get a look at the situation. The driver of the truck, a man, was doing a sobriety test, trying to place his forefinger on his nose for an audience of two state troopers. As Edie rolled away, a sliver view of the man in her rearview mirror tipping over, drunk in the early morning.

"A fucking a-hole is all I can say," she said to the road before her, then wondered why. From time to time, alone in the car, nonsensical things would come jabbering out of her mouth.

After a while, a gas station lumped among the trees. On the corner of the building was a pay phone, and Edie walked toward it along a concrete curb that served as a stoop for the adjacent twenty-four-hour convenience store. She glimpsed her ghostly outline in the window as she passed: tall trees across the quiet road behind, the reflection of a bird swooping from one side of the window to the other. On the other side of the glass, inside, she spotted a white rack decorated with snack foods. Beer nuts, butterscotch, red pistachios, and caramels, gleaming through their clear plastic bags, their red cardboard labels festooned with swirled baseball-pennant script. On the way back she'd grab a bag of pistachios, not dyed. Maybe some caramels.

The pay phone had scratched graffiti, scratchiti, all over it, mainly a celebration of the name *Ray* written sideways, perpendicular, and diagonally on the phone's silver surfaces. Edie punched in her various calling card numbers after the requisite chimes. When she heard the phone ringing she was amazed for a moment that the card number still worked, feeling like her removal from her ordinary day-to-day in New York should have somehow disrupted it.

The pleasant sound of a ringing phone—the world works, Edie thought to herself—gurgling like a child's toy. Then the voice she expected, her sister Margaret, after enough rings to cause Edie to wonder why the voice mail wasn't picking up.

Margaret sounded a little tired, a little harried. "I was on the verge of calling in the National Guard," said Margaret. "I thought you'd call last night."

"I *did* call last night."

"You're up early," said Margaret, looking at her clock. "Are you there yet?"

"I'm a little north."

"The flight's tomorrow, Edie."

"I know," Edie answered.

"Today's Friday," Margaret pointed out, then was quiet for a moment, aware she was being pushy, possibly condescending. She paused and took a breath, like Brian would remind her to do. "I'm just curious to know how he's doing," she explained.

"Sure," said Edie.

"To have your report."

"Right," said Edie. They listened to each other say nothing. Edie watched the triangular flags (car dealer flags, flags for swim meets) above the parking area wilt in the wind collectively. She watched a taupe sedan crunch along the gravel and park underneath them. The pinched face of an elderly woman in the backseat peered out at her briefly. "I'm at a gas station," Edie announced.

They laughed. A sisterly laugh at nothing but at something at the same time. "So," said Margaret, wrapping it up. "I'll talk to you when you get there. We're all heading off to the doctor here."

"Okay," said Edie.

"Call me when you get there," Margaret told her, annoyed that Edie didn't ask why they were going to the doctor. She gave her another chance by asking, "What's that noise? Is someone laughing?"

"Crows," said Edie, looking up into the large trees. "Very loud crows."

"They sound like women. Okay, off to the *doctor*."

"They're huge," said Edie. She watched one alight on a furry branch, settling, folding in its big wings like a collapsing umbrella. It looked left and then right. Something in the style of its glance, something both comfortable and insecure all at once, made Edie think of their brother. "Where is my brother?" said Edie, out of the blue.

Margaret smiled into the receiver. That possessive thing Edie did. Margaret said, "*Our* brother?"

"Yeah. Where is that guy?"

"Beats me. But I got to get going here," said Margaret, saying good-bye, putting the phone down. She stood still at the freckled counter, the window framing the green cove of backyard, the cut basil starting to droop in its glass of water, the wooden bowl with its shriveling, oozing fruit. She picked up a molding peach, its soft side pressed flat, and tossed it into the trash under the sink. A telling *thunk*: Did she forget to put a new garbage bag in when she took out the trash? She imagined the peach smeared along the inside wall of the white plastic garbage can. She leaned over into trash territory, not wanting to clean it all but mainly not wanting to turn around to her approaching kids, trying to avoid their customary siege.

They were like hired private detectives, the way at least one of them would descend upon her after she'd hung up, demanding immediate information. Usually at least one of them was there long before the phone call ended, asking for things they already had in their hands, orbiting the room, winding through her legs like a cat, getting in her way, looking for things, even if they'd been happily involved in something before the phone rang.

The response time this morning, however, was lax. Stephen was in a hyperactive froth state, despite the fever (or because of it), striking at flies wildly with the flyswatter: tennis serves, zipping the air. Into the kitchen he jumped.

"Was it Edie?" asked Stephen, flushed.

"It was Edie," said Margaret. "Yes."

"Well, where is she, Maggie?" asked Sarah, entering the kitchen through the living room door. She looked tired, her long hair matted, the tough-life punk-rocker look of a worn-out almost-six-year-old.

"Yeah, Mags. Where is she?" asked Stephen.

"Call me Mom, please. Or Mother, if you will."

The kids both shrugged the same shrug. Their eyes were different, their mouths were different, but their bodies' shapes and the way they moved mirrored each other.

"Well, where is she?" asked Stephen. "We've been waiting for her to call, haven't we? Haven't we been waiting, Mom?"

"California."

"California." Stephen smiled. "The sunshine state."

"That's Florida, Stephen." She looked at the clock on the microwave. They'd leave in ten minutes for the doctor, she decided. "I believe California's the golden state," she said.

"What's she doing *there*?" Stephen grimaced, whisking the air with the swatter.

"Would you please settle down?" She had a headache. Or something. "She's getting Gramps. You know that."

"Gramps stinks!" said Stephen, grinning.

"Cut it, String Bean," said Margaret. She rubbed her neck, pressed a fingertip hard into a spot at the base of her skull.

"When will ol' Grampmeister be arriving?" asked Stephen.

"Settle *down*," Margaret told him, as, simultaneously, Stephen accidentally swatted her skirt. Margaret grasped his wrist, took a deliberate deep breath. "You don't seem too sick, do you?" Margaret said to Stephen. She looked him in the eyes, then at Sarah, back and forth. Another deep breath. "Do you guys get why Gramps is coming here?"

Sarah shrugged. "I get it," she said.

"Why?" asked Margaret.

"Yeah, why," said Stephen, blinking.

Sarah explained to her brother, trying to sound grown-up. "'Cause, you see, Stephen," Sarah told him, trying to incorporate her hands, flipping them, a novice hand-talker. She tipped her head sideways, mashed a shoulder to her ear. "Gramps is sick. And—well, you see, because—" Her head went side to side; then she looked up at Margaret for a finish, for some help.

Margaret could see both of them waiting. Small animals, she thought. Little heads and shiny eyes. Big facts.

"He's sick," said Margaret (for the thirtieth time), making an effort to sound gentle, "and he's going to pass away." *Pass away*, she thought. What an idiotic way to put it. As though nothing actually occurred.

Sarah squinched up her nose. "Pass away?"

Outside, a little bird had begun singing loudly next to the open window. *Tweetilly tweet. Tweetilly tweet. Tweetilly tweet.* Stephen butted in, spoke loudly over it. "Gramps is pretty much a goner, guys," he said, speaking into his index finger like it was a microphone.

Margaret lifted an eyebrow at him. She turned to Sarah. "He's dying, honey."

"Oh," said Sarah. She mulled it over for a few moments, moving air in her cheeks from side to side as though she was swishing mouthwash. "Oh," she said again. "That part I didn't really get."

"You didn't, sweetheart?"

"No. I don't really get that."

"Okay. Is it his coming to stay with us for a while that you don't really get? Or is it *dying* that you don't really get?"

"Yeah. I mean—*zoop!*—it's over and you don't even know it. Right, Mom?"

"Well, I think probably you would know. When your time comes. Maybe."

Sarah was biting her lip, thinking hard, her dazed stare looking past her mother through the back doorway's bottom screen to the empty swing set and the huge hydrangea bush at the edge of the yard. "Oh," she said, staring past her mother. "You mean like Granny knew? Prolly?"

"Probably, honey . . . I'm not sure, sweetheart," she said, feeling herself treading unfamiliar territory. Reeds and a marshy bottom. Watery, cold territory. "It's the great mystery of life."

"It is, Mom?" asked Stephen.

Sarah looked at her mother. "I thought you said love was the great mystery."

"Yeah, Mom," said Stephen. "That's what you said." His finger still a microphone, he placed it at his mother's mouth.

"Well, sure," she said into the mike. "They both are. The two great mysteries."

"Okay," said Stephen. He moved the microphone to his sister.

"Oh," said Sarah. She looked at her mother's hands. "Um, Mom?"

"Yes?"

"Can Gramps, like, talk still?"

"Sure, honey. He can talk."

"Good," said Sarah.

Stephen asked, "Will he, Mom, like, know who I am?"

Margaret spoke into her son's miniature index finger. "Yes. Yes, he will."

4

ax Bramble sits on a bench in Riverside Park. Blue sky all over the place, morning sunlight spilling through the trees into swarms of light on the green ground before him. Early summer's air on his arms and his cheeks. A frappuccino bought with cobbled-together coins from the dented silver dish by the door. A lovely wind.

Down the sloping hill, a backdrop to everything—trees, pigeons, loping dogs, joggers, walkways, pedestrians, people with strollers, people holding hands, balls being tossed, balls being kicked, a yellow Frisbee getting thrown expertly through the air—is the Hudson River, a swath of bluish-gray satin, a massive metallic mirage above the walkway's stone wall.

Along the walkway down the slope in front of him, schoolchildren are in straggled single file, clumped groups of chattering. The boys' baggy pants and moping scuffles. The girls' quicker movements, their heightened energy taut and playful like held-in laughter.

Max leans forward, elbows on his knees, the heels of his hands on his cheekbones. He stretches the skin across the bridge of his nose, looks at his feet: the same feet he's always had. Beneath them, city dirt, worn and weary, less like soil and more like compacted beige dust. To the right of his right shoe, the foil of a Powerbar wrapper (peanut butter). To the left, a spent condom wormy next to a rock.

He stands up, takes the lid off of his drink to polish it off, keeps some mashed coffee ice in his mouth, and tosses the plastic cup into a wrought-iron wicker garbage can. The plastic cup explodes on contact and uncaps, a small firework of leftover coffee whip splattering the pathway, a light spray on his sneaker. He stands there for a second, contemplating the mess. There's nothing to clean up. He walks a couple of paces down the hill to get a better view of a soccer game being played by some South American guys. The pop of the ball, its rise high up over their heads, is completely satisfying to him. One of them heads it, and the ball floats into a volleyball game farther on, the balls comingling, bouncing like dogs greeting each other.

Max starts to walk toward the soccer guys to ask if he can play, when through the fingers of leaves and branches that shade his spot protectively, he sees something, the flicker of the familiar, recognizes a familiar stride half a field away. The blond hair, the squared shoulders, coming down the steep hill beside him in a downhill walk, bracing a little, clomping. The Maclaren stroller, its periwinkle-colored awning with its fancy titanium or whatever-it-is frame, its handles curled like an umbrella's. Pudgy legs emerge from it, then the baby boy's body thrusts forward, curious, erect, like the figurehead of a clipper ship or cattle boat. His small hand points: a scooter, a wheelchair, a puddle, a bike. He bounces with excitement, both hands pointing at what he sees: a tugboat, toylike, moving slowly upriver, steady as a flatliner, its chin down, small and determined.

Once they're on level ground at the bottom of the hill, the mother stops and digs into the massive Guatemalan bag that's straddling the stroller's handles. Out comes a navy blue ball cap which, after some objection, the baby lets her put on him. After a few paces, it's quickly tossed aside, promptly picked up by the mother, and put back on the head. A few more steps: again it's tossed off. From Max's distance, it's a combination of silent-movie comedy and the sad humor found in a senile old man, serenely objecting. The mother brings out an apple, quickly takes a few bites in order to skin it, and the little boy takes it, forgetting what's on his head when the mother puts it back on.

A warm, clear day, the young mother in a pale pink dress with her toddler, a morning outing in the park, birds singing. To the rest of the world the duo is a charming one, sweetly comforting, a vision of early summer, vernal, a reminder of nature, a reminder of motherhood. But to Max, they are terrifying. Blazing like a candle, the young woman unassumingly pushes the stroller along, the sunglasses on her face, her loose ponytail falling apart into splayed strands at the back of her head, getting closer.

Max retreats behind a tree. If he scrambles up the hill, she might see him. Or, more likely, eagle-eye Rexie will spot him and start shrieking. Max gets behind another tree, farther up the hill. He can't help, however, watching them a little bit. Chloe stops and fiddles with her foot. She stands up straight and reties her ponytail, takes a swig from the water bottle in the stroller's thoughtful beverage holder, wipes her brow with the back of her forearm. She looks so free. Little Rex is completely comfortable and calm, watching the world, alone with his mother. Max imagines other people looking at her, looking at the boy, wondering what their life is like, where they live, what she does, who the husband is.

Chloe steers the stroller in a skilled curve, stops at the stone wall that looks down over the lower rung of the park, the hidden West Side highway, and, mostly, the water. She squats down to get something out of the bag. The familiar red of the box of animal crackers, filled on the sly with cookies from the health food store. When she stands up, she leans on the stone wall. She hunches over for a second. Her shoulders shudder. A quiver of her upper body. Is she crying? Coughing? Little Rex is busy watching the soccer ball get kicked around. One of the guys slides on the grass. A long streak of grass stain is left behind on his leg.

Chloe puts her sunglasses on top of her head. She rubs her eyes. She rubs her neck. Sunglasses back down again. She bites at her fingernails. Whoops, the soccer ball goes soaring sideways, nearly hitting Chloe in the head, then disappears over the walkway's ledge, down to the lower level of the park.

Max watches one of the shirtless guys apologize to her, Chloe nodding, her hand up in the air, No problem. He feels an intense pang of irrational jealousy. An urge to call out to her and come charging down the hill, push the jerk with no shirt onto the ground.

He'd have noticed her even if he didn't know her. Would have watched her anyway, probably, wondering what sort of a man she had sex with, wondering if that was her kid, was she married, was she happy. Totally beautiful to him, she belongs in a French novel about the aristocracy, wearing pumped-up bodices that show off breasts clean as a bowl of milk, with velvets and silk brocades, white cotton underthings, swishing skirts and boots with buttons, glassy earrings that match her blue eyes.

But here she is, deposited here, a Christmas tree of Ziploc bags full of crackers and Cheerios, juice boxes and sippy cups bulging from her pockets, crowding the carriage's storage nets. Her neon-green flip-flops. Her peggy legs and inward-pointing feet, her birdlike quality (a long-necked bird, an emu, an ostrich even, though she's not that tall), her big eyes and surprise tattoo—you wouldn't think she had a tattoo—that she got in Japan of a dragonfly. Here she is, deposited here in a New York City park, the mother of a son (who also belongs in some Lord Fauntleroy arrangement, the red bow mouth, the rock-star shag of blond hair), being watched through the trees by her husband on a Friday morning at the end of spring.

Max sighs. It feels like he has an ulcer. A nervous fluttering bores through his abdomen in a specific area, like a fire's poker.

It's been almost three weeks that he's been pretending to go to work. He'd been working as a producer for the last four years at a small production company begun by his friend Jake that was backed, in a very roundabout, vague, but still somehow intensely close way, by the Vivienne Communications megaconglomerate where Jake's stepfather was president of Development. It was called Foona Laguna Productions from a Dr. Seuss character (Jake himself *looked* like a character), and they'd made two short independent films and one feature, *Along Came You*, a "charming coming-of-age tale," it was generally called, that made a little bit of a splash, got good reviews, and played in theaters mostly in the city, a sort of modern-day *Sabrina*-esque story where a young woman, Abby (played by the lovely Chloe Eliot), the daughter of a deeply indebted, widowed summer cook in the Hamptons, ends up living happily ever after with a self-made katrillionaire Bill Gates type (but he's handsome, young, and hip) whose life isn't as easy as it sounds, apparently, since his father slept around all the time (even with his son's earlier *girlfriend*, surprise, surprise), and the mother had a primo drinking and gambling problem.

After *Along Came You*, Chloe got pregnant, married Max, and put her possibly promising career on hold. After all, she was twenty-six; her modeling career was basically over, she could get back into acting once the baby was bigger, and she'd wanted a baby for as long as she could remember.

Growing up, she'd followed her divorced parents around. Both worked for UNESCO: Geneva, New York, Beijing, Paris, Long Island, back to Paris, New Hampshire (of all places) for that breakdown year of her mother's when Chloe was twelve, Paris again, London, and then back to Paris, where a modeling scout spotted her eating a ham and butter baguette on the steps of Saint-Sulpice when she was fourteen. The agent, the *scout*, gave Chloe her card: The Stern Modeling Agency, a name even Chloe recognized. They arranged to meet the following day after school at a café in the Tuileries, where the scout, Genie, arrived with a photographer, a Spanish woman with skunk-striped hair who took plenty of shots of Chloe smoking cigarettes and drinking her lemonade. Genie told Chloe, straight out of the starlet discovery lore, the milkshake-counter legends, "If you play it right, kid, that face could make you heaps of cash." In the end, Chloe was never really tall enough, though she did make some nice money. In the end, Chloe never really cared.

After all that ridiculous modeling time spent in Japan, all that traveling and silly catalog work, Chloe was ready (*dying*) to just sit relatively still and take care of a small person. Have some other person, at least partly, take care of her.

Max had quit. Foona Laguna began producing more and more pre-launch promos, sales, and marketing tapes, which was fine until they started to be primarily commercials and corporate videos, jobs being passed to Jake by his bigwig stepfather. A public service announcement for the Republican Party, trying to be edgy, trying to be *young*. Next, Jake took on a local chapter of the NRA as a client, and then an assemblyman who'd practically defended the outright racist comments of a particular senator, which was one thing, but mainly Max began to disagree with Jake in terms of the production company's future. Their original idea was that all this corporate stuff, all this advertising, would help fund independent features and fascinating documentaries, when what was happening instead was Jake was becoming one of those Euro operators who visited Ibiza regularly and went to raves in the desert in Southern California. Which also was fine, good for Jake—but Max, looking at his own cute little kid and pretty wife, whom he adored but felt sort of pathetic around, didn't *like* his friend Jake anymore. He didn't like the way Jake was cheating on his semi-girlfriend. He didn't like the way he was so over-the-top himself, filling up entire rooms when he entered them, like a dopey golden retriever that's in the way all the time, his silly curly hair floating in floppy ringlets around his head.

"I feel like I'm in advertising," Max had told Jake offhandedly, not meaning much by it.

Jake had an irritating grin on his face, like either he had a girl hidden under his desk playing with him or he was on something. "It's the American way," said Jake, squeaking back in his expensive desk chair.

"What, making money?"

"Equal representation, dude."

"Like defense lawyers?"

"In a way, bro. In a way."

"Well," said Max, disheartened, confused. "I thought we were going to make movies."

"You're so idealistic," Jake told him, meaning, *Don't be so idealistic.* "We're not in college anymore."

"Why do people always say that? That college thing."

"Hey. There's a good thing going here," said Jake. "Enjoy yourself."

"I don't enjoy it," said Max. He said it again. "I'm not enjoying myself."

"Well, then leave." Jake shrugged. On another day this comment might not have riled Max. But on this day it was too much: the look on Jake's face, his heavy lids, the smugness—*was* there a girl under the desk sucking him off? —the way Jake leaned back in his chair, clasped his hands behind his head, and smiled, self-satisfied. "You can always leave, man," Jake said again, baiting him.

Max looked at him, intensely angry at nothing in particular, wanting to say something, a real zinger, but what came out was, simply, "Okay," with an unfortunate nervous quiver underneath it. "Okay," said Max again, this time casually, and as he walked out of the office he felt incredibly relieved, incredibly gratified, but then not at all relieved when he thought of Chloe and where he'd left her that morning: surfing realtor.com compulsively as she did daily, Rex on her lap scrawling with crayons, attacking the keyboard, or down on the floor pulling out all the towels and sheets from the low cabinet. "Look at this one," said Chloe, calling to him.

Max was on his way out the door, but he came back in. A picture of a wooden A-frame in some dark woods. "Where is it?" he asked.

"Long Island. North Fork."

"I couldn't live in that house."

"It has *four* bedrooms," said Chloe. They currently lived in a glorified studio.

"There's no way there are four bedrooms in *that*."

"It *says* four," said Chloe, always a little bit by-the-book.

"It's built of that lumber that's coated in arsenic," said Max, knowing that would curb any enthusiasm.

"How do you know?"

"Because that's what it looks like. I can't live in that house. I can't live out on the North Fork."

"It's definitely cheaper."

"I can't live out there."

"Well, then, where *can* you live, Max?"

Max slung his bag over his neck like a messenger, put on his sunglasses, and left. Why didn't Chloe get a job? She was the one who could make the quick money just by putting on nice clothes and posing for a camera. Why was all the pressure for earning money on him? It was a tough break you got when you were a young man in the world.

Max watches Chloe take Rex out of the stroller and wedge him onto her hip for a better look at the tugboat. Where is she going? What is she doing way up here? The ulcerous feeling rises into Max's chest, up into his throat. She's up here to surprise him. That's it. She's up here to drop in and see him and have lunch. Max takes out his tiny cell phone, rings Miriam.

"Foona Laguna," answers Miriam, sounding bored.

"Hi, Miriam."

"Max!" exclaims Miriam happily. Then low. "It sucks here."

"Did Chloe call you today?"

"No."

"She didn't?"

"No.

"Are you sure?"

"Why, as a matter of fact, *yes*, she did call. And she mentioned that she has this *feeling* that you haven't been going to work for the last— Of course she didn't call! I told you I'd call you if she called!"

"She didn't?"

"No!"

"Is Jake in the office today?"

"No one's in the office today. That Yoo-hoo shoot."

Max sighs. "I could go for a Yoo-hoo," he says wanly, watching Rex have a small tantrum in Chloe's arms.

"Well, come and get 'em. There's a tower of them in the supply closet."

"I think Chloe's planning on surprising me there today."

"I'll tell her you're on the shoot like everyone else."

"Perfect. Okay."

"Okay."

"Wait. No one will be in all day?"

"Right."

"You know what? I'll call her. I'll call you back."

Max dials Chloe's number as he watches her through the leaves. A blur of laughing kids passes her. It takes Chloe a moment to realize it's her phone that's ringing, then she hurries to find it, presses the button.

"Hello? That's so weird you called!" She touches her forehead. "I was just about to call you. We're up near you in Riverside. We're meeting Jane and Alexander."

"I thought Alexander had chicken pox."

"That was like a month ago, Max," she says. Rex is standing before his stroller, clipping and then trying to unclip the clips on the safety belt.

Max watches Chloe look around the park, put her hand on her hip. He feels like a sharpshooter. "So. Can you have lunch with us?" she asks.

"If you're having lunch with Jane—"

"No. They've got to go somewhere. We'll just walk over to your office when we're done."

"Let's eat in the park," says Max. He's aware of two teenage girls huddled near him, giggling.

"I'll get some of that take-out sushi," says Chloe. "Who's that?"

"Who?" The clear giggles like palm fronds being shaken behind him. "Oh. Some girls."

"Some who?"

"Just some girls."

"What girls? What are they laughing at?"

"I don't know, Clo. Let's meet at the rock spot. At noon."

"No. I'll meet you at work since I don't know what time."

"I'd rather meet in the park," says Max. "It's so nice out."

"Why are there girls in your office?"

He starts to walk away, suddenly afraid that she can somehow actually hear him through the air. "I'm not at the office," he says. "I'm at Starbucks."

"Oh," says Chloe. She's quiet for a moment. "Quiet Starbucks."

"Then come by the office," he says, wincing, a pang of guilt, "whenever you're done." He hangs up the phone without saying good-bye: something he learned from his father, also a man who dislikes the telephone, and something Chloe has learned not to be offended by.

The two girls giggling are cute, long hair, low-waisted jeans. One has a tank top with Ganesh on it, the other a white T-shirt with a leather lace-up at the neck. He senses they're following him as he climbs the stairs to the street, hears them laughing and is sure of it. When he gets up to Riverside Drive, they're still behind him. He turns around. "Can I help you two?" he asks, trying to be friendly but not too friendly.

The smaller one squishes her face up. "Um," she says, then composes herself. She has a pen in her hand and holds it up like a wand. "Can we get an autograph?"

He'd had the feeling even though this hadn't happened in a while. Then again, he needed a haircut, which was when it tended to occur. "I'm not who you think I am," he tells them.

They look at him. "Hello?" says the Ganesh girl. She's turning bright red.

"No way," says the taller one.

"I'm not kidding," says Max.

"No *way*," says the taller one again. She's stunned.

"Yes, way," Max tells her.

"That is *crazy*," says the other girl. Both the girls are looking his face over, not at him but his nose, its nostrils, his ears and hair, looking for a clue. "Yo," she says. "Do people, like, stop you all the time?"

"No."

"But you, like, know who we're talking about." He sees the flash of a silver barbell pierced on her tongue.

"I do." He nods. He shrugs. "Sorry." He glances back at them after he crosses the street. The girls are still watching him go, dumbfounded. The shorter one waves. He waves back, rounds the bend, and practically mows over a short slight woman, bumps flat into her. "Sorry," he mutters, righting her by her elbows.

"Max?"

He looks down at her face, a pretty face, older. It's Mimi Woods, a friend of his mother's. Someone he would avoid, ordinarily, by crossing the street if he saw her coming (which would be highly unlikely since she now lived in Maine and South Carolina) or not looking up if he saw her enter a restaurant (also unlikely). Not because he didn't like her, but instinct somehow, his first impulse, made him avoid things specifically related to his mother. People in particular.

Now, looking at Mimi's face, there's the reason why. He sees a sparkle of his mother in the irises of Mimi Woods's eye, a vivid liveliness, part mischief, part grace, as though his mother is somehow channeling through but hiding, here to tell him to shape up. It's like a bright light, glaring. Max has to look away.

"Max Bramble!" The wide smile. She always had a touch of Brigitte Bardot in her cheeks and mouth. Her perfume smells of lily of the valley.

"Mrs. Woods?"

"Oh, Max. You can call me Mimi by now," she says, patting his arm.

"Sorry for mowing you over," says Max.

"For heaven's sake. You didn't mean to, did you?"

"Did I hurt you?"

"It keeps happening. I'm unaccustomed to city walking. The slow lady from up north blocking the road. But at least this time it was *you*! We're in town visiting my sister. Where's Howard. Howard?" Behind her, near a square of vegetation with a tree growing out of it, is her husband, tall and starting to hunch with age like a top-heavy orchid. On his leash, a small dog, its lip sneered, sniffing at the ivy.

"Howard, get over here!" calls Mimi. "It's Max Bramble, of all people."

Howard looks up serenely. "Max!" he says, smoothing his hand over his bald head.

"We're here visiting my sister," Mimi says again. "Her god-awful dog." She points at it with her chin.

"Is that a Jack Russell?" asks Max. He's been thinking about getting Rex a dog.

"It's so old, all it is does is snap at people. We hear that your pa is coming to live with Margaret!"

Max remembers that this woman Mimi is, in fact, Margaret's god-mother. Or maybe she was Edie's. "Yeah," says Max. "Edie's gone out to get him."

"I think that's perfect. Just where he ought to be."

Max thinks of Chloe coming strollering up from the park any second. He turns his back to the phalanx of trees across the street. Howard approaches. "Beware of dog," Howard announces, as the dog arthritically leads him to the edge of a building, sniffing daintily along the way. The poor dog seems barely able to control his back hips. "A lion in lamb's clothing," says Howard affectionately.

"Isn't it *amazing* that we run into you here on the *street*," says Mimi, raising her hands up and looking over the ground that they're standing on. "Right here on this *corner*."

"My office is nearby," remarks Max.

"I hear your baby is adorable. You were an adorable baby." Mimi's smile purses into concern. "How *is* your father?"

"He stopped the chemo a while ago," says Max. He looks at Mimi's face again. It's there. In the tilt of her head, in a certain reflective depth in her eyes, the ever-so-small double chin, the vertical creases on her bottom lip, covered lightly with lipstick, that smooth out when she smiles. His mother watching him, undercover.

"Oh, Max," says Mimi kindly, and then it's his mother who takes his hand and squeezes it, who touches his arm and presses.

Max feels like he might choke on something. He looks at the ground, at the toes of Mimi's espadrilles.

"And your beautiful wife?" asks Mimi.

"Fine. She's great. Yeah."

"Kate's moved to Alaska," Mimi informs him.

"Alaska? You're kidding!" Max kissed Kate, one New Year's Eve at the Woodses' apartment when he was thirteen, when Kate was still pretty. His first older woman. A coat closet smelling of mothballs, the crack of light shining across Kate's ear. He recalled vaguely the recent saga that his sisters had latched onto of Kate being left by her blond powerhouse moneymaker of a husband who turned out to be gay.

Mimi continues. "She's working for a radio station in Juneau."

"Max?" calls Howard. "Please tell my wife what street the Armory is on."

"Don't listen to him," she says, swatting the air by her head. "I know exactly where it is. When is your father arriving? Maybe we should pay him a visit."

"Um. You know, I'm not exactly sure. How long are you here?" The last thing his father would want would be visitors. Or would he?

"Mmm. Well," says Mimi slyly, nodding. His mother's eyes, twinkling, saying, *I've got your number.*

"We leave on Sunday," says Howard, coming to stand closely next to Max. Howard elbows him with a grin. "You look well," Howard tells him, his white eyebrows move eaglelike, heavy snow over windshield wipers.

"Thanks."

"Tell Max about Juneau," prompts Mimi.

"You were there?" asks Max politely.

"Remarkable. Real wilderness. An amazing place."

"And the radio station?" prompts Mimi.

"A sorry outfit," says Howard, shaking his head. "Run by two drunks. A man and a woman." He shakes his head back and forth, dismayed. "The two of them as large as polar bears."

"Howard!"

"You asked me to tell," he says. "It was unfortunate."

"Yes, well," says Mimi. "Our Katie will see to that."

"To think they want to drill into that massive expanse of pristine land," says Howard, shaking his head again. "It's an outrage."

Max is surprised; he thought Howard would be all for it.

"Can you come back to my sister's?" asks Mimi. "Have a cup of coffee with us? No one's there. Just us and Frightful over here," she says, shrugging a shoulder toward the dog. The dog is straining to get away, wheezing with a lolled tongue, choking itself, snarling at a small poodle that sits, the picture of domesticity, as it waits with its owner to cross the street.

"That would be great," says Max, "but I've got to get back to work."

"Mmm," she says, his mother says, suspicious but not; and then, "We should have called all of you Brambles, shouldn't we. But honestly, we're here for only a few days—"

"No, no. Some other time."

Howard calls to Max from the edge of the sidewalk. "You still work in television, Max?"

"He works at a production company," says Mimi. "Remember?"

"That's television, isn't it?"

Max shrugs, shakes his head yes and no, ready to explain.

"It's Edith who works at NBC," Mimi tells him. "Remember?"

"Mimi, darling, I have a hard enough time keeping track of our own children," he says.

Mimi rolls her eyes. "You go on to work," she tells Max. For a moment her eyes catch something in the direction of the park, pause on it for a second. Max's cheeks tingle. "Is that . . ." Mimi starts softly, focusing on something in the near distance. Max feels sick, pictures Chloe and Rex arriving at the top of the staircase across the street, her pretty head surfacing like a periscope, surveying the area, catching Mimi Woods's eye, recognizing her, waving to her cheerily. "Is that," repeats Mimi, narrowing her eyes, "is that a *child* on that woman's back?"

Max turns around partway, sheepishly, to look.

Relief washes over him. Across the street, overlooking the park, a woman with large bell-bottoms is talking to a man with a completely bald head. On her back is what appears to be a baby, splayed in an **X**, hanging on to her like a monkey. They look closely. It's a doll, a doll made into a backpack by some cutting-edge fashion plate.

"It's a doll," they say collectively, sighing, laughing.

"A bag, for goodness' sake! Is that *fashion*?" asks Mimi.

But about half a block farther down, Max sees them for a split second, Rex and Chloe stationing themselves on a bench.

"I wish I wasn't in a hurry," says Max.

"You're in a hurry?" asks Mimi.

"Well, yes." Max's back pocket begins ringing.

"What a busy bee!" says Mimi. "You're so grown up! Phones! Jobs!"

"Well . . ." Max lets the phone ring.

"Max is leaving, Howard!" she calls. Howard is at the street corner, idling with the dog, looking cattycorner, south, directly *at* Chloe and Rex down the street, not seeing a thing.

"Goodbye, Max," he calls kindly. "Will we see you this summer?"

"We'll be on Moss Island starting tomorrow," Mimi tells Max. "Wouldn't you come visit like the old days? Oh, I'd love it!"

"Depends on Dad, I guess."

"Remember that you can always stay with us. We'd love it," says Mimi. "Any of you. We really would love it." She gives Max a motherly hug, then pulls back to look at him. "I'll have to call your pa to tell him we saw you," she says.

"Now come, Mimi," calls Howard. "Let's get rid of this dog so we can get to the East Side before lunch."

Mimi looks at Max, curves an eyebrow at him. "My master calls," she says deviously, a restrained sexiness that makes Max feel, very briefly, both shy and pleased.

•

The Foona Laguna office is actually the parlor-floor apartment of a four-story brownstone. Max can see Miriam through the dirty window when she buzzes him in. She's on the phone, a football coach headset on, a new arrangement that Max hasn't seen. It reminds him of the headgear Edie had in junior high.

Miriam looks great in a sort of cross-wrap top that matches her nail polish, the color of a UPS truck. Miriam finishes up her phone call anticlimactically, without having to hang up. "Okay, good," she says. "I'll give you a call next week," then simply presses a button on the phone with her finger. She stands up, pries the headset off her head, and tosses it onto her desk. "My mother," she says, rolling her head, stretching, her long hair falling around in a way that makes Max worried—not aroused, really, but suggesting that the possibility exists. "Sometimes I wish she'd just die," laughs Miriam, infused with adoration.

"Yeah," says Max. He picks up a software catalog, leafs through it.

She raps her forehead with the butt of her hand. "Sorry, Max," she says.

Max shrugs. "Where are the Yoo-hoos?"

"I'm not sure if we have enough." She motions toward the corner. At least a dozen cases are stacked into two piles, one of them ripped open, assaulted, as though a raccoon pried its way in.

"Whose stuff on my desk?"

"Charlotte. She used to work for Tanya Ball."

Tanya Ball taught a documentary class at NYU when Max was there. Louise Nevelson haircut and cowboy boots. She'd made one documentary about arranged marriages in the United States that got all sorts of accolades and was never heard from again.

The phone rings. "Chloe's coming here," he says over it.

Miriam acknowledges as she answers. Max motions that he's going out, twirls his finger around to indicate he'll be back. He's got an hour or so to kill, surely, before Chloe and Rex appear. He'll avoid the park.

His days have been passing strangely. He avoids movies because he knows he'll unwittingly let slip talking about one of them, like he did twice already, and Chloe will wonder when he saw it. He's spent lots of time in various record stores, listening to new music on the headphones. A couple of days ago he went up to the Cloisters, high up over the Hudson as though you're in the trees, and then walked home on Broadway, all the way downtown. Chloe was annoyed when he went to bed so early that night. Last week he took the Circle Line. Phalanxes of slow-moving tourists were looking about eagerly in raincoats, even though it wasn't raining. A teenage couple was making out along the railing, the guy tucking his fingers into the back of the girl's pants. Behind them, the shiny skyline like a miraculous rock formation, reverse stalagmites, crystallized, rising from the water, the absent space of the World Trade Center like huge uprooted teeth.

When Chloe comes in carrying the stroller through the threshold, banging her shins with its wheels, its bars, little Rex is out cold, drooling, his head thrown to the side like someone just clocked him. Chloe drapes a blanket over the stroller's awning so the light won't wake him.

"This morning? Two girls thought I was you-know-who."

"Two girls?" asks Chloe.

"They asked for my autograph."

"Oh, you mean . . . That hasn't happened in a while."

"I think I need a haircut."

"Your hair looks great," says Chloe, sounding tired. "I got some sushi from the take-out place."

"Excellent."

"Where is everyone?"

"A shoot in New Jersey."

In the office, Chloe surveys the place, notes that no one's there except for Miriam, whom she greets pleasantly, but it bugs her that Miriam's been alone in this place with her husband all morning. She parks the stroller by the door, flicks the brake on with her toe. Max tells her to sit down at his desk.

"Open the bottom drawer," he tells her.

"Whose stuff is this?" asks Chloe.

"Open the drawer. There's a surprise for you."

"Is this still your desk?"

"Open it!"

Chloe slides it out. At first, nothing. She looks at Max. Then, on top of the folders and printer cartridges a small paw, another one, the furry face emerges, pokes its head up into the air, a pup, maybe part husky. It jumps out, falters on its own front paws, prances a few paces with a smile—ta-da!—then lies down on the floor, its head on its paws.

Chloe starts laughing. Max laughs too. Chloe starts crying. Full on tears. The puppy dodders toward the commotion—her—sniffs at her feet, starts licking her toes and the rubber of her flip-flops.

"Oh, boy," says Max.

Chloe snorts at him, tears everywhere. "Oh, boy?" she says. Her face looks chafed. Good thing Rex is asleep, thinks Max. "Oh, *boy*?" she says at him, her face crumpling. She puts her face in her hands and sobs. If Max didn't know she was still nursing, he'd think she was pregnant.

Max stands there. He watches Miriam walk discreetly toward the cubbyhole area with the fridge and cappuccino maker.

The dog is being super cute, falling over, tugging at the hem of Chloe's dress. Chloe's head is in her hands. The puppy thinks it's funny or a game and starts barking at her faceless blob of hair. "Rrrrr-raff! Raff! Raffraffraff! Raff!'

"Shut up!" she yells at it.

"Ruff!"

"Shut *up!*" she yells again. This time it wakes up Rex, who pouts out his bottom lip, about to cry, but then is delighted to see the little dog scratching around on the floor, scrambling.

"Whoa," Max says to her, as though she's a spooked horse. He's scared to touch her.

"Don't *whoa* me," she snaps. "You think I don't know?"

Max's chest seems to liquefy.

"You think I don't know you're *sleeping* with someone?"

5

argaret presses the window's black Chicklet button so it hums all the way down. She motions to the beleaguered looking blond woman who's hit them to move to the side of the road. The woman comes to Margaret's window regardless. "Oh!" the woman's saying, her voice exactly as Margaret expected, high and frilly, wound up like a fiddlehead. "Children? Is everyone okay?" She peers into Margaret's window. "How many children are in there?"

"Move away from the road," says Margaret loudly. Cars slice past one another, Benihana-style. A man's voice loops out an open window, "Yo, laydeeee . . ." whizzing past. Margaret grabs the woman's elbow— "Watch it!"—as a big truck skins where she's standing, honking like an ocean liner as it barrels past.

"Jesus Christ," says Margaret, alarmed and thoroughly annoyed. She motions to the safe hillock hump of grass.

The blond woman freezes at the loud noise, puts a hand to her chest for an extended period of time, and then finally comes around the car to the safe side. Margaret clambers out the passenger side, muttering "Jesus" again, a word that all her children perfected as toddlers, along with its conjoining heavy sigh, since they heard it so often. "Oh, my Jesus," they'd say, shaking their small heads back and forth, looking sidelong at the ground.

"I'll be right back," Margaret tells everyone, off to survey the damage. The whir and swish of cars, the sounds of a washing machine, the sounds of paper getting ripped or crumpled. Margaret grits her teeth. "Damn it," she says loudly, camouflaged in the din of the traffic.

The back door's crushed a little. It opens, but not smoothly. One of the brake lights is cracked. The bumper's mussed up. Nothing too bad.

Still, it'll have to go to the shop for a few days, probably a week, since it's a lease. That'll be interesting. Like giving up something as essential as her bra. She can see herself already, cramming the kids into the sedan the rental place will give her.

Up ahead, she circles it: not a scratch on the mighty Range Rover.

"It doesn't look so bad," proclaims Margaret, shouting over the whoosh of cars. She climbs back into her seat. "Have a seat in here," she tells the woman. "I'm kind of in a hurry."

The woman gets in, closes the door, and takes an exaggerated deep breath. "Oh, *goodness!*" she says, exhaling. "I didn't see you folks! Is everyone all right?" She looks back at the children, then at Margaret, pulls her chin into her neck. "What lovely children," she tells her, eyebrows up.

"Thanks," says Margaret. "We're all fine. Right, kids?"

Vague nods ripple through the backseats.

"Thank goodness," gasps the woman. Her eyes are red-rimmed, bugged open.

"Nice car," Margaret says to her. Then looks. "Are *you* all right?"

"Me?" A pink hand to her chest again. "Oh, I'm fine," she says, shaking her head. Her watery rabbit eyes water up some more and she starts to cry. She sniffles, reaches into her pocket, and then holds a crumpled Kleenex to her face. "I'm sorry," she squeaks.

Margaret glances in the rearview mirror. The kids are rubbering their necks around to get a better look. Adult tears.

"Here, here," Margaret says to her gently. "No one was hurt."

"I know," peeps the woman.

Margaret glances at the clock, tries to sound gentle. "If you give me your information, I'll write it all down."

The blond woman has the appropriate cards in her puffy hand. Margaret notices a ring strangling her finger. The woman blows her nose with a fart noise that makes Sarah and Stephen giggle. Margaret gives them a look—*Not now*—a rectangle flash of her eyes in the rearview.

"I'm Margaret Bright," says Margaret. She looks down at the license she's been handed, and reads, "Tammy Lopney."

Tammy looks up at her. "That's me." She smiles, then sputters into a cry again.

"Everyone's fine, Tammy," Margaret tells her.

Tammy blows her nose again into the shriveled tissue. "Oh, it's not that," she says, flicking her wrist.

"Ah," says Margaret, offended. "Well, in that case . . ." and immediately busies herself with quickly writing down what she needs—policy number, expiration, insurance—boring words for boring bureaucracy, while Tammy blubbers a bit more, her face in her hands. "Okay, Tammy," says Margaret, only halfway patient, "I've got to get these kids to the doctor. We're late."

"I'm sorry," sobs Tammy, "I'm so sorry."

Margaret looks back at the kids and shrugs at them, which makes Stephen grin nervously. "Tammy? What's your phone number?"

Tammy stutters it out as she regains her composure. Margaret's ballpoint is losing ink. She presses hard, retraces, hoping she'll make an imprint successful enough that she'll be able to read it later. While she waits for Tammy to collect herself, she watches a teenage boy on the steps of a bank building pick up a girl and then kiss her. They look vaguely familiar. Probably lifeguards at the pool.

"Sorry, Tammy," says Margaret, "but I've really got to get going."

Tammy opens her door. "So," she says, moving agonizingly slowly as she gets out. "I guess I'll . . . call you?"

"Sure," quips Margaret, "if you need to." She reaches across the passenger seat to close the door. "Bye. Sorry, thanks. Thanks."

" 'Sorry, thanks,' Mom?" says Stephen as they pull away. "What's that supposed to mean?"

"Being polite, Stephen."

"Why was she crying, Mom?"

"I don't know, Sarah."

"Look. She's still standing there."

"Was she hurt, Mom?"

"She, like, wouldn't stop crying," says Sarah.

"A bad day getting worse," mumbles Margaret, back in command of her Odyssey, steering it like a horse.

"What, Mom? Mom, what?" says Sarah.

"Look, kids!" says Margaret, diverting attention.

Much energy is spent diverting. It took her a long time to learn, in fact, how essential diversion was. She used to try reasoning and explaining. A complete disaster with a flailing two-year-old. *I told you, sweetheart, that if you clean up the blocks and stop whining—*

"Look!" Margaret says again, drawing their attention, trying to find something to address. "The miniature *golf* place closed down!"

"I love that place!" peeps Sarah.

Stephen snorts at her. "You've never even been there."

"Yes, I have. With ballet," says Sarah, pronouncing it *bow-lay*.

Margaret wonders whether she herself is shook up from the accident and unaware of it. It was, after all, a crash. She wonders this even as she coasts through a red light on Pine Street. The man about to cross the road whom she practically runs over stops to watch her reckless trail blaze, right to left, as if it's a parade.

Florence opens her eyes. "Mom?" she says, squinting into the sun. "Was that lady before really a man?" Flo's *A*s are all soft. Man is *mon*. Ham, *hom*. Banana, *bahnahnah*.

"Who, honey?"

"That lady who hit us."

"Was she what?"

"Was she a *mon* or something?"

"A man?"

"Yeah, Mom. Was she like a *mon* or something?"

"No. She was a woman."

"Oh."

They drive on, Margaret puzzled. "You thought she was a man, Flo?"

"Yeah. No," answers Flo softly. "Kind of, I guess."

"She reminded me of the one where the sky falls," says Sarah.

As Margaret turns into the parking lot she hears Stephen. "Chicken Little," he says gently, against his window's glass.

•

Dr. Perretti belongs in Hollywood. He drives an orange Hummer with vanity plates that say DOC4KIDS, which he parks in the showboatiest parking spot in the lot so everyone can see it. "The kids like it," he says, with a whisper and a wink, raising his shoulder like a showgirl. He looks vaguely like, or at least as if he's aiming to look like, a certain actor who drove a talking car and later became a leader of lifeguards and who has, Margaret recently learned from Edie (who's chock-full of pop culture that no one needs to know), an unbelievably enormous following as a pop singer in Germany.

He's a show-off, Dr. Perretti, an arrogant jerk, probably, but Margaret has no complaints. He's always taken good care of her kids, certainly no alarmist, which is a relief, compared to the young female pediatrician Stephen had when they were still in New York. That doctor constantly wanted to put Stephen on antibiotics *just in case* of ear infections and was incredulous when Margaret said she'd rather wait to see if he actually got sick. She advised Margaret to use a bulb syringe on the baby's nose so often that it got bloody from irritation. Dr. Perretti shrugs off the bulb syringes. "Nah. I don't believe in those things," he says, always chewing gum, snapping it.

His office is well run, maximizing income, no doubt, but it makes for barely any wait despite a usually packed waiting room, and he always takes calls from parents. Even when he's examining someone, he'll get right on the horn; no problem. More than once Margaret has heard things she'd rather not have heard: Dr. Perretti booming into the phone as he checks on oozes and listlessness, while at the same time peering into Sarah's ear or eye with his little light beam, shouting colorful things into the phone for the entire office to hear "Sounds more like a rupture!" or "It could be fifth disease! Or scarlet fever! Come on in!" or "It doesn't matter if the vomit is vibrant! All shades are fine but we don't like to see coffee grinds!"; "Is the baby blue?"; "Bright yellow or green puss is totally normal!" To which Sarah looks at Margaret and mouths "Gross," her pained expression saying, *Get me out of this place.*

Sarah runs ahead, aiming toward the Tootsie lollipop she knows is coming at the end of the appointment. Stephen follows after her, while Margaret lags behind, carrying Florence. "You're getting too big to be carried," Margaret tells her.

"I know, Mom," says Flo. "But I like it so much."

As she walks, Margaret notes a pain in the ball of her foot that she's been noticing on and off, driving her to wear the most basic shoes for fear of damaging her feet further. It burns.

In the waiting room, Stephen's already busily seated with a copy of *Highlights* in his lap. Sarah's standing, looking up at the TV hanging from the ceiling in the corner. One of the morning shows is on. A blond fitness trainer, with her hair pulled back from her face as if she's about to splash cold water over it, is demonstrating the correct way to do a sit-up, which looks nothing like your ordinary sit-up at all. Florence finds a piece of yellow pipe cleaner left on the table and promptly starts twisting it into the shape of a flower.

Margaret glances about the room, wonders for a moment about sitting down on the tired tweed chair before her, and thinks of the invisible bacteria and viruses, those shapes in Stephen's book, teeming maggotlike on every surface of the place: *Coxsackie, streptococcus, RSV, roseola, influenza, chicken pox, bird flu, SARS. . .*

A carnivorous-looking plant adorns the reception desk. "Look, Mom," says Flo, twirling the pipe cleaner around her finger, pointing at the big plant. "It looks like Stinky."

"Who, honey?" she says, not listening.

"It's a plant, Mom," explains Stephen. "A puppet plant. Like it talks and stuff."

"Sure, sweetheart," she says vaguely. She rummages through a pile of magazines, their glossy finishes softened by many perusing fingers, her fingers tentative as though sifting through garbage. A minefield of germs. But she'll risk it. *Fitness,* no, *Time,* no, *Child,* no, *Money,* no—and then jackpot with a tabloid, months old but with starlets in their Academy Award gowns on the cover.

"Here, Mom. Sit here," says Flo. "Sit down next to me"—pointing to one of the dirtier chairs. A waxy wad of ancient gum is stamped in its center.

Margaret sits on the edge of the chair, flexing the muscles of her legs, and flips the magazine open. An Irish actor in a cigarette boat in the south of France. Two married tennis pros playing goofy for the camera at a fund-raiser with their baby, who shares the same trendy name with a mega–movie star's son in a picture on the opposite page. No mention that the kids are named the same. A fashionable pop singer with a bad choice of hair but an excellent choice in earrings: gold chains as thin as angel-hair pasta that drip on both sides of the earlobe. Like an exhale, reading this stuff. Like shopping or watching sitcoms. A May–December couple in matching ball caps, hand in hand, hurrying along a sidewalk. Now, *that's* intriguing, thinks Margaret, studying the picture, her shoes, his sneakers, her sunglasses, the bend in the sidewalk where they've just turned a corner, the worried shape of her mouth like they're being followed, which they are, obviously, by photographers trying to get this stupid picture so people like Margaret, she realizes, can look at the picture in a place like a pediatrician's office. Look at it and wonder whatever they might wonder, which in Margaret's case is, What about your wife? Where are your kids? Nice shades. Where's *your* little boy?

Sarah comes over, leans against her mother's thigh without turning around. "Mom?" asks Sarah.

Margaret scans the pages before her. "Mmmm," she answers.

"On the TV, Mom. Who's *that*?"

Margaret looks up to see that the morning show is showing a clip of a young blonde's gyrating, mostly naked, dancing body.

"Um," says Margaret. The girl is clearly grinding against the back of a chair. "She's dancing," says Margaret, practically embarrassed at the sight. She leaves it at that and looks around the room to see if other children are watching. A small boy, mouth agape, stares up at the screen. Next to him sits Stephen, head down, heavily absorbed in *Highlights*, deciphering a word puzzle with the nub of a pencil the size of a thumb.

Flo comes over too, leans against Margaret's other leg like a cat. "Mom?" she says. She gets close to Margaret's ear and whispers "Mommy," low and throaty, so closely that it tickles. "What's wrong with her?" whispers Flo, pointing her elbow toward a young girl waiting alone. "What happened to *her*?"

Margaret looks. Across from the receptionist is a little girl in a sundress the color of a buttercup, bald except for a slight fuzz of hair. She's looking down at her hands in her lap, almost too precious to be true, when she's interrupted by a voice calling her name.

"Alexandra, sweetheart?" calls the receptionist, the phone tucked under her ear.

The little girl looks up. "Yes, Debbie?" Her voice belongs on Broadway or in the movies.

"Your mom will be here in ten minutes." The receptionist holds the phone out. "You want to talk to her?"

"No, that's okay." The girl smiles. "I'll see her in a sec."

"Mom?" whispers Flo. She pokes Margaret in the neck.

"Later, honey," Margaret tells her, pushing her away. "Where did that flower you made go?"

Margaret tries not to watch but discreetly watches anyway as the little girl smooths her dress over her legs. On her feet, a small pair of Chinese slippers with yellow sequins. On her lap, a blue suede purse with Pocahontas fringe.

Margaret looks back down at her magazine, feels faintly like she's going to vomit as she imagines momentarily what this child must endure. Aside from the shunts and the prodding, everyone looking at her, so pretty, so sick, a martyr already, beguiling people left and right, whether she likes it or not, like an angel visiting from its gauzy realm. *Please God, keep my kids healthy.* The shunt on her father's arm, kept in place with a giant piece of transparent duct tape. The time it was improperly put in so fluid like a camel's back ballooned on his forearm. "Why didn't you say anything, Dad?" Margaret had asked him when she arrived in California, seeing the end result: his arm still puffed up, black and blue as if it had been beaten.

"I presumed it was perfectly normal," answered Arthur. He shrugged. "I've never had chemotherapy before." He glared at her, but with a small smile. "Have you?"

When Dr. Perretti opens an arm to guide the Bright troop through the door into his examining room, he has a new aura of hero about him. It never really occurred to Margaret that he really was a *doctor*, actually saving lives, dealing with terminally ill kids.

Margaret feels partly compelled to ask him what's wrong exactly with that girl Alex, but mainly doesn't want to encourage his tendency to gossip. "You know that big huge guy on *The Sopranos*? His kid was in here. Abscess in his gum." Or, more dramatically, "We had a woman come in here yesterday and leave her baby *behind*," he pronounced once, one eyebrow raising like a rubber band. "She *forgot*." This is the kind of gossip he reports.

"Really?" Margaret thought of the times when for moments she couldn't find baby Flo anywhere. *Did I leave her in the car? She's not in the crib!* "She's right *there*, Mom." Little Stephen would smile, pointing to infant Flo curled like a raisin in the Baby Bjorn on Margaret's chest, thinking his mother was feigning confusion for his own amusement. Or the time when Margaret got pulled over. "Sorry. Was I going too fast?" She was less than a mile from the house. Stephen and Sarah sacked out in their car seats in the back.

"No," said the police officer. "But can you tell me why the infant isn't in its seat?" Again, Flo was on Margaret's chest, asleep in the Baby Bjorn. Margaret had even adjusted the driver's seat so they'd fit comfortably together behind the wheel. At least she'd buckled up.

In the examining room there's a new poster. A cross-section of a head and chest, diagramming the head with emphasis on the ear, nose, and throat areas. The kids all point at the yellowish lymph nodes and the fatty tissue, yellow and puckered like the peel of an orange; *eeeew,* they say, shivering their laughs, *eeew eeew.*

"Look, Mom," says Stephen, pointing to another poster, "a strep."

Margaret looks where he's pointing. A portion of a purple necklace, five round beads beaded together. She reads the tiny italics under it: *Streptococcus bacteria.* "Wow, Stephen. Maybe you'll be a doctor after all."

"After all what?"

"After . . . I don't know," says Margaret.

Dr. Perretti barges in without knocking, almost creams Flo, who's playing idly with the doorknob (the vector of all vectors, thinks Margaret when she sees her daughter hanging on it). Flo scurries to her mother, stands safe in the furrow of her mother's legs. "Strep again, eh?" he says, looking down at the kids like a clown at a birthday party. "We'll check all of you." He winks. "You too, Mom."

The doctor presses the wooden paddle down on Sarah's tongue. Her sandaled feet kick back and forth, *scrunch scranch scrunch scranch,* dangling from the papered examining table. Full of life, full of movement, her little-girl body completely contained, working absolutely. Margaret looks at her daughter's face, its pink tongue as healthy as a dog's, her skin so clear it's as though she's been dipped in some kind of cleaner. Margaret says a quick prayer to keep cancer away forever from Sarah's body, away forever from all their bodies. She thinks of her father. She makes her way onto a padded stool, wobbling with worry, thinking of Sarah in the place of that little girl Alex, thinking of herself in the place of her mother on the airplane, wondering in a flurry why *more* people aren't dead. Life is so fragile. This accident they were in this morning—

Dr. Perretti looks at her. "Margaret? Are you all right?"

"Yeah, Mom," says Stephen. "You look weird."

"We had an accident coming over here," she says.

"Oh, *really*," says the doctor.

"Nothing big," she says. "Just rear-ended."

"Hmm," says Dr. Perretti. Dr. Perretti comes close, angling in at her eyeball with the scope. "Would you like some Xanax?"

His pink gum, the curled lip close up, as he squints through the tiny flashlight. She catches a scented wind of his breath, thankfully smelling like his gum. She's surprised by his choice (Juicy Fruit).

"Some Zoloft?"

Margaret remembers her friend Regina telling her how she had asked Dr. Perretti about a sore elbow once and in response he asked her if she wanted some Xanax. "Not yet," says Margaret. "My father's coming to live with us." Why was she telling him this?

Dr. Perretti steps back. "I *see*."

"He has cancer."

"What kind?"

"Liver, stomach. That whole area. Throat."

"Mmm-*hmm*."

"Stage four." Why not give him the whole rundown. He's a doctor, for God's sake. And if they all have strep. . . .

Dr. Perretti respectfully closes his mouth for some pensive gum-chewing with his front teeth. "How old?"

"Seventy-six."

"Is he still doing the chemo?"

The kids are beginning to disturb the adult talk, "No, it's *my-ee-een*," Flo is whining.

"Don't whine," Stephen tells her.

"Give it," whines Flo.

"No. No more chemo," says Margaret. What can another doctor tell her that she doesn't already know? She could ask him what she should expect. She considers this. "Stephen, give your sister back her *tiny* piece of *pipe cleaner*," says Margaret without needing to look, knowing instinctually that Stephen took it from Flo and was taunting her with it.

"You have a hospice lined up?" asks Dr. Perretti.

"Yeah, yeah," says Margaret, wanting to end the conversation but also aware that this was her *family* doctor, that he could give her some valuable information.

"I'm sorry," says Dr. Perretti. "Let us know if you need anything. If he does. You know what I mean."

"I'm dealing with Dr. Smart. Do you know him? He's the one my father's doctor in California referred."

"Couldn't do any better," said Dr. Perretti, opening the door, moving over to the counter, flipping lids, folding things up.

Sure, thought Margaret. Say that whether it's true or not. After all, poor Dad's in the can already.

A fly comes in through the open door, does an entire revolution about the room, and backtracks, looking for a place to land, zigzagging like an ink-jet printer above Sarah's head. Margaret watches it, rolls up her magazine to swat at it. She has done what she often does compulsively, like her quick prayers: made a Margaretism, as her husband calls them. *If that fly lands on someone, that someone will get cancer.* She doesn't take them seriously. But then how can she ignore them? Sometimes they don't happen for a few days; sometimes they're constant, worse when they become an avalanche all day long. *If I catch this ball, Flo will get into a good college. If I empty the dishwasher before the phone rings, all the kids will sleep through the night for the rest of the week. If I make the toss into the trash can, he'll love me forever.* Making order of the unorderable. *If I forget to turn the dryer on again, I have to tell Brian that I'm not using birth control. If I— slawapp!*

"Ow!" Sarah cowers.

"Sorry, honey," says Margaret. Everyone's looking at her as though she's lost her mind. She shrugs. "There was a fly."

"Mom," says Sarah.

Margaret looks at the doctor, who just watched her hit the top of her daughter's head, and sees the act as though she's watching it herself: an insane mother walking across the room to bonk her daughter—So *there!* —with a magazine in the middle of a medical exam. Now *there's* some gossip. Dr. Perretti looks at her queerly. "Watch out for your mom, kids!" he says with a grin, chewing his gum, and then leaves with the swabs, which he repeatedly calls *swaps*.

Margaret puts her hand on Sarah's arm. "Um," she says. "Sorry, honey. There was a fly." What was the proprietary thing about mother-hood that made her feel like her children were not just hers, but were actually *her*, part of *her*? That to swat her daughter's head to kill a fly was like swatting her own arm? She would never in a million years do that sort of thing, without thinking, to anyone else in the world other than one of her kids! Well, or Brian (the time she plucked a nose hair from his nostril at a cocktail party as though she were grooming herself in the mirror.). Again, befuddled faces all around her, Brian holding his nose, stunned but smiling politely, "Ouch, Margaret."

Sarah's trying to be brave but she's alarmed and startled. "Just warn me, Mom, next time," she whines.

At this, Margaret feels some tears welling up. The borders of where her children end and she begins are vague, always have been, but now that they're getting bigger she needs to reevaluate, she's told herself, set them clearly apart from herself with respect and consideration, so that she recognizes them as complete people instead of fascinating creatures that are parts of her like her own wrists are parts of her, that she can flick things on and off of, that she can tell what she thinks are funny stories about them in front of them, as though they are her pets: "So then Sarah pushed Flo off our bed and said, *Put her back in tummy, Mama!* And Flo—this tiny infant!—had a *huge* goose egg right on her head. She landed, like, *two inches* from the door stop—that's a big chunk of *rock*—so I mean she would have probably cracked her head open and—" to be interrupted by her sister, Edie, nudging her, motioning quietly, point-ing out Sarah standing nearby, swaying from side to side, covering her ears in shame.

So they're growing. No longer the toddlers that called her Princess Mama, Mama Power Ranger, Daddy Mama, and (her favorite) Doctor Mama. No longer the little babies that she can grab and kiss on the mouth, flatten her cheek against their fat ones, mash her nose into theirs and let them suck on it, squeeze juicy thighs and elicit goofy giggles. No longer infants, so tiny. And then those smiles finally, oases amid the drudgery, succulent berries—well, a lot of that was gone. Now their eyes were always thinking something, heading down their own paths of discovery and craggy landscapes, shooting off into their own lives, their own selves, which was all exciting and everything, but—

"Mom?"

"Mommy?" The small voices are like pebbles being tossed into the air around Margaret's head.

"Why are you crying, Mom?"

"Yeah, why?"

"I'm fine," says Margaret, confused also. She tells herself she must be shaken up from the fender-bender.

"Everyone's crying today!" Sarah laughs, putting the bright face on. "First that lady, now Mom. First that lady Flo thought—"

"I'm not crying," says Margaret, licking her upper lip.

Stephen looks at her warmly. "Mom." He smiles; his eyes roll ceilingward. "It's only strep throat."

"Oh, honey," she says, but she's thinking how she hasn't told Brian she threw the birth control pills away. She's thinking of the for-crying-out-loud argument she had with Edie, which continued with Edie saying, "You can't *wait* for Dad to get here. You *love* taking on all these burdens."

"Burdens? Dad being sick is a *burden?*"

"You love this martyr stuff," said Edie.

"*Martyr?*" Margaret felt her nostrils flaring, her face hot. Somehow she felt like she was wrong. She splurted out something she wasn't even sure of. "I think when he's dead, Edie, you'll wish you'd spent more time with him."

"Is that how you feel about Mom?"

"What?" Margaret considers it. "Maybe."

"What about work, Margaret? Should I not go to work?"

"Edie, this is the sort of thing that people don't go to work *for*."

"That's easy for you to say, coming from someone with no responsibilities."

Margaret snorted, laughed out loud. "Yes! One big party all the time here! Not a care in the world here!"

"There's the martyr."

"Why are you so angry with me?" said Margaret angrily. "Why do I always feel like I'm letting you down?"

6

After hanging up with Margaret, Edie checked the pay phone's coin slot for any coins, walked around her car's hood, hot from the sun, and opened the heavy door. She sat down in the driver's seat, one blue-jean leg dangling out the open door, and began crying into her arms on the steering wheel, the seat-belt reminder dinging, the open-door alert buzzing like the end of a kitchen timer, until they both stopped.

"You all right, miss?"

She looked up to see a torso, a red T-shirt with a small but mega-international gas logo on it above the wearer's heart. "These yours?" A young man, about her age but probably married with kids, mildly handsome, wearing wraparound mirror sunglasses the same shade of the windows of a certain Lexus SUV that she kept spotting out on the road. On the hook of his finger dangled a dyed purple rabbit's-foot key chain. For a second the sight of it horrified her. Her key chain was actually an animal's *foot*.

"Yeah," said Edie, sniffling, automatically placing herself in a bad movie again. The omniscient deep voice of the trailer's narrator: *She was in distress, until a perfect stranger came along. . . .* A Perfect Stranger. Sense the mystery of what's meant to be. . . . *AperfectStrangerratedRnowshowingnationwideblahblahblah.*

"You left them on the counter," he said.

"Woopsy daisy." Sobbing. Smiling through a sob.

"Um. Do you need some help?" asked the young man.

"No." Edie wept. "Thanks. Wait. Which way— Is this road heading east?"

"South."

"I mean that's what I meant to say. South." She sniffled. "Thanks," she said, looking up at him, taking the keys.

He smiled partway and turned around to go back inside, not at all interested, but why should he be? She dug around in the rectangular key well for enough change to buy a bag of Mary Janes. Cinnamon Dollars? Then she remembered she had a box of Dots in the glove compartment, remembered also that she told herself she wouldn't have any sugar today, wouldn't eat anything at all until noon. When she had envisioned driving out to California, part of the appeal for her was in terms of eating. She'd be out of her usual routine. She could fast most of the time, drop a few pounds, get back to normal, *purify*, *detox*, all that. Maybe do a juice fast for the whole trip. But then she decided against it because she didn't want to be too drowsy, hypnotized by the road, a general menace behind the wheel.

Unfortunately, it had turned into a game of compulsion, of bingeing and purging, transforming generally monotonous, relaxing days in the car with the radio and changing scenery where she could have learned a lot about her country if she paid attention, where she could have thought long and hard about . . . something—her *self*, her *life*—but instead managed to infuse most of the stacked hours with a frenetic sense of lost control, wrought with spiraling, riddled with what felt like her failed will gone haywire. Where to eat? Where to stop? What to get next? Salty? Sweet? *Thirsty*. Her eyesight passing over the local interests, the new surroundings, for a craved Golden Arches, a Taco Bell, or a regional franchise like Dairy Queen. Bloated, gassy, cleansed, disgusted—all in the matter of a morning. She'd get breakfast at a drive-through, gorge on some homemade fudge picked up at a tourist office, drink bottles of water, stop at a depressing rest area with wood chips all over its landscaping efforts to stick her finger down her throat in a bathroom that was sometimes empty, sometimes full of people, but almost always possessed the lemon candy smell of cheap but effective disinfectants.

Something's clearly wrong, she'd tell herself vaguely, as she looked at the smooth white porcelain, whirled like a conch shell, inches from her face, as she found herself internally plugging up her nose to avoid any offensive smells, seriously wondering what would be the best position to *kneel down in* to do this. She wasn't even fat! Yet. This was *her* Bush doctrine, preemptive: Get the food before it has time to amass into her flesh.

An RA at SUNY had told her once that, in the freshman girls' dormitory she monitored, they had to redo the pipes in the bathroom because they were so eaten away by girls' vomit. That old urban myth. But the girl, Kelly, had actual stories that went along with the myth so it was myth no longer: Some girls would eat a gallon of ice cream or entire boxes of cookies, a whole chocolate cake from the bakery in town, alone, then barf it up in weird places like the top drawers of their dressers. Or they'd have whole eating parties, a roomful of girls who would all go and puke together. At least she wasn't like *that*, Edie told herself. She was simply *struggling with her weight*, as they say. A passing phase. Or was it?

It was this newfound boredom. Doldrums like a forest of drooping trees surrounding her in the fog. Every day, inertia. Cigarettes no longer satisfying. Exercising just one big drag. Every day now has been very similar. Even when it's different, it's still the same. Every day she's woken in the semidark of her nearly windowless studio by the click of the radio alarm and then the drone of the familiar voices of NPR.

Every day she listens to the same but also very different, vaguely interesting, sometimes profoundly compelling news stories and feels the same feeling of helplessness born of her recent bored state helixed with the truly bad news and silly nature of things going on, so sad and never to be undone, that are reported by the radio, that come blaring at her through the television sets that are littered about the offices at work.

She listens closely like her sister, every day, for the weather threads, as she relies on their updates for her attire. Her office, however, is always freezing cold in summer, boiling hot in winter. The dingy window in her studio looks into an airshaft, faces a brick wall the color of crap. If she cranes her neck around, mashes her cheek to the windowsill, and looks up awkwardly, she can see, way up there, a thin rectangle of sky, a shard, almost always a muted white even when, once she's outside, the day is blue.

Into the little stand-up shower, olive green plastic, flecked in gold, the same shampoos standing upside down to bring their paltry contents to the fore, teetering at the top of the shower's ledge. She shaves her legs and armpits while conditioner sits globbed on her head. The water off, her ears back to the low blare of the radio as she gets dressed, lately into the same uniform of black, straight leg pants with a slight stretch and a slight flare (Gap) and a long-sleeved scoop-necked shirt which she's started wearing untucked, sans belt. A lot of her pants don't fit her anymore. Some shirts too. Even the quiet security guard at the elevator bank at her office, who ordinarily gives a half-nod twitch to acknowledge her passing, had looked up at her, the first small smile she'd ever seen creaking out of his face to say, from the side of his mouth, his eyebrow raised, "Putting on some weight?"

A nervous sweat overcame her for an instant, a spray of surprise. "I am," she replied, as though she'd been trying. She hurried past. She poked the round lozenge UP button that turned sherbet orange when she did so and then waited, feet together, bag in hand, looking up prayerfully at the old-fashioned arrows above the elevator doors.

After getting dressed she brushes her hair, tosses the excess hair from the brush into the toilet, wonders momentarily (every morning) if the hair will eventually clog the pipe and who will deal with that. She finds something to tie her hair back with and wraps that elastic or scrunchie or whatever it is around her wrist. Then she finds her bag and loads it up with what she needs, which isn't much: money for coffee, a muffin, something, maybe a bagel; her Metrocard.

Walking had been her usual route. A decent spurt of exercise, about forty minutes, and not much different time-wise from taking the subway after going upstairs, going downstairs, waiting on the platform. Plus, it was rare time spent outdoors. All the time indoors in the city; it was ridiculous. Was that what was getting her down, dulling her, the fluorescent lights? For the winter months, she was basically at work from dark until dark. The morning commute provided her with glimpses of weak winter light that hurt her eyes. Walking also gave her a sort of community in the people she'd regularly see each morning: the people at the French coffee shop on her street who seemed to refuse to acknowledge her regular appearance, every morning, nine o'clock, to order a café au lait. Either the young Algerian woman or the woman in braids would ask, every morning, Yiz? And every morning Edie would say, Café au lait, please.

One morning she tried *Hi*, as she entered through the door, bells tinkling atop it. Smiling brightly, if I'm to do this friendly thing. *The usual*, she said cheerfully. The women stopped in their tracks and looked at her as though she'd insulted them.

"I vish I could read your mind," said the woman with braids dryly. On her tiny T-shirt, a yellow smiley face with a red prohibitive slash through it.

"A café au lait, please," said Edie.

"Café au lait," the woman registered quietly, and proceeded to go about making it.

It was claustrophobic, seeing the same people at work, the same traveled channels of the city, the sky so far away. There was the weird occasion when she'd see the same people, strangers but repeated faces within the labyrinthine streets: that woman with the navy blue hat with pink fur in the earflaps whom she saw at the soap store in SoHo, at the Chelsea Piers carrying a bucket of golf balls, at the take-out lunch counter near her office, and then hurrying along the sidewalk way up on the Upper West Side late at night. There was the man who looked sort of like a stretched-out version of one of America's favorite actors whom she saw at Battery Park as she Rollerbladed one day, then saw again at MoMA, and then on both the R train and the B train at completely different times of day. Or the dark-haired woman with twins in a double jogger stroller that she saw sitting on a bench outside the Fat Gourmand store, then at Penn Station, and once in the window of a Crunch on Lafayette, where Edie could see the woman running very quickly on a treadmill, her ponytail jittering, a necklace around her neck bouncing at her chest while her two babies slept in the stroller parked nearby.

After a bout with a bad ankle when she had to forgo the walks to work for the subway, which spat her out in her office building in true spaceship style, she took on a fondness for the cookies down at the coffee shop on the shopping concourse, the praline ones with the soft centers, as well as the pasta at the Italian take-out underneath the mezzanine;

their penne alla vodka and their bread was great too, and the mozzarella and prosciutto. Around the office there were always little jelly beans in bowls and jars like bright Easter egg hunt finds, bite-sized chocolates like Reese's or Snickers in dishes on desks or tucked offhandedly by someone—who?—into the inside of the fridge's door where the mini Evian water bottles were kept in a straight line. There were donuts and bagels at the morning meeting in the conference room when it was someone's, anyone's, birthday. Had all these foods always been surrounding her at work? The answer was yes, but Edie had never noticed before. The chocolate Hugs that were in a glass jar out at the reception desk, that she was now obsessed with, grabbing handfuls whenever no one was around, she had formerly passed by. "What are those?" she asked once, leaning on the desk as she wrote a note for a segment producer. "Gold kisses?"

"Yeah," said Minerva, the fantastic, unflappable receptionist who'd since had a baby and moved to Philadelphia with her boyfriend. Minerva could've run the show if she'd stuck around.

"Didn't know they came in gold," said Edie.

"They're Hugs. They have an almond in 'em."

"Mmm," acknowledged Edie, finishing her note, not even thinking to try one.

Now she was counting things all the time in her head: counting minutes or hours that were passing from when she last ate to when she'd eat again, counting M&M's with which she'd reward herself: one for each hour she went without eating, five if she walked up to the office instead of taking the elevator, four if she didn't smoke a cigarette for two hours, and so on. Forget about carbs and fat content and all of that mumbo jumbo. She was counting the old-fashioned way: calories from a dog-eared paperback book almost as old as herself that she picked up from a street vendor and kept in her apartment; she didn't travel with it, didn't admit to anyone that these things were going through her head. Counting hours or days that she went without purging. Hours or days she went without eating.

It was *where* she was transported when she tasted different tastes, particularly sugar, particularly fats, and felt different textures sliding and crunching in her mouth. Away to a nondescript place. *Away.* What else was there like tastes to take you somewhere away from yourself? At other times in her life, she'd have been able to answer readily: sex, laughter, people, music, creating, learning, air, smells, discovering. Eating was what preoccupied Edie now; what to eat and when, how to keep it under control, when to exercise, when to barf.

Ever since the sore ankle, exercise has become much more difficult to begin; her body feels somehow too soft, as if it wouldn't be able to manage whatever task it might be given. Edie feels embarrassed when she thinks of her ungainliness in attempting something like a jog or a Pilates class. A yoga class like she used to go to with Margaret. But body, shmoddy. That wasn't the issue and she knew it. But what was? Edie would look at herself in the mirror and wonder, Where have I gone?

Now Edie is driving, though plainly crying, the gas station and the phone call with Margaret behind her, heading south toward her father. She turns the radio up, crying still, and distractedly through tears sings along, shouting "*Can I get a witness?*" through her melting, crying face.

"What's wrong with me?" she cries. "Where am I going?" she says, musing over what she sees before her: the road that tilts off to the left down a hill.

The DJ's all upbeat, speaking smoothly: "If you're headed into the valley, it's hot hot hot. . . ."

"Hot!" says Edie, imitating the DJ, her face collapsing into another cry. "Oh boy oh boy oh boy," she says, through her drippy face.

Edie cries as she drives along the winding roads of the craggy, toothy coast of southern Northern California, or northern Southern California, wherever she is. As far as she's concerned, it's like Purgatory. She keeps lighting those butts religiously, significantly, blaring the music on the all-Beck hour out of Santa Cruz—*who's gonna love my baby, when she's gone around the bend?*—opening all the windows so that her hair will blow around like she's having fun, strands getting singed by cigarettes.

The huge Hearst mansion. Saint Elmo? San Remo? She can't remember. It appears looming in the distance up on her left. On her right along the beach there are hordes of sea lions—elephant seals, a nature sign tells her—speckled on the beach, adding to the amusement-park nature of things, Sea World down there, but desolate too in the immense open air. The wind wrinkles the water, limbers up the squat trees. Some sea lions look washed up, bloated like stunted bowling pins toppled in the sun on the sand. Another bunch are wriggling, as though struggling to untie themselves with their non-hand flippers, squirming like maggots. Another thing she can't remember: What would it be, a pod? A pride? Not a gaggle. Not a symphony. Should be a bark: a bark of sea lions. A seethe; they're seething down there. Bright sky. Windy clouds. Arrows of angled light, coming from the west, dart off of the massive Pacific, hurting her eyes when she looks. Pride probably right. *San Simeon*, right. The subtle, gratifying waft of relief that comes with successful recollection of the trivial.

After the Hearst estate, Edie stops crying. She focuses on the roads, the varying lanes and exits. She roams inexplicably, ending up first on a massive freeway and then, eventually, on a very flat main road through level acres of fruitless fruit trees in very straight lines followed by row after row of nonspecific squirts of low leafy vegetables. Spinach, maybe. Alfalfa, probably. Plenty of others, most likely with their important business going on beneath the soil: carrots, beets, turnips, potatoes. How do potatoes look as they grow? She didn't know. One crop in particular intrigues her, low and weedy-looking. She sees her name on a white sign, hand-painted in red—EDIE'S STAWBERRIES!— as she passes. Smiles at the exclamation point. Always a little bit of fun, she thinks, to see your name somewhere, particularly on a sign selling strawberries.

With nowhere else specifically to go pee, Edie signals left to pull off onto a smaller service road that looks like it'll plunge straight into the center of the mysterious crop's territory. She stops, blinker blinking, looking over the sweep of solid land ordered in green sequence, think-ing, How would it be to live here? How would it be to be an Edie selling strawberries? Straw hats and baseball caps. Pickup trucks. Lots of crates to cart around. Tying things up with twine. Steinbeck. Hay bales. Rolling cigarettes. Flapjacks.

With her left arm out the window, waiting, she surveys the road she's about to turn onto, narrowing like a pool cue into some grove. She turns her attention to the oncoming traffic, sees a break coming up after an approaching orange semi. Waiting. Then, psychically, a quick premonition, a distinct feeling of general approach like the ghostly awareness that someone has entered the room. She glances up at the rearview mirror and, sure enough, sees a large white car zooming up upon her. In disbelief, she turns around, left arm still hanging out the open window, to get an actual nonreflective view of the status of things when—yup, here it comes—a huge white car with what seems to be a faceless maniac behind its dark windshield, someone cinematically trying to ram her, comes slamming into the rear of her car, sending her flying forward.

The pack of smokes on the dash goes flinging into the backseat. The dashboard flips open, ill-folded maps popping out like jack-in-the-boxes. The passenger seat flings back to recline. The car stops rolling forward. The engine stalls. A frantic clatter under the hood is followed by a faint *sssss* of something whistling like a nostril. but Edie hardly notices any of it since she felt her arm snap somehow deep within. Felt the bone break and all the miniature disruptions of muscles and flesh that surround it. To Edie, the air feels very thin. All she wants to do is hold her left arm close to her stomach gingerly, like it's an infant.

Just as the pock-faced young man at the gas station appeared in her window earlier, now another man appears beside her in the window of her driver's seat. Awfully quickly. And a cop! A basic California cop straight out of central casting: middle-aged, cop sunglasses.

He leans in. "You all right?"

Edie watches the fuzzed blond hair on his forearms shiver in the wind. "I broke my arm," she says.

The policeman laughs, a display of extremely white Hollywood teeth. "Let's take a deep breath." He takes a slow deep breath as a prototype, a California yogic breath: in, out. "Now then," he says. "You all right?"

"I'm pretty sure my arm's broken."

"Which arm would that be?"

"This arm," says Edie, pointing at it, limp in her lap, with her chin. The pain is starting to frighten her. Her vision. Everything is tinting green like before a tornado.

"Mmm. Can you bend it?"

Edie looks at him. It's a cruel, perverse request. She looks back down at her arms and slowly, tentatively, begins to lift her right arm up and away from the wounded left. Before she has a real look at the injured arm—what she does see of it is all completely wrong and bent—she can't control her impulse to attempt to lift her left pointer finger. Before she's aware of the pain it will cause, she begins: brain telling finger *lift* and, like a switch or a pull cord, at the instant of command, a brief rush, a suffocating feeling of gray-green silver, nausea, a sprinkle of stars tingle at her face, and she passes out.

•

It's not that Edie didn't want to go see her father once they learned he was sick. It's not that she didn't want to help him and keep him company the way Max and Margaret managed to do. The first time she went to see him, alone, it had been practically excruciating. She was uncomfortable, literally. The clothes she wore in New York, the clothes she wore regularly, seemed markedly depressing, unoriginal and urban, even ill-fitting, when she went to see her father. They seemed to stink of cigarettes, something she never noticed in New York, no matter how much she washed them or how often she changed. Walking down a New York City street, all that concrete, that sky and wind, she could feel herself looking attractive, or at least at times imagine that she was, the sound of her steps, her steady gaze down the long avenues, an anonymous girl (did she look like a woman?) on the move, heading to an anonymous destination. When she was in motion—going to work, heading home, climbing the smelly stairs of the subway, the warm subterranean wind forming a miniature cyclone of trash on the landing, hailing a cab, leaving the movie theater—things were better. Sometimes her body would fall away from her self, like swimming, and all she'd be left with was what she saw, what she thought.

This barely ever happened when she was at her father's house. Even when her mother was alive, when she went home to Merrick, she felt lumbering and awkward. All the rest of her came crowding in. Her skin felt flabby and pale, her jaw double-chinned, her feet smelly, teeth yellow. She felt she was sitting still, and a restlessness like cabin fever, weepy and impatient, came over her, even when she made the effort to get up and move about, walk down to the pharmacy or jog under the freeway to the fancy hotel at the end of the beach.

She'd forget about the stasis sometimes, while she and her father ate dinner (string beans, pork chops, Minute Rice; broccoli, steak, Minute Rice; string beans, pork chops, baked potato), or when he was talking to her, really talking, telling Edie about her grandmother, which he'd never done before. Edie had only barely known her. She could recall simply an aura of civility and kindness, a certain brown velvet scarf with satin trim, the smell of lavender. An active thumb, back and forth like a windshield wiper, as a caress on a knee or an arm.

Her father had never talked about her very much but now Arthur's face would relax with so much relief as he spoke of his mother that it almost made Edie jealous. What about *her* mother? Shouldn't he be thinking of her?

Her father would sigh wistfully, like he was high, which he very well could have been from the medications. He'd look off, mooning like a teenager. "She'd tell stories of the Dillinger gang. She was a *very* funny woman. She was a very, very *smart* woman."

Edie would listen, storing the information away somewhere since she knew it was important, knew it applied to her somehow: her genes, her past and future, the family history. It was something she always told herself she'd learn about later, get to the bottom of later, when it mattered, when it made sense. But then her mother died and now here her father was dying. Who would be her supplier of family lore? Everyone was dead. The "diaries" of Aunt Betsy? Everyone knew she had a tendency to embellish for the worse. "They never *fed* us! We were hardly ever *fed!*" When, in reality, there was an Irish cook for more than twenty years.

Being with her father, being as close to home as she could get, made her lonely. It reminded her that her mother was gone. But she was lonely before that happened. It reminded her of how lonely she was all the time. She was fine. She was always *fine*. But, frankly, Margaret and Max had families to go home to after they saw Dad, and Edie—well, Edie would rather stay in her apartment in New York so she could avoid eating a meal with him, eat instead whatever she wanted alone so she could puke it up afterward in her empty bathroom without worrying about him hearing her.

"Edie, my love?" She heard him on other side of the bathroom door. She thought he was at the neighbor's, bringing in their mail for them, watering their plants while they were away.

"Yeah, Dad?"

"Are you all right?"

"I—I'm just sick to my stomach, Dad."

A large pause. "Can I do anything for you?"

"No, thanks, Dad."

"Very well."

•

When she woozes out of it, coming to, Edie finds herself with the car door open. She's sitting sideways on the seat, sparkling pavement a few inches from her face. She can look under the car at its newly ruptured engine. Dark pipes dangle. She thinks of the rabbits Max brought home from school, the ones that started to tear each other apart in the hutch after they got bigger, both males. Edie came to feed them one morning and the white one was bloodied, hopping about with some entrails coming out of its belly.

The policeman has tried to push her head between her legs. But I've already fainted, she wants to say. She thinks, Where's my bad arm? She can hear the policeman, murky talk. When she lifts her head up, she's overcome with nausea. An older cop, hatless, with twinkling blue eyes like Archie Bunker, squats down. A kind face. What a good villain he'd be in a film.

Edie cradles her arm, looking at him. "I was waiting to go left," she says. Then it's there again, woozy and silver, and she rests her head on the seat's headrest.

"Can you tell me your name?"

His tender voice causes her to start weeping a little. "Edie," she says.

"Edie? Can you tell me what day it is?"

She starts laughing while she's crying because she really hasn't the slightest idea, lately, what day it is. Then she remembers Margaret telling her the flight's tomorrow.

"Thursday," says Edie. "I mean, Friday."

"We'll have someone here to help you shortly, Edie." He claps his hands down on his squatted knees like a big-hearted coach.

"Registration in the glove compartment? You mind if I fish it out?"

Fish. Glove. "That's fine," says Edie.

He helps her into the police car where, once she sits down, she sits still, aware only of the frenzied ache in her wrist that won't settle, that's carrying on its own electric life up and down her arm, into her belly. She vaguely watches the man go over to her crumpled car, reach around in the front seat, and come out with her silver shoulder bag, her small black duffel from the backseat. Off to the side, she sees the driver of the car that hit her, an elderly diminutive woman with a head of mauve-colored hair that keeps shaking.

The kind-eyed policeman comes to speak to Edie, his head framed in the passenger-seat window, the mountains behind him like shoulder pads.

"Thanks," Edie says to him.

"They'll fix you up," he tells her. "Here comes Al."

Al, a younger officer, gets into the front seat and radios something on the radio. After a brief unintelligible correspondence over barking static, he speaks to Edie as he turns the car around. "Looks like that's it for your Volvo," he says, sounding like *vulva*. "I had one like it myself. Great car." He glances at her arm, whistles a glissando. "That's got to hurt," he says.

She smiles weakly. She is eager to know the procedure here: How far is the hospital, where are they going, what's with the car?

When Officer Al says shyly, "I'm sorry, but I've got to buckle you up," she hears it as *button you up*, her mother, doing up her coat, doing up her boots, doing up her sweater. He clumsily pulls the seat belt over her body and finally clicks it in, the satisfying sound, and she feels nicely secure for the first time in a while. Being buckled in, even if it is while she's injured. Being driven. As children, they'd climb free-for-all around the station wagon, Edie's domain the way back, straddling down into the backseat on top of Margaret and Max, climbing up into the front, leaning against her mother.

Edie rests her head on the doorframe, closes her eyes, and thinks about that big station wagon—The Tank, they called it—thinks about her mother driving, how she used both feet, one for the brake, one for the pedal. She pretends that her mother is driving, that her mother is beside her. She does this in her apartment: She imagines her mother on the couch, imagines her mother is in the bathroom, about to come out.

The car slows down, a red light probably. Edie keeps her eyes closed but sees, feels almost, the movement of her mother's right arm coming out, extending like a guard rail, an automatic boom, out in front of Edie in the passenger seat. Do mothers do that anymore? With kids in the back, kids buckled up, car seats, booster seats, kangaroo seats, air bags?

Edie opens her eyes, tipped to the side of her passenger seat. She sits up. The pain is starting to become too much to bear. She looks at the road, all the people driving somewhere. All the people with things to do. She tries to think of something to keep from thinking of her arm. Something to say. Something to remember. San Simeon. Edie glances over at the policeman, her driver. "Did you know that Patty Hearst has been in some John Waters movies?"

"Ahh," says the young cop, taking his eyes from the road for a second. He looks quickly at her face, her knees, smiles, then back at the road. "Yeah. Yeah, I did know that. As a matter of fact, I auditioned with her once."

·

At the hospital, Edie doesn't know which way is north, which way is south, but the tiny medical room that they put her in has a decent view. Out the window, on the other side of a parking lot, the green hills are like odalisques, fallen down, hips jutting up. They look artificial, as though they've been rolled with a rolling pin. Somewhere in this theme park of a state, her father is expecting her.

Inside, in this hospital where nobody knows her, she is in a precarious position. The bone of her arm is being set. She had no idea that this was how it was done. She imagined, as in Westerns, a doctor or two tugging at her arm, bracing themselves with a foot heel upon the examining table. The contraption they have her set up in is completely medieval, chain mail and all. Her arm is in the position it would be in if she were waving. Thimbles made of woven metal cap each finger like tips of gloves and are pulling her hand upward through a small but incredibly efficient pulley system on the ceiling. A nurse, a doctor, *someone*, straps some weights around her elbow, which immediately pulls her arm down while the pulley pulls up, lengthening her forearm.

A woman with white hair, thankfully, upon her arrival—and after gruffly using goops of Vaseline to grease off a ring from Edie's hand (her mother's wedding ring, the early version, thin and gold, not the platinum one she was wearing when she died)—had shot her arm full of something that has numbed it, made it mellifluously warm and pleasantly itchy. With the weights going down and the pulley pulling up, Edie feels extension in her forearm, feels it being stretched, and then hears clicking sounds, jarringly loud but muffled, like the sounds that come out of an old oven as it's preheating or the noise of a car's engine after it's been turned off after a long journey. There's an especially loud one, muffled in the flesh—*cleck*—that old joke of a fingernail flicked against the tooth when you pretend the nose is being moved.

The nurse nods at Edie with eagerness. "That's what you want to hear," she says brightly.

"Really?" asks Edie, giddy with pain relief.

"That's everything moving back into place, dear," says the nurse. This nurse is a woman, probably not much older than Edie, maybe even younger than Edie, but who uses the word *dear* to a peer. The nurse has a mildly round body, a friendly face. She could be thirty. She could be forty-five.

Once the bone is set, there's a second round of X-rays: before and after. The doctor studies them, then smiles at her. "These final X-rays indicate that you won't be needing surgery," he says. English is his second language.

"Surgery?" she answers. She's shocked.

"Like I said. You very fortunately will *not* be needing it."

"Oh. Great," says Edie, as the doctor, an Indian man who clearly had a severe acne problem at one point, streams out of the room.

Edie sighs and groans a little like a whiny baby since there's no one in the room. "How far is Santa Viola?" she complains to herself.

Then, from behind her, "You're very close, dear," answers the nurse. "Now's the fun part. You get to pick a color for your cast."

Edie picks the one that glows in the dark, thinking Margaret's kids will appreciate it. The fiberglass looks like it's yellowing, a chalky lime color.

•

"Your cast is the color of urine," Arthur points out, shortly after her taxied arrival at his house.

"Yes, Dad. Thanks."

"Is it not?"

"It glows in the dark."

"Glows in the dark? Isn't that nifty."

"I thought the kids might think so."

"Of course. Could you please water the freesia for me? I'm unable to do so. As you'll see, there are terrible weeds under the rose on the trellis."

"Don't you think, Dad, that since we're leaving here tomorrow it doesn't really matter if I water the plants?"

He looks at her blankly. "Do as you like," he says, almost bitterly. "Alice will take care of it."

When the phone rings, Edie realizes she has to answer it. She's on duty. It's Margaret, checking in. Edie tells her, in a thumbnail version, that she's broken her arm and the car was totaled. After a moment of listening to her sister, Edie blurts out cheerily, "Margaret was in an accident too!"

"Wonderful!" says Arthur.

"They're fine. They got rear-ended too."

Arthur shakes his head back and forth. "Good grief," he says.

Edie sniggers. Then she starts laughing, laughing hysterically. "Good grief!" she repeats, barely managing to hang on to the phone. She doesn't really know what's so funny. Maybe it's the painkillers or the strange relief of finally seeing her father. He looks bad, but not that bad. He actually looks pretty good: slender and limber, younger than usual. She keeps laughing, stutters to Margaret that she's got to hang up. A glimpse of her father's expression as he watches her makes her laugh harder: He's bemused, almost pleased, smiling slightly, but he looks concerned as well, almost frightened.

It all seems so silly: her going to the hospital when here is her father, terminally ill; her puking into toilet bowls dotted across the country; her longing for something, for someone, for what exactly she has no idea. She is alive and doesn't know what to look for. She leans on the counter. She laughs harder and harder, her nose starting to run, her eyes watering, the muscles of her stomach beginning to burn. To be a grown adult and to feel so lonely. . . . It was just ridiculous.

7

Needless to say, after Chloe's outburst regarding infidelity and the couple's reluctance to address it, what follows is not a great lunch for the young family Bramble. They fumble outside together, foggy-headed, the lovely day glaring after Chloe's tears, and settle for the Foona Laguna stoop rather than an effortful, brooding walk to Riverside Park. Flies from a mysterious source swirl about their heads, occasionally touching down on their eyebrows and the tips of their ears. Mother and father eat California rolls that taste like they're from a deli salad bar lined with sneeze guards: wheaty, pickled, a little bit fishy. Max chews on a lot of ginger to compensate, glances around with the general worry that he might see Mimi and Howard Woods pass by again, with an ensuing explanation to Chloe, the look on her face as a result: Oh—smiling suspiciously, nodding but friendly—*you saw them earlier?* Her expression quizzical but nonchalant. *Near the park?* A pause. *I thought you were at Starbucks.* Another pause. *Isn't that on Broadway?*

Chloe doesn't speak and works at avoiding her husband's glance by focusing on baby Rex as she tries to get him to eat his bagel, then some Veggie Stix, then a hard nectarine with a label still stuck on it. Rex occupies himself by busily flipping open and closed the brass mail slot of the brownstone's front door, a distressing repetitive clanking that ordinarily Max would calmly and promptly put an end to but that under the circumstances he endures, so as not to seem impatient or abrupt. The puppy, initially alarmed by the clatter, then intrigued, is now uninterested. He's tied to the wrought-iron railing at the bottom of the stoop, flopping around on the sidewalk, sniffing at the bags and clear plastic containers, then cleaning his paw with slow, deliberate licks.

"Clo," says Max.

She smiles at him nervously, a slightly barbed glare. "Let's not talk about it now," she says, her jaw tight. "But we *will not* keep a dog."

Max doesn't say anything. She so rarely uses declaratives that this crisp show of surety somehow annoys him. Her sudden upper hand. Her sudden control of the situation.

Chloe continues. "Then again," she says sarcastically, but softly, "maybe it's a great idea! I'd just *love* to tie a big ol' *dog* to the stroller and spend my time scoopering up shit. Rex can help! And, well, we have *plenty of room!*" She starts to cry again. This time, hearing his name, Rex notices. His round face looks up at his mother and squints as though sprinkling rain is falling in his eyes, his lower jaw jutted out, bagel in hand, staring at her. He looks to his father. What is this? Are we scared?

Max picks him up, plops him on his lap. Rex studies his father's face, close up, pronounces, "Ded," with a pat on the cheek, "Deddie," and squeezes Max's nose, scraping him with long nails (can't she keep them trimmed?), before sliding off his father's thighs to go investigate the puppy.

Max looks at Chloe, whimpering. He looks at his son, sitting directly on the dirty pavement, and the oblivious smiling puppy that has to go back to its hot shaving-filled window on Eighty-ninth Street. Chloe sniffles, blowing her nose into a napkin with a Japanese name on it, while Max makes fleeting eye contact with a passerby. A woman who looks like Madonna (that newsboy cap) takes note of Chloe's tears and the baby and looks Max's way briefly, dismissively, as if to say *pig*.

Chloe clears her throat loudly. "*Plenty* of room," she says again, flailing her arms out to demonstrate how very little room she actually means.

·

Their apartment, actually, was a fantastic deal. Max bought the lease from a tiny girl he used to wait tables with, with whom, yes, unbeknownst to Chloe but long before he'd ever met her, he had slept one drunken night—the only one-nighter of his life, really—when he ran into her on the street and she took him to a party, the focus of which was making caipirinhas.

The rent was cheaper than anyone's Max knew of. A one-room studio with an actual foyer in a prewar building in Chelsea. The huge bathroom (meaning two people could stand in it) had both a bathtub *and* a window, with a tiled floor of tiny white octagons and a thin ribbon of black around the border of the room like hockey tape. Rex's crib was set up in the orangey-red foyer, preventing the front door from opening entirely. Chloe had hung some light blue mosquito netting from a hook on the ceiling over the crib for some added privacy for Rex, creating a sort of Moroccan-vibed entryway.

The kitchen "area," made semi-alcove by a red Chinese divider that Chloe shined up with numerous coats of polyurethane, was on the far wall of the main room, abutting the wall with three large windows that looked down to Eighteenth Street. The bed took up most of the main room, but Chloe usually managed to keep it inviting and clean, the sheets militarily taut, the plentiful pillows fluffed up and cushy. In the corner, the raspberry-colored iMac in front of which Chloe was regularly stationed, robotically trawling the Web, looking for real estate on Long Island, New Jersey, Connecticut, Westchester, upstate New York, Pennsylvania, Vermont, and, one odd wintry afternoon when Max came home early with the flu, Arizona.

"Arizona?"

Chloe shrugged. "I'm not really sure how I ended up here, but it's kind of neato."

"Neato?"

"It'd be great for your allergies."

"I don't have allergies."

Chloe looked at him.

"Those are attacks," said Max, referring to the sporadic occurrences when his nose is overcome by *something*; when it waters; when it reddens and sneezes. "They're reactions," he said.

"Well. It'd be great for your reactions," said Chloe, clinking away at the keyboard.

Her real estate fixation began one night, in one single moment, like a stray snowball hitting a window, as she lay in bed, seven months pregnant, the unknown baby boy kicking away tirelessly inside of her. Lying there in the dark, their apartment as much a home as some sort of container, she listened to other people, strangers, in their own containers above her, below her, and alongside, their faint human noises. From above, chair legs backing away from a table. From below, a muffled paroxysm of male anger, possibly a reaction to a sports play on TV. Beside her, the shower whistling in the neighboring bathroom, the sound of a bar of soap being dropped, clonking the side of a tub. The heavy front doors everywhere, creaking open, creaking closed, the people alone above her, alone below her, the traffic sounds down on the nighttime streets, sirens from an ambulance stuttering through traffic, the churning of the trash compactor in a garbage truck, the impatient honks sailing through the air and up toward the sealed-shut windows of their apartment—where Chloe lay, suddenly gripped with nightmarish fear.

It wasn't terrorism or any of that—specifically. The city was just too scary, too much noise for a baby, too dirty, too many people to eye him with evil eyes, invading his privacy, invading his *life*. Was she being irrational? She'd always loved New York. But a postage-stamp lot of greenery, a shack in the woods in Minnesota, Montana, Maine, wherever, *anywhere* with more than a room and a half, somewhere with a front door that brought you out to level ground, a patch of grass beyond that door, the view of a *tree* out of a window (imagine!), a pot of dirt to grow strawberries in, a real live bush, a window with more than a quadrant of sky—it all seemed somehow safe and secure and, with pregnancy-induced irrationality, utterly *necessary*.

Chloe lay there, spoke into the darkness. "We've got to get out of here," she said. She knew Max was sound asleep but she said it again, feeling dramatic. "We've got to *get out*," she said, the pressing whisper of a starlet, as if her life depended on it, the actress within her relishing the solitary moment of deep feeling and the image she saw of herself, flat on her back in the dark, round with child, trapped in a sooty metropolis, lying in bed awake, staring at the wall while her husband slept. She indulged in theatricality. "I can't take it anymore," she said, into the dark, because it seemed to be the thing that someone like herself would say on film; it seemed to be the right thing to say.

She got up out of bed, sat down at the computer, googled *real estate* and effortlessly wound up on an extensive realtor website, and found herself fascinated by houses as though they had never occurred to her before.

That panicked anxiety, that stricken imperative of leaving the city, naturally subsided. Along came Rex during a late snowfall, and Chloe went on to enjoy motherhood even more than she thought she would (which she thought would be a lot). She jaunted happily about town with him rag-dolled in the Baby Bjork, as Max called it, strolling from store to store, visiting friends in their apartments, coming home, and, while Rex napped, diving headlong into the e-soup world of e-real estate.

She became a sort of real estate Web searcher aficionado, knowing what realtor.com was good for in comparison to the smaller, more local homepages. She could fluently discuss (primarily with her friend Rena, the only interested audience [she had also recently had a baby]) odd samplings of school districts and remember where Westchester stood in relation to various counties in New Jersey when it came to average property value and the local tax rate. She undeliberately maintained a directory of open houses in her mind whether she was interested in see-ing them or not, without ever having written them down, as though she were some kind of top-secret messenger safeguarding wartime coordi-nates. "Did you just mention Montclair? Hmm. There's an open house at Twenty-two Chestnut Street from three to five on Sunday. Colonial. Four bedrooms, two full baths. Eighth of an acre. Corner lot. Eat-in kitch—"

"That's . . . okay, honey."

Words and terms that Max had never heard cross his wife's lips came fluming out of her like cool falling water, sounding surprisingly attrac-tive since their source was her lovely mouth: ARMs, balloons, lenders, APRs, fixed rates, principal, monthly payments.

"Maybe *you* should have gone into real estate," Max told Chloe, as he watched her stare at the computer screen, as she clicked closed a graph of New York's mortgage rates.

Chloe shrugged as she studied a large picture of a Tudor in Nyack. "I know," she answered wistfully. With her deep sigh, for a moment, there she was, on the lawn of her big Tudor homestead, calling the kids down from their tree house, ratatouille simmering on her nice big Viking stovetop in a shiny copper-bottomed pot, some white sheets of an unbelievably high thread count tossing about down the hall in a silent dryer in the laundry room (a laundry room!), and a baby sleeping upstairs (an upstairs!) with its monitor on in its own bedroom (its own bedroom!).

Max sat down in their lone armchair still wearing his raincoat, watching his wife, wondering how they'd ever drum up enough cash to buy a house, to buy anything. True, they were due some money from the Maine airline for the crash that his mother was in. The airline, however, was having Chapter 11 issues to begin with, and he and his siblings weren't holding their collective breaths (though each of them certainly had various very-much-alive plans for what they'd do with the money). His mother's life insurance had all gone to his father and would come their way eventually, if there was any money left. Arthur seemed to imply that there wasn't. But what about buying a house the old-fashioned way, with capital that he'd earned and saved himself? What about that? Shouldn't I be able to do this? he'd wonder. Shouldn't *we*?

•

Max watches his son at the bottom of the stoop. Rex pats the puppy tenderly with toddler slapdashery, against the grain of its fur. "Dap," Rex says to it. "Dappy."

"Dog," corrects Max.

"He's saying *puppy*, Max," Chloe says dryly.

Rex is all glee, suddenly fully aware of the puppy again, cooing at it, humming to it. Chloe and Max, gleeless, sit side by side, putting syrupy containers into grease-streaked paper bags to cart them off to the trash. The largest one, saturated with soy sauce, breaks apart when Chloe picks it up, the pieces of trash skidding down her legs, strewn over the stoop like an exploding party favor, soy sauce trickling down her shin. At the bottom of the steps, she lets the puppy lick it off while she watches a $100,000 (she knows this from her World Wide Web education) silver Mercedes SUV, the military-looking one, boxy and gleaming, drive past.

"Aren't people ashamed to be driving that?" she asks, trying to look in and see who *is* driving it. It's the first regular thing she says since she said she thought Max was sleeping with someone.

"Oh, yes. I think they're very ashamed."

"I'm serious," says Chloe. "Won't just a standard luxury SUV do?"

Max smiles, feeling slightly off the hook. "Honey," he says to her. "There's nothing for you to be upset about. I promise."

Chloe stands there, curbside, watching the light traffic rev past along the leafy street. "It's one thing if you're driving around in Greenwich or Beverly Hills," she says. "But to drive through New York in one of those things? It's just . . . embarrassing."

Max wonders about the logic here. First, New York is one of the richest places on earth, really. Second, the logic of Chloe's fantasy about living in a nice big house isn't exactly Marxist. Surely Chloe would enjoy a multimillion-dollar home, seaside, if she had the chance. Wasn't that more show-offy than a car?

Instead, he guffaws. "What's another fifty Gs if you have it to spare?"

"Exactly," says Chloe. "Tell that to this guy." She tips her head toward an approaching black man, on cue, with a crippled foot.

"Spare some change for the United Negro Pizza Fund?"

"Look, chief," Max says to him. Max has seen this guy around. It was about time to know who he was. "What's your name?"

"Jerry."

"Jerry? I'm Max. Look, Jerry. Now's not a good time. Okay, man?"

"I understand. I understand that. But as you can see"—Jerry motions down to his severely inward-turned foot—"now's not a good time for me almost *all* the time."

"Are you hungry?" asks Chloe. "You want this apple?"

"No. No apple," says Jerry. "I could use some change." Jerry glances down at Rex. "Hello, little man."

"Look," says Max. He looks down at Jerry's twisted foot. "What's up with this? I've seen you more than once walking without a limp at all."

"You must be mistaken. I've been in this predicament my whole life long."

"No. I've definitely seen you."

"Leave him alone, Max. God, if a man has to fake a limp—"

"I've seen you walking up by the Cloisters totally fine. Does the pity thing really work?"

"Well, yes, it does. Yes, it does."

"What?" asks Chloe fiercely. She looks at Max briefly as she clips Rex into his stroller, her expression getting shrill. The puffiness of her eyes makes her look as though she's been doing a lot of swimming.

"What what?" asks Max, shrugging.

Sensing an ensuing argument, Jerry quietly moves along.

Chloe turns to Max, her face narrowing into a wrinkled prune. "What were you doing up *there*?"

Max is perplexed. "Up where?"

Chloe's face, tired and wan. Chloe's face, distressed and frail, blinking at him, her mouth all curled up, chewing on its lips. When he glances at her directly, allows her eyes to bore into him, their airy blue: all of those streets she took him on in Paris, walking day and night, how surprised he was at how good her French was, how amazed he was in the hospital when she was in labor with Rex, where he thought she'd be a raving lunatic (after the stories Margaret had told him)—instead she became queenly, stern and brave, retracted into herself. Max couldn't see her, didn't recognize her. He felt as though he were in a hospital room with someone dying—or someone divine. He felt as though he wanted to cast a net over her, trap her, as though this new woman might hurry along on her own once she was done and the baby was out. What would she ever need him for? When she reappeared, after Rex came out, he fell in love with her all over again—that old cliché—but it was true. He'd lost her for a spell of time, seen a part of her he'd never have predicted. And then she came back. Now, this spring afternoon, her eyes are tinny and blue, her eyebrows thoroughly downturned, sad and pleading. "What were you doing?" Chloe wails. She sobs into the bowl of her hands. "What were you doing up by the *Cloisters*?"

Max rummages for words. He looks away, down the street, feeling as though he's being pushed down from above like a birthday candle getting poked into sponge cake. The glimmering pavement looks hard. The angry underbite face of the stout mailbox. Everything is cross with him. The puppy starts to yelp. Rex begins to whine. Max tugs at the hair on his own head to get some blood flowing, let off some tension. He takes a deep breath. Oh, how he longs for a neck massage, some firm-fingered attention to his trapezius muscles, his temples. "Oh, Chloe." He sighs.

"Oh, *Max*," she says sharply.

"Let's talk about it later," says Max, nodding toward Rex. Rex is whining toward the street. "But I am *not* sleeping with someone," he whispers at her.

"Let's go, Rexie," says Chloe angrily, feigning cheeriness.

Rex is whining. "Dappy," he says to his mother. "Dappy dap."

"The puppy has to go home now," quips Chloe.

"Ded! Me dedda!"

"Daddy has to go back to work," she says, as she picks him up.

Rex screeches. "Dappy dap!" he screams, lurching his back into an arc, almost head-butting his mother. "Me dedda!"

"Daddy has to go to *work*, sweetie," she says sternly, placing him in his stroller.

"Dappy! Dappy!" screams Rex. Max approaches the stroller to help buckle him in.

"I've got it, thanks," Chloe says curtly to Max.

"Me Dappy! Dappy! DAP! HO HO!"

"It's the dog, Chloe. He wants to see the dog."

"No. He wants to take the dog *home*, Max."

"Here let me," says Max. He reaches to fix a buckle that's twisted.

"I've *got* it," says Chloe. She clicks it in and then veers away quickly. "Good-bye," she says sharply, swerving.

Max watches his wife and child continue along the sidewalk. Chloe glances back at him, or back at the steps, her face tear-bedraggled, almost smiling. Smiling? For a second, Max's heart lightens, he's overcome with an inflating feeling of respite, of tension abandoned, everything's over! Truce! She's not *upset*! It's all comedy, after all! Or maybe she's squinting. Yes, she's squinting. He can see her sobbing again, walking away quickly. Rex's continued screams loop out of the stroller as they make their way toward the corner. Max lets out an audible groan.

Chloe's pretty body, her pretty hair and face, the pony prettiness of the whole package, the fresh sight of the stroller with Rex in it, and now the motion of them moving away, the two of them one unit, mother and child, his wife, his son, his own family—the sight of all this makes him feel so claustrophobic, so unworthy. Not claustrophobic in the low-down dog sense of wanting other women or wanting to *break free*—he loves his wife, he knows that, and he loves little Rexie. But the effort of it. The burden. The fact that it *is* a burden, that somewhere in the marriage arrangement he feels that: the *burden* of it. This is his problem. The tiny apartment that they're in. This *job* situation. How he's letting them down. How could she think he was sleeping with someone else? Does that mean *she* wants to sleep with someone else? (Who told him once—maybe it was Margaret—that mates get jealous because really they're thinking unfaithful thoughts themselves?) Does that mean *Chloe* is sleeping with someone?

Chloe. The first time her ever saw her—it was so silly—it was as though the sky cracked open for a second, that old saying, all that stuff, the room in this case the lobby of a Loew's movie theater. He had the sensation that living in the world was like living inside of a hollowed egg, an egg that was lit like a Constable painting. And here was this face, her face, partly a face that he'd known forever, partly a face like nothing he'd ever seen before but somehow imagined. There she was, constantly arriving. She smiled at him, shook his hand politely, and it seemed almost ridiculous that she was being so civil, as though they didn't even know each other yet (which they didn't), when it was so apparent to him that she belonged with him. She looked strange to Max, managing in her life alone, without him. He never told her this, how clear it was to him that he loved her, or something like it, from the first moment he saw her. It petrified him to tell her so.

Max wonders, Does she think she made a big mistake marrying me? Of course she must. What can he do? Which way to turn? For the moment he is thankful that Chloe no longer has a father—what an awful thing to be thankful for! But if she did: a suspicious man constantly watching Max's moves? And thank God Chloe's mother wasn't more aware of her daughter's life—what an awful thing to thank God for!—instead of living in Geneva with that Spanish count, shopping all the time. If her parents were around, would he be stronger for her? If his *own* mother were around, would he be bucking up better? But of course there *is* his own mother, it seems, spying on him.

Chloe never got to meet Florence, is always asking, Was his mother kind of like *her*?—pointing out a nice-looking older woman in the park. Max would shrug. Kind of, I guess, he'd say.

"But she was also kind of like *her*," he'd say, pointing to another woman, more polished, more coiffed.

Chloe would bite her lip, watch the said woman gather her newspaper and roll it into a cylinder, stick it into her bag. Chloe would say softly, "Well, see now, that throws me."

Max walks aimlessly, finally plants himself on the grand steps of Low Library at Columbia University, pretending to be a student, pretending to be a professor, watching the summer students crisscross the wedge-shaped greens along spokes of paths. Butler Library dreams of a cumulus cloud with a gorgelike valley. Max leans back on his elbows, rests a foot on his knee, his toe punting the thunderhead, his retro Adidas shell-top sneaker—did Chloe know he'd had the same pair as a kid when she bought them?—taking him back to those bus rides to school when he'd trace their ribs with a ballpoint pen, coloring in the field, his warm breath on the cold glass, the bare brown tree limbs outside, the slight vibration of the engine, his coziness, the swish of his CB parka, all giving him a slight fleeting erection.

He'd spent a lot of times watching people on this college green, wondering different things. In the early days, as a freshman, when he looked at girls, watched them, he generally wondered what they looked like naked. Surprisingly great. Surprisingly bad. Unsurprising. What they were like in bed. Sultry and soft. Spicy but submissive. Loud and angry. Maybe like a pop star, self-conscious and mechanically aerobic.

Once it's almost dark, he goes home, tiptoes in. Toys have colonized the entryway. He steps on some gadget, an electronic book. *That oughta stop ya!* it says. *Parker!* The Batman book with the audio buttons. He winces, looks to see if he's woken Rex. Rex isn't in his crib. The sheets are flat, empty, slightly rippled, a still shot from evidence photos of a kidnapping.

She's left me is the first thing Max thinks. *They're gone.* But then around the corner he sees them, both asleep on the bed. There's nowhere to sit. There's the chair, but it's too close to the sleepers. There's the stool in the alcove of the kitchen, but not there. Not at the desk. He wants to leave again, but also doesn't. He goes out on the fire escape, partly hiding, partly not, and watches the two of them sleeping together. All around him, the glassiness of late spring, the light blue light of evening filtering through the apartment and across their silky heads as though the two of them are stems in a vase, bright and wavy through the thick shining glass. What life there is here, all fresh! What is he doing out on the fire escape? What is he doing, period?

Chloe stirs as though she heard something when in fact, as Max witnesses, there was no noise. She wakes up abruptly. "Hello?" she says, then remembers the baby is asleep. She hurries to the door and looks out through the doorway's tiny hole, which presents her with the long warped hallway. No one. "Max?" she says softly, which makes Max feel sad. She gets the baby from the bed and places him in his crib. She watches him settle for a moment and then gets back into bed.

As night falls, the action picks up. With lights on in the windows, Max can see a woman studying at her kitchen table. Two buildings over in the rear, there are glimpses of people doing capoeria in the large windows of a dance studio. Some nights people are on stationary bikes or energetically kickboxing; other nights it looks like an AA meeting. Directly across from him, a man is talking on the phone while he shakes something in a frying pan. Across the courtyard, down below, there are some people on a much-envied patio huddled around a tiny café table with candles on it. The flames look lemony in the darkening blue light. Max can smell something sweet like honeysuckle. He catches a faint whiff of marijuana. From an indeterminate open window, he can hear that Strokes song playing that he hears everywhere he goes.

Later, when it starts to rain and Max finally comes to bed, Chloe rolls toward him in the smudgy dark. "Where have you been?" she asks. The tone of her voice doesn't sound terse. She doesn't sound mad. She doesn't even sound regular. She sounds sleepy and sweet.

Max takes a deep breath, lies down on his back beside her, and sighs, looking up at the ceiling. He puts his hand on her supple thigh and squeezes it, closes his eyes. "With my other woman," he says.

He tucks the sheet in lovingly around her shoulders. He puts his big hand on her face, edges in next to her. She is smiling at him, her eyes closed.

They hold each other, clasped. The roar of the rain. The quiet, loud rain. Her love for him, smooth as a tooth.

8

In the evening, when Brian comes home, Margaret follows him upstairs to talk about Edie.

"This again?" he asks. When he first met Margaret, she was a person completely untouched by death. Everyone around her was still alive. Her grandparents were dead, but that had happened almost before she was born. Then there was the accident with her mother. And now here was her father dying. Somehow, though, it was as if the events hadn't caught up with her yet, hadn't yet penetrated her death-free existence. Always Brian had delighted in her deadpan, her matter-of-fact manner, the serious look on her face when she wasn't really a serious person at all. Her general manner shed of anything frivolous. He couldn't help smiling at her: the way she walked, the way she talked. "What?" she'd say, her face expressionless. "What?"

"I don't know what I'm going to do," says Margaret now, referring to Edie, how to approach her sister, how to befriend her again.

"Oh, you'll work it out," says Brian, tenderly but borderline dismissively. Brian has little (no) patience for melodrama. His life began as a melodrama. His mother died of brain cancer one Halloween evening when he was six years old. In the Boston hospital he remembers crepe paper streamers shaped like candy corn and ghosts looping down the hall. Paper jack-o'-lanterns taped to the indigo windows. His little sister Sinead asleep on his uncle Bobby's lap. There was a troupe of small trick-or-treaters traveling en masse from room to room to cheer up the patients. Still today he remembers the glance of a little girl in the group, his age, blond but with dark eyes in a squaw costume, peering in the door. His cheek was squished against his aunt Mary's shoulder as she held him. The small girl's eyes, soft and intelligent, bored into him. A girl Brian always thought he'd find one day. A girl he always thought he'd marry.

Brian's father, a demolished man left with five kids all under the age of ten, did the best he could. He drank a lot, understandably, and three shaky years after his wife's death, on his way to pick up the oldest, Liam, at hockey practice, his Country Squire swerved wildly on an icy road and, according to a woman who was collecting her mail from her mailbox at the time, accelerated headlong into a tree.

The five kids were raised by their aunt Nora, a woman with Louise Brooks hair, dyed black even now at eighty-two, who had moved to Florida and sang tunes like "If You Were Mine" and "Under the Sea" at her retirement community, Southern Winds.

Margaret sits down on the edge of the bed and watches Brian change out of his work clothes. "She just makes me feel like I'm letting her down," she says. Flo climbs onto her mother's lap.

"Maybe you are. *Have* you let her down?" Brian's taking off his pants. His dark socks have slid partway off his feet, like an elf's.

"That's not what I wanted to hear," says Margaret, watching Brian look in his drawer. "I wanted you to tell me I'm a great sister."

Flo pats Margaret's cheek. "You're a great sitter, Mama," she says solemnly. Margaret puts her down.

"Edie's obviously unhappy, Margaret," says Brian.

"She is?"

"Look at her."

"Look at her?"

"I don't know. There's sort of a rootlike quality to her lately. She's a great-looking girl, but lately she looks like she's come up from the dirt."

"She does?"

"*Bloop bloop,*" says Flo, moving her body in one piece. "This is all water, Mom. *Bloop bleep.* The house is a tank and I'm a fishy."

"She has that stunned look," continues Brian. "Like she's shocked."

"She does?"

"Here come a shark." Flo cowers in Margaret's legs.

Brian unfolds his shorts, shakes them out. "Drained, kind of. Clogged."

"Clogged?"

"Listen to you," says Brian. "You're like an old lady sometimes."

"I am? Flo, honey, let go."

"You hardly laugh anymore."

"I don't?"

"Mom's an anolomy. Git down!"

"I'm worried about you. A little bit."

"You are?"

"I think you need to relax."

"You do? Let go of me, Florence."

"I know it's been a tough few weeks. But this frown line here is starting to be permanent."

Margaret reaches up, feels with her fingers the oily space of skin between her eyebrows. She frowns. "It is?"

·

Morning comes. The kids have all turtled their way down the stairs. Trace noises come up the stairway in ribbons, various whines, occasional mumbles, but mostly the whirls and whoops of a morning cartoon: *Doing-oing-oing . . . Splat! "No sign of Shag and Scoob!"* The sounds of her own youth as well.

Margaret luxuriates, stretches out in the empty white bed, king-size, a cloud, plentiful pillows, Leona Helmsley for a moment, for God's sake. An airplane careens down loudly in the distance, headed for Newark.

She relaxes, thinking about airplanes, thinking of her mother. She'd never have predicted that was the way her mother would go. A small-plane crash! Amelia Earhart: Where was she? That snappy red plane she flew. Buddy Holly. The Lindbergh baby. John-John off the Vineyard. She speaks to Brian as she stretches, her words stretching out as well. "So," she says, "Carolyn Bessette. Getting her toenails painted over and over for the perfect shade of lavender." Margaret yawns, a great huge dog yawn that causes her to shiver, almost drool.

Brian is busily getting dressed. His entire office has been participating in a workshop for the last week and a half called "Facing Ourselves, Our Past, and Our Future" which to Margaret, frankly, sounds like far too many directions to be facing, part-time, over the course of two weeks, but it certainly was raising lots of intriguing questions, questions about morality, questions about truth, questions about justice and responsibility, questions that Margaret—let's face it—had practically forgotten about.

Here in the bedroom, Brian focuses on the issue at hand. "Carolyn's toes," he muses, as he combs his wet hair, as he looks at himself in the mirror. "Did they hold up the departure? Did they really *need* to be perfect? Was the poor woman actually being *judged* by the shade of her *polish?*"

Margaret smiles but also considers it. Everyone *did* scrutinize everything about the woman, it was true, head to toe. Carolyn's "buttery chunks" of hair, as Margaret once read, a description that strangely, inexplicably, still loiters at the forefront of her awareness with disconcerting frequency. Margaret hugs a pillow as though it's a flotation device.

Brian puts his hands on his hips and looks at his wife, her hair all over the pillows like groundcover. "And what *is* perfect?" he says. He claps his hands together briskly like chalkboard erasers. "Let's break up into groups—"

"Mom?" It's Stephen, sauntering in with a concerned head tilt, looking at the floor. Sometimes he looks like a bad-boy tennis pro, impish and athletic.

Brian keeps combing his hair, looking into the mirror. "How come no one asks for me anymore? How come none of you kids say, *Dad? Hey, Dad?*"

"Okay, Dad," says Stephen, looking up at him. "Dad?"

"Yes, son."

"That lady who—hey. How come you're dressed for work? It's Saturday, Dad. Remember?" Stephen starts laughing, as if the prank was for him and he was clever enough to catch on.

Brian blinks and looks at his wife for confirmation as he stops buttoning his shirt.

"Mom? That lady's in our backyard."

"What lady, honey?"

"The one in the car who hit us yesterday."

Margaret springs up. "What? She's at the door?"

"No. In the back."

"That woman who hit us? Is she looking for me?" Margaret gets up, reaches for her bathrobe, and Brian enjoys the momentary sight of his wife in motion, nude. Her breasts look great after all the kids—why were people always talking about them stretching and sagging? Margaret's had gotten bigger, more robust; they'd taken on a life of their own. Above the breasts, Margaret's face, troubled, as she dodders out of bed with wild hair. "What is she *doing* here?" Margaret asks no one out loud.

Downstairs, Flo and Sarah are leaning on the windowsill, looking out. Sarah explains. "She was right there. Then she went over there. Then there. Then she left that way."

"Yeah," says Flo, nodding.

Margaret scans the lawn and garden, the same backyard that it always is, looking at the bushes, looking up toward the trees. With the solemn youngster concentration surrounding her, she feels as though she and her children are looking for a phantom alien that came and went: Big Foot, the strange green bird with suction cups that Brian claims to have seen suction-cupped to his bedroom window when he was eleven and feverish.

Margaret is standing there, arms crossed on her chest, scowling out the window when her annoyance is swiftly swept aside. "Oh, I get it," she says, lifting up her head, everything clear now, nothing to worry about. "That's a good one, guys."

"What, Mom?"

"You had me for a sec."

"No, Mom," says Stephen. "Really. She was *right there.*" His small palms face up, little pleading fingers like a sea anemone.

"Yeah, Mom." Sarah gently stamps a foot. "*Really.*"

"We *swear*," says Stephen.

Margaret moves along toward the kitchen to get the coffee under way. "Good one," she tells them.

"But Mom." The three of them trail her. Her tired white silk bathrobe with the Chinese dragon on the back, her deft feet. She looks back and winks at them. The enigmatic smile. A goddess for a moment.

A large white angel. They watch her. Who is she? Getting the coffee grinds from the freezer, her hair loose and tangled like a tousled heroine's. The kids all watch her, for a moment hypnotized as though she's some kind of witch. Was she right? Did they not see anyone at all?

But then Stephen looks out the window. "Mom!" he shouts. Margaret looks at the garden, the swing set, the shed. Nothing. She looks at the garage. Alongside the garage, a woman. Hunched. Bumbling in the trash like a bear. Lifting up a cardboard box.

Instinctually, Margaret calls out the screen of the open window, raps on the glass up above. "Hey! Hello?" and then—why this?—politely, almost eagerly, "May I help you?"

The figure scrambles. A cardboard box falls soundlessly onto the driveway.

Margaret looks at the kids, and rushes outside, out the front door since the back one's locked, and then around the house, the driveway, jogs toward the garage, and peers into the trees. "Hello?" She hears sticks cracking in the near distance, like a deer passing through toward the Prices' brick house. She calls after it. "Wait!" There's a hurrying sound, a breaking through brush, and then it is quiet.

This small swath of suburban woods is thick, the maple leaves like flattened hands showing her their manicure jobs, some limp in coned bunches, some humped like parasols. Through the green, Margaret can make out smatterings of color, the houses of all of her back neighbors, their large presences like small ships run aground, the steel blue (Carolina Sky) of the Mackenzies' house, the staid brown (Northfield Taupe) of the O'Neills', the no-nonsense white (Alabaster Statue) of the DiGiovannis', the playful orange (Salmon Brook) of the Steins' Victorian.

Behind her is the choke cherry that's growing around the roof of the garage like a boa constrictor. To her right, the fort that Stephen and his friend Angus built out of plywood. Angus had whacked his finger with the hammer. "They were *nailing?*" his mother asked, aghast, when she picked him up. "With real *nails?*"

Margaret looks inside the fort, pokes her head into the slanted roofed doorway. No one is there. The slab of silver wallpaper that Sarah was fixated on putting up. Some string and a Bionicle. A Super

Soaker water gun. Underneath a heavy rock, a magazine, the damp pages swollen up at the edges. Is it *Nintendo*? Is it pornography? She lifts up the rock. It is, alas, pornography. A blond woman with a body builder's plasticized body in an army camouflage thong holding a Kalashnikov. Her scarily large breasts look like a giant scrotum. Margaret feels light-headed. Oh, she has been negligent. Is she so naïve? She rolls the softened pages into a thick cylinder, can't help wondering if those breasts could possibly be real.

As she comes up the driveway, Martha, an older, portly, kind woman from two doors down who runs a literacy program in Newark, is walking her yellow lab, Portia. "Morning, Martha," says Margaret, waving the baton of porn. Martha nods. "Morning, Portia," Margaret says to the dog.

The boy culprit greets her at the door. "Did you see her?" Stephen's eyes are eager. "Why was she in our *trash*?" His squinty eyes like thistles with their huge long lashes.

"Come with me, Stephen," Margaret says curtly, pinching his shoulder as she passes.

"What happened, Mom?" asks Sarah. Flo, mouth open, stands in front of the television, staring into it.

Margaret leads Stephen upstairs. Where is Brian? She tells Stephen to sit on the bed, plants him there with her hands on his shoulders. Stephen shrugs, smiling. Sometimes he likes being bossed around, manhandled.

Margaret finds Brian in the bathroom sitting on the toilet when she barges in. "Look at what I found," she tells him.

"I'm going to the bathroom," says Brian.

"Look at this."

"Surely this can wait," says Brian.

"This was in Stephen's fort." She places it on his lap. "Peruse it at your leisure."

Stephen is sitting obediently on the edge of the master bed. "What happened, Mom?" He's smiling.

"I found a pornographic magazine, Stephen. In your fort."

"A what?"

"A dirty magazine."

"Dirty?" Stephen thinks, Magazine. He thinks, Dirt. He thinks, She's angry that one of her magazines from downstairs got dirty. Did he do this? He can't remember. Yes, maybe, when he and William were using the big fashion magazine as a slippery glacier for the miniature explorers.

"Yes, Stephen."

"It got dirty, Mom?" Her overreaction, her concern, seems disproportionate and strange even to him.

"He has no idea, Margaret," says Brian, entering the room. Brian looks at his son. "Stephen," he says, "does Mark DiGiovanni still go into your fort?" Mark was a sixth-grader who honestly, when he looked at Margaret, made her feel as though he were looking right through her clothes.

"Yeah. He smokes cigarettes in there with Devin," Stephen answers, ambling away toward the stairs in a formless escape.

Brian clears his throat, looks at Margaret. "Problem solved," he says to her. Margaret senses the implication, somewhere in his glance, that she jumped the gun (which she knows she did) and that she ought to have taken a deep breath before the rush to judgment, as they say.

"Problem solved?" Margaret feels jumpy. "What about the bully who's been invading our son's fort?"

"He's not a bully, Maggie. He's a hormonal twelve-year-old."

Margaret lets out a huff, as deep as a bull's snort as it paws at the ground. "Well, what about this *woman*?" she says. "What about this woman going through our *trash*?"

"This I'm not aware of. An indigent?"

"The kids thought it was the woman who hit us yesterday."

"Well, that makes perfect sense. A woman driving a Range Rover would be going through our trash."

"I don't know, Brian." She's starting to get cross now, starting to get really tense. "But did you really not remember what today *is*?" she whines. "You were really going to go to *work*? When today is the day that my father is coming home to *die*?" She collapses her head, lets her arms fall floppily at her sides.

Brian puts his arms around her. "I forget everything, honey," he tells her. "You know that." He thinks to himself that she's incorrect to have said that her father is coming *home* to die. This home (his home, their home) was never his father-in-law's home at all. But this correction— well, he keeps it wisely to himself.

"What needs to be done?" asks Brian, his lips speaking into her scalp.

She looks up at him. "You mean in the grand scheme of things?"

"I mean for your father's arrival."

"Edie's coming too."

"I know."

"I'm picking them up. Nothing. Maybe a sign to welcome him home?"

Again, notes Brian, the home thing. "A decent project," he says, considering it. The children are hog wild about projects. There are even project "tables": in the garage, in the sunroom, and out on the porch. "I'm working on my *project!*" one might scream wildly through a closed door when told that it's dinnertime. "I've got lots of projects to get to," says Sarah dismissively, shaking her head back and forth, her beads and twine kit folded tightly under her arm like a briefcase as she goes out to the porch.

"But who *was* that woman?" Margaret asks herself, heading toward the shower.

"Maybe it was Alfie." Alfie was a peculiar man who lived near the end of their street. Empty bird feeders dotted the overgrowth in front of his yellowing house like an I Spy game or connect-the-dots. He walked a lot in the afternoons, along the more trafficked roads with no sidewalks, in old Jack Purcells, no socks even in the winter. The nice house had been his parents'.

"I'd have recognized Alfie," says Margaret.

When the phone on the bedside table rings they both look down at it, waiting for the caller ID to alert them to who it is. INCOMING CALL, it reads. INCOMING CALL . . . ring . . . ring . . . then, FENCER INS. CO. flashes up at them like a banner behind a prop plane above the beach.

"Fencer Ins. Co.?"

"It's our car insurance," says Brian.

"On a Saturday?" gasps Margaret.

"Did you report the crash?"

"Yes."

"Let it go."

"It's barely nine in the morning."

"Let them leave a message."

"Who in the world works this early on a Saturday?" asks Margaret.

"Everyone works anymore," says Brian.

It's his use of the word *anymore* that puzzles her. Her mother used it the same way. Using it without a negative. "Hmm," murmurs Margaret, taking off her robe. She walks naked toward the bathroom, suspicious of everything.

The tiles in the bathroom are pale pink. Not their first choice when they bought the house, but they were clean, intact, at least stylishly old, and not a bad shade, after all. The best thing about them, for Margaret, was the warmth they gave her in wintertime, rosy and inviting.

A shiver of winter is there with her in the shower, fleetingly, this warm morning with everything up, sprouted and leafy, flourishing even further, and Margaret feels a pang of sadness already, a melancholic twang of a guitar chord, that all the flowers and bushes will shrink shriveled back into the earth—*again*—at the end of summer. The little steamy window is cranked open, giving her a couple of inches to look out, the same familiar quadrant of treetops scrubbing up against the sky, a portion of the driveway, a slab side of the garage, the edge of the garden where the delphiniums will be bright blue in a few weeks. The white climbing rose on the trellis looks great; the red one looks even better. The butterfly bush is starting to perk up. She wonders about the morning glory, why there's no sign of it yet.

That's when she sees someone at the garden's edge, hunched next to the fence like a bullfrog, crouched as if at the start of a race. The face pokes up. A man? A woman? Down again. A quick peer into their yard, their life. Then it's behind the fence, the top of his/her head visible like a toupee.

"Brian!" yells Margaret furtively, softly but urgently, around the shower curtain. "Brian!" She gets out of the shower, shakes her wet feet like a dog so she doesn't trail too much water out of the bathroom. She grabs a towel, a swimming cap of shampoo still on her head, and starts downstairs, the shower still running plentifully behind her. "Brian!"

Brian is in the kitchen buttering toast, looking partly amused, partly alarmed. "What is it, sweetheart?"

"She's next to the fence."

"The fence?"

"That *woman*. Someone. Look."

Brian looks out the kitchen window, through the screen. "I don't . . . see anything."

"By the *corner*." Margaret looks out the window too. "Damn it. She's crouched down. She *was* crouched down."

"Crouched down?"

"I'm going out there," says Margaret, turning to go. Her towel is lime green, very short, skimming the crotch line. She is sopping wet.

"You're naked, Margaret. I'll go."

Brian goes out the back door that he always unlocks, first thing. Margaret watches him from the window. She watches him walk toward the fence. He looks up at the coin of her face in the window, shudders with pretend fear of the fence as he approaches it. He gets there, leans over, looks up and down its length. He looks back at his wife, raises his arms up in the air like Atlas holding up the heavens, then, as an afterthought, makes his hands into victory fists and pumps them into the air.

Margaret calls out the window, "No one's there?"

Someone's crowding her thigh. "What's going on, Mom? You're dripping everywhere."

"Nothing."

"Nothing?"

"Where are the Polly Pockets?"

"Look in the drawers."

"Mom. I really need her, the Pollies."

Then Stephen. "Mom? Who's Dow Jones?"

Someone else. "Hey, Mom, there's still shampoo on your head."

Another one. "What are you looking at, Momma?"

"Where, Mom? Where . . . Are . . . The . . . Polly . . . *Pockets*?"

"That whining is awful, Flo," says Margaret, straining to see out the window.

Flo puts her small hand on the back of Margaret's wet thigh. "Mom? Can we—" They were swarming her.

"Hey, Mom, the shower's still—"

"What are you trying to see, Mom?"

"Everybody mind their own business!" says Margaret. "Everyone just back off for a second!" She calls out the window to Brian. "Hey!" she calls. She can see that he's inspecting the white climbing rose. He's scrutinizing a leaf. A slight rusty fungus problem. His dawdling seems intentional. Margaret sighs, yells, "Will you look behind the garage, please?"

Brian looks in her direction, decidedly calmly to illustrate her excessive frenzy, before he disappears behind the garage. After a moment, he emerges on the other side with his arms raised, Atlas again, signifying the no one that he has encountered.

Margaret is looking at him, her face cross.

Brian shrugs. He can see Margaret's frowning face in the shadowy window. He shrugs again, then shouts at the garage for good measure. "Stay away from my family!" He faces into the woods. "Who do you think you are?"

They hear the scraping rattle of a window getting pulled up next door. It's Scott, the more handsome half of the gay couple who live in the neighboring house. The dream neighbors, perfect neighbors. Their house tastefully painted and landscaped. Their good humor and consideration. The two of them work, work a great deal, at a glossy art magazine in Tribeca. "What's up?" asks Scott.

"Sorry, man," says Brian. "Did I wake you?"

"No."

"Everything okay?"

"Fine," says Brian. "Margaret thought she saw someone out here."

"I did!" clarifies Margaret. "I did!"

"She *did!*" Brian corrects himself. "She *did* see someone out here."

"Oh, brother," mutters Margaret. When she glances down, hangdog and harried, at the kitchen counter, there is Brian's toast, partly buttered, an image of domesticity, its homey smell. There are two pieces, dry, on another plate that surely he was about to prepare for her. A novel idea, some toast. When was the last time she had *toast?* She would have toast on the morning of her father's arrival, this regular daughter with her kids in suburbia. She'd have some coffee before heading to

Newark. She'd sit down and eat. She'd butter her toast and *enjoy her toast*. Maybe even eat it on the front porch for the picture of sylvan Americana. She'd be damned if she wasn't going to find some jam or marmalade somewhere to slather onto it as well.

She pulls the child-sized stepstool chair out of the bathroom in the hallway, careful of the loose screw in the back that she hasn't repaired— only covered with duct tape so no one will get scraped because of her negligence—drags it to the cupboards, and forages maniacally through the "pantry" shelves, the highest out-of-reach shelves that are filled primarily with Campbell's soup cans they never eat and brick-hard boxes of salt and sugar.

"What are you doing, Mom?" She hears the vague questions behind her, below her, begin to gain momentum again. Why is it that, when there are only three children, they sometimes feel like a herd? As she's reaching around some white wine vinegar for a squat jar of raspberry jam, Brian's perplexed voice: "Honey?" He so rarely sees her at this particular cupboard, so high up.

When she turns around, her entire family is arranged in a choir semicircle at the base of her chair.

"Mom?"

"Momma?"

"What is *that* stuff?"

"What are you going to do with that *jam*?"

"I'm going to try to *open* this jam," she says, exerting herself, trying to twist the lid off.

"Are you going to try to eat it, Mom? Do you want to eat that jam?" Much of raising children, Margaret realized long ago, is providing a blow-by-blow account of what, exactly, is occurring and how. And why. "Are you going to eat it, Mom? Do you want to eat that jam?"

"I'm dying to eat it, kids. I am just *dying* to eat this *jam*."

"You better go get dressed," Brian tells her. "Aren't you going to the airport soon?"

Margaret looks up at him from her crouch of exertion, "I'm ready," she says calmly, standing on the miniature chair in her tiny towel. "I'm totally ready."

"I'd call first to make sure it's on time," says Brian.

"I'm completely ready," repeats Margaret.

Brian glances about the room that surrounds her. The kitchen cabinets are for the most part all flung open in varying degrees, many drawers are partway ajar as though the house has been ransacked, as though a poltergeist has come tearing through. Brian notices her helmet of shampoo. Her hair is a plastered cap. The suds have shriveled so that they look like dried spit. Brian hears the water in the pipes in the wall. "Were you planning on turning off the shower?" he asks. He heads to the stairs.

Margaret calls after him, "Wait!" She scuttles off the chair, hurrying through the goaltending line of her children. "Wait! I have to rinse off!"

The three kids stand there, a crowd not yet dispersing. "But hey, Mom!" calls Sarah. "You forgot your jam!"

9

The flight to Newark. Clouds like pulled wool. A stadium of blue sky. The sun screams through the window into Arthur's face like something medical, a scan technique, jarring and intrusive. On the window, scribbles of frost are formed on the outer glass.

"I don't like this," mutters Arthur, his restrained tension heightening. He squints at his lunch tray, looks up at the curved catacomb ceiling, the little air streams above him with their clickety knob adjusters, person after person, face after face, all side by side, in front and behind, their heads like eggs cradled neatly in containers.

He's short of breath. From every metallic seam, every rounded plastic edge, every button and switch and *bing* of the seat-belt alert come pieces of Florence: her healthy hair, her walnut smell, her way of chewing on her bottom lip as she listened on the telephone. Florence's plane twirling like the nose of a maple seed, pinwheeling from the sky.

Arthur looks at his tray. "I have trouble with this food," he musters.

Edie's cast goes up to her mid-forearm, not such a bad break after all. But she has Percocets and an awkwardly shaped hook of a left hand. Edie rips open the plastic bag holding her father's fork and knife with her teeth. "You unwrap it and eat it," she says. "This is chicken. No, pasta. And this is—let's see, a bean salad."

"You used to be offered a choice, were you not?"

"Pretty soon they won't serve you anything, Dad." Then she realizes the death implication. "Pretty soon they won't give you food." Wrong too. "Airlines are doing away with food altogether," she says.

"Get me a scotch, please," he says.

"Sure, Gramps." She snickers. He hasn't had a drink in years. Edie looks at him. Or has he? "You haven't had a drink in years," she says cheerily, mostly for the benefit of the woman seated in front of them who Edie can tell is listening. The woman's head is still, elevated just so, a frosted dome.

A flight attendant with a waxy complexion pauses next to them, holding up an institutional stainless-steel water pitcher and some frightening prongs. Her smile is relieved, as though at last she has finally reached them. "Would you lack s'mass?"

Gramps cups his hand to his ear to hear what she's saying.

"S'mass?" she repeats.

"Pardon?" he says.

"*S'mass?*" She smiles, mannequin-like.

"I'm sorry," he says, squinting.

"*Ass?*" still smiling. "You lack some?"

Gramps sits back, turns to Edie. "I think she's asking me if I'd like some ass," he says, dumbfounded.

"Ice," explains Edie. "Would you like some *ice*. In your water."

Arthur nods, throws his palms to the air. He coughs loudly.

Edie watches her father pull at his collar. Then she remembers. She forgot the diabetes. Margaret had told Edie to call in advance to reserve the special meal. The sort of thing Margaret would never forget. She feels awful that she forgot. She almost wishes that she never remembered and could sail on through the flight unaware. She can hardly bring herself to ask, "Can you eat the pasta, Dad?"

"If I want to lose a digit, yes."

"Sorry, Dad. Let me get you a diabetes meal." She cranes up like an egret.

"The bean salad is ample," Arthur tells her.

"Here. It'll only take—"

"The bean salad is *sufficient*."

His lips look dry. His mouth is smeared back in a smile of discomfort. For a second, like something revolving that you have to wait to look at to see it turn your way full view and then pass, Edie wants to drape herself on top of her father like some kind of blanket that could provide him relief, hurl herself on top of him. But she feels divided, set back. Only then does she remember the bottle of Valium or whatever it is that his nurse, Alice, gave to her. She digs into her silver carry-on bag: the grit of frayed cigarettes mingling with lint; a piece of naked cinnamon chewing gum, conglomerate with grit and hair; the mellow scent of shredded tobacco.

"Dad," says Edie. She rattles the amber prescription jar in the air. Regrets it when she looks ahead at the listening head of hair, sees it twitch ever so slightly at the clatter. "You want another one, Dad?"

Her father looks at her brusquely. "Yes."

Groggy sleep follows for both of them.

When Edie wakes up, the airplane fills her ears like a giant seashell. Everyone seems to be asleep. She looks at her father's face with its lines, the relaxed down-turned corners of his mouth slack like the Cowardly Lion's. She thinks of things, like a laundry list, like Post-its stuck all over his body, that she would like to ask him, questions she knows she'll never ask: Was he happy? Was he proud of her? Was he proud of *himself*? It was clear that he had loved her mother, but did he ever love anyone else? Did he like being alive? And in terms of life overall . . . could he *advise* her somehow, please? Could he please pass along some wisdom that she'd cherish and try to abide by forever? What about those papers she found at the Woodses' house in Maine?

When Edie and her father approach the arrivals gate Margaret is there, waving from behind the velvet rope. She tiptoes up with a wave. "Hi!" she calls. "Hey!" She's been to the airport, gone home, and driven back again, since the flight was delayed nearly three hours.

"Thank God," Edie says, when they get near, smiling knowingly at Margaret.

Margaret looks at her. If Edie thinks that was tough, she has no idea what it's like to have children.

"Hi, Dad!" says Margaret. She's happy to see him. She kisses his cheek.

"My dear," he mutters.

"This way, Dad," says Margaret, touching his arm. "I have one of these golf cart thingies."

Arthur looks up at her. His face brightens. "Wonderful."

"Nice cast."

"Thanks."

"Very Gaultier. It's the color of a margarita. Does it hurt?"

"Uh . . ."

"How was the flight, Dad?"

"Edie drugged me so I slept the whole way."

"Valium," says Edie.

"It's called a Sonata," says Arthur.

Edie mouths to Margaret, *Valium*.

"It's called a Sonata," Arthur says again.

"You should have seen us trying to board. All the pills we had. We're like drug dealers."

Margaret shoots Edie a look, implying this is a rude thing to say.

"I mean all my Percocets," Edie tells her, trying to correct it.

In the car, the bleary travelers are subdued. Margaret is a little gun-shy when she looks in the rearview. Every approaching vehicle looks like they'll ram her. She has the AC on as high as it will go, and the cool air, the absence of children, and her slight fear of the multitude of cars behind her make her feel alert and focused, ready to talk. About anything.

"Do any decorating this week?" coming from a feeble Edie in the back, as though Margaret ventriloquisted the question, was an ideal opener.

"Yes. I'm after that *Stuart Little Two* look. Good colors. Not your everyday shades of orange, yellow, and green."

Edie leans up between the seats. "The mouse?" It is now completely clear as day that her sister Margaret has fallen into that cushy bake-puff world of Familyland lite.

"Like *Far from Heaven*," continues Margaret. "Did you see that movie?"

"No."

"Everything sort of matches autumn. Bright autumn. When there's still green around. When the leaves are bright bright orange."

"People like bright bright orange in their house?" asks Edie.

"*Far from Heaven*. It looked great. That movie was definitely of the *Stuart Little Two* school."

"Is that what you tell your clients? That you're of the *Stuart Little Two* school of decorating? That must be a great sell."

"Did you see *Far from Heaven*, Dad?"

"I haven't the slightest idea what you people are discussing."

"A movie. It came out a few years ago. I think you and Mom saw it."

"I thought you and Brian never went to movies," says Edie.

"DVD. Move it, you jerk!"

Gramps groans.

"Sorry, Dad."

•

The three kids are out in front of the house. They're playing something on the porch steps, heads tipped forward like bent spoons. Margaret beeps since she doesn't see the sign up. Beeps again and the kids snap to, struggle with it, call to their father. They stand up, waving awkwardly.

"It's a welcome sign for you, Dad," says Margaret, pointing it out.

When she left for the airport they were painting it in the garage. Amid the clamor of the three of them, Stephen calmly waved good-bye to her. A full-fledged boy. Looking back now, an only child seemed so incredibly manageable. Almost boring. Almost a joke. Stephen, all alone. Yet somehow the chaos seemed compounded with the first one. Margaret would stare at him constantly, inspecting every inch, wondering about the red blotches and infant acne that come and go like breezes as though they might be smallpox—the pressure on the poor kid!— waiting for him to laugh again, desperately *trying* to make him laugh again. His baby cries often petrified her: Was he hurt? Was he choking? Was he sick? *Very* sick? The times when his nursing seemed frantic, when Stephen seemed frantic. What in God's name did this infant want when he'd bang his head against her bumper breasts repeatedly, when he'd wag his tiny head back and forth like a dog trying to break the neck of its prey as he readied for a chomp, a latch-on, to the nipple?

Everything seemed so dire, as though his terrier-sized body contained where he had come from (which was *where?*); it might burst, and what would happen in his future? His heartbroken face when he had to burp, the agony, his face crumpling up like tissue into a scream, the giant scream of a cartoon baby, like someone screaming for his life, screaming so he can be heard downtown, screaming about the infinity that he just came out of. Of course the girls did all the same things, the wagging of the head, the stiffening, the uncontrollable jags, but with them everything else carried on—they were babies, for heaven's sake, and that's what babies did.

Soon the days came with the girls when she could put the manual breast pump together like a rifle, quickly, efficiently, all ten tiny plastic and rubber parts fitted into their mysterious valves and levers and holes. After a while, she'd forgo the pump altogether, lean over the small plastic bowl for the baby's infant rice cereal, and squirt her milk into it by squeezing her teats like a cow's. Nursing. The babies plucking on and off her breast, stretching her nipple like the neck of a clam, kneading her bosom like a cat about to settle to sleep. She misses it. She can summon the feeling of her milk dropping so easily, can almost will it to occur, can recall it as easily as that nausea from pregnancy, that sick dull feeling high up in her throat.

She got so capable at it, nursing the girls as she moved about the house, as she got Stephen's dinner, as she sat at the computer to pay bills (pillow on lap, infant on pillow, a slight lean so baby could reach her nipple). But in Stephen's early days, the chaos of one. Towels all over the bed, her breast milk spraying on everything: enlarging the pixels on the computer screen, bleeding the ink on bills, accidentally firing into the baby's eyes, into *Brian's* eyes or plate of food. Margaret's incredible thirst all the time, more than with the next two.

The famous time, on a drive back from upstate, Brian pulled in to a gas station so she could get a soda or something and nurse screaming Stephen (an incident where, with one of the girls, they'd have probably continued driving, Margaret maybe clambering into the back and hunching over the car seat to shove her breast into the baby's mouth, or simply waited until they got home, would even have been able to gossip leisurely with Brian about Max's new girlfriend through the infant's shrill cries, as opposed to snapping at each other, tense as piano cords, barking at one another over how best to deal with Stephen's wails).

This famous time, after Margaret had finished nursing him, she buckled a limp, sound-asleep Stephen back into his car seat and went into the diner to use the bathroom. On her way out, she bought a pink lemonade and a bag of potato chips.

As she got back into the car, Brian was reading the newspaper. He crumpled the paper away, looked at her as if to say, Ready? But instead, "Oh, sweetheart," he said, shaking his head back and forth. He put his forehead to the steering wheel.

"What?"

"Look."

"Look at what?"

He pointed to her chest. She looked down. Between her pulled-down black camisole and bra and her pulled-up black T-shirt was her nipple, still out, round like a large button, a big pink lozenge. "Oh, no," she said. She looked out the window at the gas station attendants, the masses of people flowing in and out of the door to the diner, the line of people at the kiosk next door where she bought the chips. A middle-aged black woman had nodded at her, she remembered now, and said "Miss," with a purposeful nod. Margaret had thought the woman was simply prompting her toward her turn at the cashier.

•

"It's a welcome sign they made for you, Dad," Margaret says again.

"So it is," he says.

Margaret expects to look at her father and see him looking in the wrong direction, across the street, up ahead, down at his thumbs, some-where else. But when she looks at him he's looking right where he should be, right out his window at the children, an amused expression on his face. "We did this sort of thing for you children when you came home from—when we got you at—when you came home from the—"

"Hospital," finishes Edie. She's got her head crouched up between the two of them in the front seat. "When you *got us* at the hospital."

"Thank you," says Arthur, "yes." His hands are clasped together in his lap, one hand holding the other's wrist. "Is that *Stephen*? And there's your handsome husband with no shoes on. Pansies. Verbascum. Scabiosa. Dianthus. Salvia. Dead peonies that need to be staked—"

Margaret reads the sign out loud as they pull in: "WELCOME TO GRUMPS." Doesn't notice the misspelling but wonders why Brian put TO in there.

"Welcome to Grumps indeed," says Gramps. He opens his window, buzzing it down sedately as though he's in a limousine. "Hello, children," he says. "Get away from the car." He shoos them. "Move away from the automobile."

Simply because he's old, or simply because he's their grandfather, they always obey him. "Get off that," he says, simply, and the kids get right down. "Don't touch that," and the eraser-pink fingers recoil.

Brian shepherds them aside. Margaret puts all the windows back up before she turns off the engine, saying, "It's gonna rain." She looks at her father. "Do you want to lie down, Dad?" Margaret asks him.

"Right *here?*" he asks.

Margaret smiles. She can tell he's glad to be here, the way he's looking around. "You'll be in Sarah's room," she tells him. "She's bravely ventured into the attic."

"She *has?*"

"You look good, Dad," says Margaret, noticing that the kids are now waiting politely, gathered near a granite rock on the edge of the driveway.

"Don't I smell?" asks Gramps, looking through the windshield at the kids. "That radiation gave me the most awful smell."

"You smell fine, Dad," says Edie, trying to say something, then realizes that she just implied that he *does* smell.

"I would like to lie down. Yes." Suddenly the kids start clamoring at his door, the tops of their heads like creatures coming to attack, groupies at a rock concert.

"It's like a nightmare," says Margaret, watching their heads bob and their small hands smear the window. Her gaze turns into a vacant stare for a moment as she wonders to herself, What was I thinking to subject this old man to a house full of children? She imagines a phantasmagoria of inappropriate behavior: the three of them jumping on Gramps's bed when he's in pain, a shrill argument in the hallway while Gramps is asleep, Gramps really sick (like he is) and dying (like he will).

"A pleasant nightmare," says Gramps.

Brian opens Gramps's door. "Welcome," he says, extending an arm. He tells the kids to stand back.

Arthur looks up at him. He's always liked this young man, this broad face coming toward him. Arthur says to the face, "I thought I saw you, and then I didn't see you. But here you are. Barefoot. Fancy-free."

"The spirit of summer," says Brian.

"Don't you have a job?" Gramps asks him.

"I quit," says Brian, his dry jokes that people often take literally. Brian smiles broadly at his father-in-law. "I said, *To hell with you people.*"

Margaret cringes, readies herself to explain to her father that Brian's only joking. But then she sees her father smiling at her husband. The first real smile. "Good for you," Gramps says to him, patting his back as Brian helps him to stand. "Good for you."

Margaret gets out of the car. "Where's Max?"

"The baby has a fever."

"Sure he does."

"Well."

"Hey, Gramps?"

"Yes?"

"Gramps!"

"Did you see our sign, Gramps?"

"Yes I did. You called me Grumps."

"We did not, Gramps. It says *Gramps!*"

"Grumps. See there, the U? Don't you know your letters, child?"

"Hey, Mom," calls Stephen. "Gramps is the same. He's like he always is."

"Look at her cast!" yells Flo.

"Where's the cancer?" asks Sarah.

"Yeah, Gramps. Where's your cancer?"

"Right here," he says, pointing to his throat, his chest, his belly button.

"Look, Gramps!" they cry. "Mommy! Gramps!"

"Okay, chickens," Margaret tells them, squatting down, "go get your socks on and stuff and we'll go for a ride."

"Our socks?"

"I'll take you to get some ice cream," says Edie. "That place with the stamps and stickers."

"Yes!" they cry. "Mommy!" they cry. "Mom! Mom!" They keep saying it, so easy, and it sounds so good. Their word of all words. The greeting hasn't been sufficient. They'd like to keep rosying around. The three of them start to amble in loops, running aimlessly with excitement, bumping into one another and laughing, kicking the grass like flappers doing the Charleston or football stars kicking off.

Standing on the sidelines slack-shouldered and tired, the adults watch them, smiling anyway.

•

When she gets inside, Margaret calls Max from the phone in the kitchen, whines at him that he missed their father's arrival.

"Rex was having febrile *convulsions*, Margaret."

"Come on," says Margaret, slapping a wet sponge around on the countertop. "You were probably just arguing with Chloe again."

"Right. I probably should have left my wife *alone* with my *sick son in the emergency room* so I could hurry out to your house to hold up a *sign* for Dad."

A pause. "How did you know they held up a sign?"

"Who, the kids?"

"Yeah."

"They did? On, like, paper?"

"Yeah. Poster board. It said *Grumps*, though."

"Well. Probably appropriate."

"Is Rexie okay, then?"

"He's fine," says Max, deflated, confirming for Margaret the lie.

"So come out here tomorrow," she tells him. She peers out the door, looking for her father. "The hospice woman's coming again. Did I tell you the hospital bed got delivered?"

"You sound so happy about it."

"It took forever. I don't know if we even need it. Dad! Over here! Come in here." She aggressively rakes a chair out from the kitchen table, checks the floor to see if the legs' black rubber feet marked it up. Then she watches her father stop in the front hall, sit down awkwardly on the front stairs. She approaches him. "Are you all right?" When he nods, she thrusts the phone at him. "It's your son," she tells him.

Arthur takes it. "Max," he says into it. Waits a moment. Passes the phone back to Margaret. "I don't hear anything."

"Dad?"

Is he all right? His mind is suddenly void, like in a cartoon when buzzing flies trace out the NASA emblem above someone's head to show the person's been knocked out. He's not knocked out, but it's as though all the objects surrounding him have lost their sense.

"Dad?"

A small dog, something personable, seems to be settling next to his knee in a friendly manner. He touches its head like a blind man.

"Not right now, Flo," says Margaret. "Dad?"

The dog rustles next to him. The hallway's wall across from him, the corner of a mirror, swirls back into its sense (it is a *wall*, it is the corner part of a *frame*, which is a decorative and functional thing). What's present comes returning pointillist style, falling pixels getting rearranged again, splattering the surfaces of what has been emptied. It returns: the house with its summer wood smell, the sloping lawns, the bad taste in his mouth like he's been sucking on a penny, this plentiful life, the warm presence of a small animal beside him, his granddaughter still a little bit canine. He's aware he's supposed to say something. "Sit," is what comes out, in a blurt of command.

"Sure," says Margaret. "You sit, Dad. I'll get you a glass of water. We'll head upstairs."

A few minutes later, sitting on the step still, Arthur has that rejuvenated look of someone who's just recovered from a taxing experience, someone who's passed a kidney stone or recovered from a violent bout of food poisoning or eaten some bad mushrooms. "Mimi Woods called me yesterday," he booms toward his daughter.

"Just to say hi?"

"She ran into Max on the street."

"In New York?"

Arthur doesn't answer. It's a stupid question. But also he's seeing some residuals from the episode he just experienced. The doorway through which Margaret is standing in the kitchen is unpromisingly two-dimensional. Flo, who stands four feet away from him, seems somehow to be in another room. This disagreement causes him to shout, "Bruno!" hopefully to scare the little dog into the room where it belongs.

"Dad?" Margaret comes, not rushing but not slowly, touches his shoulder delicately like she might pop him. She hadn't bargained on this.

"The dog," he says to her.

"Sure," she says, as if it makes perfect sense.

"What dog?" asks Brian, coming in from outside.

"Mom?" It's Stephen, trailing in like an undone shoelace. "Is there a dog in here?"

"We're getting a dog?" shouts Sarah. "When? Where?"

"I love dogs!" cries Flo.

Margaret looks at them all from one to the next. These people. Sometimes she wonders, Where did they come from?

Gramps pulls through. "No dog. Nonsense. You've got *me*." He puts his hands out like he wants an embrace but implying, Someone please help me to stand. Margaret does and then walks with him into the kitchen, plants him on the chair she'd pulled out. His glass of water, Margaret's handprint on its frosty side.

Margaret fills the water pitcher as she looks out the window. Edie's out there dragging on a cigarette, looking pretty but pathetic, pigeon-toed, sitting wanly on a swing.

•

Upstairs, Sarah orbits around as her grandfather gets into bed. "I'm up in the ackett—I mean attic, Gramps—with a big giant fan."

"I'm eternally grateful, my dear, that you've so graciously—" He can't remember the rest.

Sarah shrugs. She's fiddling with her body the way five-year-olds do, trying to sit on the narrow windowsill, slipping off, trying to sit again, slipping off, busily looking out the window at the same time. "What are they called, Mom? Those big tall ones?" Lately she has been asking the names of flowers and plants, amazed they all have such specific names themselves, strangely thrilled whenever her mother says, "I'm not sure, honey."

Margaret glances down. She'd cheated, bought them at the nursery almost full-grown already, and planted them up against the fence. "Hollyhocks. Don't sit there. You could fall out the window." She pauses, scanning the backyard like a mother robot. "It's starting to rain," she says. "Where's Edie? Weren't you going to go get ice cream?" She leaves the room to go look for her.

"You'll be wearing dresses instead of smocks, when you grow as tall as hollyhocks," says Gramps, after watching Sarah for a short time.

"How tall are hollyhocks?"

"When you'll be wearing dresses instead of smocks."

"Look, Gramps," says Sarah. "Two birds."

Underneath the eve of the house next door, perched on a ledge just their size, a pair of sparrows, puffed up and bedraggled, sit side by side like a married couple, watching the rain, not knowing what to make of it.

"So there are," says Gramps. It's been a long, long time since he's heard the rain, so he lies there listening to it change its tones, forte-piano, going from stadium roars to the rapid light steps of a tripping stream until he's hypnotized by it and the real rain stops, the soaked summer ground vibrant and loamy. The outdoors is a big huge room, green and misty, thick with trees. Sarah's room, now Arthur's room, is a cube set inside it. Close to his window, bunches of waterproof leaves, the pearls of water held steady in their seams, like mercury, there and then gone.

Max's train rattles slowly through industrial New Jersey. Cranes like praying mantises, plumes of smoke. Parking lots full of new cars.

"Well, when *will* we talk about it?" huffs Chloe.

With all those bright shiny cars in those parking lots, armies of them gleaming like pills or bullets, Max wonders, Would anyone really notice if only *one* went missing?

"When, Max? Just give me a time and date."

"A time and date?" Max winces. "I don't want to get into an argument again," he moans.

"You think I like arguing, don't you," says Chloe gently. She resigns herself to the idea. She looks glumly out the window. "I just want to know what's going on," she says, mostly to herself.

The train pulls forward in a molasses jolt, kicks into gear, and then finally speeds up.

"Tomorrow," says Max. "We'll talk about it all tomorrow. Today, let's just visit my dad."

"When tomorrow?"

Max looks at his hand, picks at some skin. "Tomorrow morning, Chloe. Okay? Nine-oh-two. Or no: Nine-oh-eight would be better for me."

Rex is asleep in his stroller with its sun visor down, the train rhythmically rocking him. His loose feet dangle, his head lolls to the side. When they disembark, his parents carry him tenderly off of the train as though his stroller is a stretcher. They walk silently down the stairs into the subterranean underpass with its murals—paintings of sailboats, swimming pools, snowmen, and fruit trees—and then up the stairs to the street.

Magnolia Heights feels empty. The usually bustling little village is relatively quiet, as though the entire town is attending the same event somewhere, a hanging or a wedding. The amber light of the sun seems to have honeyed everything over, reddening bushes and the sides of buildings so they have the subdued fieriness of red hair. The summer haze, the orangey light, its tincture of gold, are all like a soft-core movie or a seventies postcard. It relaxes Max but sort of depresses him: the deathly emptiness of a Sunday. Where is everybody? He feels glad for a moment that he's seeing his family. Then he feels dread, Sunday dread.

On the short walk to Margaret's house, Chloe looks hungrily at a brick house with a FOR SALE sign, restrains herself from discussing it.

They walk up the driveway. Chloe parks Rex near the side of the house in a shady spot, and then they round the corner to the world of the Bright backyard. The kids are all skidding through a sprinkler set up on the near end of the lawn. Brian and Edie, playing croquet in an abbreviated course near the vegetable garden, look up at the newcomers, wave lazily in greeting, not shouting. Despite the kids' shouts, Brian puts a finger to his lips, motions to the patio where Gramps is in an upright chaise in the shade of the umbrella. A white cotton sheet is over his legs. Max is struck by how regal he looks, reclining, slender. The white sheet like a Roman toga, Margaret's big planters like urns full of herbs and annuals. Gramps is dozing off, his hands clasped comfortably over his heart, his chin resting firmly on his chest, his mouth sagged down and relaxed.

Max sits down in the weathered cedar chair next to him. "Hi, Dad," he whispers.

Arthur opens his eyes without moving his head, stares straight ahead at the children in the plumes of spray. Max can see a yellow tint to his father's eyeballs, an ocher glaze over the pink corners. After a moment, Arthur closes his eyes again.

"Hi, Dad," Max whispers again.

This time, Arthur looks at him. His sleepy eyes take a moment to register before he smiles. "Max," he croaks, then clears his throat. "You're here."

"Here I am," says Max.

"With the enchanting Chloe Eliot," says Arthur, as Chloe approaches.

"Chloe Bramble, Dad."

"Of course."

"Hi, Mr. Bramble."

"Good afternoon, Chloe."

"I didn't wake you, Dad, did I? I mean, you're not *trying* to sleep, are you?"

"If I wanted to sleep this clearly would not be the place," he answers, eyeing the squealing children. "We were all waiting for you people," says Arthur, suddenly indescribably at ease. He feels surprisingly relaxed. Not hot, not cold, not hungry. No pain, no nausea. "I feel quite well," he announces, before anyone asks.

Sarah and Flo, wet and wiry, shiver across the driveway to crowd Rex's stroller. Chloe hurries over to quietly steer them away. The small girls scurry off in a uniform gesture like dogs being shooed from a garbage can, like a sail catching wind.

"How was your flight, Dad?" asks Max.

"Why is it people always ask that about air travel. They're all the same, are they not?"

Max smiles. "Sometimes things happen, Dad. I don't know. Sometimes there are good stories to tell."

"I suppose." Arthur sighs.

Sarah runs over, presents herself before them, her gymnast body, her breastbones jutting out through her metallic-pink swimsuit. She touches Max's wrist. "You want to come in the sprinkler?"

"Not now, thanks."

Margaret comes out the back door. "You made it!" she shouts. In one hand she carries a pitcher of lemonade, a stack of plastic glasses that look like real glass in the other. She looks around. "Did you leave your baby on the train?"

"He's right there."

"Where?" asks Arthur.

"He's sleeping in the stroller, Dad. Over there in the shade."

Chloe unloads the towers of glasses in Margaret's hand. Edie approaches from the outfield of the lawn. She's wearing army-green shorts and an army green tank top. Ordinarily, almost anything on her would look graceful and inviting. What has happened? wonders Max, watching her come slouching off the lawn like an athlete who should have retired a couple of years ago. Something about her seems dowdy and mousy. Her carriage is downtrodden. Her body type is all-around different. She approaches hangdog, slumped to the side and listless. "I broke my arm," she tells Max with a yawn, raising it like a torch.

"I heard."

"Did it hurt?" asks Chloe.

Edie looks at her. "Guess," she says, monotone, only halfway trying to sound like she meant it playfully. It's not that she doesn't like Chloe. It's not that she even knows Chloe very well. Edie still can't get over the fact that her older brother Max married someone five years younger than her. Granted Max is only a year and a half older than Edie, and Chloe is very worldly and everything—but Edie was always the young one. No longer. Plus, she never sees Max anymore. Plus, it wasn't that she wanted to find a spouse herself, it wasn't that she was jealous of that, but Max has found *something*. Before, before he met Chloe, he seemed to just *bing bing bing* along happily despite what was happening in his life. Whenever Edie would start to feel blue and bored, she'd think of Max and think, *Well, Max doesn't love his job either and he's basically living the same life that I am, and he manages to be happy and content*, and it would pull her toward happiness and contentment, even if she was faking it a little. Now here was Max with a wife, with a baby, living a very different life, a life she rarely even got to hear about.

"Of course it hurt," Chloe says diplomatically.

Edie kicks a beach ball to Stephen and follows it back onto the lawn.

"A little bird tells me that you ran into Mimi Woods on the street," Arthur says to Max.

"And Howard. Yes."

"You didn't tell me that, Max," says Chloe.

"Right. Friday," Max says to his father.

"Friday?" asks Chloe, her face squinching up. Max looks at his wife quickly, nodding with a casual smile. Had that only been Friday? Oh, it has been a long, long couple of days.

"She said you almost knocked her to the ground." Arthur chortles .

"I guess I almost did," says Max.

"Edie is going to visit them in Maine," says Arthur.

"Really?" Max is surprised. It seems like a strange visit, Edie visiting friends of her parents. "Mimi didn't mention that."

"She's going today, I believe. I believe they just arranged it when Mimi called yesterday."

"You sound good, Dad," says Max.

"Why? Because I'm talking coherently?"

"No, just—"

"You'll remember that Mimi is Edith's godmother."

"Right," says Max, watching the lawn activities. Edie and Brian are now playing croquet hockey, the preferred sport with the croquet mallets. It's like field hockey, only it's usually one-on-one, and the goals— there are two apiece, sometimes three—are the tiny wire arches. Stephen abandons the sprinkler to join them. Max can hear Brian reminding him, "Keep the balls on the ground, remember. All balls on the *ground* or we stop playing."

Margaret, faceless, screams from her surveillance station at the kitchen sink, yelling instructions out the window. "Balls on the *ground*, Stephen!" A moment later, they hear her again. "And no lacrosse balls!"

Max calls to Margaret, into the dark square of window above them that is the kitchen. He can't see a thing. "What are you doing in there?" he calls to her.

"Me? Shit!" They hear something large and plastic—a bowl, possibly —bounce on the floor. "Me? Getting you some food!"

Max heads inside, aware that he's leaving Chloe stranded with his father. Why stranded? She's a grown woman. She's a mother, for heaven's sake. She can make small talk with her son's only grandfather.

In the kitchen, he finds Margaret sweeping frantically with a child-sized broom. "Wow. What's the hurry?"

"Hurry? No hurry. I'm just cleaning."

"You're sweeping so . . . quickly."

She pauses for a moment, looks at him. "I'm sweeping." Then she tells what happened. "That plastic pitcher knocked a peach out of that bowl and then the peach knocked over that box of rice."

"Like dominoes."

"Exactly. Now, rice everywhere."

"Don't you have a better broom?" The broom is about three feet long, its three primary parts in the three primary colors: red shaft, blue bristle holder, yellow nylon bristles.

"A better one? Oh, I don't know where the other one is." Long ago, she resigned herself to her children's tools, which, unlike her own, never seemed to disappear: the little training scissors and tiny nail clippers, the miniature snow shovels and rakes, Fisher Price flashlights, the orange plastic garden hoe, the red plastic spade, since she can never find the real one they gave her for Mother's Day. The calculator on the toy cash register is where she balances the checkbook, usually with a dehydrated felt-tip pen—in orange or hard-to-see yellow—from a marker set.

"So. How's it going?" asks Max.

"It's been one night. It's weird. But everything's fine. Sonia, the nurse, came and will keep coming. I mean, I don't have to change his diaper and stuff yet."

"His diaper?"

"He's still up and around. As you can see. I mean, he doesn't wear diapers. As you can see."

"Actually, I haven't seen."

"I gotta say, I can't believe you're only coming out here now." The sweeping gets a little more frantic. "Your father has terminal cancer and he's been here for two days and you live just twenty minutes away, Max." She talks with one hand, thrusts it out for emphasis, despite the swift sweeping.

"It's only been one day, really, for the record," says Max, "and I told you—" Here, Max is aware of the sets of ears outside. Can Chloe and his father hear Margaret's whining? Can they hear him? He didn't mention to Chloe that he'd falsely said Rex had convulsions.

Max looks out the window at them. His wife and his father are smiling together. Chloe is relaying something with a great deal of animation and pleasure. What could she be telling him? She hasn't given Max that much vivaciousness in a long time. "I told you," Max says to Margaret in an aggressive whisper, poorly trying to hide that he's whispering, "Rex was sick."

Margaret collects everything in the dustpan, stands up. "Oh," she says, whispering back. "And is that a secret?" She turns around to shove the little broom into the clutter closet, to throw away the mound of rice, its falling cascade into the garbage bag sounding farmlike, grains of wheat pluming through a silo chute.

"Okay." Max sighs. "How can I help you here?" He's afraid of the terrain that his sister is touching on, afraid she'll start talking about Chloe, afraid she'll start talking about their father.

"You can cut the watermelon," says Margaret, as she exuberantly mixes up a goopy bowl full of miniature mozzarella balls, tomatoes, and basil. "Did you see Edie's cast? Just a few slices so it'll stay fresh."

"Yeah, I did." He lifts the lid on the big pot, peeks in. "Mmm, corn," says Max, pleasantly surprised.

"Yeah. I meant to grill it, but . . . I didn't. Will you stick it in that caldron?"

"You mean colander?"

"Caldron, colander, coriander. Whatever. We were in an accident too, you know. Me and the kids." She sprinkles some Parmesan on a green salad.

"When? Is everyone okay?"

"No we were all severely injured, Max. Of course we're okay! The same morning as Edie."

"Weird."

"Yeah."

"Is the car—"

"The car has to get fixed." She hip-checks the drawer to close it. Max thinks, She must be nervous having Dad here. He hadn't really thought about it. Really. Margaret keeps talking. "Most importantly, though, I was afraid the kids had *strep* and then they'd give it to *Dad* and what a disaster *that* would be."

"And?"

"And they're all deathly ill, as you can see. They're fine! But you—you should keep Rex away from Dad if he really was so sick."

She was punishing him. He could never explain to anyone the bottomless delight he felt when he saw his father holding his son. "Well," says Max, "the doctor said it wasn't contagious."

"I'll bet he did. Have you talked to Edie lately?"

Max shrugs. "Not really. Dad just told me she's going to visit the Woodses in Maine."

"That's weird, right?"

"I couldn't imagine visiting them."

"She's going *today*." Margaret snorts.

"She is?"

"I don't even want to get into it," says Margaret, shaking her head. "I thought she'd be around to help out with Dad while she was on vacation."

Max doesn't know what to say.

"I think something's wrong," Margaret continues. "I think she's really unhappy." Margaret peers out the window, making sure Edie's not under it. Edie is sitting on the grass at the edge of the lawn, smoking. Brian and Stephen are whacking balls back and forth with the croquet mallets, laughing. There's a certain laugh that Brian gets out of Stephen that Margaret, for the life of her, can never elicit. "Forget about the watermelon," directs Margaret. "Cut the steak." She takes it out of the fridge, out from under its aluminum foil, and places it on the plastic butcher block with her bare hand. "Nice and thin. Here. This knife is excellent."

"Mmm," says Max. It smells of teriyaki, the congealed grease around the edges. Tiny sesame seeds like teardrops aiming this way and that.

Margaret pauses, looks at the plastic butcher block, and is reminded of something she heard on the radio recently. A woman, a food expert or epidemiologist, was talking about mad cow and contaminated foods and how the place that's actually the most threatening for harboring any kind of threatening bacteria is one's own kitchen, particularly in sponges and cutting boards. A sponge after only a couple of days can become a big glob of teeming microbes, and when it's Zambonied around on tables and countertops to tidy up, it just spreads them more. The woman pointed out that plastic cutting boards in particular trap reams of bacteria and microbes in the knife grooves, even after they've gone through the dishwasher.

"Wait," says Margaret. She pulls out the big wooden cutting board, transfers the meat onto it.

"What are you doing?"

She slides the plastic board into the trash can. "Good-bye to that," she says. "Edie said she kept trying to call you at work," says Margaret. "She wanted to know what you did with all that stuff you packed up for Dad."

"Yeah. I missed her calls."

"She said she kept getting that girl Miriam."

"Right. Because I was missing her calls."

"Mm. How *is* work?" asks Margaret, clamoring around for plates.

Max cuts the meat, wondering if this is a trap. "Um," he says. "Fine."

"That's good. I mean, I guess what else can you say, really. Who really wants to get into it, talking about *work*?"

"How's *your* work?"

"Actually it's going pretty well. There was this couple that moved from Tribeca that bought a house . . ."

Max tunes her out, managing to nod and listen halfway, but doesn't hear what she's saying as he gets busy slicing the meat, thinking about his absence from work, thinking about Chloe and all the jet-setting she used to do and how she probably wants to live some high life that Max will never be able to attain. But then he hears Margaret again, when the tone of her voice changes and she comes weaving back to—"upset with me, always doing something wrong. I don't know what it is. It's like she doesn't want to talk about it, but I don't know how to approach it. Is it resentment? Am I unaware of something? I don't know."

"Wait," says Max. "Who? The people who hired you?"

"No!" Margaret groans. "Our *sister!*"

"Oh. Wait. Back up, back up. I'm listening now."

"Forget it," says Margaret, wheeling out of the kitchen with the plastic polka-dot plates.

"Hey! I'm listening!"

"Maybe later," says Margaret. The screen door slams shut behind her.

Max leans against the counter. In the center of the kitchen, just above head level, a swirl of flies are looping around one another.

Outside, Margaret puts the plates down on the table, heads over to her father. "Are you comfortable, Dad? Do you want to sit at the table to eat?"

"I'm fine, my dear."

"Maybe you'd like some steak?"

"Maybe."

Chloe finishes the story she's been telling Arthur. "So anyway"—she smiles—"from then on, my mother swore she would never set foot in the Danube again." Chloe is smiling, her blond head floating before Arthur and Margaret like a lovely paper lantern. Margaret is perplexed, wondering what the story was about, while Arthur is admiring Chloe's pretty eyes, her young enlivened face, her general effervescence, when, from behind her, both he and Margaret see what's approaching: a small boulder, a meteor, sailing through the air. Chloe's smile continues, slomo, until—before either Margaret or her father can do or say anything—the red croquet ball with the white Saturn stripes beans her, hard, on the back of her head. The sound is as though the ball has hit concrete. Chloe lets out a sharp cry, pained, her hands go flying up to the site of contact, and she crumples to the ground.

Her cry wakes up Rex who, after looking around for a moment like a hatched chick, starts to wail. Margaret helps Chloe to a chair. She checks Chloe's head. "Is it bleeding?" whimpers Chloe. "It feels like it's bleeding."

"It looks okay," says Margaret.

"I'm dizzy," says Chloe. "Really dizzy."

Brian has jogged into the kitchen. He comes out with two bags of frozen green beans, Max trailing behind him. Edie has picked up Rex, who's still crying but then is interested in her cast. Sarah and Flo sit on the foot of Arthur's chaise while Stephen, lurking guiltily, stands uncomfortably next to the trunk of the beech tree, edging behind it. Once Max is with his wife, Margaret beelines for Stephen, practically takes him by the ear, and gruffly leads him inside.

"S-sorry, Mom," says Stephen.

"Don't say sorry to me, pal," says Margaret, gritting her teeth.

"Ow, Mom. You're pinching me."

In the dark of the dining room, she levels with him. "What if you had hit Gramps, Stephen? What if you hit *him* like that?"

Stephen doesn't say anything.

"Do you realize you could have *killed* him?" It escapes out of her, like those fast little green lizards Stephen has that dart out of their aquarium case every time you lift the lid. The velocity of her anger and where to put it. The look of horror on Stephen's face as a result.

"Oh, honey," she says. "I didn't mean that," but the anger rises back like a bubbled bullfrog. He could have, couldn't he? She looks at him squarely. "But I'm *really* mad," she says. "Go to your room until we eat."

Stephen obeys, scampering off toward the stairs.

Brian comes in from outside. "Shall I go talk to him?" He sees that Margaret's biting her lip, tears welling up in her eyes. "Oh, sweetheart," he says.

"What if it had hit Dad?" says Margaret, starting to cry. "Right in the head?"

"Oh," says Brian. He rubs her arms up and down. "He'd have been all right."

"I think I scared Stephen." Margaret smashes her face into Brian's armpit. "I'm not cut out for this," she muffles into his shirt.

"Honey, you're doing great. Who would be better cut out for it? A nurse in a hospital? Alice out in California?"

"Probably," she says, muffled, meekly. But partly she meant not being cut out for parenting

"You're doing great, Maggie. Everything's fine."

Margaret comes up for air. "Is Chloe okay?"

"She got badly nailed in the head, but she's fine."

Margaret leans on Brian's shoulder. She looks emptily out the window at the front of the house. The glare of the pavement on the street, the massive magnolia across from them that they get to look at all the time, the special pear trees that look so harmless now but that shed their miniature mushy fruits all over the sidewalk every autumn, causing hazardous treading, slipping, and injury. She has a mild headache. She allows herself to relax a little bit more, consciously tries to lower her shoulders, relax her neck, and then feels like she could fall asleep. Outside, the mesmerizing greenery, the verdure of summer, a lone thick-legged pedestrian on the other side of the street who's stopped to read a posted sign—a missing dog or cat, a garage sale—tacked to a telephone pole.

"Wait," says Margaret. She lifts her head up, looking at the pedestrian. "There's that woman!"

"What woman?"

"The one in our trash!"

"What?"

"The one who hit us!"

She hurries to the front door. She flings the door open, hurries down the steps. "Tammy?" she yells, louder than Brian expected. "Tammy Lopnop!"

Outside, the woman is gone.

·

When they all assemble to eat at the table outside, Chloe and Arthur both remain on their chaises. Arthur isn't hungry, and Chloe is recuperating from her blow.

"She was in your trash?" asks Edie, spooning some mozzarella onto her plate.

"Yes. And she rear-ended our car," says Margaret busily. She is preparing plates for her children, cutting up the sirloin into tiny pieces. "The thing is," she continues, "she had no *insurance*. But she stopped and acted sweet and gave me all this fake information."

"Yes," says Edie, making a face, "we've heard." Margaret doesn't even notice the implication that she's mentioned it a great deal. "But you did *not* mention that she was in your trash."

"No? Well." Margaret sighs. She surveys the food in its bowls on the table. All she wants is to sit down, be quiet, and eat.

"There was a woman in your garbage?" asks Chloe, confused, her head on the pillow of frozen beans.

"Picking through it," says Margaret. "Looking for something. Or something."

Brian gives Chloe a look. Chloe giggles.

"What?" asks Margaret, looking around. "She was. There was a woman. Right, kids?"

All three kids are silently eating, their wet heads polished shiny in the sun. "Right, Mom," says Sarah, amplified by her glass of lemonade as she takes a sip.

Margaret brings out two metal mesh domes that keep the flies from plaguing their dinners. She puts one over the steak, another over the mozzarella. The salad will have to fend for itself. She sits down next to Brian and starts chomping on her corn on the cob in the fashion of a typewriter. Everyone eats, keeping to themselves. For a moment they can't hear any cars anywhere, no ambient neighborhood sounds. A while ago, the music stopped. As the kids eat diligently, Margaret thinks to herself how, when they're active, they eat. A cicada rattles loudly, quiets down, and then picks up again where it left off, getting louder, getting softer. They eat and listen to the rustling trees shimmying in the wind.

Gramps, his hands clasped on his belly, looks peacefully at the shadows on the flattened dirt at the edge of the patio. The roots of the nearby cypress tree bubble up through the ground. Gramps looks up at the big pine trees, the maples, a splotchy sycamore with milky limbs, a locust. The sun is gleaming through the crisscrossed boughs. Arthur clears his throat. "Where's that pen?" he shouts.

The children all laugh. "That scared me!" laughs Flo.

"Oh, my God, me too!" laughs Sarah.

"What, Gramps?" Margaret smiles.

"I asked you for a pen, did I not?"

Margaret jumps up. "Yes! Sorry. You did! Hold on."

Margaret returns from inside with a small pad of paper and a ballpoint pen. Arthur takes the pen in his hand, is faced with the lined white paper before him. The piece of paper seems awfully small. He puts the pen to the paper and has the tumbling sensation of a déjà vu on top of itself, a déjà vu having a déjà vu. Whatever he's meant to write down has slipped his mind, wisped away like cannon smoke. His busy mind—hadn't it been busy?—was like a bubble of clear air. Now it's like he said yesterday to Margaret's friend Andrea (or was it a he, a Bob or a Mark?). Or was it actually Margaret herself? And was it not yesterday but several days ago? To Alice in California? Or in a dream? Or something or other: "Children? My children? Yes . . . Their faces . . . they come up to me—hello—and then they go away."

A summer breeze blows through the yard, swaying the swings in the swing set. Flo drops her fork on the patio's bluestone. "Do you need anything, Dad?" asks Margaret.

Arthur looks at his daughter blankly. "I'm having a *senior moment,* as they say."

"Me too," groans Chloe from her nearby chaise.

"Would you . . ." Arthur says to Margaret, insinuating the finish—*please go away*—with a tilt of his head.

The stereo suddenly kicks in, starting at the beginning of its rotation again. Some energizing music, Joe Strummer's "Bhindi Bhagee," starts rattling up out of the speaker in the window. Sarah snaps to, floats out onto the grass, and starts dancing energetically, shimmying around freely, a big wide smile like a figure skater's, bobbing her head like she's seen in the Bollywood movies she watches at the babysitter's house. She has her arms out, twirling at the wrists, relishing the music like it's something that's smoothing over her body. Some graceful little goat hops: hop-hop-hop-swoop, hop-hop-hop-swoop. Her arms are long and outstretched. She rotates her wrists, rotates her shoulders, her body like a belly dancer's, swimming on top of the music. The metallic fibers of her pink bathing suit flash in the sun.

Everyone watches her. Max, particularly spellbound, feels a kind of inspiration and humor that he hasn't felt in a long time. If only *he* was like a rock song, a trapped vault full of energy, full of tale and expression, full of *verve*. "Go, Sare!" says Max. "Whooo!" yells Brian.

The first time Sarah did this—erupted into a dance in the living room to the same song: that big smile, all her movements as though they were breaking free—Brian and Margaret looked up from reading their respective papers, delighted to see her. Her arms and legs seemed tremendously long. They were expecting her to stop shortly after the initial outburst of dance, but she kept going until the end of the song, like a Hindi movie mixed with funk, overfilled with elation and energy. Margaret and Brian both got misty-eyed, smiling at the surprise enthusiasm of their daughter, the amount of joy in her, the concentration and focus, the looseness and unreserved release.

"That was great, honey!" says Margaret, after the song is over, through the general applause.

"Thanks, Mom," says Sarah modestly.

"Marvelous!" says Gramps.

"Where did she learn that?" asks Edie, edging up next to Margaret on the patio.

"Her babysitter, Marina, watches lots of Bollywood movies."

"Yeah, but who taught her *that*?"

"No one. I don't know. She just *does* it."

"But she's *really* good."

"I know. I know it." Margaret looks at her father, at the pleased look on his face, watching his grandchildren amble out onto the lawn again like players after halftime. Determined, Rex walks the Frankenstein walk of a toddler across the wet grass, ignoring the drizzle of the sprinkler, to reach the bottom of the slide on the swing set. Stephen gnaws at an ear of corn. Brian holds a football, motions to throw it to Max, who runs long.

Margaret thinks of something. "Here, Dad," she says. She drags over a little drink table and places it next to his chaise. She picks up a big planter full of deep purple rambler petunias—she was never a petunia fan, but this "wave" variety was bright, vigorous, and rambled really well—and places the planter on the little table next to her father. "Here, Dad," she says again. "Can you clean this up for me?"

Arthur can smell the geranium-like tinge to the plant, almost coniferous, a little bit peppery. He surveys the pot, touches a silken leaf that wilts in his hand almost immediately when he picks it off. The velveteen of the petals. He plucks off some dead flowers and browning stalks, the familiar stickiness oozing from the stems. He takes his handful of refuse and lets it fall on his belly, the array of greens, the purple and faded purples like petals for a honeymoon bed.

He glances down at the trace dirt on his finger, up under his nails. He looks at the pot and then purposefully sticks his forefinger into the dirt, as though his finger has been burning and finally it has found something perfectly soothing. He pushes it in as far as it will go, as though planting a crocus bulb, as though inside his wife. He lets it rest there in the cool soil. He closes his eyes and sees a large red tomato from years ago—not many seeds, a Big Boy? Beefsteak?—in the vegetable garden in Merrick, wiping it off on his shirt and biting it like an apple, its meaty flesh tasting resplendent and mineral, its trapped sunlight inside his mouth. Its summertime.

II

Another plane for Edie. This time a little one that hums and dips through the clear Atlantic sky. The plane buzzes over a quaint harbor town. She sort of knows the buildings, knows the roads. She drove up there one wintry long weekend, solo, to see the place, the town that was closest to her mother's plane when it crashed. Why didn't she tell Margaret? Why didn't she tell Max? She wasn't sure. Partly because she was afraid they would want to come with her, partly because she felt sort of pathetic that she had the time to do it, that she felt the need to go.

She stayed at the only open inn near the harbor. She was the only guest, and the innkeepers left a basket of warm muffins with a chambray dish towel over it every morning outside her door. She drove around in the old Volvo, smoking cigarettes and going over the same roads, and stopped doing that when she passed more than one person for the third or fourth time, the person seeming to peer into the car as she passed, curious about who she was. She took a lot of baths and watched cable, wondering what she was doing there.

Today, slight winds cause the harbor to goose-pimple, the plane to bob. The small boats at their moorings delicately turn in unison in the same direction, as if from a remote control. As the plane starts its descent, she can see a path through a woods leading to a meadowed clearing with whirled grass around the smudge of an old fire. A place for parties, no doubt, where cars are parked and trucks backed up with kegs and speakers on the flatbeds, where all anyone can see is the twinkling stars and vague outlines of the spruce trees, vague outlines of people, a baseball hat, a ponytail, no one dancing, just standing around, leaning on cars, cigarette embers slowly smoldering here and there.

It has been a long time since she went to a party like that. It has been a long time since she's been in a summer where she *felt* like it was summer, with her bare feet navigating grass and pebbles, trees crinkling in the wind and warm air, her hair crunchy with saltwater, weathered cheeks, the smooth coolness of sheets after a day of being blown around.

Until she was about fourteen, her family had rented a little shingled house on Moss Island, just outside of town, almost every summer. After that, as the kids all got bigger, her parents would head up there once a summer to visit Mimi and Howard Woods but otherwise stayed closer to Merrick and a three-week rental on Long Island's North Fork. Edie never went up there again until the summer after her freshman year in college, when Mimi, her godmother, hired her to be her cook for the summer.

Mimi had inherited from her father an amazingly large, rambling, black-stained shingle house with a matching smaller guesthouse, where Edie stayed. There was a tennis court, where bushes of rose hips climbed the lattice fences, and a wide vegetable garden where Mimi grew things that Edie had never seen before: freckled lettuce and black green beans, white eggplant and purple tomatoes. Behind the boathouse were tall tangles of raspberry and blackberry bushes that Edie would get tangled up in herself, picking them, using the berries to make tarts in July (raspberry) and crumble in August (blackberry), and in cream whenever, the easiest dessert of all.

The Woodses' spread seemed to belong in Newport or the Hamptons. It sat high above the water on its hill. The bleached wood yacht club sat a few hundred yards below on pilings and stilts above the water. Little kids scampered up and down ramps, learning to sail. Older kids in their early teens screamed annoyingly through various forms of water fights. Anonymous adult voices floated up in the evenings, their accents from another era, like Hollywood starlets in 1940: "Whatever happened to the *When and If*, Richard? Wasn't that a *wonderful, marvelous* sloop?"

It was weird to begin with, that Edie had been offered the job. She had no previous experience as a real cook, though she'd cook at home from time to time. She worked for a caterer while she was in school, folding little filo doughs into triangles, rolling flaky pastry around sautéed mushrooms, skewering shrimp on toothpicks with that festive colored plastic wrap twirled at its tip, slicing the filet to just the right thickness, dolloping things with their appropriate dollop, but in terms of cooking real, big-time meals, day in and day out, to big people on big plates, that was something she had never done.

"You've been *catering* all these long months," said Edie's mother cheerfully, talking to Edie on the phone.

"Mom. I'm told what to do and I do it."

"Well, I think you're a tremendous cook."

"Thanks, Mom. I don't know what I've ever cooked for you."

"Your carbonara is the best in the world."

"It's *your* carbonara, Mom."

"Mmm."

"Does she really always have a cook? I don't remember them ever having one."

"Um," said Florence. "No."

Edie was quiet.

"But she wants one."

Edie didn't know what to say.

"You're a terrific cook, Edie," her mother told her.

"Oh." Edie sighed. "Thanks, *Mom*."

"And wouldn't it be fun to spend a summer up there again?"

Edie glanced out at Broadway. A man in a cape waving his finger at someone. A plastic bag the color of caramel getting blown in the wind, landing matted against the window in front of her face. "It *is* really nice," she said.

"It's beautiful! I can't wait to come visit!"

The summer *was* lovely. She felt completely removed and industrious. Sleeping in Mimi's guesthouse made her feel as though she were working all the time, which she liked. It set her apart from her regular self. It made her busy. It made her feel as though the rest of her life was on the back burner. She thinks of this as the plane descends. The farther down the plane slowly falls, the more Edie can see: the terrain, the colors, the field grasses way below in their distinct shades of scratchy green. She'd forgotten all about sea lavender. She'd forgotten all about some of the different younger feelings, airy ones, summery ones, that were flooding back at the sight of the water, the rocks. Wouldn't she like it if her job made her travel—We need you in Tokyo! They want you in Rome!—with the feeling that she's having on the descending plane: an absence of dread, a true excitement at the prospect of the new fresh air that will meet her as the plane sits on the tarmac and the door snaps open to foreign smells and territory.

Now, as the plane lowers and the ocean begins to take on its familiar posture as a flattened firmament, she is reminded of nature, the behemoth of it against her tiny apartment creaked among other apartments. She watches the small surf below furl and unfurl along the shore, the light on the ocean make patterned designs that shoot crazily all over the place. Over and over she keeps thinking of the same thing—why this?—of running down a path as a kid, the light on the water twinkling through the evergreens, her bare feet, running behind Max—he had a Red Sox T-shirt on (the things she remembers!)—the ground cushioned with tassels of rust-colored pine needles, her head feeling ten feet tall, her body feeling young and alive, light and effortless, like it might bounce into the air, *boinggg*, up, into, and over a tree, to fall slap onto the water, where she'd float happily like a bubble astray, drifting in the lively wind.

It was such a boring, adult question: Why was she so *tired*? Why did she feel so heavy? It was the kind of question she imagines someone her father's age asks himself. It was the kind of question someone dead like her mother doesn't have the luxury to ask.

They had been in Margaret's backyard before Edie left for California to get Dad, the night trees sizzling with insects, Edie smoking her cigarette. "Why don't you go talk to someone?" Margaret had asked her, feeling light and easy after a glass of wine, talking about it with herself before she spoke out.

"Me?" Edie took offense. "About what?"

Margaret backed off. "I don't know. You seem kind of unhappy. To me."

Edie's eyes welled up, glossed over. "I'm not unhappy," she said.

Margaret could see her sister's face in the light from the hurricane lamp go from a tranquil Georges de La Tour to slight torture. Edie's lip

quivered. Margaret had the dreaded feeling that they were headed somewhere she was ill equipped for.

"I guess sometimes I just feel like my life's a *waste*," said Edie, the
buzz from the last beer easing it out. "I don't know what's wrong." She
smiled, feeling phony, feeling like an actress in an after-school special,
wiping away tears.

Margaret curved a strip of Edie's hair behind her pink ear, felt the
urge to pick her sister up, hold her on her lap. How do you comfort an
adult? Brian never needed comforting. Margaret put her hand on her sister's cheek, cupped it, then sensed that Edie didn't want to be touched,
so she sat back quietly like a dog watching another dog that's sick.

"It's hard having them both die," said Margaret. She rolled her eyes
to herself: a brilliant comment. Jesus Christ.

"Yeah," said Edie. Maybe it *was* all about mourning her mother. She
knew it wasn't. Edie sniffled. "Nice earrings," she said to Margaret.

"I'm wearing earrings?" Margaret reached up to feel them. "You gave
me these."

"I know."

•

Edie knocks on the wood frame of the screen door. "Hello?" She lets
herself into Mimi's house, sees first the painted black wood floors, a
straw rug, a bunch of pink spray roses on the table at the foot of the
stairs. On the thick round table in the entranceway is a bouquet of sea
lavender the size of a small trash can, surrounded by a neatly arranged
assortment of mussel shells and sea urchins. Held down by a smooth
granite rock, a note in Mimi's bubbled hand.

> Edie, dear—Am at the dump. Now known as the transfer station.
> (Their hours are demanding!) Back momentarily. A pot of tea in the
> kitch. prob. still warm.

Edie puts her bag down on the stairs, walks through the living room,
out onto the wraparound porch. She goes to the railing and holds on to
it. The steep hill below is covered with scruffy grass and bushes. The
ferry hums at the harbor landing as cars and trucks creak onto it, heading back to the mainland.

Edie can't remember exactly the last time she was here. Her mother was alive, she was certain of that. They'd stayed in this house while the Woodses were in Europe. Was it four years ago? Stephen and Sarah were born. She remembers Sarah, her fat cheeks and perfectly straight posture, sitting on the rocky beach on Butter Island, cramming pebbles into her mouth like popcorn. She remembers walking to the general store with baby Sarah on her hip and Tom Tagg assuming that the baby was hers.

Edie scans the water, the island across the way. The Woodses' boat-house is off to her right. She allows herself to remember something from that summer she lived here. She had walked down there to smoke a cigarette, drink another beer. A moonless, starless night, the boats so still it was as if they were grounded. She sat on the edge of the ramp, looking out at the flat black water with its garbage-bag sheen. It had been a dinner party, fifteen people. Crabmeat and crackers. Mussels to start. Lobster and a romaine salad. Nothing demanding. Strawberry shortcake afterward.

The boathouse was nothing much. A couple of sailing race flags hanging from the rafters. A small mural of a vase of flower power and an American flag with 1776 painted across it. KILROY WAS HERE, the partial cartoon face, in Magic Marker. A peace sign painted in white but mistaken into a Mercedes-Benz. When the Woods kids were younger, the place was a command center of party life. Beer bongs and smushed cans. Music thrumming across the water in the dark.

Edie had lit a cigarette off the one she was finishing and inhaled as much as she could when a figure emerged out of the dark to her left. It slipped on the damp grass, cursed. Edie recognized the voice. It was a man who had been at dinner, Ralph, the boyfriend of Mimi's niece Amelia. He was handsome in an obvious way, brassy-haired, faint freckles the color of cinnamon. Edie had found herself refilling his wineglass more than the others, not because she favored him at all but because he was drinking a lot. At one point she thought she'd felt his hand on her hip as he thanked her when she took a plate mounded with mussel shells away.

She felt the warm blur of the two beers she'd drunk and sucked at her cigarette, annoyed by the intrusion. The figure lay still, groaned.

"Are you all right?" she called finally. A foghorn in the distance groaned as well. Another even farther off.

A dribble of laughter from the ground. "I could use some help getting up," he said in the dark. "My knee."

With cigarette in hand, Edie went over to him. She reached out a hand to take his. She took both his hands and righted him. He wobbled and then clutched her waist. He slid his hand down her pants. "No," she said, prying it out. "Stop it."

"You're so *sexy*," he said messily, and they tipped over.

"Get off," she said. "Get *off* of me." She pushed him but that didn't do anything, his clumsy body suddenly strong.

Afterward, a hulk of dead weight on top of her. She pushed him aside, a push backed by another push, rolled him off. As he rotated, he woke, like a person out of a nightmare, unusually alarmed and defensive, to whack her on the side of her head with his forearm and then sloppily with the back of his hand. Edie got up, hurrying away.

The next morning, Mimi was getting coffee in the kitchen. "My God. What in the world happened to your face?"

"I slipped on the ramp of the boathouse," said Edie.

"It's quite swollen." Mimi frowned, seeming to imply—Edie wasn't sure—that Edie had drunk too much and fallen down. "Should you see the doctor?"

"I'm fine," said Edie. Edie still didn't know what to call her—Mrs. Woods? Mimi? so she avoided calling her anything. And she *was* fine. Was she? She was angry. She was humiliated; how could she have let that happen? But somehow nothing about the incident surprised her.

She went outside to take the bucket of leftover mussel and lobster shells from dinner down to the water to throw them overboard. On her way to the dock she saw some luggage sitting on the grass outside the back door. Amelia and Ralph were getting ready to leave, clearly. She looked around for them. She'd been mulling over whether to speak to him or just ignore him—why bother saying anything?—if she saw them before they left.

She looked at the two bags as she approached them. One was pink gingham, the other a brown leather duffel. A large tennis shoe was jutting out of the partly opened duffel bag. She could see the edge of a man's toiletry kit; it was clearly Ralph's bag. She glanced about her. She quietly unzipped his bag, opened it wide, and then upturned the bucket with its chumlike contents into it. She let the grimy water dribble out all over the shirts, the socks, the camera, and the cell phone and then gently zipped the bag back up, all the way this time, its outside leather as neat as a pin.

12

Margaret heads back upstairs. The late-afternoon sun shines through the windows of Sarah's bedroom, falls in toppled rectangles, parallelograms squashed across the floor. Margaret fusses, adjusting the air conditioner so it shifts gears to an alto hum, closing the door on the television laughter tinkling up from downstairs, and then hands her father the blue felt-tip pen he's asked her for.

Gramps is sitting up in bed. "Thank you," he says as he takes it, exasperated, looking into Margaret's eyes with a glower, as if to say, *Finally! the pen I've been asking for forever*, as though he's the boss and everyone he's employing is a complete idiot. On his lap, a spiral notebook opened and folded over to a blank page.

Gramps holds the pen's tip about an inch above the paper and lets it roam back and forth in the air like a divining rod as he contemplates something—what to write? where to begin?—a sketch artist about to take the plunge. When he does take it, it's not with a quick flourish but with lots of hesitation. He writes slowly, his mouth sagging with concentration, his hand shivering out some spidery letters.

After some rounded quiet where Margaret listens patiently to the scratchy-smooth squeaks of the felt tip on the paper, as she takes note of the rampant floccules of dust under Sarah's dresser, Gramps makes a period, more like a comma, the stalled finishing swipe of a contract signed, then nods to his daughter, who's standing by like a good footman. "So I don't forget," he says to her, statesmanlike, king of a country. He taps the notebook repeatedly with his forefinger, handing it to her. "Keep that somewhere," he instructs her.

163

"Sure, Dad," says Margaret, playing along. She takes the notebook from him, looks at the writing on the page before her, leggy and jittery, an all-out bizarre evolution from the handwriting she's known her whole life. The letters drip, creepy-crawly, tumble down a hill far beyond the standard chicken scratch of old-person writing. Margaret's surprised, overjoyed even, that her father can actually still write at all, but then simultaneously feels mortified, almost irritated, that he can barely form the letters anymore. To Margaret—she'd never thought of this but it was just now dawning on her—her father's handwriting has always looked more like *him* than anything else in the world. She feels choked up, momentarily panicked, the road of his deterioration suddenly so apparent, so absurdly obvious.

Margaret holds the notebook in front of her face, up close and then away as if she's nearsighted, farsighted, one of the two. She squints, reads the two words together out loud. "Hazey," she says, searching. "Hazey," she says again, the vague word into a fog bank, a test into a microphone that doesn't work. "Haze swirl? Lazy . . . crivil?" waiting to be corrected, careful not to ask her father directly—*What does it say, Dad?*—just as she'd been careful not to praise him effusively when she saw he'd written two words, just as she's careful never to say to one of her kids, *What the heck is that?* when they present her with a drawing they've done. She starts trying out different combinations for herself, almost whispering. "Dazzle? Daisy? Hazey swivel?"

Gramps, annoyed, frowns at her. "So I don't forget," he says again.

"You want me to remind you, Dad? That I have it? To remind you so you don't forget?"

He is looking the irritated boss again, his expression saying, *And now be on your way, please, thank you very much.* Behind his scowling head, Sarah's Powerpuff Girls poster, the cartoon trio with their bug-eyed glares.

"You want me to remind you sometime?" Margaret asks again. "That I have it somewhere?"

Gramps lets out a sigh, sinks into the pillows, closes his eyes, and promptly falls asleep, as if he's just been karate-chopped in the neck.

As Margaret leaves the room, notebook in hand, a taffylike pull from behind, a cresting arrival at the top of a hill. The question: Did he just die?

Margaret turns around to look back at her father. She waits a moment. His head is turned in profile, squished deeply into the pillow as though he fell backward from a great height. He's small but weirdly healthy-looking, hallowed and mystical like a Tibetan monk. Then she hears a deep breath, sees her father's nimble-looking hand pull on the blanket. Margaret goes back and pulls the blanket up better. The white hair springing out of his ears. His sour-smelling mouth. His skin tenderized and supple like a fine fawn purse.

In the upstairs hallway, the heat is like warm water. The banister is warm to the touch as though it's been on low bake. Margaret pauses as she goes down the stairs, looks at the page again, feels a curdle of nervous sweat forming on her upper lip. She can't believe it. He's *really* dying. It strikes her. She would maybe sit down and cry, maybe sit down and think about her father and what she wants to know from him, what she needs to tell him before he goes, mourn for him and herself, think about her mother, feel something for a moment, but—a child's voice— "Mom?" calling up the steps tentatively; "Mom?" a little more urgently, "Mom?" bordering on loud.

"Shhh!" she chides, whispers urgently. "Gramps is dying! I mean, *sleeping.*"

"Mom?" Stephen has the cheap lacrosse stick that she got him at the drugstore. "Look what happened, Mom." The stick's shaft is curved, melted in the hot sunlight of the foyer window, bowed out into a sloppy **L**.

Margaret holds the notebook in her armpit, takes the stick from Stephen, bends it over her knee, rights it, eyes it, bends it again, straightens it for him.

"Thanks, Mom."

"Sure, honey." She goes into the kitchen, rips off the page from the notebook, the holes frizzed like confetti down the left margin, and sticks it on the fridge with a SpongeBob SquarePants magnet, Gramps's shaky words now the name of the refrigerator, center label, in the midst of snapshots and reminders crammed on the freezer's door, as though the house is some sort of a think tank and this was their central goal in some way, *Hazey Swivel,* something to keep in mind constantly, to ponder as they open and close the fridge door, as they hurry in and out of the kitchen, as they go about their lives. *Hazey Swivel,* something to not forget.

Margaret puts it up there on the fridge for no reason that she's aware of, maybe because she has a feeling it's the last thing Gramps will ever write. Or maybe because it has a weird kind of beauty about it, the words together mysterious (what did it mean?) and sad (nothing: a man whose mind is filling up with holes). But most likely she put it up there for the same reason she tapes up the paroxysmal paintings and precise drawings done by her kids, as a method for trapping time somehow as their long little lives race ahead so quickly like tossed balls of yarn. And now it was her father—wasn't it weird?—whose mind-set was going *backward*, toward a kid's, or maybe it wasn't; maybe deterioration was *progression* in some weird way, the departure of it. It didn't seem to matter. It didn't even seem to matter that these two random words were melded together in Gramps's frayed mind, that he had harnessed two words out of the hodgepodge, wrestled them down.

Her father, here in her house. Something she's been expecting, dreading, and looking forward to for some time. Should the TV be in his room? Would he like to listen to the radio, some music? The things she hadn't considered. The hours to pass. Or, rather, the things she'd considered in her mind as though they were rotating on a lazy Susan: How long will he live? Will she be able to leave the house? To leave him alone? What will he want to do? How long will it last?—turning, turning, toward the forefront of her thought and then receding, circling away, to be approached and resolved at a later date. She lets the ideas retreat again, and with Gramps asleep and the kids somehow occupied, she takes the opportunity to make the dreaded call to her car insurance company.

"So you're telling me that a woman driving a Range Rover is driving it without insurance?"

"Yes, Mrs. Bright. Just as I told you on Saturday morning."

"And *I'm* going to be paying the deductible. Even though this woman bashed into *me*."

"Insurance fraud is a gargantuan problem in New Jersey."

"I see. Gargantuan."

"Yes. Very big."

"I understand. But the five-hundred-dollar deductible. I'm to pay that."

"That's right."

"Terrific."

"If and when our Collections Department recoups the money that this . . . *Ms. Lopney* owes us after the work is done, you'll get your deductible back," explains the insurance agent, her voice buglike on the other end of the line.

"Well that's . . . hopeful," says Margaret.

"I wouldn't hold your breath," responds the agent.

"Great." Margaret sighs. She watches a squirrel scamper along the top of the fence, small humps, like a wave machine at the aquarium. "What if I call the woman myself and just ask her to give me five hundred bucks?"

"That would be against the law, Mrs. Bright."

"Mom?"

"Just a minute, Sare."

"Mommy?"

"I'm on the phone, Sarah."

"Gramps is awake again."

•

As Margaret climbs the stairs she can hear Florence playing in her room, the sound of the battery-run infant baby swing that Florence herself spent many an hour rocking in and which is now a central toy for Flo and her dolls. The mechanical, monotonous push and pull, its quiet creak back and forth, the digital chiming burbling out, one of two alternatives; tinny versions of "Home on the Range" or "Let Me Call You Sweetheart."

Gramps's door is open. Margaret pauses in the doorway to see him gazing out the window at the stately eastern trees. Gramps sings along, full-throated, with the twangy music from across the hall, his deep voice Tommy Dorsey–like with forties-style velvet smoothness, *Let me call you sweetheart, deedee dum, da, dum. . . .*

"Dad?" Margaret enters nonchalantly, bringing a bottle of water for his bedside table.

"My dear."

"Did Sarah wake you?"

"No, she did not."

Her father looks so small. His oxford-blue pajamas look as though they'd fit her. "Sharp-looking pajamas, Dad."

"Alice purchased them for me."

"So, Dad. Alice said you were listening to the Teddy Roosevelt biography?"

"I was. The Adams biography as well."

"Did you finish them? Do you want to listen to anything? Music? Tapes?"

"I'd like you to read to me."

"Do you want me to bring a TV in here? The thing is, there's no cable, so—"

"I would like you to read to me."

"Sure, Dad," says Margaret, flustered that she hadn't offered. Her mind feels frazzled at the idea of reading to him with three kids in the house. "I'm reading *Huck Finn* to Stephen," she says. She is fibbing. She had read Stephen the first three pages about a month ago. "Would you like to hear it too?"

"No. 'The Night Before Christmas.' "

"You'd like me to read it?"

"I'd like you to read me 'The Night Before Christmas,' yes."

"Okay, Dad," she says cheerfully.

" 'Twas the night before christmas,' " he says.

" 'And all through the house,' " says Margaret.

"That sort of thing."

"I'll find a copy. I think we've got one."

"Every holiday, my mother—" mutters Gramps.

Sarah comes in. "Can I lie down in here with you, Gramps?"

"Certainly."

"Honey, maybe you shouldn't crowd him."

"Please do crowd me," Gramps says to Sarah.

"Can I come up there too?" asks Flo.

"Of course."

The girls climb up on the bed. Margaret looks at them. Where do they get this boldness, this ease? What little she remembers of her own grandfather, she had a hard time even looking at him, let alone talking to him or touching him. She had never climbed onto her own father's bed the way her kids were doing, had she? She rarely ever went near her parents in their bedroom. The agony of having a nightmare had to do mostly with the anguish of staring into the dark, weighing the pros and cons of getting out of bed and braving the black hallway, opening their door—the only door ever closed in the house—and then enduring their bed, the two of them sound asleep almost immediately after her arrival, their bodies hissing and wheezing like a full, sedate sea, and Margaret lying there, stiff and straight, thinking of Edie back in the bedroom that they shared, abandoned, sleeping unaware in the dark. Margaret would inevitably get up, scare herself down the hallway again, and get back into her own bed or get into bed with Edie, who would wake up, completely alert immediately. "What's wrong?" Edie's little face would say, her skin in the dark the color of the moon, and then she'd move over to give Margaret the warm part.

One night, that same bedroom, the satin ribbons holding back the curtains, the white wicker desk, Margaret woke up to Edie crying quietly in the murky dark. Margaret got into bed with her, put her arms around Edie, and inadvertently felt the jiggle of her sister's brand-new breasts, felt her torso quiver with a cry. Margaret said *shhh* and felt good being the comforting older sister. When Edie stopped crying, Margaret dozed off only to wake up to a shudder from Edie's body and Edie saying, full-voiced and breaking, "Sometimes . . . I don't *feel* very well!" and at this statement, as though she'd finally said it, Edie wailed and wailed, big choking cries that made Margaret recoil a little, made her move back, to let Edie cry on her own. There were times after that when Margaret woke up to hear her sister, her muffled sobs, and would lie there listening, sometimes with her eyes open, sometimes with her eyes closed, not knowing what she should do, somehow scared to do anything, but waiting awake with her until the crying subsided.

Sarah's hair untucks from behind her ear, falling in a curved wave over her eye as she unselfconsciously edges up next to her grandfather. Flo scrambles up more closely on his other side. Arthur smiles slightly. Sarah says, "Can I tell you a story, Gramps?"

"It would be my pleasure."

" 'I know an old lady,' " sings Sarah, and then stops. "I guess it's more of a song," she clarifies quickly, out of the side of her mouth.

"Yes."

She sings.

> *"I know an old lady who swallowed a fly.*
> *I don't know why, she swallowed a fly.*
> *I guess she'll die.*

"Do you know this one, Gramps?"
"I certainly do. Please carry on."

> *"I know an old lady who swallowed a spider,*
> *that wriggled and jiggled and . . . tickled inside her.*
> *She swallowed the spider to catch the fly;*
> *I don't know why . . . she swallowed the fly.*
> *I guess she'll die."*

Margaret sits down on the windowsill. The cold air from the nearby AC blows out onto her thigh. Through the closed window, summertime: the glare of the hot sun, green lawns, patent-leather-like beach balls bouncing through sprinklers, the pavement getting soft.

She's thought before that her life is simply made up of snippets, a connect-the-dots of moments of clarity, of instants, big and small, where life softly explodes in her head, which remain with her either because she simply decided to remember them for no reason at all or because it was something that was seared into her consciousness as if with a branding iron (Stephen's glistening body raised up into the air in the delivery room—who was holding him anyway, Brian? The doctor?— or the miniature of her own face, orbed and shiny like a Christmas tree ornament, reflected on the iris of one of Brian's eyes). Sometimes the dots are close together, and then sometimes there's a big long swoop of lagging line, like a sail that's lost the wind, like a stretched-out elastic. Margaret is aware that here, in Sarah's room, she is at one of those instants where the elastic gets pulled taut, the slack sail is given its breath of wind. It's the image of her father in bed, sitting up, her girls surrounding him, Sarah's lilting voice singing this gentle, eerie song.

For the moment she is aware of exactly what she is: a mother and a daughter in a room with her dying father, her healthy kids. There are always so many problems in the world. There are poor people, people getting screwed over, people taking advantage of other people, people not caring about anyone's outcome but their own. One of the factoids that Brian brought home from work: The amount of money spent on cosmetics in a single year would be more than enough to educate every single person alive in the world, all the way through college. How someone came to that conclusion . . . well, it didn't matter. The abundance surrounding her. The luxury of the supermarket she frequented, its produce clean and shiny, stacked judiciously, unblemished. The opulence of a hot shower, which she took every day. A refrigerator full of food, paper towels galore.

And what was she doing? What difference was she making? What volunteering or outreach effort in her community was she doing? Nada. Zip. Zero. She was involved at the preschool co-op, because she had to be. It was required that she help out in class from time to time, blowing noses, putting the plastic dinosaurs and farm animals, the train tracks, and the peg blocks all into their appropriate bins; that she unscrew paint jars, the powder of dried paint flaking off around the lids, that she vacuum up sand from the sandbox table, change the occasional diaper of a slow-to-the-potty kid. And even that would be coming to an end, because Flo's last year there was coming up.

Wasn't it good enough to be raising three kids, giving as much as she could to them, as often as she was able? Wasn't it good enough to be nursing her father, bringing him into her house? Wasn't it good enough to be waiting hand and foot on little people, hardly aware of what she was wearing, of what she wanted, of who she was anymore? Wasn't all that good enough, to be immersed in her abundance of children, allowing them to take over?

Margaret can remember so many instances of abbreviated adult conversation, of dialogues that might have been fascinating if they had been allowed to progress. She remembers once when her friend Gloria started saying something fascinating: "And then it occurred to me—I'd never thought of anything like it before—I mean, *everything* was suddenly *completely*—" to be interrupted by a crazed, "Joseph! No! That's *Ariel's*! Hey! Don't you dare run away from me!"—as Ariel shrieked and wailed, followed by breakdowns and punishments, the ensuing treaties.

"Anyway. You were saying?"

"Oh, God. What *was* I saying?" Gloria asked herself as she watched her son gallop away, checking that he didn't immediately misbehave again.

"Something that occurred to you."

"What *was* I saying?"

"Something you hadn't thought of before."

"Really? God, I have no idea."

Meanwhile, their friend Kathy was changing her baby's diaper on the grass. The baby's fist came up to grab a clump of Kathy's hair. Kathy spoke in the direction of Margaret and Gloria. "Don't you ever feel as though you're in some kind of purgatory?" asked Kathy gloomily. "That you're just waiting this out until life begins again?"

Margaret shrugged. "In a way, I guess." There was a skirmish on the other side of the lawn. "Give it back to her, Flo! No grabbing!"

"Not me," said Gloria quickly. "I've never felt so alive." Margaret saw something burnished in Gloria's eyes—Is it hunger? Is it love?—as she watched her two kids scramble around the crickety-looking apple tree.

"God," said Kathy wearily. "Really?"

"It's like the moment that I had kids, I woke up to the world," said Gloria plainly.

"Really?"

"Yeah. I don't know what the hell I was doing before. Taking myself too seriously. Taking everything too seriously. *Way* too caught up in myself."

"Really?" Kathy sighed as she wadded the dirty diaper up into a ball and tossed it, *thud*, in the direction of her diaper bag. "Maybe that's my problem," she groaned.

"In fact," said Gloria, "if I had to pick the best time in my life—a certain age—it would be now. This child-rearing stuff, as much as it's a drag sometimes, feels the rightest. I feel the most comfortable in my own skin right now."

"Wow," said Kathy, looking at Gloria dumbly. "I never thought of it that way." Poor Kathy looked tired, washed out. "I don't know when that time would have been for me. Junior high, maybe? College?"

"I'd never go back to junior high," said Margaret.

"How about you, Margaret?" asked Kathy, frowning. "What period of your life seems the most like yourself?"

"Oh, gosh," said Margaret, "I don't know. When I met Brian? I don't know. Hopefully I haven't come across it yet."

It was true that she still had a hard time accepting herself as an adult, even with the kids and the house and the husband and everything, had a hard time actually looking at the bank balance and the credit card bills. But a large part of her looked forward to being an older mom, even a grandmother, with all her people around. She'd be working again, everything orderly and clean, but then she'd miss her little kids' bodies . . . being able to grab them when she wanted . . . squeeze them hard, like pillows.

Margaret felt both ways: worn-to-the-bone numb at times, flying off the handle, bored but mostly enraptured by her kids. The key was to separate herself from them (i.e., her "job") for an hour or two at a time regularly; otherwise it was hard to see them as likable and distinct from one another. It was hard to see them at all. They became like your own face when your face drives you crazy. But after an hour or two or, better, three, she longed for them again. A thrill when she saw their small faces, their clothes, their hair, just the way she left them but already they looked like they'd grown. How was *school*? Did you have *fun*?

Feed the children; then the children need to eat again. Unload the dishwasher and fill it right up. The washing machine is always hungry, its open-hatch mouth as wide as a bullfrog's, waiting for more. The floors are swept, the clean clothes all folded and put away, the bathroom glistening clean, the refrigerator and freezer stocked to the brim, and Margaret would get the feeling, Well, that's *done*—as if it all didn't have to be done again and again and again—and contentedly sit down for a moment, trying not to think of the chaos hidden inside some of the kitchen drawers, the messy filing job in further disarray in the so-called *office*. Where were all the kids' birth certificates? Where were the bonds for the kids that Brian's brother had given them? Where was the actual deed (not a copy) for the house? Where were the excellent baby pictures of Flo that she hadn't seen in about a year? And what about that great summer dress she couldn't locate anywhere?

Margaret would sit calmly, her thoughts inevitably turning back to the children, and find herself thinking, Well, at least they're not tod-dlers anymore. Pick up the crayons, the crayons get thrown. Pick up the blocks, the blocks get dumped. Clean the wall, the wall gets scribbled on. A sippy cup received into their little hands with fresh juice, consid-ered momentarily—something's horrendously wrong: the color of the juice? the level of the liquid?—and then hurled insanely against the wall. The ensuing wail and then, illogically: *I want juice!* The lunacy of actually trying to reason with a two-year-old. That's what she was reduced to for a number of years, arguing with a two- or three-year-old, whoever it might be, trying to one-up them before taking a step back and realizing who, exactly, she was squabbling with. A small small per-son. "Bad Mama!" Stephen used to yell when she dealt him a low blow (sarcasm, gruffness, outright impatience).

"Mama?" Stephen asked once, three years old. "Are you and Sarah having an argument?" Sarah was one and a half, had just learned the word *No*, which she pronounced *neow*, like *meow* for a cat, with a major nasal twang. Margaret was seriously engrossed in a yes/no volley with her toddler daughter: "Yes!" "Neow!" with the thrust forward of a tiny fist. "Yes!" "Neow!" "Yes!" "Neow, *neow*, NEOW!"

Even sleep couldn't shake her out of the hysteria of a toddler day. Brian coming home to her after a work dinner, rousing her in their bed, Margaret basically still asleep but keeping him abreast of vital informa-tion, reporting sleepily: "Well, so then this afternoon . . . I bought a bop bag for 'em . . . which was a big hit . . . But then it broke . . . and everyone fell apart. . . ."

Oh, it was a happy-sad state of affairs, it was true. Now here she was: a suburban mom blasting hipster music while cleaning the kitchen, somehow trying to attain that thread of grooviness that she had once had. Didn't she have it, once?

•

After the kids have their dinner, it starts to rain again. The children head to the TV room to see what's on while Margaret rifles through Stephen's bookshelf to find "The Night Before Christmas."

In Gramps's room, Margaret starts to close the windows that she'd opened a little earlier. "Leave them," says Gramps.

Margaret stands there. The gray-green light engulfs the trees and the garage. There is an electricity in the drizzle.

Margaret sits down on the edge of the bed next to her father and begins, the singing hush of the rain outside.

> " 'Twas the night before Christmas, when all through the house
> Not a creature was stirring—not even a mouse;
> The stockings were hung by the chimney with care,
> In hopes that Saint Nicholas soon would be there;
> The children were nestled all snug in their beds,
> While visions of sugar-plums danced in their heads—"

"Brains," says Arthur, butting in.

"What?"

"It should say *brains*."

Margaret wasn't sure. Perhaps her father was using his own creative license, editing as he saw fit, throwing in a suggestion of how it should sound. "You think brains sounds better?" offers Margaret, as if to a child.

"No," says Gramps. "The original word is *brains*. Originally, that's what was written."

"Mmm. . . ."

"*Mmm*, indeed. I'm telling you so. Read on."

Margaret continues, "'And Ma in her kerchief and I in my cap—'" and like she's a pied piper, one by one her children come drifting into the room, settling about quietly on the bed and the floor like cats waiting to be fed.

> "Away to the window I flew like a flash,
> Tore open the shutters and threw up the sash.
> The moon on the breast of the new-fallen snow
> Gave the luster of midday to objects below . . ."

When she finishes, Gramps has his eyes closed. Margaret motions to the kids to move out of the room. She looks around, some Christmas amid the summery light. As she clicks the light off, her father speaks. "I don't want to discuss it," he says. "That's plenty." He nods to them, opening his eyes droopily for a moment to see Stephen look at him with a nervous smile, but Gramps is nodding to a gas station attendant circa 1940 who's selling him night crawlers. "Thank you. Thank you very much," says Gramps, and then he is in a skiff with an outboard going fishing, alone, one of the nicest places he's been in a long time, skimming along the water, flying over it like a bird about to dive, the light shimmering along it in chips.

·

In the late evening, Brian reads what's posted on the door of the fridge. "Hazey Swivel?" He raises an eyebrow. "Sounds like fun," he says, eating some cantaloupe straight out of the halved melon, leaning back against the counter.

"Oh," says Margaret. "You mean like a sex thing?"

Brian shrugs. "No." He raises an eyebrow again at her, and for a moment she feels the thrill of wanting to run up the stairs and get in bed, to stand on his bare feet and kiss him passionately.

Instead she says, "It sounds like the name of a drink. Or a carnival ride."

Through the open window they hear the plastic garbage cans next door getting tipped over onto the driveway.

"Raccoons," says Brian.

"Or the Fennessys' cat," says Margaret, spacing out. They hear a dog bark down the street.

"Have you noticed that cat?" asks Brian. "It looks like David Bowie."

"It has two different-color eyes," Margaret says absently. They hear a dog bark down the street, a car peeling out in the distance. She is puzzled. She is tired.

"And that other cat, the stray," says Brian. "Have you ever noticed? That one looks like David Byrne."

"The black one," says Margaret, zombielike. "It's the shape of its head."

Stephen comes into the kitchen lazily and sits down at the table.

Brian takes another scoop of melon. He points at Stephen with his spoon as he heads out into the front hallway. "What are you still doing up?"

Margaret stares into a daze. "He took a nap today," she says vaguely. A place? A boat? A recipe? A person? Margaret stops wondering, snaps out of it. She'll simply ask him tomorrow! Of course, she thinks, it means nothing. "Sonia was here," says Margaret, spacing out.

"Isn't she here every day?"

"She actually gave him a bath."

"Isn't that what she's meant to do?"

"And Deidre was here." Margaret sighs.

"From the hospice?"

"She's nice," says Margaret lazily. "I really like her." She thinks of her father upstairs. The glass of water by his bed.

"Sweetheart," says Brian. He's struggling with something in the front hall, a package of some kind.

"What?"

"This is getting out of hand."

"What?"

"How many more do we need?"

"What?" Margaret gets up to see what he's talking about.

"This is becoming a serious problem."

"Oh," says Margaret distractedly. She watches him open a large rolled rug. "Oh, right. The rug stuff. Yeah."

"Wow," says Brian. "This one's nice."

Margaret sighs. "I didn't know Japan put plague in fleas and unleashed them on China."

"Wow," Brian says again. "What a beautiful rug."

"Did you know that?"

Brian doesn't need to say yes. He knows everything. Instead, as he moves around to roll out the rug, he asks, with an amused expression, "What made you think of that, my darling?"

"That rug with the cocaine. Remember? Why was I afraid of anthrax?"

"Everyone's afraid of anthrax," says Brian, surveying the rug excitedly.

She smells the sweet, almost rotten smell of Brian's melon sitting on the front hall table. It occurs to her. The plate of scrambled eggs that her father barely touched. The little pieces of cheddar cheese she ended up eating herself. The slices of cucumber. The bean soup where, honestly, the beans were undercooked. "You know something?" says Margaret. "I don't think Dad's actually eaten anything since he got here." She pauses. "I mean, I've given him stuff." At this realization, she feels as though she might throw up. It's like someone playfully socked her in the stomach, but it hurts. How could she have let this happen? She rises abruptly and goes outside to stand on the front porch.

In the dark, the spray of the rain mists onto everything, almost silently. The trees droop in the dark shadows. The rosy light of the streetlamp down the road is smothered in the moisture, a glowing globe with indeterminate edges. Night is everywhere, crouching in the dormers, straddling the rooftops, clinging to raindrops and the undersides of leaves, to every particle of air that floats in and out of the house, over the quiet streets, and upward into the blanketing night sky that looks both limitless and near.

13

In their apartment, Max and Chloe are having sex. Chloe feels impatient, only marginally aroused. Looking up at Max's face on top of her, his head and body moving in a sort of repeating oval, swooping over and over in a robust movement that ordinarily transports her, right now the whole thing feels perfunctory. She notices other things, like the dampness on her pillow from the rain outside the cracked window, the hangnail on her baby toe that keeps getting caught on the sheets like a fishhook. Worse, she senses that Max doesn't even sense her impatience.

"Did that feel good?" she asks him angrily afterward.

"Um," says Max, his heart sinking. "Yeah."

She rolls away from him. She doesn't know what else to say. The tears begin, quietly and in the dark, as she stares at the bricks on the wall, the same bricks she always stares at, tracing the vague outlines of the dimly lit mortar making Ts and backward Ls, unfinished capital Cs and solid Hs like field goals.

Max's tired hand falls heavily onto her hip, pats it a couple of times, and soon thereafter Chloe hears his heavy breathing. She bumps him with her butt, wanting to rouse him, wanting him to say something. "Um . . . Max?" she whispers. She turns around to face him. "Max?" He's deeply asleep. She uses her voice at regular volume, a little stern, and shakes his shoulder. "Max."

His eyes flicker open, then close again. Chloe starts crying. "I don't feel good," she tells him.

"Ohhh," he says sleepily. "It's okay, Clo," and puts his arm around her.

She wiggles out from under his arm. "Max!" she says again.

He's returned to heavy breathing already. She tries coughing close to his ear. No response. She pinches him a little. "So what is it?" she asks.

She's up on her elbows. Max doesn't answer. Could he truly be sound asleep already? Did he drink a lot of beer? She hadn't noticed. "Max," she says, controlled and close up, as though being firm with a dog.

"What is it?" he mutters.

"Please don't sleep right now. What have you been *doing*?"

"Doing?"

"Every time I call you at work, you're never there. You don't pick up your cell phone—"

"I've been busy," he says mildly, closing his eyes again, an almost tranquil, close-lipped smile on his face.

"Busy? Plus, you never call us anymore."

"Us?"

"Me and *Rex*! Remember him?"

Max takes a deep breath. "Oh, Chloe."

"Wake *up*! I hate to sound like a nag, but I also don't want to be standing around like an idiot."

"Standing around?"

"We're married people, Max. I want to address things."

"You think I'm seeing someone."

"Are you?"

"No," says Max. He pauses, his face apparently wide-awake now, his eyes defensive and beady in the dark. "I've been seeing *three different people*, Chloe."

For a moment she believes him. Her entire body seems to rigor-mortis itself, then relaxes at the sight of the sarcasm in the positioning of his mouth. Then she feels simply nervous, a soda-froth whirlpool, sick to her stomach.

Max continues. "The four of us have sex together, all the livelong day, in different hotels."

Chloe pauses for a moment, looking at his face, his handsome mouth. "That's not funny," she says, and turns to face the wall again.

Max is silent for long enough that Chloe turns around to say, "*Something's* going on. For the record, I'm noticing. Note me noticing," she says tearfully. "Since you hardly notice *me* anymore," she says, starting to cry again. For a moment, Max can't help but hear a strain of comedy in her high voice, her tearfulness.

"Maybe I don't notice you enough," he says, closing his eyes again.

Chloe sniffles toward the wall. "And your dad's basically *dying*, and you haven't even really said anything about it."

"What's there to say?"

"Anything. I don't know. Something."

In the quiet, some dreamy whimpers come scampering out of Rex's crib.

"Great," says Chloe.

"He won't wake up," says Max. "He's dreaming or something."

"Okay, expert," says Chloe, wondering how she'll ever finally fall asleep.

Her mind ambles into the day she's just completed and winds up thinking of Margaret's house, the bump still there on her head—why was Edie always sort of rude to her?—Mr. Bramble on the chaise. Did Mr. Bramble have a feeling, she wondered, of how long he would live? Do dying people think about that? Or do they just take each moment as it comes and try to avoid thinking about dying, just as she was trying right now to keep herself from thinking of Max, lying beside her, and the thoughts about him that shook her up.

Max takes a deep breath. Couldn't Chloe just leave him alone? Did marriage really mean 24/7 attention and consideration? Of course not! Well, yes, it did. He knew it did. What was wrong with him? And what would be the worst thing that could happen if he just told Chloe the truth? People quit their jobs all the time! Why couldn't he be proud of it, and then she'd be proud of him? If he'd just told her from the beginning, the day he did it, that would be a different story. Now he'd sunken himself into a mass of quicksand. It wasn't *that* irresponsible; he had a tiny bit of savings to fall back on, right? Plus, he didn't *like* it there. Jake was a jerk!

The thing about marriage was that *his* business was all *her* business now, and that was hard to get his head around. Not all marriages were that way, he thought to himself. Some married people carry on with their own affairs (*business* affairs) all day long and then meet at the end of the day, often not discussing a thing about what they accomplished. That wasn't strange. But he knew. He knew that if Chloe had been moonlighting some modeling job and not telling him about it, he'd be suspicious. What was he hiding? What was he doing? He wasn't sure. Was he hiding that he was ashamed? He didn't want to think about it. Why doesn't *she* go get a job? Why was it such a given that *he* make all the money anyway? He could take care of Rexie. It certainly wasn't that hard, as far as he could tell.

Why couldn't he and Chloe just relax and lie together, enjoy each other, instead of being immersed in all this tension, all these small tart remarks that chipped away at the other's soul. "I can *do* it, thank you." Or his own dismissive, "Oh, Chloe." All brewing resentment and withdrawal. If things didn't feel so brittle. . . . He tried to remember his wedding day, the warm, heightened happiness he felt at City Hall. Chloe was always smiling at him then instead of frowning. How could he get her to smile at him again? She was right. Sometimes he purposely didn't look at her so he wouldn't have to see that frown. In fact, he wasn't sure of the last time he actually made specific eye contact with her.

Max tossed in the bed, away from his wife. Did his parents ever feel this way? Of course. Right? Max didn't notice his mother frowning at his father very much. But then his father never pretended to go to work for three weeks. His father. Chloe was right, Max wasn't addressing it. How *to* address it? I'll think about him right now, thinks Max. Will that do me any good? A sadness wells up in him for a moment, thinking of Rex, thinking of his dad, thinking of his own new little family and the regular distance he feels from his wife. Like Chloe, Max thinks of earlier in the day. He pictures his father on the chaise, summons up the scene of Flo bringing him over a rose that broke off the trellis. "Careful of the horns, Gramps," she'd said.

"I will certainly be careful of the *horns*," he said, holding the flower on his lap.

Flo shrugged. "It's pretty. Right, Gramps?"

"How old are you, child?"

"Free," she said, holding up four fingers.

"Free?" he asked. He gently pushed down her pinkie for the correct number of fingers. "I thought . . . you were only one."

"I'm free!"

He frowned. "Are you sure you're not only two?"

Flo was smiling, nodding a lot. "It's a buddhaful flower, right, Gramps?"

"Mmm."

"But it's not perfect. 'Cause look, it ripped. And this part's all floppy."

"Perfect things are never *buddhaful,* as you say," said Gramps. His old finger, the pad of it puffy and leathered, a little bit deflated like a lion's paw, touched one of the thorns gingerly, then pressed a little harder to feel the point.

"Right, Gramps. Ripped stuff's best."

"Yes."

"Ripped stuff's my favorite."

"Of course. Me too."

"But you can't go running all over town ripping things up."

"No, you cannot."

"Wouldn't it be funny if all around the town everyone was crying, and they like cried so much they filled up rivers? All around the town?"

"That would be . . . not funny. No."

14

From the porch on Moss Island, chez Woods, Mimi and Edie can see the fog coming in, a wispier band of darkness that smothers the lights across the harbor. Mimi is on her third glass of wine. Looking at Edie, sitting with her on the porch, she almost feels as if her old friend Florence will come and join them at any moment.

She'd met Florence when Howard and Arthur were lawyers together in New York. She and Howard were already married with two babies. "A glamorous dancer" was how Howard had described Arthur's new, younger girlfriend. When they first met in Central Park, Florence was wearing a yellow dress the color of a taxicab. A colored pencil (turquoise green) held her hair in a chignon. Arthur's dapper gray hair made him look older, which he was, yet it was clear to Mimi even then, as she came walking toward them down the path, that the two of them shared what people look for, a certain tribal similarity, a particular charge that Mimi could feel buzzing out at her when she stood near them.

Florence had taken off her shoes because the little heel had snapped. "They were terrible anyway," Florence said to Mimi.

"Would you like to wear mine?" joked Arthur.

"You won't believe this," said Mimi, "but look what I have." In the white canvas bag that she carted to and from her part-time job at the museum in those days, crammed with proposals and grant applications, Mimi pulled out a pair of black rubber flip-flops that she'd picked up from a bin at the drugstore during lunch.

"Where did you come from?" Florence smiled. "Are you my fairy godmother? The sister I never had?"

It delights Mimi now, looking at this young woman, her goddaughter, listening to her talk about her job in television, the things that go on in the studio: the tantrums in the control room, things overheard in the office from the studio feed, greenroom requests of particular guests. Oysters for one pop star (at ten in the morning!). Three heads of iceberg lettuce for an upcoming starlet. Nothing red—pillows, pictures, *anything*, and no one knew why—for a solid B actor. Caffeine energy drinks for a good number of people.

Edie lights another cigarette, her feet up on the porch railing.

"Well, it's all quite a difference from when you were cooking in our little kitchen that summer," says Mimi. She looks out into the dark. "You all grow up so quickly." She sighs and, even as she says it, feels silly voicing such a cliché.

She remembers Edie—now a grown woman!—as a baby: her big wide eyes, the sweet shape of her little head, Florence carrying her in a straw bag once, like a puppy, when they went out in the boat on a picnic. Her own children were even older. Only Kate, her youngest, didn't have any children, out there in godforsaken Alaska, but that was all right.

"Isn't that a stupid thing to say?" says Mimi, reining in her thoughts. "But it's true. It all just zips by." She gets a little teary. "It's not fair that your mother got so royally gypped."

Above everything else, Edie notices the use of the word *royally*.

"And now your dear father—"

"That summer," says Edie. Despite the Vaseline-lens effect of the wine, Edie feels her heart begin to thud in her chest. She knows she's about to say it. "That summer," she says again—she's a little short of breath—"there was something I wanted to ask you about."

"Yes?" says Mimi.

"I found something."

"Found something?"

"There were some papers."

"Some papers?"

"That seemed to indicate some kind of an adoption or something."

"Oh, dear," says Mimi, without a pause.

"Oh, dear?" Edie says gently.

"Yes. Yes, I know what you're talking about."

"You do?"

"This is something your mother was in charge of."

"In charge of?"

"This is something your mother planned to talk to you about."

"To me?"

"And your brother. And your sister."

"Are we all adopted?" Like that, the question just comes out, thinks Edie, and, buzzed warm with wine, she feels the lighter for it. After all, it's only a question, words strung together. What took so long to string the words together?

"Yes. No. Not exactly," says Mimi.

"The papers were weird. They were unclear and weird."

"Why didn't you ask your mother about them?"

"I planned to, I guess. Eventually." Edie's heart no longer feels as though it's thudding, galumphing along in thwacks.

Mimi takes a deep breath. "Do you think you should talk to your father about this?"

"Do you?" asks Edie.

"Those were legal papers."

"Legal papers?"

"Howard drew them up. You see, your mom—well, I guess, here we go—had trouble getting pregnant."

"She did?"

"So your mom and dad found someone else."

"To carry us?"

"Bear with me," says Mimi, trying to clear her mind. She looks out into the dark. She pictures her old friend's face. "Florence," Mimi says out loud, then settles into her chair to remember.

They had been walking. Here and there among the trees dead firs had fallen, silver-barked with lopped-off branches, their stiff trunks cradled in the feathery green limbs of younger trees, frozen like a finale to a modern dance routine.

Florence walked along one tire track while Mimi walked a few paces ahead of her on the other. The Maine fog was lifting. The women wore blue jeans and canvas sneakers, their flared pant legs darkened with a stripe of moisture around their ankles from swishing through the dewy grass. On Mimi, a pink wool sweater. On Florence, a thin yellow raincoat, unzipped. The two women's clothing the only bright colors amid the muted grays and browns, the vibrant greens and piney tones of the overcast forest, hushed wet and still.

The two of them were enjoying a "Grand Real Estate Tour," as Mimi had referred to it before their departure: a brief getaway to the mainland to look at some real estate they certainly didn't intend to buy as a diversion from the monotony of the fog socking them in on Moss Island. The grand tour had so far consisted of the following: (1) a wet ferry ride to the mainland, (2) spending the night at the Captain Ro Motor Lodge, where they ate pizza and drank cabernet out of waxy Dixie cups while they watched *Spellbound* from their shared queen bed with its bright orange bedspread, (3) rising in the morning and driving up the coast in a burgundy rental car through misty rain, and (4) getting a little lost, backtracking, arguing briefly over directions and routes already taken before successfully finding the small nameless gas station where they were met by a big-toothed realtor named Barbara. Barbara then showed them two houses on the water. One was lovely—stone— but nevertheless tiny while the other one was dark and cabinlike with hardly any windows. Afterward Barbara took them to a pretty piece of property that sloped toward the water where there had been a farmhouse that burned down.

The final place they looked at was a fantastic empty captain's house atop a hill overlooking the bay with a wraparound porch, fireplaces in almost every room, and dense spray roses along the path leading down to a small beach of smooth stones. After lots of *oohs* and *ahs* they said good-bye to Barbara, took her card, and went for a walk along a dirt road until they came to a fork where they steered onto another road, more grass than dirt, knowing it was curving toward the water.

They'd been walking for about fifteen minutes through the windless woods. Thick ferns, beautiful ones, bellied up to the bases of trees in clumped islands.

In the distance, through the basket weave of woven branches, just in front of the water, was a shack or a cabin. "Mmmm," said Mimi, nibbling on the inside of her cheek. "A boathouse? It looks like a barn."

She moved without hesitation into the thick brush. "Maybe there's a beach over there."

"My God, you're fearless, Mimi. You should have been a mountain climber," said Florence, watching Mimi's head disappear into the woods.

"What on earth do I have to fear?" Mimi called over her shoulder.

"Just the way you forage on through, bushwhacking like an explorer."

"I love the woods." Mimi giggled. "And I live in the city! You forget that I'm a country girl, after all."

"It's the same way that you swim in freezing cold water every day."

"It's wonderful!"

Then, out of the trees, came a familiar sound that was completely unexpected there, completely nonsensical. Both of them froze to listen, stretched up taller, women in the wilderness suddenly, turning their heads to listen better with animal instinct.

"It's a baby crying," said Mimi.

"Yes," said Florence. "So I suppose there are people in that cabin."

"One would hope." Mimi smiled. "Let's go see."

"Oh. We don't need to bother them."

"Come on, Florence. A little *exploring*, for God's sake."

"Oh, Mimi, let's keep going," she said, nodding in the direction of the worn road. "The last thing those people want is a visit from us. It's probably a young couple, walking around in the nude."

The baby was wailing now. Mimi had already decided, was already smashing through the underbrush. The baby's cry seemed to be entering her body like X-ray waves, slivers of memory broadsiding her as she lifted branches and crouched under them. The nervous energy that would accumulate itchily in her body as she listened to her children cry, trying to train them to go to sleep on their own. She remembered Kate, the baby, standing screaming in her white crib in the middle of her peach-wallpaper bedroom, crying before a nap, so stubborn she probably never ended up taking one, and Mimi finding Jane—she must have been about five—sitting with her legs crossed in the hallway outside Kate's door. Jane looked up at her mother as she approached. "I'm keeping watch, Mommy," she had told Mimi, her little-girl face all business, "since you're making her cry so much."

"Are you coming, slowpoke?" Mimi called, a hand on her hip, waiting.

Florence found Mimi's trodden path and followed it. "Here I come," she answered.

The baby's howl suddenly seemed more urgent, its pitch more that of a toddler, less rattling than an infant's. As Mimi moved quickly, she turned her head awkwardly into the tip of a dead branch that poked the side of her forehead. She put her sleeve to it and pressed, thinking it must be a toddler having a tantrum. The parents must have taken a fork away from its little hands, or forbidden him to climb a certain table or chair. "Hurry up," called Mimi. "I'm going to knock on the door."

"Go knock. I'm right here," answered Florence, almost there, and came to Mimi's side at the door—a barn door at the front of what was clearly a neglected boathouse, with a ramp that sloped over rocks into the sea at high tide.

Mimi put her head close to the door, one ear up against its bleached gray wood. "Hello?" she called. The crying stuttered for a moment, then stopped. "Hello?" she asked. Then the crying began again with a flared screech.

Mimi said, "It's okay, sweetheart," through the wooden slats. She nudged Florence. "Just open the door," Mimi said to her. Mimi looked around hastily. The tide was low, making the rocky beach look drained and dirty. The rocks were covered in seaweed. Farther out, the water was green and still. Was anyone anywhere? "Open the door!" she told Florence.

"I'm trying," said Florence, hunched over the iron handle, yanking at it. "Here," said Florence. "Help me push *down*—"

The door skittered open. Standing before them on the gray floorboards, stamping his feet quickly back and forth as he cried, was a tear-streaked baby boy—or was it a girl? Mimi thought at the time—wearing a light blue sweatshirt that fit like a dress. His eyes were magnified with tears. His mass of yellow hair made him look like an angel or a troll, glowing up out of the darkness. For a moment he stopped crying and stared up at them, stunned; then he fell backward on his bottom and started to cry again.

Mimi picked him up. "Shhh, shhhh," she told him, patting his back. His diaper was sopping.

Mimi remembers calling, "Hello?" up toward the rafters; screaming, "Hello?" out the big open door to the beach, her voice echoing over the flat calm.

·

Upstairs in the guest room, Edie surveys the top shelf of the bookcase that serves as her bedside table: Lampedusa's *The Leopard*, a biography of Margaret Wise Brown, Richard Yates's *Revolutionary Road*, Evelyn Waugh's *Scoop*, art books on the Wyeths, Eve Peri, Fairfield Porter, Gardner Cox, Robert Motherwell, *Architecture of the Penobscot Bay*. She hasn't read any of them. She opens up the architecture book, then decides to have a cigarette instead.

She smokes at the windowsill, not thinking about her mother or her father, or her brother or sister, but remembering a guy she had slept with in college. She met him at a party she didn't mean to go to; she was dropping off an essay that someone had paid her to type and stayed for a beer. He was in New York for a long weekend from Chicago, where he went to school, staying at his aunt's apartment, watching her cats and visiting friends. He and Edie fell together. They playacted as a couple for three days, staying in bed, making meals in the kitchen, feeding the cats. The second night they were together, he went out to buy some beer and came back to the apartment with a six-pack and a new red dress for Edie, asking her to put it on with her hair up. When she came back into the living room wearing it, the expression on his face changed completely, glazed over, and without speaking he pushed her forward onto the back railing of the couch, hooked aside her underwear, and screwed her with an intensity that was different from the rest of the weekend, like real lust.

It was sort of a big deal for her—she didn't have boyfriends—and he was fairly attentive, at least physically. Since the weekend was fleeting, she thought about him a lot; whether she was actually thinking about *him* or the idea of him, she wasn't sure. She thought less about what happened after: how when she went to meet his flight a few weeks later—they had spoken a little bit on the phone and she planned to surprise him—when she went to meet his flight, she stood in baggage claim watching the people from his flight come down an escalator, streaming out, one after the next, none of them him. Later, back in her dorm room, she called his cell phone, planning to leave a casual message. A woman answered with many voices in the background, men and women, mostly women laughing, and then Edie could hear the woman's heels or boots clicking through hallways and rooms to find him and give him the phone. "Hey!" he said jovially to Edie. "I got here yesterday. Or, no, the day before." She thought of the airport, the empty baggage carousel after everyone had taken their bags. "We should try to get together," he said, sounding as though he wouldn't be trying very hard. It was only later that Edie thought of that time with the red dress in a different way. He hadn't wanted *her* like that. He was dressing her up, pretending she was someone else.

Now, with all the information that Mimi has just planted in her head, why, Edie wonders, is she still thinking about this? Why is she sitting here mooning over someone—hardly able to remember his face let alone the sound of his voice—almost ten years later? Enough of that. What was wrong with her and men? If only she was attracted to women. She had only had one boyfriend, David, who she went out with for most of senior year, then on and off sporadically for a couple of years. He would seem really engaged sometimes and then his mind would drift off, wanting to be around groups of people all the time, falling asleep next to her in bed, side by side, barely interested in touching her. She was old enough to know it was her own choices, her own decisions, that put her in places like that—lying next to some guy, wondering why he wasn't more attracted to her, being used for the weekend by someone pretending she was someone else—but what was up? She told herself that it didn't matter if she never fell in love. It didn't matter if someone ever loved her like that.

"That guy should want to have sex with you all day long," she remembers Margaret saying to her, when she mentioned that David wasn't always interested.

Edie smiled, appreciating her sister's protectiveness. "That . . . would be nice," Edie muttered in return. Margaret always had men around. And when she had problems with them, the problems seemed fun and exciting, not tedious or psychological. Then, to top it all off, she met Brian, her obvious mate forever, with his perfect imperfections.

She forces herself to think of something else. Her mind automatically turns to consider her daily caloric intake, her numbers often way off, starting with the coffee on the airplane (85, with milk), the small bag of roasted peanuts (150?), the half crab roll at the ferry landing (God only knows, 300? 800?) She makes herself attempt to consider what Mimi has just told her. But how to approach it? Where to begin? What about her dad?

She thinks of the photograph she has of her mother holding her as a newborn, her mother's gentle smile looking triumphant and weary. She thinks of Margaret. Was it too late to call her? I'll wait, thinks Edie, to see her in person. Or maybe that's silly. This is big news, right? Is Margaret asleep? She imagines Margaret asleep in her king-sized bed in her Bright family life. Edie places her own head in the same place, sees it alone in a bed on a pillow.

•

In the morning, the fog's gone, blown out by an early wind that now flutters the white curtains in Mimi's kitchen. Mimi shakes some coffee grounds out of a Ziploc bag into the coffeemaker. The disclosed story from the previous night hangs lively in the air around her. It makes Mimi feel younger and light-footed. "So . . . did you make any plans?" she asks Edie kindly.

"Not really," Edie answers. Edie's sitting at the open window with another cigarette. Mimi smoked for years so is sympathetic. She brings her an ashtray, places it on the sill. "I guess I should go home," says Edie. She inadvertently clonks her cast loudly against the windowsill.

"Goodness," says Mimi. "Does it hurt?"

"No."

"Where will you go? Back to your apartment?"

"To Margaret's." Out the window, Edie sees a small rowboat moving toward a dock, its oars dipping in and out of the water like wings. "I don't know whether to tell them or wait until he dies," she says.

"Now that you know, you should tell them," says Mimi simply, pouring water into the tank.

Mimi's frankness—the implied simplicity of it all or something in Mimi's tone—annoys Edie. "Well," Edie says, "I've known something was up for years and never said anything."

A sunny wind balloons the curtains. "That's remarkable," says Mimi, looking out the window with the view of the water, shaking her head. Again, Edie is annoyed at the comment. Remarkable that Edie's kept a sort of secret from her brother and sister for so long? Mimi was the one keeping secrets. Remarkable that Edie was considering waiting until after her father died to tell her siblings? Remarkable that Mimi had told her goddaughter a secret that her friend had made her promise never to tell anyone? Was the weather remarkable? The day? Or was there simply something remarkable out the window that Edie couldn't see: a gigantic cattle boat, a sloop knifing through the bay, the odd appearance of a luxury cruise ship like a chunk of hotel, bobbing like a giant ice cube in the water? What exactly, Edie wanted to know, was *remarkable*? But Edie didn't ask. She didn't want to get into it if it was what first jumped into her mind: her knowing for so long that something was up, finding those papers, and not saying anything for so long, even when her mother was alive.

"Do you have to get back to work?" Mimi asks her.

"We have next week off as well," says Edie.

"What a lovely long vacation you get!"

"It's the payoff for working so much the rest of the year."

"It's marvelous."

Edie watches her mother's friend heat up some milk at the stove. She can tell that Mimi is relieved. Mimi might as well be humming. Right on cue, Mimi looks at Edie plainly and says, "I know it all must be a shock for you. Or I don't know how it is. But I must say, knowing that you know makes *me* feel a little lighter. And relieved."

"I can't believe Dad never said anything."

"He made a promise to your mother, just like I did," she answers breezily. "Plus, you know your father. Leaving well enough alone. Coffee?"

Edie nods. The red wine from last night has left her with a mild headache but, more important, has left her feeling long and lean since she didn't eat very much yesterday. She feels taut, at the ready, her feet flexible and strong, armed with information she somehow hasn't allowed to penetrate, information she sort of wants to keep to herself, to keep as her own.

"I guess I'll fly back down." She sighs. She looks at her small bag, crammed with magazines and garbage, in the same place where she left it when she first arrived, propped against a chair leg in the kitchen. It looks game and ready to get back on a plane. Edie reaches for it, looks inside to start cleaning it out a little. "Do you want any of these magazines?" she asks Mimi.

"Do they talk about gardening?"

"Gardening? No. They're tabloids."

"Oh, God," says Mimi, "I hardly have the energy for my own problems, let alone theirs." Mimi pours some coffee. "Shall we call your sister?"

"I'd rather tell her in person," says Edie. "I'd rather tell her when I'm home."

"I'm thinking of your father," says Mimi. "To check in."

Edie remembers when Mimi called him in California, when she was there picking him up. From where she stood, Edie could hear Mimi's voice come tinselly through the receiver, tiny and high. "Hello, *Arthur*! It's your old friend Mimi Woods!"

Arthur listened, smiling sideways. "*Mi chiamano Mimi*," he sang softly with a smirk, sitting sunken on the couch with the receiver to his ear. He looked at Edie. "I have your goddaughter here," he said.

As Edie completes the memory, something enters her, softly, gently, a tenderness of paternity, thinking of his face, the idea of him sick at Margaret's house, the image of her father as a young man, holding her as an infant with his sleeves rolled up, the two other toddlers around, her mother scooping them up. Her father was *her* father. He was *hers* like no one else.

•

On the ferry back to the mainland, Edie stands in the stern, watching the sea boil up from the propellers in an inviting froth. Farther out, the water is navy blue, almost black in places, dark green in the near spots where the white foam erupts on its surface. Was it silly to be leaving after spending only one night with Mimi? She could get more details later. She's distracted. She realized moments ago that she left her bag and her pocketbook in the ferry terminal on Moss Island. Miraculously, she has her cash card, credit card, and license in her pocket, which is basically all she needs to get home. She hasn't made herself vomit for almost three days. She hasn't eaten much either. Her cast is starting to look ratty.

She feels full of vagueness but full of new history, inflated with it. She's still not sure if she'll tell Margaret when she gets to New Jersey tonight. Where would she begin? "Hey, Margaret! Get a load of this one!" No. "Once upon a time, Mom and Mimi came across this kid in the woods." No. "Did you ever wonder, Maggie, if Mom really wasn't our real mom?" Or, "Guess what? Mom and Dad hired a *surrogate mother* to carry us all!" Or, "Boy, do I have a lot to tell you!" Or, "Did Mom ever say anything to you about her labors when we were born?"

The hum of the engine and the roiling ocean mesmerize her. For a moment, standing there at the stern alone, Edie sees, ghosty-like, her mother and father standing at the rail together, looking out over the water. Their backs are to her. Her father's arm is around her mother, the wind in their hair. Her mother's head is tilted, leaning against her father, contented and relaxed. Edie wonders. Is she remembering them standing that way on a trip they took on the ferry when she was smaller? Has she seen them standing there that way before? It is the first time since Mimi told her everything that she is actually thinking of her mother and father *together*, the two of them as the people they were, newly married, her mother wanting to have a family, her father wanting to make her mother happy, the two of them going through it all to please each other.

Edie is overwhelmed by a bizarre feeling that she *is* her mother, willing to do anything. She can imagine strapping on the various-sized pillows that Mimi made for her to pretend she was pregnant. She can imagine wanting to wait to tell her own children until later in their life, or even deciding not to tell them at all. What did it matter? She did everything she could to bring them into the world, to bring them to her.

Edie starts laughing. Her mother! Her father! Seeking her out! She has never felt so touched, so special and unique, in all her life. She starts laughing and crying. They wanted her so! And yet here she stands in the stern of the boat, alone, with no one to watch her, no one to wonder what she's doing.

The hum of the ferry's engine moves down an octave as it slows. The water below looks inviting, green and calm. An assortment of docks is only a few hundred feet away across the mottled water. It seems so silly to go all the way to the ferry landing, wait for the cumbersome boat to alight, wait for the ramp to come creaking down, for each and every car to disembark, before the pedestrians are allowed off. It seems ridiculous to go through all of that when she could just . . . swim. She has her credit card and license in her pocket. And her shoes? They were sandals that were on their last legs anyhow. She slips her feet out of them, leaving them neatly poised at the edge of the stern where the boat's wake churns like Jacuzzi bubbles.

When Edie steps back, however, the sight of her sandals, solo, poised as a pair above the roar of the engine, seems too ominous. She picks them up, tosses them into the trash can next to the door to the ladies' room. She knows just the place in town where she can pick up another pair of shoes. She can even get a sundress there and a bag to put her wet stuff in. Isn't this what life is for? To do things you want to do as long as you don't hurt anyone or hurt yourself?

Edie climbs up onto the railing where she had imagined her mother and father standing, arm in arm. She glances about the ferry to be sure no one is watching. A flapping flag behind her, its halyard clinking, prompts her forward. She jumps in, dives out sideways from the railing to avoid the undertow, and then smiles broadly underwater as she arcs down and then up and begins to swim.

15

The kids all like to linger around in Gramps's room—for the most part they're surprisingly respectful and quiet—since that's where the action is, but also it's the only room with an air conditioner that really works. Only now they're not in there for the air conditioner. They're in there because Gramps is practically comatose. His body is still. His eyes are open, the eyeballs in a constant slow motion, roaming back and forth in the shape of a rainbow, searchlights on the highway, slowly and steadily, not changing their speed or pausing to focus on anything.

Earlier, he was moving but strangely unconscious, rolling over, fussing with the sheet, pulling it up and down carefully as though checking on the status of his feet. The kids and Margaret sat in there with him, weirdly transfixed, watching him gently put his head under the covers over and over like a baby learning peek-a-boo. Margaret pulled her act together enough to call Deidre, the hospice nurse.

"Floccillation," said Deidre.

"Excuse me?"

"Aimless plucking at the bed linens."

"There's a word for it?"

"I'd gather your family, Margaret."

"You would?"

"I can call your husband for you," offered Deidre, and Margaret had the odd notion, momentarily and out of place, that Deidre wanted to call Brian simply because Brian was so handsome.

Gather your family. Margaret heard it again in her head. "But that was so fast," she muttered.

"There's no timetable here, remember," said Deidre, both sweetly and sternly.

"How do I know he's not in pain?"

"Well. You don't. Usually you can sense the discomfort. It sounds to me as though your father's comfortable. But you can certainly give him the morphine if you'd like."

"But he said he didn't want it."

"Well . . ."

"Yeah?" asked Margaret. She wanted to be told what to do.

"Morphine can cause bad dreams and images, remember. Do you want me to come over?"

Margaret paused. She thought of Brian. She thought of Max and Edie. "We're all right. For now, I guess. Thanks, Deidre."

She calls Brian. Brian's assistant. His front desk. Voice mail. Edie. Edie's cell phone. The Woodses' in Maine. Why in the world don't they have an answering machine? Max. Max at work. Max's cell phone. She leaves a flurry of messages. Chloe at home. She looks up Chloe's cell phone on the master list she's posted on the side of the kitchen cabinet. Where *is* everyone?

Margaret goes back into the room, the air AC-crisp, holds her father's hand for a while and then has the strange feeling that she is holding him back, literally, as though she is the one staying still, stagnant there at the bedside like a post here on earth, a cleat on a dock, while he is actively moving away.

She decides to go make a pitcher of lemonade, carry it up to the kids, try calling everyone again. As she's listening to her voice-mail messages—maybe she missed one of their calls, the air conditioner is so loud; why didn't she take the phone into the room with her?—she's stacking plastic glasses to carry them upstairs,

"Um, Mom?"

She holds her finger out, shushing Sarah, trying to hear the message. Flo tends to press all the buttons on the phone, inadvertently toying with the volume adjustment. Margaret can make out that it's a client, a woman she chose some colors for. From the tone alone, Margaret can't make out whether the woman's thrilled or disappointed. She is adamant about something, however, her pitch rising and falling like a heart rhythm.

"Mom?"

"Shhh," says Margaret, vaguely catching the woman's saying an emphatic "of *all* the choices!" But again, is she pleased or horrified?

"Mom?"

"Something something . . . to come down the hall to this Owl Feather *gray* . . . something something something . . . that deep Hanover *blue*—"

"Mom?"

Straining to hear, Margaret walks into the front hallway, away from Sarah's gentle insistence. With the woman's faint voice singsongy in her ear, Margaret notices a figure, a plump woman's torso sitting like Humpty Dumpty at the edge of their stoop down by the sidewalk, facing the street. Some ash-blond hair pulled back in a little piglet ponytail. The torso is pear-shaped, the T-shirt the color of an Anjou. Margaret pauses at one of the long rectangular windows that frame the front door. Is it someone resting? Is she okay? The way the shoulders are slumped down, stricken, resigned, the weariness of an overweight body.

Margaret hangs up the phone with the *bleep* of the button. She waits a moment, watching to see if the woman is about to rise and carry on to walk away somewhere. How long has she been sitting there?

"Mom?"

Maybe the woman is overheated, in need of some water. Margaret opens the front door. The glare of the sunshine. The waft of summer heat.

"Ma-*uhm*," says Sarah.

Margaret peers down the walkway to where the woman sits. She tries to say it politely. "Can I help you?" Margaret calls to her.

The woman sits up a little straighter.

"I mean," says Margaret, "do you need some help?"

When the face turns around and starts to rise, Margaret sees that it's the woman who hit their van in the Range Rover. Margaret squints at her to make sure.

"It's . . . I'm Tammy," she says, getting up. "Remember me?"

"I remember. Tell me. Were you in our trash the other day?"

"Um . . . *Mom?*"

Tammy comes lumbering up the front walk, stiff-kneed, shaking her head back and forth. She heaves out a world-weary sigh. "I rang the bell before and no one answered," she says.

Margaret clears her throat, unsure of how to approach this. "I've heard that you have no insurance," she says, standing in the doorway, the first thing that truly comes to mind.

Tammy's mouth forms a grin, more like a wince at the doom and gloom of the cloud that seems to hover around her body. Her voice is high, speaking through the grinning wince. "Yeah, that's—"

"Mom!" At this point Sarah pokes her mother in the thigh.

"What *is* it, Sarah?" She looks down at her daughter.

Sarah looks up at her with narrow eyes, whispers urgently. "Gramps *is breathing funny*, Mom."

The screen door slams on the figure of Tammy on the threshold. Margaret hurries up the hall but first nonsensically checks the baby monitor, realizes it's not making a sound, swats it, and hears crinkling static, a tinkling lullaby from a mobile, probably the kid two doors down.

When she comes into the room, Stephen and Flo are standing at the foot of the bed. Gramps is not struggling for breath but his breathing has completely changed. It's not breathing anymore but rather a series of breaths linked together rhythmically, small socks of gasps, soft pops of inhales, gentle puffs of pleased surprise similar to the sound one might make on opening a welcome gift while trying to be quiet about one's reaction. *Hup!* A pause in between. *Hup!* His eyes are no longer roaming. Instead they are fixed and specific. Dulled. He is alive, but he is gone.

When Margaret leaves the room to get the telephone, she hears someone downstairs cough. She walks down the stairway halfway, far enough to see Tammy standing at the edge of the living room, looking at some pictures on the wall.

"Hello?" says Margaret. She stays on the stairs, craning her neck down. "Right now's *really* not a good time to talk," Margaret tells her.

"Oh," says Tammy. "Oh." But she stands there.

"You can let yourself out."

"Oh. I'm not in any hurry."

"Please let yourself out," says Margaret.

"Huh. Okay," says Tammy, implying that Margaret's tone is huffy.

Margaret goes into the master bedroom to get the phone. When she glances out the window, she sees Tammy's lumpen figure settling down on the stoop. Margaret—and she wonders why she is taking the time to do this as she does it—opens their bedroom window wider and calls down to her through the screen. "Excuse me," she calls.

Tammy turns her squinting face toward the house, finds the right window with Margaret in it.

"Now is *not* a good time," Margaret yells down to her.

"I'm not in any hurry," says Tammy with a smile.

"Hurry or no hurry, I can't talk to you right now."

"Oh. Is it one of those kids?" asks Tammy, with a gosh-darn-it quality in her tone.

"Please go," says Margaret, meaning, Get the eff off our stoop. She feels like she's about to cry. Her tone, however, is one of maternal no-nonsense. "Now," she says firmly, as though commanding Sarah to give her back a lighter or a sharp knife. Margaret closes the window enough so a child won't fall out of it and walks away without turning around to see Tammy's response.

In the whirring AC room, Margaret calls Brian's assistant again and learns that he's already on the train home anyway. She leaves a message for Edie on her cell phone—Come *now*—and leaves another message for Max. She sits in there on the bed, reading the paper but not reading it, and the kids come in and out, still docile, moving about as quietly as cats. Sarah has a giant drawing pad down on the floor by the door that Flo sits on as though it's a raft.

When the pauses between his huffs start to grow longer—it's almost as if there's no exhale happening, only sips of air, inflating, inhaling— Margaret starts to think that this might be it. Could it be? What about the death rattle? The agony? Should she call for help? She calls Deidre again.

"Is your husband home?"

"He's on his way."

"Good."

When she hangs up the phone, places it on the windowsill, and looks at her father, his breathing has stopped. "Oh, man," she says softly, and goes close to him.

"He went like this, Mom," says Stephen. Stephen makes one of the *hup!* inhales and then stops, frozen, for a few moments. "And now he's just . . . like *this*." Stephen's face remains there, frozen, looking askance.

Sarah puts in her version. "Mom, he went—" and she does her rendition of the last pouf of breath, but just as she finishes it, Gramps gasps one more time. One determined, subdued, but hungry breath of air like he's about to swim the length of a pool underwater.

They all sit quietly, looking at his pleasantly surprised–looking face. "That's it, Mom? He's dead?"

Margaret touches her father's cheek. It's firm and cool as though he's just been outside on a cool day.

"Mom?"

"Yes, honey?"

"That's it?"

"Is Gramps dead?" says Sarah.

"Yes," says Margaret. She looks at the kids, the arrangement of them, three stems, looking at her calmly.

"He is?"

"Yes," she says. Her head feels as though it's about to melt apart into pieces, starting with her throat. *Is that it?* Margaret wonders this as well. From one moment to the next, just like that?

"Can I touch him?" asks Sarah.

"Sure, honey. You all can."

Sarah hops up close to his head, practically sitting on his shoulder. She places her hand on the top of his head, cupping it proprietarily, then looks up at her mother. "Aren't you going to cry, Mom?"

"That was fast, Mom, wasn't it?" says Stephen. "I thought Gramps would be here for a while," he says. "I really thought that, Mom," he says. His eyes start to well up, a bloom of water; then the overflow quickly recedes.

"Look at his *eyes*," says Flo with nervous giddiness, as though she's entering a darkened room, as though she's awaiting a big wave coming her way at the beach.

Arthur's eyes are frozen, looking indeterminately at the upper edge of the window to his right. His mouth is open, the mouth of a dead man. Didn't the Romans stick a coin in it to pay for the passage across the Styx? Or something. Wasn't that right? He would know, but now Margaret can't ask him.

Stephen's gotten up on the bed next to Margaret. He sits on the other side of Gramps's head. "Can I close them, Mom?" His hand hovers above the old man's open eyes.

Margaret nods, thinking for a second that Stephen has seen that action too many times on TV, probably. The drama king Stephen. But then Stephen does it with such grace, such an assured unsqueamish maturity, that Margaret feels a pang of self-loathing. Why undermine her son? Why think of television?

Stephen looks up at his mother, his chin puckered like the skin of a walnut. He rests his hand roughly on Gramps's shoulder as he steadies himself, causing Gramps's body to jerk a little. "Sorry," Stephen says to him, like he might have hurt him.

Margaret smiles at her son. "He can't feel it, honey," she says.

The four of them are sitting quietly when the door opens and Brian comes into the room, tugging at the tie around his neck, looking at everyone expectantly, sweat like a sealant shining on his forehead. At the sight of him, Margaret begins to sob.

"Daddy!" says Flo. She runs to him. He picks her up.

16

In the city, Max is home, going in late to "work" since Chloe has a toothache she has to get checked out. Father and son have headed out to the coffee shop around the corner to get some donuts. Max carries Rex on his shoulders. Occasionally a young woman, a mother on her way to work, smiles at him. Or maybe she's single and flirting (it was true, after all, what he'd heard before Rex was born; kids are chick magnets). But for the most part—well, for the most part people don't notice father and son at all, but the majority of the people who do look at them do a double-take; they look up at Rex's little face up there atop his father's stride, then look back down at Max as if to ask, Is that *all right*? Won't that child *fall*?

Max noticed a similar thing when Chloe was pregnant. People would stare at her, fascinated, as though she were some kind of wild animal, as though the sight of a pregnant belly on a young woman was a window toward another world, as though looking at her made some people ask themselves, *That's* still going on somewhere? Somewhere humans are actively *breeding*? It was completely different, no novelty whatsoever, in neighborhoods like Park Slope, or out in Magnolia Heights where Margaret lived, where the sidewalks and streets were clogged with children under ten, where there were pregnancies and kids all over the place, strollers parked doubled up, playgrounds with rubber floors, toy stores and ice cream shops, franchises of Gymboree and Paintin' the Plates. That was the kind of place he needed to move his family to: somewhere, anywhere, where strollers were left safely parked outside buildings or houses, where playgrounds were clean and looked like wooden castles or tree houses, where Chloe could make friends with people who were doing the same thing that she was.

It occurs to Max that he is running out of money. He is lying to his wife. His father is dying half an hour away, and here he is holding on to Rex's little ankles with one hand like a bow tie, pushing the door open to a coffee shop.

Practically before he sees her figure, he can tell it is happening again, the spectral presence somehow there when he opens the door. The first person he catches sight of is a young woman sitting in the corner next to the window. Her back is to him, her head dropped forward a little bit, reading something, revealing the back of her neck. Her hair is short, boyish, and he can see the tiny clasp of a thin necklace catch some sun and glint at him across the room. His insides flutter. The shape of her head, the shape of her neck bowed forward, the positioning and contour of her arms and the way they are rested on the table, one wrist flexed to the side, is his mother. A young version of his mother. He takes in all of this in a matter of seconds, wanting to look longer, not wanting to look anymore.

At the counter, Max puts Rex down so he can put his nose to the glass and ogle the pastries. Max glances them over as well, as though the pastry case is a magnet, to avoid the draw of looking over at his mother's figure again. He distractedly orders the donuts and an iced cappuccino. Rex points excitedly at the glazed donut with chocolate frosting. "Eat dat!" he shouts.

The guy at the espresso machine starts talking to Max. "Hey, man," he says. "I didn't know you had kids."

Max looks at him: a fellow with a short ponytail. Surprisingly skinny calves jut out of his oversized shorts. "Do I know you?" Max asks him.

The young man faces Max. His cheeks are rosy. His face, leonine, a Helios. The fringe of little hairs around his hairline stick straight up like he's been electrocuted. "I saw you, dude," says the rosy face, "in that play last year at the Circle. You were great. I'm an actor too. I bet everyone tells you they're actors." When he says that, Max pictures him dressed up in regional theater garb, a colonist or a Renaissance player.

"Oh, no," says Max. "I'm not him. I just look like him."

"Dude," says the young actor. He solemnly (and convincingly) retracts a hand as though he just touched something hot. He probably does mime work. "Dude," he says again. "That's cool, man. I'll back off."

"No. I'm serious." Max laughs. "My name's Max Bramble." He has his wallet out anyway since he's paying. "See?" He shows the guy his license.

The young actor smiles. "Bro, I'm usually so excellent with faces!"

"Max?" The womanly voice comes from the direction of where his mother redux is sitting. He's afraid to look. Why? "Max?" it asks again.

Rex is tugging on the paper bag with the donuts. Max picks him up and turns to see—what was her name? He knew her. They worked at Intrepid Films together . . . no, she'd been an intern at Locomotion . . . she was a friend of Chloe's; they went to high school together?

"Amber," she says, reminding him as she approaches. He squints at her. The window behind her is bright light, but also there seems to be a silvery shroud of his mother—the way she's moving, the shape of her shoulders—that's been dropped down on this woman's silhouette, an angel approaching.

"Amber," he says, partly unsure of the use of her name.

When she gets closer, he can see her face with its oddly placed beauty mark: a large freckle on her eyelid there playfully when she blinks. He remembers that sexy detail, can see it through some very hip-looking pearlescent eye shadow that she's got on, and then thoroughly remembers where he knows her from. They were APs together on a pilot about partisan politics. He can picture her desk, the cute leather skirt she wore with shit-kicker boots and suede jackets lined with sheepskin, her dark complexion and fresh face making her look like she just walked down from the Andes. Her scruffy-looking Italian boyfriend with some name like Fabrizio or Matteo or Antonio.

"You cut your hair," says Max.

"Yeah," she says, touching it.

Max notices that the charm on her tiny gold necklace is the busty girl that you see on the mud flaps on trucks. Amber smiles: Healthy white teeth and pink gums. Perfect skin. How does someone get the whites of their eyes so white?

"Is this guy yours?" she asks, mussing Rex's hair.

"Yeah," says Max. Even though it's only been moments, he can't remember if he greeted her properly. Did he kiss her hello? Did he give her a hug? How well *had* he known her? Had he noticed before that there was this weird resemblance to his mother?

"What a cutie," says Amber.

Rex shoves the bag out in a clenched fist, proud of its contents. Amber smiles.

"What are you up to?" she asks Max. "Do you live around here?"

"Right around the corner," says Max.

"I saw your movie. Way back when."

"Yeah?"

"Yeah. I liked it. Whatever happened to that actress?"

"The star? I married her."

"All right!" says Amber, showing her specimen teeth. "Marcello and I got married last fall. 'Member him?"

"Congratulations. Sure," says Max. He stops Rex from pulling reams of napkins from a dispenser. "So, do you guys live around here too?" He is having a hard time looking at her. When he does, it's as though the glare is too bright.

"We live in Williamsburg," Amber's saying, "but I'm working on Eighteenth Street. Listen. Do you have a *job*?"

"What?"

"Do you want a new job?"

"What?" Max looks at her. The sly playfulness in her eye is his mother, saying, Isn't this silly? That I can just *do this*? Max quickly looks away, helps Rex climb into a chair to eat one of the donuts.

"Um. Actually," says Max—it is the first time he's saying it; he says it to Rex's interested face—"no. I don't have a job."

"But you were working with that guy at—"

"Foona Laguna. I actually quit."

"Well." Amber laughs. "*I've* got a job for you." The idea of working alongside her, Max thinks to himself, this mother thing—or is it attraction?—might be impossible. "Marcello and I are moving to Milan in, like, a month."

"Cool."

"Yeah. He's got some stuff to shoot there, and I'm putting together a documentary on his grandmother's family."

"Cool."

"Yeah. It's actually cooler than it sounds—his grandmother and stuff. I've got a grant, a production company into it. But *anyway*, I've just started this job here, which is great. It's like a *Frontline*-type series. It's not all news—not, like, *all* serious—more like mini-documentary-type things."

Max nods.

"And it actually has money"—Amber smiles—"since various backers are backing it. Bravo, for one. But *anyhoo*, I've got to leave and so do a couple of other people—no one thought it would get picked up—but here I am sitting here in the coffee shop looking at résumés on my laptop and in walks Mr. Perfect-for-the-Job."

Max is stunned. "Gee," he says. "It sounds too good to be true."

"Dead!" cries Rex, jubilant over his donut. He's called Max *Dead* ever since he started trying to say *Dad*. Max would watch him in his crib, banging a book haphazardly, his chore of pushing board book after board book through the slats of his crib like it was his godforsaken lot in life to forever empty out a crib of its contents, then strangling a stuffed animal, smashing its nose up to his own nose, looking at it cross-eyed, muttering in a deep gravelly voice, *"Dead dead dead dead."*

"Enjoying your donut?" Max asks his son.

Rex smiles, puts his hands up in the air like he's on a roller-coaster ride.

"Guess that's a yes," says Amber.

Max looks at his son dreamily.

"So," says Amber. "You interested?"

"In the job? Definitely. Is there someone I should call or something?"

"Yeah. I'll give you his name," she says, reaching into her bag. "I'm so psyched I ran into you. It's perfect! I don't know why I didn't think of you to begin with. And you're not working! This is amazing."

"Yeah. Pretty weird."

"Well," she says. She looks up at him from writing on the back of one of her cards. "Things happen for a reason," she says. Did she wink? That freckled eyelid seemed to have winked at him. He looks at Rex. Donut in his cheeks. Rex winks at him too. "Write down your number," says Amber, passing him a card.

"Good thing we came out for donuts, huh, Rexie?"

"Dat!" shouts Rex, pointing at the huge clock on the wall. "Dis!" he calls, pointing at the ceiling fan.

Amber looks at the giant clock. "Ooh," she says. "I'm almost late already." When she looks at him, it's so silly—Max feels as though he's in a schlocky movie—it is his mother speaking when Amber says lightly, "I need to say good-bye." She looks up at him with a smile. "Well . . . I'm glad I ran into you." Her eyes are the *color* of amber, hon-eyed and deep. "Have a nice job!" she jokes.

"I'm glad too," says Max. He doesn't know what to say. "Maybe I'll see you when I call this guy or whatever."

"Maybe."

"Good luck in Italy."

"Thanks. Okay. Gotta go." Max leans forward to kiss her cheek while Amber does the same thing. They end up simultaneously planting the kiss on each other's lips. They hold it there for a second, shocked—she tastes of vanilla—and then pull apart.

"Whoops," says Max.

"Well, that was sort of a little bonus." Amber laughs. "I guess I'll have to tell my husband about *that*."

"Yeah." Max smiles and, simple as that, like specks of dust being vac-uumed up to heaven in a tornado twirl, his mother has left the room. Something releases. Something unfolds. He looks at his son. Rex's face seems to have opened up somehow. The blue sky seen out the window of the coffee shop looks four-dimensional. The green leaves luffing on the tree there look endlessly active. The passers-by look eager and happy to get where they are going. There's a lovely girl cupping her hands around her eyes to peer into the window who is—who is his *wife* looking in, peering in at him, who just saw him kiss a girl, not just any girl, but someone small and dark with a perfectly proportioned strong and slight little body. Just the kind of girl that Chloe always imag-ined—if Max was ever to cheat on her—that he would be drawn to.

•

Max hurries out the door of the coffee shop carrying Rex. He can see Chloe through the sidewalk crowd, her light blue dress, rounding the corner of their street up ahead. When he and Rex turn the corner themselves, he expects to see her, slightly pigeon-toed, walking away. She's not there.

"Where'd Mommy go, Rex?" Max is full of clear energy, partly because he's afraid of Chloe's reaction but mostly because he's finally ready to tell her everything.

"Momma!" yells Rex. He found her. He points to Chloe sitting on a stoop right next to them. Max looks at her. She's not even crying.

"Hi Rexie, honey," she says sweetly.

Max looks at her. "Listen, Clo—"

"I'm not even surprised," she says, looking at her feet. "Look at me. I'm barely even upset."

"Chloe—"

"At least something's *happened*."

"Chloe—"

"Stop saying my name. But why would you bring this one with you to meet her?"

"Chloe." Max can't help smiling. She's got it all wrong. "I just ran into that girl. I worked with her on that DC thing."

"What *DC thing*."

"That show on Capitol Hill. Before I met you."

"Is she an old girlfriend?"

"No."

"What's her name?"

Max shrugs. "Amber, or something."

"Or something?"

"Amber," says Max definitively. "Her name's Amber."

"You just *ran into her*—"

"Yeah."

"And kissed her?"

"It was an accident."

"An *accident*? You mean like you crashed into each other like *two cars*?"

Max smiles. He loves his wife, the way she says things. "Sort of." He smiles, trying to touch her.

"Don't tou—" she starts to say, but looks at little Rex trying to chip black paint off of the wrought iron. Her mother always said dismissive things like that to her father: *Don't touch me.* Or, *Leave me alone.* She'd say them in front of Chloe and Chloe always noticed, felt bad for her dad. She promised herself she would never say the same sort of thing in front of Rex.

Max tries to explain. "I went to peck her on the cheek good-bye, and she did the same thing. But we met in the middle."

"How convenient," says Chloe.

Max sits down next to her. "There's a job that sounds really interesting that she told me about."

"Great."

"Chloe. Listen. I'm sorry I've been behaving so weirdly the last few weeks. I quit my job at Foona Laguna."

"You quit? Wait. Wait. Are you trying to get off the subject of *Amber*, here?"

"I quit, like, three weeks ago," says Max.

"Wait. Are you sleeping with that girl?"

"No. I just ran into her. But I quit my job, and I was afraid to tell you."

"I want to go home," says Chloe. "I don't want to talk anymore."

"Three weeks ago. I quit." Max wants to say it over and over.

"I want to go home," repeats Chloe, as she gets up.

"Come on, Rex," says Max, picking him up.

Chloe walks quickly, a little bit ahead of them. "Three weeks?" she mutters. Now she sounds angry. "So what have you been *doing* for three weeks?" she mumbles.

They're quiet on the ride up in the elevator. Rex jabs at all the buttons, lighting them up. At the end of the hall, Chloe works at unlocking the door.

"How was the dentist?" Max asks her.

"I need a root canal," she answers glumly, her back to him, then shoves open the door.

When they go into the apartment, it feels like the heat is on. "It feels like the heat is on," grumbles Chloe.

"It's just stuffy," says Max. "I'll open the windows more." He opens the gate to the fire escape, pushes the window up higher.

Rex immediately tries to climb out onto the fire escape, knocks over the pot of basil that Chloe has growing there on its edge. "Uh-oh," says Rex, after it crashes down, looking at the cracked terra cotta, the thick rope of soil strewn diagonally across the floor like coffee grounds.

"The heat *is* on," whines Chloe, touching the radiator. "Pew! Did you poop, Rex?" She stands in the middle of the room grimacing, looking around wide-eyed and motionless, as though the items surrounding her are drifting away. "Where's the *diaper bag*?" she whines.

The phone rings on the low table next to Chloe's knee. She looks at the caller ID. "It's Margaret," she says, biting her lip. She picks it up. "Oh," she says into the phone, after a pause, and then starts to whimper. "He did?" she asks, and then bursts into tears. She holds the phone out to Max. "He died," she tells him gently, her tears streaming down. Max's face is white as he takes the phone from her. Chloe collapses around his feet. "Oh, honey!" she cries softly, hugging his knees.

17

It's only an hour or so before two women, arranged through the hospice nurse, come in a huge dark-blue SUV to take Gramps's body to the crematorium. Margaret and Brian help them move his body from the bed to the stretcher and then get the stretcher down the stairs. They leave through the side door, Margaret aware of whether neighbors are watching—she sees none—imagining that the scene must, from an unknowing distance, look macabre. "Well," says Margaret, puffy-eyed, leaning on Brian at the door, "Dad would be thrilled to be taken away by two forty-year-old babes."

"Who wouldn't?" says Brian.

Margaret sighs. "Now what?"

"Did you call that client?" asks Brian.

"What client?"

"That's why I came home, remember? To watch the kids?"

"You think I should go to *work* right now?" Margaret winces.

"No. I'm just reminding you, sweetheart. The woman might be waiting."

"I guess. I'll call her."

"I'll take these guys down to the park," says Brian.

"And leave me alone?"

"You want us to stay here?"

"Yeah. Please. Well. Do you want to? I don't care. Go."

"No, we'll stay. I'll stay. I thought maybe an hour for you alone might be nice."

"I could take a bath," says Margaret evenly.

"Do anything. Go lie down. Make phone calls."

"Hmm. Those are two very different things."

"Max is on his way?" asks Brian.

"You guys could meet them at the station," says Margaret. "I wrote down the time on the counter."

"Okay. So. We'll leave you alone?"

Margaret bursts into tears. "Okay," she squeaks.

"Oh, I'll stay here with you."

"No. You're right." Margaret sniffles. "I'd like to have no one in the house for a little while."

"Where's Edie?" Brian asks.

"I don't know," peeps Margaret. "I've left her lots of messages on her cell phone. Mimi doesn't answer."

"Go lie down," Brian tells her. "Do we need anything at the store?"

"No. Yeah. Lots of stuff. Milk. Paper towels." She sits down clumsily at the kitchen table. "Get some beer."

•

Being alone in the house, it already feels like the eventual day after a death when all's supposedly back to normal, when family disperses, bills need to be paid, bathrooms cleaned. It makes Margaret think of when her babies were born, that deferment of time and reality with its disrupted sleep and emotions like you're on drugs. She feels suspended, as though she's been gently pulled up into a wave.

The client that Margaret was meant to see called shortly after Brian and the kids walked out the door to say that she was still on Martha's Vineyard. The seaside wind scuttled into the cell phone.

"I was practically leaving for your *house*," said Margaret, not bothering to explain, allowing herself to let off a little steam by sounding borderline rude.

"I'm really sorry," said the woman, Lydia, sounding bothered that Margaret was bothered to begin with. Through the roar of the coastal static, Margaret could hear the nasal whirr of a weed whacker starting up.

"Usually I charge people who don't cancel within twenty-four hours. Like dentists do," said Margaret crossly. "But I guess I didn't make that clear to you, since I didn't think it would happen." Margaret had never met this woman, but from the sound of Lydia's voice and their brief conversations, Margaret could tell that Lydia would be heavy on the yellow beiges, favoring colors with names like Straw and Twig. Cancun Gold would be a shoe-in with Lydia.

"There was a death," said Lydia, probably lying. "If you need to know."

"There was a death here too," said Margaret, then hung up.

Almost immediately the phone rings again and Margaret picks it up on the second ring, ready to apologize to this woman Lydia.

"Margaret Bramble?" A woman's voice, authoritative and sexy.

"Yes?"

"Please hold for Jack Rawlings."

"Excuse me?" Al Green blares into her ear, golden and twangy. She waits there. *How am I doin'? Oh well, I guess I'm doin' fine . . .* Where have all her CDs gone? How do they just disappear? Margaret hangs up.

She gets back to the matter at hand—not a bath, not a tranquil cup of tea while lying in her bed or making phone calls but rather the underworld of the sink, the crammed quarters of dishwashing-liquid bottles, bleach containers, squirt bottles of Windex, Seventh Generation, Mr. Clean, Murphy's oil soap, all standing shoulder to shoulder like people in an elevator, facing the door, waiting to be used. She's disassembling the arrangement. A happy discovery of an unopened value pak of six light-blue sponges with dark blue abrasive.

She's got all the bottles out of there, is cleaning the white wood with Windex before laying down some liner, is scrutinizing some small black flecks. Are they mouse turds? Dirt? Black rice? Rolled lint? Dead ants? The phone rings again.

"Hello?" The waft of antiseptic lemon from her hand is noxious.

A man's voice. "Margaret?" It sounds like someone who knows her, the lilt of her name like a sheet being shaken out over a bed. She can't place the familiar voice.

"Yes?"

"Margaret Bramble?" The possibility of the familiar is gone with the use of her last name. Surely a telemarketer. And she'd put her name on that Do Not Call list. When would it ever kick in?

"Margaret *Bright*," she says, exercising the rudeness she reserves for unsolicited calls, for people whose faces she can't see, like strangers who call during the middle of dinner, long-distance representatives who call just as a child is falling asleep, bubbly women with "free" trips to Orlando or nights in a new Catskill resort; the chimney-sweep scams; the murderous fury she feels when she races to the phone, dropping groceries in the doorway, putting aside a needy child, thinking it's Brian, thinking one of the kids is in trouble somewhere, to hear a chirpy, "Hi, this is Joanna! I've been meaning to get in touch with you for a long time," and when Margaret tries to interrupt, the voice keeps talking: a *recording!* A *recording* calling her home, interrupting everything, disrupting everything with a recording! Oh, it makes her mad. "Margaret *Bright,*" she says again, clenching her jaw.

The line is quiet for a moment. Then, gingerly, "Margaret Bramble Bright?" says the man. He pauses. "Now there's a mouthful."

"What can I do for you?" she says.

"My name is Jack Rawlings."

"Mmm-hmm." Recognizing the name again, the character actor from movies like *These Days* and *Intersection* and the quirky *Captain Birch.* She might not know who he is if her brother Max wasn't mistaken for him regularly. Or used to be.

"My assistant just called you," he says. "Sorry. I wanted to call you myself."

"Yes?"

"I'm an actor."

"Sure," says Margaret, starting to smirk. She leans against the counter, her mind filling up with completely senseless explanations. It's either Brian pulling something by having someone call, trying to make her laugh—but Brian's home. And is this funny? Maybe it was a pre-planned gag he forgot to put off—or Edie put him up to it as some sort of thing for her dumb show. Could this possibly be an on-the-air phone call? But since when was *Chew the Fat* getting people like Jack Rawlings involved? Maybe it was a friend of Max's at Foona Laguna. Max trying to cheer her up. But why would this *cheer her up?* What was she thinking?

"Um." The man groans. "This is awkward."

"Is this Brian somehow?"

"Sorry?"

"Will you put my husband on the phone, please?" But knowing that her husband was at the park with the kids.

"Look. I have some—ah, strange information, so—"

Margaret laughs. "You really sound a *lot* like him."

"Like who. Your husband?"

She hangs up the phone. The cleaner is making her nose ache, as though it's capped with a metal thimble. Back on her knees, a faint wail from the room above her. Flo stirring. Then, nothing. A faint sound again. Margaret freezes, raises her neck like an emu, a wild animal in the forest listening for her young. She stays still. Nothing. Of course there's nothing. The kids are all out of the house.

Most of the time (all of the time) she hears phantom cries, yelps from the upstairs rooms, calls from the outdoors, blended somewhere within the static of the washing machine, the dishwasher, the silence, a car passing outside, a certain frequency of the running shower when she is in it, a faraway lawn mower or chain saw. She'll hear her children crying, calling her name. Mom! Momma? She'll round the corner into the TV room asking, "What *is* it?" fed up, the three of them looking up at her listlessly from their respective stations—bean bag chair, rug with crayons, table with the fake toaster oven—wondering what she's talking about. Even tonight while she is sleeping she will be woken by the grumbling sounds of her father, calling to her from his room. She will automatically get out of bed. The open window in the hallway, a swaying branch, the leaves hissing in the wind. The dark air outside looking like deep water. Traces of clean moonlight. She will be more than halfway to his bedside before she remembers that he is dead.

The phone rings again. "Ms. Bright?" It's the authoritative woman's voice. Gentler now and more friendly, closer to the phone. "I'm really sorry to bother you. My name's Danielle and I'm Jack Rawlings's assistant."

"Oh, *really*," she says.

"Yes, really." Margaret hears an audible exhale of a cigarette. What offices can you smoke in anymore? "I'm not sure if you're familiar with him as an actor—"

"I know who he is."

"Okay, then. If it's possible, Jack would like to meet you. I believe you're fairly close to New York City, right? Magnolia Heights is—"

Margaret snorts. "Does he want to put me in one of his movies?"

"Um. Jack's never made a movie of his own. Hopefully in the future we'll—"

"I'm joking. What is this?"

"What is what?"

"What do you want?"

"Mr. Rawlings would like to meet you, ma'am."

"Mr. Rawlings? Oh, now we're all formal?" She feels suddenly especially angry. Quickly. Angry that she's exchanged words at all.

"Well, it's that he—"

"I don't mean to be rude, but tell whoever it is that I'm not in the mood for a joke right now, okay? Thanks." She hangs up the phone.

Later on, dusting the table in the front hall with a yellow feather duster like Lucille Ball, paper-toweling the cordless phone, the phone with all the doohickeys, the locator bleeps, the intercom button that blurts out the dial tone as she cleans it, the receiver falls off its cradle. When she places it back in its place, the caller ID lights up from the last call: H SWIVEL PRODS.

Margaret stands up straight. Her chest balloons into her throat, bullfrog, and then falls back down again. She presses the buttons, hastily going through the caller history: H SWIVEL PRODS, H SWIVEL PRODS, PRIVATE CALLER, MANNY AUTO, PRIVATE CALLER.

She stands there. Presses the button that automatically dials the number back. After one ring, "Hazey Swivel," bleats a young woman's voice, almost inaudible.

"What is this?"

"Hazey Swivel Productions," says the receptionist, with wry pronunciation.

"Excuse me? Could you say that again?"

"Who's calling?"

"I'm sorry. I see here on my phone that you called my house. I'm wondering who you are."

"We're a production company."

"Oh. What sort of production company?"

"Um, a film production company."

"Is Jack Rawlings . . . involved somehow?"

"Who's calling?"

"He just called me."

"Who is calling?"

"Who *am* I?"

"What is your name, ma'am?"

"Margaret Bramble."

"And he has your number?"

"He just *called* me."

"I'll give him the message."

"It's not a *message*, I'm wondering why—" and the receptionist hangs up. Hangs up! Margaret still holds the phone to her ear.

She gets back to the sink, sits on the floor, and looks up at the refrigerator and the notebook paper with her father's scribbly handwriting: *Hazey Swivel.*

The phone rings again and she picks it up off the floor. "Hello?"

"Hi."

"Max! The weirdest thing—"

"Margaret? This is Jack Rawlings, calling you back."

"Sorry. I thought you were my brother!"

She hears him clear his throat just as, out the window, perfectly framed by its panes as though it's a Stephen King movie, Tammy Lopney appears, so large and strange-looking that Margaret jumps, startled. She drops the phone.

"Holy shit! Excuse me. You scared me," Margaret yells at her. Then she is angry. "What *is* it that you want?" she asks loudly. Tammy smiles awkwardly through the screen.

Margaret picks up the phone. The pleasant male voice inside of it is low and contemplative, saying, "Um, Margaret? Is everything okay?"

"Everything's *fine!*" But for a second, Margaret is scared. Is this woman a raving lunatic? Should Margaret run and lock the door? "Who *are* you?" Margaret asks her.

"Shall I call you back?" asks Jack Rawlings.

"Please," Margaret says to him, and presses the button to hang up. She glares at the large woman standing outside her window.

"Rough day?" asks Tammy, without a single trace of irony.

"*Tammy*. Please leave me alone."

"Rough day," she says again, this time less of a question but as though she's proud of herself for inferring correctly.

"What can I *do* for you?"

"Um." Tammy smiles. She raises her eyebrows creepily with a smile. "I know about your brother."

"What?"

"I know who your brother is."

"Good for you," says Margaret. Clearly, this woman is insane. "Please leave me alone. Honestly. Should I call the police?"

"Gosh. Am I that bad?"

"It's been that bad a day, *Tammy*."

"Can I help at all?"

"I guess I should lock my doors. Is that what I should do?"

"No. I just wanted to ask you something about your brother."

"I don't want to be . . . *talking*," says Margaret, wishing there were a door she could close and walk away. Should she close the window? But then there's only glass between them, and it's hot today. "I'm closing the window," Margaret announces, and as she does so, Tammy begins talking, but Margaret can't hear her once the pane is slid down past her large talking head.

Margaret walks away—to where? Where should she go? In the living room, Tammy would be able to see her through the windows at the front of the house. In the dining room, there's the window near the driveway. She goes upstairs into Gramps's room. The AC is still on, the cool air a fresh surprise. She lies down on the crumpled white sheets, buries her head in the pillow. "Dad," she says quietly, and saying it makes her start to cry. She closes her eyes, trying to relax, then quickly stands up and starts stripping the sheets off the bed.

•

A little later, Margaret sits on the back terrace with a glass of white wine loaded with ice cubes, a box of tissues, and the telephone handy. She stares out at the garden, dazed. The nasturtiums are finally filling out, some foxglove poking up out of the columbine. Where was the rudbeckia? They were the hardiest things in the world, those black-eyed Susans, giving flowers almost until Thanksgiving last year, and now there was no sign of them. Mullein spindly against the fence, the lupine flowers already going, bee balm and buddleia drawing the butterflies that Sarah liked to go after with the net. Margaret gets up and walks out there to the beds, looking down at the deep burgundy verbena, the lovely rose mallow, phlox, the zinnias and cosmos coming up, Saint-John's-wort, bachelor button, the splotches of herbs at the start of the vegetable garden, the bushy yarrow that jumped across the yard to spread on the other side, the rogue hollyhock that came out of nowhere.

Now she knows what her mother and father were doing when, as a girl, she'd look out the window of the house in Merrick and see one of them standing next to the flowerbed, peering down at the ground with their hands on their hips, walking along its edge as though it were a shoreline, surveying plants, inspecting what was missing and what was growing. To her as a girl, they looked insane, occasionally muttering to themselves or stooping down over the dirt but mostly just standing there, staring down at an area of garden as though they just saw some-thing move and were waiting for it to move again. Watching her father staring that way, Margaret would wonder aloud, What is he *doing* out there?

She immediately thinks of her father's funeral—and of what flowers they would use. It'll depend when we have it, she thought, though glad to have something to consider about him, something logistical.

At the nursery a few weeks ago, the owner was on the phone, then hung up flabbergasted as Margaret waited at the cash register to buy some flats of blue pansies. He looked up at her, dumbfounded. "Have you ever heard of a *yellow peony?*" he asked her.

Margaret shook her head. "No."

"Well, this guy tells me he'll sell me some."

"How would it look?" asked Margaret. "Yellow like a daffodil or sort of off-white?"

"It looks like a rose, is what he said," said the owner, ringing her up, which didn't leave Margaret with the visual she was after, but that didn't matter because on the way back to the car, something about it bothered her. It seemed invasive and artificial. But right now, the idea of a yellow peony seems unbelievably lovely. She pictures it pale yellow, like butter. That would be nice for the memorial: big bunches in glass vases . . . low bunches . . . maybe those round glass vases . . . they were cheap enough . . . Peonies not so cheap, but—

The phone rings. Margaret picks it up.

"Margaret?"

"Oh, Edie!" says Margaret, how else to say it? She didn't have anything planned. "Dad's dead," she blurts out.

Edie's not surprised. "He is?" she asks. She starts to cry.

"He died so quickly, Edie."

"He did?"

"And he was so graceful and quiet about it."

"He was?"

"The kids and I were right there."

"You were?"

"Yeah." The two sisters snuffle into the phone line together, like holding hands.

Finally Margaret comes up for air. "So can you come home tomorrow morning?"

"I'm in Boston," peeps Edie.

"What?"

"I'm on my way home," she says again, louder.

"You are?" Margaret smiles.

"I get to Newark at five."

"I'll be there. Downeast Air?"

"Yeah," chirps Edie, still crying.

"Okay," says Margaret, glad for a task. "I'm a-coming."

They say good-bye, but Margaret wonders, as she's hanging up, "Hey. Hey?" she calls to Edie out in the air. "How come you're back?"

But Edie's already hung up—the dial tone inflating in Margaret's ear—already walking away, heading for the bathroom and then outside to smoke cigarettes before her next flight.

As Margaret hangs up, she hears some clanking around in the house. "Who's that?" she calls.

"It's us," says Max. He and Chloe come out the back door, holding hands.

Margaret blows her nose. "Don't you two look lovey-dovey."

"We renewed our vows on the train," says Chloe, looking willowy and flushed.

Margaret chuckles.

Chloe sits down. "Max had this idea that all I care about is *content* and *money* or something," she says, clearly still on a roll from their train heart-to-heart. "It's not about what we have or don't have, it's about the *quality* of what we have *emotionally*. It's about *interaction*. It's about *family*, right? And being *kind*."

Margaret takes a sip of her wine. "I can get down with that."

Chloe continues. "We only live once, right? It's always so important to keep—"

Max playfully sits down on her lap so she'll stop talking.

"Ugh!" Chloe laughs. "Hey!"

Margaret watches them. "Where's Rex?"

"Sleeping," says Max, standing up. "Where's Dad?"

Margaret looks at him dryly with a little bit of a smile. "Dad is dead, my friend."

"I mean, did he go to some funeral home or something?"

"Should I have kept him here?" asks Margaret, truly concerned. "Would you have wanted to see him?"

"Oh, no. No, no," says Max. "Don't worry."

"Two women took him away in an SUV," she says.

"Really?"

"It has been a *very* strange day," says Margaret flatly. "*Very* strange."

"Here comes your brood," says Max, glancing into the house.

Stephen comes out the back door carrying a manila envelope. "What's this, Mom?" he asks, trailed by Flo.

"How was the park, honey?" asks Margaret.

"We got some pizzas, Mom," says Flo. "Dad brought them to the kitchen."

"What's this, Mom?" Stephen asks again. He holds the big envelope up over his head.

"You tell me, sweetheart," says Margaret.

Flo climbs onto her mother's lap.

"Here, Mom," says Stephen. "What is it?"

"Where did it come from?" asks Margaret, only halfway paying attention.

"Someone left it at the front door," says Stephen, playing with the little rope that ties it shut.

"Open it and see," Margaret tells him. She breathes in Flo's citrusy-smelling hair. It's a mystery how her children end up smelling the way that they do.

Stephen unwinds the string and opens it. "It's . . . some *guy*," he says, disappointed, and then bolts for his bike in the driveway.

Margaret is lost in the hair at the back of Flo's head, nudging her nose around in it as Flo giggles.

"Who's that guy, Mom?" asks Flo, eyeing the eight-by-ten photo that Stephen left faceup on the table. "Is that Uncle Max?"

Margaret peers around her daughter's small head to see what she's talking about. It's a dated-looking headshot of the actor Jack Rawlings. Stuck on his ear is a pink Post-it with squiggled crazy-person writing ballooning across its surface saying:

Only just looking for an autograph, please . . .
Thanx!

Tammy

18

Rosedale Crematorium has the feel of a Frank Lloyd Wright house with its angular hallways and walls of glass, its camel-colored furniture and subdued oriental rugs. It's one level, like a space ship, like a mountain resort house with a focus for its views. The building is set on a hill, mid–tree level, so the spectacle is one of flappy leaves at varying heights. Sunlight falls stippled through hoops of branches.

The three Bramble siblings sit in seats lining a wall, facing the big—what else to call them?—ovens. To their right through a full-length window, as if they're in a tree house, are thick bunches of leaves like heads of Bibb lettuce, the full spectrum of greens.

Margaret is reminded of an oncologist's office in California, something in the positioning of the seats in the waiting room, the way the hallway comes to an end and then turns. Margaret had sat across from her father. Gramps was looking at *Time* magazine while an incredibly good-looking brunette with long shiny legs was seated next to him. Margaret couldn't place her. She must have been a movie star, or someone must have wanted to *make* her a movie star on more than one occasion, out there in California. Margaret found herself daydreaming about the woman's life, her daily routine of carefree exercise and self-maintenance. She probably surfed every morning with two or three towheaded kids, shopped at open-air markets for fresh vegetables while lowly passersby turned to watch her go. Her own husband probably still couldn't believe that he had landed this babe. Gramps didn't seem to notice her.

A nurse came in and stood in front of Arthur and the bombshell. "Are you two together?" the nurse asked Arthur.

"Uh, no," said Arthur. Then, without even looking at the brunette, he looked at the nurse squarely and continued, "But I wish I could say that we were."

"So what *else* did Mimi say?" asks Max. They'd had a late night last night, Edie explaining to her brother and sister what Mimi had told her on Moss Island, first outside on the patio and then in the kitchen while they heated up some pizza. Margaret had gotten out a piece of paper to write things down and try to keep everything straight, jotting down notes like she used to do during lectures in school:

- Mom and Mimi walking in the woods.
- Find blond baby boy (Jack Rawlings) abandoned in an old boathouse.
- Mom & Mimi take him to sheriff (Myrtle, Maine).
- Baby's father left him in boathouse.
- Baby's father=Trouble, crazy. Estranged from baby's mother— HAZEL SWIVEL!!
- Baby's father lived in Buffalo, came & took baby from crib while Hazel slept—to get Hzl's attention? To make her mad? Unclear crazy behavior.
- Hzl wouldn't pay him attention. Hzl: schoolteacher, 5th grade.
- Mom and Mimi meet Hazel @ sheriff's, H can't thank them enough. M & M spend the night w/H b/c it doesn't seem weird.
- Get to talking about kids. Mom says she can't get pregnant. Hzl says she can help.
- Hazel dead of breast cancer in '96. Mimi says sort of looked like Mom.
- Dad helps with Jack Rawlings (pays for Vassar).
- Howard Woods: legal issues guy.
- Jack R's father never around. Hzl told Mom he died of alcohol poisoning in Fla in the '80s. His brother, a good guy w/family, lived near Hzl and Jack in ME.

"So we have a history of breast cancer in our family. That's important to know, you know," said Margaret.

Brian, in the background, leaning against the counter, nodded to her supportively.

"That explains where Dad's money went," said Max, not at all bitterly, simply as an observation.

"Yeah. *All* Dad's money," joked Edie, since they're all aware there was never very much.

"So did Dad *sleep* with the woman?" asked Margaret.

"I know. I don't know," said Edie. "I didn't get into that."

"What about our birth certificates?" asked Max.

"I know," said Edie.

"Well, we were all born in Maine," said Margaret. "No matter what time of year it was. Which I always thought was weird."

"Mimi will explain."

They were silent for a moment, their minds abuzz with it all. Max looked at Edie. "Are you *serious.*"

They all smiled, stunned and weary.

"Mimi will explain," Edie said again. "We should all go visit her sometime when we can. We can grill her; she said so. She'd like that."

"Yeah," said Margaret thoughtfully. "The kids would love it up there."

"Yeah," said Max, getting tired. "*I* loved it up there." Max rubbed his head, scratched at his hair vigorously to rouse himself. "But what about this *half brother?*" he asked playfully. He raised his arms up in the air for a large stretch, then let them rest on the backs of two empty chairs on either side of him as if they were pretty girls. "I'm not the only man in the family now. Right when I get my big chance I have to compete with *Jack Rawlings?*"

Margaret and Edie grinned. "He sounded . . . nice," said Margaret, smiling. Her crooked smile turned into a snicker, and then the snicker dissolved into a silent laugh attack. Edie started laughing too. Nothing was funny. But that was a laugh riot.

"Nice?" asked Max. "Well, that's a start—"

"Wait!" chirped Margaret, laughing, doubling onto the table. "I—" but the rest of the sentence was indecipherable, sounding like a guttural *happa settee.*

"Happy city?" asked Edie, trying to clarify, her eyes watering with hilarity.

Margaret got up abruptly, almost knocking her chair over like a drunk. Her laughter was beyond her control, wheezing, the kind of lunatic hormonal laughter that happened to her postpartum or when she was pregnant.

"Oh, boy," said Max. "Take it easy," he said, making his sisters laugh harder.

Margaret opened the drawer of the table on the way to the front hall. "Oh!" She sighed, wiping her eyes. "Look at *this*," she said blearily, the look on her face about to break like a cracked egg into hysteria again. She placed the picture on the table. "He e-mailed me *this*," said Margaret, laughing silently, crumpling to the floor.

"He melt? What?"

"Oh, dear." Max smiled, watching Margaret hold her stomach. "I haven't seen you do this in a while."

"E-mailed, e-mailed," Margaret managed to say.

"E meld?" asked Edie, coming around the table to look at what Max was holding.

"*E-mailed*," said Max, understanding. Margaret nodded vigorously, pointing at Max like he got the clue in charades.

Edie sat down next to Max and looked at the picture. The sight of it made the laughter stop, the three of them studying it with reverence and wonder. It was their father, no doubt about it, a younger Arthur Bramble, his shirtsleeves rolled up, his belt buckled, standing slack-armed and still with a pleasant smile on his face, his right hand holding the hand of a small boy who looked kind of like Max, who squinted into the sunlight, one eye squinched shut, a rascal smile, a baseball glove on his free hand. Behind them, the Essex Green of spruce trees, black-green, hushed and dark as night.

"It's a photo," said Edie. "Dad looks so handsome," she said.

"I remember that belt," said Max. It was brown leather with a square brass buckle.

"I remember that shirt," said Edie.

"It looks like all his shirts," said Max, studying the picture.

"It always reminded me of Pilgrim shoes," said Margaret from the floor.

"Pilgrim?" asked Edie.

"The shirt?" asked Max.

"The buckle. The buckle." Margaret sighed. "I've got to go to bed."

"Why didn't you show us this before?" asked Edie.

"I forgot," said Margaret. "I . . . totally forgot."

"You're allowed to forget things today," said Max, looking at the little boy's face. It looked like him, but a little nobler, sort of smoky. Max knew his own face had a jollier edge, more chummy, less striking.

"He sent this too," said Margaret, getting the other thing. It was a copy of his high school yearbook picture.

"Why did he send this?" asked Edie, looking it over.

"To show us his name. And see? Myrtle, Maine."

"Oh, yeah." The three of them looked at it, fascinated. Jack looked like Max put into a different casing. The strangeness of genes shining through the actual eyeballs, the lips, a certain curve in the brow and cheekbone. Underneath his picture: Jack Swivel, soccer captain, basketball. *King Lear, Pajama Game, Bye Bye Birdie, Zoo Story*. Pet Peeves: The term *pet peeve*. Likes: Music. Dislikes: Musicals. Most Likely to Be Seen: On the silver screen.

"I always hated that word too," said Edie.

"Did he always know about us?" asked Max.

"He said his wife's about to have a baby," answered Margaret. "He wants to get things in order family-wise."

"What's that supposed to mean?" asked Edie.

"I don't know. Reach out. Clarify things. Know who his *relatives* are."

They sat quietly in the kitchen. Margaret dimmed the light so it wouldn't be so bright. They picked at the pizza. Edie reached for another slice, aware that she wasn't telling her brother and sister about the papers she found when she was a cook for Mimi Woods that summer. And then, being aware of that thought, wondered whether she was actively lying in any way. She was also aware that she might try to throw up her pizza before bed. How to do it without making any noise? Should she go outside? Say she's going for a walk to have a smoke?

"I can't explain it, but I kind of like the whole idea," said Margaret, her voice curling up out of the silence like an ornate plant.

"What whole idea?" asked Max.

"The convergence of everything. I mean, you think it's a coincidence that Mimi was telling Edie everything practically at the same time Jack Rawlings called me up? And Dad dying? And that weirdo woman popping up in my window? Don't you think it's, like, *Mom* doing something?"

"Mom?" asked Max excitedly.

"Like her way of telling us?" asked Edie.

"You think that weird woman might have been Mom?" asked Max.

"Well. That might be pushing it."

"Yeah, what *about* that woman?" said Edie.

"She's a fan of Jack Rawlings, apparently," said Margaret, too tired to get into it any further. "She's been following him on and off for a couple of years. He got a restraining order after she took a bunch of stuff from his garage. Personal papers."

"Personal papers?"

"That was the term he used." Margaret yawned.

"Stalking him?" asked Edie.

Margaret shrugged. "He called a cop."

"You think Mom can see us?" asked Max, still thinking about it.

His sisters shrugged.

"In a way," said Edie.

"Dad *did* write down Hazel Swivel's name," said Margaret, looking at it on the fridge. "He must have had plans to—I don't know."

"Maybe someone told Jack Rawlings that Dad was dying," said Edie.

Margaret shook her head, watery-eyed from another yawn. "He said he had no idea."

Chloe came around the corner like a sleepy animal, squinting. Max grabbed her by the waist and pulled her to sit on his lap. She wiped her cheek with her hand, looked drowsily to the floor.

"Did you fall asleep with Rex?" Max asked her.

"Yeah. He's in the Play and Pack now."

"Pack 'N Play," corrected Margaret automatically. Then checked herself. "Sorry."

"I'm hitting the sack," said Chloe.

"I'll pull out the—"

"I already did it," said Chloe. "That's what we fell asleep on."

Max squeezed her around the waist. "Uhh." She smiled. "Careful. I feel a little icky."

"Your stomach?"

"I'm just tired."

"It's been a long day," said Margaret.

"I'll be right in," Max told his wife. He turned to Edie. "Where are you sleeping, in Dad's bed?"

Edie wrinkled up her nose. "Maybe tomorrow night. Tonight I'll be with Sarah." Sarah was in the double bed on the third floor.

"I'm heading up," said Brian, coming in from some contemplative time out on the patio, after locking up all the doors.

"I'll be up in a sec," said Margaret, almost wistfully.

The brother and sisters sat at the table. Edie picked at the candlestick wax. Margaret ate some grapes. "I feel kind of sick too," said Margaret, thinking of Chloe.

"Does it make you mad?" asked Edie. "I mean, for myself, I would think I would be mad—but I'm not. Maybe I will be later. Are you mad?"

"I'm not *mad*," said Max. "I mean, I guess they had their reasons . . . and maybe Mom died too soon to straighten it all out. But I'm a little freaked."

"Me too," said Margaret. "It's freaky. But I also can't *believe* that Mom and Dad—especially Dad!—would go through so much trouble to have us. I mean, it doesn't *change* anything, but in a weird way it makes them more, like, *multidimensional*, doesn't it?"

"Does it makes you think of the two of them before they had us? With a life of their own?" asked Edie.

"Yeah. Exactly," said Margaret.

"Yeah," said Edie. "I like thinking of them that way."

"Me too," said Max, thinking of himself and Chloe.

"Isn't it *weird*," said Margaret, her eyes in a daze, "that people feel the need to bear children over and over?"

"I don't feel that need," said Edie.

Margaret leaned her head back on a chair. "But you know what I mean."

"Think about sleep," said Max. "Isn't *that* weird? Whole portions of the country, of the world, going unconscious at the same time?"

Margaret remembers coming home from the hospital with her first baby, Stephen. The idea of falling asleep made her panic. At the hospital there were nurses and doctors and lights, always someone to peek at him if she should be asleep while the baby was awake. But at home, the idea of his tiny vulnerable body opening its big black eyes to a world where the adults were snoozing away petrified her. What if he stopped breathing? What if he got tangled up in his clothes in some silent conniption? What if, by some fluke, the bassinet should collapse? Anything could happen while she was sleeping. She might as well have been dead.

"Well, he had a decent life," said Edie, looking out the window.

"Who?" asked Margaret, thinking of infant Stephen.

"Who do you think?"

·

Some commotion can be heard coming from down the hallway. Around the corner come two well-dressed men pushing a gurney with a human-sized cardboard box on top of it. "Good day," say the men, with polite nods. Written diagonally on the cardboard box, the name *Bramble*, in black Magic Marker, above, they could only assume, their father's feet. His high arches. His yellowed toenails. The milky-white tan line from his socks. And then, beneath the name *Bramble*, in ballpoint, *124 lbs*. Edie notices that her father weighed less than she does. She wonders if that weight includes the box or is just his body. She looks at her sister Margaret's crossed legs, wonders how much she weighs.

"How much do you weigh?"

"What?"

"How much do you weigh?"

Margaret shrugs, unsurprised by the question since she obviously noticed the weight written on the box as well. "I have no idea. One twenty? One twenty-five? Maybe one thirty-five or forty?"

"That's quite a range," says Edie.

"Beats me."

The older, funereal man returns to oversee placing the box in the oven. "Are we ready?" he asks the Bramble children, like a schoolteacher. They nod.

"It looks like a brick oven," whispers Margaret.

"It *is* a brick oven," says Max.

"I mean for pizzas."

They watch the box get placed in there, the low flames looking like flowers blooming up around it.

Margaret thinks of her father just a couple of days ago, that same body lying in the bed upstairs, looking tiny, awake and alive. Margaret came into his room. "What is this wonderful music?" he had asked dreamily.

"It's the Beatles, Dad," said Margaret.

"What is this marvelous music?" he asked again.

"The song's called 'She Said,'" said Margaret, listening to it come soaring up from downstairs.

The Brambles sit quietly for a time. The door to the oven looks like a low-security bank vault or a door you'd find in the interior of a submarine. The three siblings sit in their chairs and stare straight ahead at it.

"Remember the DiGiovannis' pizza place?" asks Edie.

"Yes," says Max.

"Yes, we remember," says Margaret.

The three of them sit there. "Weren't they square?" asks Edie.

"The DiGiovannis?" asks Max.

"No, you dope! The pizzas!"

"Wait," says Margaret, shaking her head. "You're mixing it up. The pizzas at *school* were square."

"Right. I thought the DiGiovanni ones were too." Edie smiles, suddenly shy. She bursts into tears.

Max pats her on the back. "You can believe they were square if you need to, Eed."

Another man comes around the corner, butlerlike, tall and gray with a beaked nose. "Is there anything you need?" he asks, bowing forward with an appreciated but also annoying elegance.

"No, thank you," says Margaret.

"How long does it usually take?" Edie asks him, overcoming her tears, even though Margaret has told her. She's conditioned, from work, to always double-check everything people say. Or maybe it's not from work.

"Quite a while," the man tells her. "Most families don't feel compelled to stay the entire time. I'll return shortly to seal it shut," he says, motioning toward the vaultlike door. He disappears around the corner.

"Okay. Should we read this thing?" It's a poem their father liked,

John Masefield's "On Growing Old." Margaret remembers her father listening to a recording of it being read by F. Scott Fitzgerald.

"You read it," Edie tells Margaret.

"I'll read it," says Max.

He takes the piece of paper. "Did you get this off the Internet?"

Margaret shrugs, nodding. "I couldn't find a book."

Max reads thoughtfully but not pretentiously.

> "Be with me, Beauty, for the fire is dying,
> My dog and I are old, too old for roving.
> Man, whose young passion sets the spindrift flying,
> Is soon too lame to march, too cold for loving.
> I take the book and gather to the fire,
> Turning old yellow leaves; minute by minute
> The clock ticks to my heart; a withered wire
> Moves a thin ghost of music in the spinet.
> I cannot sail your seas, I cannot wander
> Your cornland nor your hill-land nor your valleys
> Ever again, nor share the battle yonder
> Where the young knight the broken squadron rallies;
> Only stay quiet, while my mind remembers
> The beauty of fire from the beauty of embers.
>
> Beauty, have pity, for the strong have power,
> The rich their wealth, the beautiful their grace,
> Summer of man its sunlight and its flower,
> Springtime of man all April in a face.
> Only, as in the jostling in the Strand,
> Where the mob thrusts or loiters or is loud,
> The beggar with the saucer in his hand
> Asks only a penny from the passing crowd,
> So, from this glittering world with all its fashion,
> Its fire and play of men, its stir, its march,
> Let me have wisdom, Beauty, wisdom and passion,
> Bread to the soul, rain where the summers parch.
> Give me but these, and though the darkness close
> Even the night will blossom as the rose."

Margaret leans across Edie to give Max a kiss. "That was lovely," she says, the words sounding, even to her, like her own mother's.

"Really nice, Max," says Edie, nudging him.

"What's that smell?" asks Margaret.

"It's my cast," says Edie. "I know. It stinks." Edie repeatedly brushes her head, her face, as though someone tossed sand at her.

"Are you okay?" Margaret asks her sister.

"I feel like I have cobwebs all over my face," answers Edie.

"What?"

"I feel like I have cobwebs all over my face." Edie makes a strange gesture, as if she's gently trying to pull off her nose in slow motion. She looks at Margaret. "Do you see anything there? Strands of hair or something?"

Margaret looks closely, sweeps her hand over Edie's cheek. "No. There's nothing there."

"I feel all itchy. Like I need to wash my face," says Edie.

"Then go wash it," Margaret tells her.

"I'll stay here for a little longer."

Just as she says it, the older man returns, nods to the three of them, and then clamps the door to the furnace shut like a vault.

The three of them look straight ahead, watching the digital temperature on the furnace rise. With their mother, they didn't stay to see this happen. Margaret takes Edie's hand. "Jesus," says Margaret softly, squeezing it. On her other side, Edie takes Max's hand and squeezes it, passing it on.

•

The sunny day turns overcast. The ride home is quiet until they get closer to Margaret's house and the musings of the car's passengers begin to float out of their mouths.

"I love my wife." Max sighs, sitting in the back.

Margaret smiles at the approaching road in front of her, glimpses her brother in the rearview mirror. "Well, that's promising," she says.

"I love my life," says Edie curtly.

Margaret looks at her. "You do? Are you being sarcastic?"

"Why not?" says Edie, resigned, watching the sidewalk wind alongside the road like a towpath along a canal. "Who lives *there*, anyway?"

asks Edie, as they approach a particular house of disarray on the corner: a half-done paint job, the old paint molting like the skin on a snake, areas of matted clay dirt, overgrown grass like the shag of a beard, plastic swing sets and kiddie cars all cockeyed, hidden in the high grass and weeds. Plastic garbage cans are tipped over next to the crumbling stoop.

"We don't know."

"Do they have kids?"

Margaret shrugs. "We never see them."

Edie imagines the house as her own body, with its disorder and chaos. Why not at least put the toys *upright*? Or get rid of a couple? Or right the garbage cans? Or yank a weed or two every time you go out to get in the car? Edie understands why they don't bother. But starting right now, she is going to make herself tend to herself, and then she'll see what follows. She'll pretend she is taking care of someone else, feed that person (herself) properly, see that the person (Edie) gets enough fresh air and exercise and sleep, make herself at least mow her proverbial lawn and right her proverbial garbage cans. Wasn't it strange how things happen without things *happening*? How something so invisible, a change of mind or something revealed, can change so much of your outlook? Riding along in the passenger seat, Edie feels something akin to belonging while still she feels solo in the world, with herself, and that independence is suddenly an exciting thing. She can do anything. If she pretends to take care, maybe real care will follow.

"It's starting to rain," says Margaret. "*Again.*" Tiny needles of rain chicken-scratch on the windshield.

"He told me to always put my wife ahead of everything else," announces Max.

"Who did? Dad did? Really?" asks Margaret.

"He told *me* to pay special close attention to what I love the most," says Edie.

"He did?" asks Margaret.

"Yeah. When I was in California."

Margaret drives on silently. Then she asks, not meaning to whine but whining all the same, "How come Dad didn't give *me* any golden kernels of wisdom?"

"Maybe you didn't need them," says Edie.

Margaret isn't sure if her sister is complimenting her or dissing her but leaves it at that.

She remains quiet, driving onward, tentatively delving into her head to try to remember something he'd told her, something he'd said.

"I bet he did, Maggie. You're just not thinking of it," says Max from the backseat.

"He told me to have an open mind," says Margaret as they approach her house. "He said life is much easier that way even though you'd think it would be harder."

"He did?"

"And to keep a sense of humor about everything."

"See. There you go."

"And to enjoy the moment. Keep your chin up! Look on the bright side! Love will find a way!"

"Wow."

"No," says Margaret, pulling into the driveway. "He didn't say any of that. I'm just thinking on my feet."

She pulls into the driveway, notes the heeling lilies that need to be staked. They get bigger every year, these things, more and more of them practically taller than she is. The light drizzle has already darkened the pavement to an oily sheen.

As they get out of the car, Margaret sees her, standing by the garage, of all places. "What the—" mutters Margaret, slamming the door and walking right up to her. "What in the world is going on?" Margaret asks her.

Tammy Lopney stands there. "Did you get that envelope I left?"

"Tammy? Please go home. Please leave me and my family alone." Behind her, her brother and sister watch curiously, protectively.

"I don't mean to be bothering y'all," says Tammy. *Y'all?* wonders Margaret. Was she southern? Margaret thinks of George Bush calling Al Qaeda "these folks" after 9/11.

"Us *all?*" asks Margaret. "Well, I can guarantee that you're bothering *me*."

"All I want is an autograph," says Tammy, smiling.

"You are creepy," says Margaret. "I can't get you any autograph." She wonders why she's even talking to this woman. She turns around to walk toward the house.

"But he's your brother," says Tammy in a whinnied drawl.

Margaret is storming toward her house. How did this woman *know? Personal papers.* Margaret hears the words in her head. Who *was* she?

Margaret is continuing toward her front door, listening for her siblings behind her, when Tammy calls after her with a singsongy, "I'm a longtime fan," as if that would be the clincher.

Margaret stops in her tracks. She thinks of the Range Rover looming large behind her car, right on her butt. She thinks of Tammy's weird expression when she climbed into the Odyssey to exchange information. Margaret stares at the pavement in front of her, astonished, asks, "Did you hit my car on *purpose?*" She turns around to see the reaction.

Tammy, lug-headed and doughy, smiles at her with a shrug.

Margaret walks back toward Tammy with something like fury loose-winged in her chest. She sees the stunned expressions of her three kids, strapped in their seats in the Odyssey after they were hit. An energized surge jolts through Margaret's body like an electric shock. She clenches her jaw and, with a good amount of force pent up within her, belts Tammy Lopney across the face.

Brian is coming out the door as she does it. "Sweetheart, sweetheart," he says, hurrying toward her.

Tammy, holding a hand to her cheek and crying, bustles past Edie and Max, waddles toward the street.

"Where is she going?" asks Edie. "Does she have a car?"

"Sweetheart?" says Brian, unsure of what to make of what he saw out the window. "We don't hit people, honey," he says, in the tone they use when they say it to the kids.

Margaret starts crying, snottily and strongly, her face drooping like a bloodhound's, hanging on Brian's shoulder. They go to sit on the patio. Edie and Max follow. Edie comes back outside with a glass of water for her sister. Some tissues. "Thanks," says Margaret, honking her nose. "I mean," she says, blowing her nose again, "he died so *quickly.* I didn't even get to *help* him." She sobs.

Edie looks at her sister, is tempted to ask angrily, So this is all about *you,* Margaret? About your showmanship at his bedside? But she doesn't.

Max addresses it gently. "That's a *good* thing, Maggie. For Dad."

"I know," says Margaret slurpily, dabbing her eyes. "I'm just being selfish." Brian smooths her hair, erasing the minute beads of moisture that have landed there. Margaret leans into him and groans, shuddering.

"I might have a new job," Max announces when it's quiet, for something to say.

Margaret smiles. "That's great!"

Edie smiles too. "You do?"

Brian asks, "What is it?"

"I quit Foona Laguna, like, three weeks ago."

"Why didn't you tell us?"

"I didn't even tell Chloe. Where *is* Chloe?"

"She and Rex are napping," says Brian.

"She's been exhausted," says Max. "She thought I was going off to work the whole time I wasn't working. She thought I was having an affair."

"Eeew."

"Ouch."

"Yeah."

This might be Edie's moment to tell them she's got eating problems. But it's her problem. It's not that bad, anyway. Plus, right now *isn't* the moment. Plus, with all the activity of new information and dying, she doesn't feel as bored and flat. Maybe it won't return. She'll head back to her studio apartment in a few days, and the first thing she'll do is buy some new curtains and clean the place up. Maybe she'll join the new gym on the corner. Maybe she'll try to get a new job, too, one that travels. "So what's the new job?"

"It's not definite or anything. But I'm pretty sure. It's a series of mini-documentaries. Kind of like *Frontline*, I guess. But not always on serious subjects."

"That sounds great," says Margaret, her pink eyes looking like she has hay fever. "Really great." A distinct pallor passes over her face like a glum cloud.

Brian looks at her. "Sweetheart? Are you all right?"

"Yeah, Margaret," says Edie. "You look kind of green."

Margaret looks blankly at her sister. She looks emptily at her husband. She feels puny and gigantic at the same time. She watches her brother say "Maggie?" with a concerned look on his face but hears his voice scrambled as though through a voice decoder. She turns her head to the side for a much-needed deep breath of air and vomits onto the bluestone.

"Honey," says Brian, partly laughing. There is something comedic in her body language, the suddenness of her getting sick after clocking a strange woman in the driveway. "Are you all right?"

Margaret wipes her mouth with the back of her hand. She looks up at her husband. "We're having another baby," she says flatly, and in her eyes Brian already recognizes the hormones all a-glimmer.

•

Inside the house, the kids are interested. They abandon watching *Chitty Chitty Bang Bang* to hear about the cremation. Margaret explains the process for the twentieth time, this time with more confidence. "So then they put him in the big pizza oven so he"—how to avoid the word *burn* here?—"turns to ash. When we want to, we can scatter his ashes somewhere special."

"Do they cook pizzas in there too?" asks Flo plainly.

"No. It just *looks* like a pizza oven, Flo. Like the brick ovens downtown at Marco's."

"Where are his ashes *now*?" asks Sarah suspiciously.

"They're keeping them at the crematorium. We'll pick them up sometime soon."

"What brick oven downtown?" asks Flo. "Who's Marco?"

"Marco's. The pizza place," says Brian.

"The place with the shaker things full of Farmer John?" asks Flo. *Farmer John* is how she says *Parmesan*.

"That's the one."

"Are kids allowed there?" asks Stephen.

"At Marco's?" asks Brian, mocking shock.

"No! At the place where they burned up Gramps!" says Sarah. Her fingers busily mimic flames, up and down in the air in front of her, like a hippie girl on acid. "With all the fire!"

Stephen ignores her. "Are kids allowed there, Mom?" he asks again.

She should have taken him, thinks Margaret, looking at Stephen's face, his curiosity, to see the progression of death. "I'm not sure, honey," she says. There will be time for his reflection.

Margaret sits back, watches her children mill around the kitchen, and has the feeling again—she'd had it before when she came across the fact of it—of responsibility and leadership. She is at the top of the family now. She is the oldest, even if it is only by a couple of years (barely). No aunts, no uncles, no mother or father. She can't help it but immediately fast-forwards to the terrifying time when she herself will be dead and Brian too, when her kids will be dead, when *their* kids will be dead—when no trace or memory of any of them will exist.

She thinks of the eerie things her kids say at bedtime sometimes, out of the blue, strange and abstract, minimalist and simple in the twilight of their bedrooms, often having to do with mortality. Flo with her first headache, her face wincing on the pillow, moaning, her face pale like a sick child's in the sixteenth century. "Right here," she groaned dramatically, whispering softly as she touched her forehead. "It's all silver for dying." Or the time Margaret came to say a final good night to a restless Sarah, and in the darkness Sarah muttered, "There's a ghost child in my bed," causing Margaret to panic but remain calm and hurry downstairs to follow Brian around. Sometimes the questions are dizzying, coming rapid-fire: "Mom? When people *die*, does the erf"—earth—"under them get all dusty? When *you* die, will you turn into, just . . . *wind?*"

A lot of times as she looks at them, as they prattle on or fiddle with something, as they watch a squirrel dart across the grass and jump gliding onto a tree, as she watches them break into laughter at something she doesn't find remotely funny, she can't help but wonder whether they'll make it to being adults, to being parents, to being alive in their old age. They come in smatterings, usually clustered together, the close calls to disaster. Stephen getting honked at loudly by a whizzing box truck as he almost steps onto the crosswalk. Flo falling out of a friend's tree house. (She's fine, but the friend's mother looks white as a sheet as she tells Margaret how it happened.) Margaret swerving in the road as she reaches into the backseat for a fallen sippy cup, righting herself and the car just in time.

So many people in the world. More people than there have ever been, knowing more than they ever have. It makes Margaret anxious to think about it. And these three kids of hers, they're just as inconspicuous as everyone else, the billions of children, just as inconsequential to the weighted, leaden thing that is time, that is tragedy, that is disaster combined. How can she ever maintain whatever it is that makes them bubble to begin with? That was one thing having children had surprised her with: how apparent it is that baby people start out so innately good and joyful and vulnerable, longing to be near other people, fascinated by what's around them, curious of faces, their sense of loneliness and their sense of humor practically in place before they've even mastered which senses are what. She was shocked, and still is, at how little *control* a mother actually has. What *is* it, she wonders, that rises through her children, through every life, like what reaches through a tree, out to its outermost tips, and down to its deepest roots, forever pushing down into the dirt? What is that united energy that spreads through a life like the flare of a fern? What is it that's trapped within each of them, that rises up and grows, that shimmers along the edges of a life like a glistening fish, ready to burst through?

When she's apart from them, when she goes into the city or has a longish day working out of the house, she gets a feeling similar to what she felt when she was first falling in love with Brian, the thought of her children buoying her as she walks down the street, giving her more confidence, more verve. She walks about freely, unfettered, but the thought of them all, her home, her gorgeous husband, is like a secret backpack clasped around her neck. As she walks down the street, she feels as though people must be able to see it: the great sex she's just had, the newborn baby she just birthed, the band of family back at her den.

Was something wrong with her that she couldn't remember what buoyed her, what kept her going in such a way before she had them all? She looks at Edie, thinking of her sister's solitary life in the city, and tries to remember what it was that made her content and happy when she was single in New York. She wasn't unhappy then. She loved it. Didn't she? Does she miss it? She hardly remembers.

She's nauseated and her boobs are killing her. She looks at Brian. She looks at Edie, who's playing cat's cradle with Flo, something Margaret never learned, or cared to learn, to do. In the dining room, Chloe and Max look as though they're about to slow dance. Chloe's probably pregnant as well, thinks Margaret.

"I'm going outside," Margaret announces.

"It's raining," says Brian.

"It's just sprinkling." Margaret groans. "I want some air."

She stands on the patio. The neighborhood is quiet. The sound of the showering rain is like static, a low white noise.

She looks at the chaise where her father had been sitting the day Chloe got beaned by the croquet ball. She remembers a morning in California.

"Love's what it's all about," Margaret had said shlockily, poolside, summing something up sarcastically.

Her father was sitting on the edge of his chair, eating peanuts, plucking off the shells and depositing them on the ground between his feet. "It's not all about *love* at all," her father had said matter-of-factly, his hands on his knees. He didn't look at Margaret but looked straight ahead at the pool, at that little dwarfy statue that stood on the side, at the orange tree with its green oranges. "It's about the ability to do it, it seems to me. Is it not?"

Margaret walks out onto the wet grass toward the vegetable garden. Before she gets there, she sees the weeds around the mint and the basil. She kneels down to pull them up. They come up easily out of the damp soil. Healthy earthworms squirm back into the ground and suddenly the world is here, up in her face, wet and loamy, muddy and fertile. What is all this looking *up* about? It's here, she thinks, down here, in the dark dirt of the ground, what's underneath, creeping out, seeping up from it. She wants to dive into it, a madwoman, rain-soaked and dirt-streaked, all the minerals and rich nutrients, the future coming forth, efflorescing. She feels ravenous, famished. She grabs a fistful of earth, a clump of it, and holds it to her cheek dearly. She samples it with her tongue. She takes a scoop of the ground with her two hands and, as though she's washing her face, tosses it over her forehead. She lies down, plunges an arm downward into the garden, looks sideways at the wet lawn, the green grass like a close-up of a scalp, each verdant blade standing soldierly and strong, growing and growing ceaselessly, the large exuberance of growth, forever contained, forever undone.

She can hear one of her kids calling her from the back door—Is it Stephen? Is it Sarah?—calling, "Mom? Are you all right, Mom? Mom? What are you *doing*?"